A TIME TO SPEAK

A Time to Speak

The Out of Time Series:

Book Two

Nadine Brandes

PUBLISHING

In memory of my big brother, Nathan.
Though you died, you still spoke into my life,
teaching me to be the example I imagined you would have been.
My storytelling began with you,
then reached our siblings . . .
. . . and now the world.

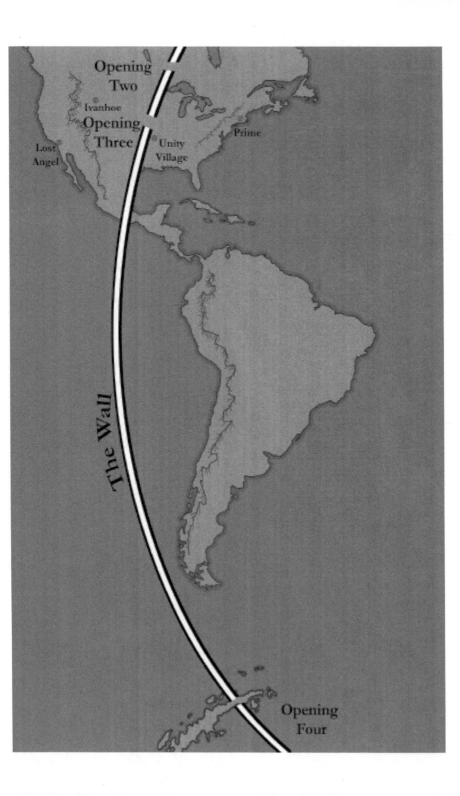

1

I've been robbed of my death.

A date was set, a coffin prepared, and a grave dug in the earth, yet I breathe against my own will as my brother is lowered six feet down. The smooth wood coffin displays the best of Father's carpentry skill. Did he originally carve it for me?

Enforcers surround the gravesite—black human pillars lined with bullets, staring straight ahead. Probably making sure I don't run.

Solomon Hawke is not among them.

A pall of autumn leaves covers the Unity Village graveyard, the only disrupted portion of ground being Reid's grave. Lumps of black earth wait to enclose him in permanent night.

Everything about this funeral feels wrong. Reid should not be buried. He should be cremated and scattered in the most adventurous locations. He is—*was*—a traveler, not meant to stay in one place. But his wife, Tawny, insisted. Perhaps she wants a grave to visit.

I try to meet her eyes. Does she blame me for his death? Her gaze is fixed on Reid, as though she can see through the lid of carved wood concealing his face. She stands with her hands folded in front of her, wobbling on the soft ground in high heels. She wears a short ivory dress with long sleeves off the shoulders and a braided tan belt.

I wear black.

Tawny takes shuddering gasps and blinks hard while tears paint trails down her smooth cheeks. I should be standing by her, creating a bond as sisters, but I'm a criminal. Because I live, her husband—my brother—is dead.

I am the last of the Blackwater triplets.

I rub my hand against my raw left wrist, growing more and more used to the space that used to be my left hand. An Enforcer removed the shackles so I can at least toss a memento into Reid's grave. The Enforcers don't intimidate me anymore. They all know I'm a Radical, but they have no harm to offer me.

"Time to go." A black Enforcer—the same one who held me captive at my hearing, sentenced me to the Wall, and shoved me through the Opening—claps the metal ring to my wrist.

I don't want to go with him. He has no heart.

"Wait." The first scoop of dirt falls like a dropped gauntlet onto Reid's coffin. I stretch my shackled hand over the hole and release my Good-bye gift—a thin lump of folded letters written on pages from Reid's old journal during my journey in the West. A reddish-brown ribbon holds them together—the one he said reminded him of my hair. He bought it for me so long ago. Another life ago.

"Let's go." The Enforcer's voice is harsh and he holds out the other shackle.

I raise my left arm. With jerky movements, he locks the metal around my stump. Does my missing hand sicken him? I hope so. It's a testament to my travels, my stamina.

He drags me away from the gravesite before I can say anything to Tawny, before I can hug Mother or Father, before I can say a true Good-bye to Reid. I've seen none of them since the fiasco at the Wall two days ago.

Do they hate me?

Father meets my eyes for a brief moment before we round a corner out of sight. A giant purple bruise spreads like a stain over one side of his face, mixing with his brown whiskers. Blasted Enforcers. They had no right to strike him.

We head away from town—away from the containment center. Away from Willow, my little albino friend. All the people I love are separated into places I hate—Mother and Father at a gravesite, Reid in a coffin, Willow in a cell, and Elm trapped in the Wall tunnel.

The soft voices of sorrow fade behind me, replaced by the rhythmic tromp of Enforcers following us. "Are you taking me back to the containment center?"

"What, two nights in there weren't enough for you?" He gives a sharp laugh.

I don't have the energy to be offended. Two nights have been far too much. I need to get moving, start fixing all the broken-ness clouding my village. I have a calling to fulfill. "Where are we going?"

"Nether Hospital, to get your medibot removed." He scowls at me and mutters, "What a waste."

"I didn't ask for it." I didn't ask for the small nano-creature to enter my skin and save my life, but God has a way of giving me things I don't ask for.

My posture goes slack. My trust in Him doesn't come as easily as it did before. I miss it.

We board the *Lower Missouri Transit* on the north side of town and plop into two hard seats. As the train gains speed, the blurred trees and wind-whipped grass remind me of riding the *Ivanhoe Independent*, only this train is much smoother. No jarring rattles or loud wind.

I want to ask where Hawke is, but the Lead Enforcer already suspects Hawke helped me. Did Hawke get in trouble because I called out for his aid? If so, I don't want to draw more attention to him. But I want to see him.

We need to talk.

The black Enforcer and I disembark, enter the red brick hospital, and walk past the front desk. He pulls me through a series of hallways.

"Ow." I stumble, but he doesn't slow.

If Hawke were the Enforcer with me instead of this hard-handed man, would he be gentle? How is he handling Jude's death? He seemed confused when I told him, as if Jude wasn't supposed to die. I need to tell him how it happened . . . how it was my fault.

I hate the idea of Hawke mourning alone.

I killed both our brothers.

We enter a small room with one bed and three cushioned, black chairs. The Enforcer sits, leaving me to stand in the middle of the room. Before I can decide whether to escape or sit down, a sharp knock precedes the entrance of a doctor. I don't recognize his face as anyone who tended to Reid when he recovered from the train derailment last spring. His frown brings me no comfort.

"I'm Enforcer Kaphtor," my Enforcer says. "You're to take out her medibot."

The doctor blinks slowly. "Patients need a scan for remaining injuries before I can remove it."

"Then do it."

The doctor appraises me with a wrinkled nose. "She's that girl who wrote the biography. Parvin Blackwater."

It's okay, talk as if I'm not here. I'm quite happy to be invisible.

"Yup, Unity's newest Radical."

For the first time, I don't mind the title of Radical. I'm proud not to have a Clock like everyone else—proud not to know the day I'll die. I'm terrified, but free from that looming knowledge.

Clock. That's all that matters to people. Numbers, not flesh and blood. Jude was right about that.

"Radicals warrant no medical care. She'd need a Clock, famous troublemaker or not."

Troublemaker? I wrote my biography to *save* Radicals—to stop the meaningless sentences. Is this how the rest of my people see me? A troublemaker?

"She's under different rules."

The doctor raises an eyebrow. "Oh really? I was unaware that government-set healthcare could change at the whim of an Enforcer."

I finally lower myself into a spare seat, since they won't acknowledge my presence, but the doctor grabs my left arm and yanks me back to my feet. I gasp as a zing shoots down my arm to my stump, pinching the scarred skin as only an invisible hand can do.

"Now that seat needs to be *cleaned*." He shoves me away. "You going to pay for the cleaning fluid? Don't touch anything."

My arm throbs. I bite the inside of my cheek. Kaphtor stands slowly, towering over the doctor. "I thought Skelley Chase contacted this hospital about Miss Blackwater."

The doctor's mouth opens and closes twice before he manages a sound. "S-Skelley Chase?" He looks at me. *"This* is his girl? This Radical?"

My nerves pop like a jack-in-the-box. That name . . .

Frozen fury forms in the crevices of my brain like glaciers. "No." My voice comes out guttural and dark.

The doctor turns to me. "You're not the one he contacted us about?"

"I'm not his girl." My right hand clenches. The shackles clink. "I'll do nothing under Skelley Chase's orders."

Kaphtor grips my forearm, squeezing like a tourniquet. "You don't have a choice, Radical."

"He murdered my brother!" Shot him. Shot Reid in the head, against his word.

Kaphtor's hold loosens. "He just hastened your brother's Good-bye. *You* didn't prepare yourself for his death."

"That's because I thought the Clock was mine."

"Enough." The doctor opens the door. "Follow me and we'll take out the medibot. We need a fresh one in our storage anyway."

"*No!*"

His eyes narrow. "Like Enforcer Kaphtor said, you don't have a choice, Radical."

My anger isn't really about the medibot. Let them take out the stupid metal creature that's been healing my body from the inside. I just don't want to do anything to please Skelley Chase, the man who got me sent across the Wall.

The man who caused all this.

If not for him, Reid would be alive, I'd be dead, and things would be right.

No. I shake my head as if to rattle my pessimism. God has a calling for me, that's the reason I'm still alive. Why was it so easy to cling to that knowledge two days ago, yet I doubt today?

We accompany the doctor to a new room, long like the start of a hallway. In the center is a flat slab, like a table, but with a screen as the surface. When the door closes, the room is almost completely dark, with just enough glow to see.

A single metal chair rests beside the table.

"Sit." The doctor taps on the table screen.

Now I'm allowed to sit? I plop into a chair and close my eyes, succumbing to his probing.

"You should know"–the doctor speaks from somewhere behind me–"I don't approve of unlawful administration of medical instruments, especially medibots, no matter who does it."

Enforcer Kaphtor says nothing.

Light penetrates my eyelids, so I open them and glance at the table. It is now covered in a colorful grid of yellow lines, green squares, and tiny blue dots.

A small metal dish is placed on the top of my skull and a series of light shocks pass through my body from head to toe. The doctor mutters, clicks something on the metal dish, and sends the shocks again. This time, they're stronger. My left wrist spasms.

"Fool!" the doctor hisses.

I cringe.

He removes the dish from my head. A virtual body now lies on the screen table to my left—or rather floats halfway out of it, face-up as though someone pushed it out of the table from beneath and it's straining against the electronic grid as if it's netting. The body has no distinct features—just a virtual human . . . missing a left hand.

So, that's supposed to be me.

A red dot pulses in the stub of my virtual left arm. The doctor places the wide barrel of a device that looks like a gun against my left shoulder. I twist to look at it, but he smacks my cheek with the back of his hand. I swallow the burning in my throat and eyes. I guess doctors are only kind to the patients who can pay.

God, I feel so alone. Reid said I'm never alone because You are here, so why do I feel forgotten? So . . . dirty? When will You return me to my family? I can't spend another day in the containment center.

The prayer coaxes my tears to the surface again. I sniff once. The gun sucks my skin with a sharp whirring. I tense in antici-pation of pain, but it doesn't come. The barrel leaves my shoul-der. The red dot on my virtual body gives three sharp pulses and words scroll across the bottom of the table screen, so tiny I can't make them out.

The doctor throws the gun onto the table. It lands with a clunk, but doesn't disturb the grid. He rounds my chair and faces Enforcer Kaphtor. "Skelley Chase is a wasteful imbecile."

I couldn't agree more.

Kaphtor leans forward. "He does everything for the well-being of others. Watch yourself."

With a wild gesture to me, the doctor continues. "The medi-bot has taken residence in her body. It never should have been inserted in the first place! There is a delicate process behind receiving a medibot. Thousands of specie have been wasted on this . . . this *Radical*."

My hackles finally rise enough to elicit argument. "Hey, I never asked for it—"

"I don't understand." Kaphtor cuts me off.

"Most medibots are designed to remain in a body until all systems are fixed and functioning." The doctor seizes my left wrist and almost pulls my arm from my socket. "Her severed hand will *never* be fixed and functioning. Amputees are not allowed medibots unless they have enough specie to permanently purchase it from the medical center."

"There's nothing you can do?" I squirm at the idea of the electronic spider living inside my body forever.

"No! Now get out."

Kaphtor stands. "Mr. Chase wants it removed."

The doctor grabs his medibot-extracting gun and walks to the door. "Well, *I* won't be the one delivering the bad news. Good day." He holds the door open.

Kaphtor jerks me after him. The shackles cut into my tender wrists. I don't know why Kaphtor uses them—my left arm can slip out at a whim.

We return to Unity via the *Lower Missouri Transit* and tromp to the containment center. On our way, we pass the county building where the electronic post board makes up one outer wall.

There I am, magnified for everyone to see—a colored photo of me on all fours with the thousand-foot Wall in the background, mid-retch. Charming. Below that picture is a headline.

Parvin Blackwater Returns . . . and Outlives Her Clock!

Well, when they say it like that, I sound like a miracle. But it was never my Clock to start with. It was Reid's Clock.

I don't know my Numbers. I don't want to know.

We arrive at the containment center. The building is made of hard wood and a shingled roof—one of the few roofs in Unity Village not made of thatch. As we enter, two more Enforcers pass in the opposite direction with a small albino girl between them.

"Willow!" I reach for her.

"Parvin!" She struggles to return to me, but we've already passed each other.

"Where are you taking her? Bring her back!" The Enforcers exit, yanking her with them. I turn to Kaphtor and abandon whatever pride kept me from cordiality. "Please. Please bring her back or let me go with her. Don't hurt her."

His walking slows and he glances at me. I hold his gaze and he blinks three times fast before looking forward again. Did I break through? Crack the hardness that seems to lay captive every Enforcer?

"She's not your concern."

No matter how I strain, I detect no softening in his voice. "What about Elm?" The anxiety of unanswered questions almost drowns me. "He's the albino boy trapped in the Wall. Is anyone going to let him out?"

Kaphtor pulls me down the hallway to the left, past the cell Willow previously occupied, and into the very last barred unit.

"It's already been two days. Someone has to let him out. He's just a *boy*. He'll starve!"

He takes off my shackles and shoves me into the cell so hard I fall to the ground. My stump strikes the wooden bench that's served as my bed the past two nights. I cry out, but can't find the energy to push myself up.

The barred door clangs shut and Kaphtor's footsteps echo off the stone. *Clip. Clip. Clip. Clip.*

I curl on the cold ground. Alone. Helpless. Willow and I are at the mercy of the Enforcers of Unity Village, where laws are ignored and Radicals are killed because it's easy.

I can do nothing. Meanwhile, an assassin is delivering Jude's Clock-matching invention to the Council—giving the Council even *more* power to control us. Once they start matching everyone with a Clock, they'll make laws by our Numbers. No work for Numbers below one year. No medical care for Numbers two years or less. People won't have a choice to reject the Clocks.

We're nothing more than clicking Numbers to them.

So many things need to be fixed, and I'm inhibited by strips of metal and wood.

What will they do with me? With Willow? With Elm? With my family?

I turn my face to the ceiling, hoping gravity will keep my tears from falling. It doesn't. They stream into my ears and my mind rests only on troubling thoughts.

Willow—my little eleven-year-old albino companion—is trapped in this foreign world so different from the forest life she's known, all because she chose to help me through the Wall. Will I ever get her back home? Will I ever get Elm—her grafting partner—out of the Wall?

It is all my doing. I never should have returned, despite Skelley Chase's threat of killing Reid. He killed him anyway. Or maybe it's because I returned too late. If I could have reached this side a day earlier . . .

I AM CALLING YOU.

"I haven't forgotten," I whisper. But if God's calling, why is He letting me sit in a cell while others are dying? Isn't my calling to bring shalom? To save lives?

I shouldn't despair. I need to see this extra time as a gift—a second chance. But, in order for me to have my second chance, Reid got a bullet to the head.

"Parvin?" A soft voice says my name from mere feet away— the sweetest word spoken to me since returning to Unity Village.

My head snaps to the left. A man stands on the other side of my door. His tall frame matches the height of the cell bars. His dark blond hair is a little longer than when I met him a year ago. The backward black *E* on his left temple still surprises me, stark against his light skin. How can an Enforcer look so kind while standing so stiff and regal?

I rise to a sitting position. "Hawke."

Something inside me relaxes as it did when he lifted me into his arms after Reid died. I meet his gaze, but no secret message is to be found. He's guarded.

"I'm here to escort you." He is still reserved, but speaks so gently.

"To Willow?"

He glances down the hall and seems to grow taller and more rigid. He pulls shackles from his belt. "Please come with me."

I push against the emotional weights and manage to stand. He unlocks the door and claps the shackles around my wrists, not quite as pinching as Enforcer Kaphtor did. I try to smile at him, but can't seem to raise my head. Sorrow's heavy like that, I suppose.

"Where are you taking me?"

He shuts the cell door and leads me down the hall. "You're being registered as a Radical."

At this, I manage to glance up. The sun flickers against the light teal color in his eyes. His posture relaxes just barely and his lips twitch in a smile meant only for me. "And then I'm taking you back to your family."

I don't know what frightens me more, the metal scalpel slicing into my left bicep, the idea of returning to my family, or the fact that Solomon Hawke and I are finally alone.

Hawke has me on a stool in a room labeled *Registration*, but it looks more like the interior of an old cement storage shed. Warped boxes lean weakly on one wall, with a smoky covering of dust along their tops. When he turned on the lights, only three of the five electric bulbs worked.

A long metal desk stretches along the opposite wall. Slits, holes, and glass doors filled with sky-blue fluid line the side of the desk. A large deadened screen covers the wall above it with a single spider in the center—a brown recluse acting rather unreclusive.

It scurries away from the light. Mid-flight it drops off the screen with a small *plink* on the desk. I turn my focus to Hawke and his scalpel.

I try to joke past the glue in my throat. "They call this noninvasive?" What do I say to this man who fought for my freedom so long ago? Who contacted me with comfort when I felt alone in the West. This man who shows the only kindness seen in an Enforcer and who might just have some answers I seek.

This man whose affections I rejected.

I can't very well say, "Jude's last words were, *Ask Solomon.*"

Or can I?

His hand is steady and the cut so smooth I don't even bleed. He drops the scalpel through a slot in the metal desk. It floats down through clear blue fluid where tiny metal arachnids meet it and tinker away with cleaning.

"Does it hurt?"

"Not the cut." My heart hurts, but I can't seem to open my lips to tell him. It's different speaking to his face instead of his electronic penmanship from my nano-book screen.

He holds a teeny flat flexible square between his thumb and forefinger, but pauses in front of the incision.

I lean away. "Is that going inside me?" More electronics invading my body. Next, I'll be a robot.

He meets my eyes. "Yes. It's a tracker." His gaze flickers from my arm, to my eyes, then to the door.

"Hawke . . . we need to talk."

"I can't do that, Miss Blackwater. I'm an Enforcer. You're a Radical."

Miss Blackwater? Why such formality? Does he see us as so different now that we can't communicate, even after everything we've been through?

Maybe he blames me for Jude.

I jump as Hawke pushes the thin film into my cut. He pulls a small strip of cloth from an open box. "Sorry this is so primitive." He binds my arm and ties a knot.

Primitive? Binding a wound with cloth? Then I guess I grew up primitive.

"Now you're a registered Radical."

Yippee.

"Probably one of the first Radicals registered in Unity Village."

It *is* rather momentous. My village has been sending Radicals through the Wall instead of registering them for as long as I can remember. Maybe I get special treatment because in town there's a giant picture of me throwing up.

Hawke rotates on his stool and taps on an electrosheet, probably entering my information. What is going on? He seemed kind moments ago when he took me from my cell.

"Um . . . Hawke?"

"Please remain silent." His tone is all business, but he reaches his hand back without looking up at me. A folded slip of paper rests between two of his fingers, extended toward me. I stare at the back of his head. Everything but his extended arm looks as if he's focused on recording information on the electrosheet.

I take the paper and unfold it. Uneven handwriting weaves all over the page in blueberry ink—Mother's homemade ink. Some words smash into each other or run off the edge, as if he wrote this without looking.

> *Miss Parvin,*
> *I'm wearing a required Enforcer Testimony Log.*
> *Sachem is monitoring everything I do, hear, and see, and sending it to the Council, especially information on how I interact with you.*
> *I'm writing this with my eyes closed, pretending to be asleep.*
> *I must remain formal for now, but this may help you rescue the boy. Be careful.*
> *- Solomon*

At the bottom of the page is a string of numbers and the word *car* in parentheses. The only cars in Unity Village belong to the Enforcers.

My heart cartwheels. Hawke has in a Testimony Log—contact lenses that record everything he sees and hears. So *that's* why he's been assigned to register me. Sachem, the Lead Enforcer, wants to see how we interact together.

What do they expect to find?

I fold the paper with slow movements and tuck it into my skirt pocket just as Hawke straightens. I want him to know it's safe to turn around, that I got his note.

"How long has this registration room been here?" It's a dumb question. The inches of dust already answer it, but small talk is less suspicious than prolonged silence.

He swivels on the stool. I avoid his gaze. "Since the containment center was built, but you're the first one to use it since I came to Unity."

"Oh."

"Let's go." He stands and hoists me to my feet.

Wait. This solitude was so . . . beautifully numbing. I want more of it, even though it's being filmed. I want to stay in this room alone with Hawke until I think of how to apologize for his brother's death.

We exit the room at the same time Enforcer Kaphtor comes down the white hall with my shoulder pack slung over one arm, dragging Willow behind him. She practically blends into the paint, all except her light purple eyes. They're rimmed with red. A thin bandage pinches the skin on her right arm.

"Willow." I reach for her. "Are you okay?"

"Good noon, Kaphtor," Hawke says.

"Good noon. This one's going with her." Kaphtor jerks his chin at me and shoves Willow forward before I can take her hand. "They'll be under indefinite patrol. You and me first, Hawke."

"Tally ho." Hawke leads our procession into the cold.

Willow is going to be with me. A coil in my chest relaxes. Even if we're in another cell, at least we'll be together so I can . . . what? Protect her? The coil tightens again. What can I do to help her or get her home? I'm powerless.

The October wind is not yet bitter, but I still exhale a small cloud. The light chill bites my tracker wound. I suck in a breath and try to shelter it with my hand.

"What's this?" Kaphtor snatches my left elbow and pulls it close to his face. I whimper and stop in my tracks. Why is everyone's touch so harsh? "Hawke, you idiot, you did the wrong arm."

Hawke shrugs. "It's more efficient, since she already has a medibot in that arm and a missing hand. All the rotten eggs in one basket, you know?" He gently tugs my arm out of Kaphtor's grasp.

Rotten eggs. That's how he sees me. Is that how everyone sees me?

"You and your obsession with *efficiency*. As long as she's tracked, I guess."

Hawke laughs. A distant, emotionless sound. "Tally ho."

"Jude-man said that," Willow chirps from beside Kaphtor.

I grimace. I haven't been able to warn her that Hawke is Jude's brother, that he still doesn't know how—or why—Jude died.

Hawke gives no response and I close my eyes for a long second, forcing my feet to keep moving. I think of Jude. I ache for Jude.

Walking through Unity Village again is like a slow trek across hot coals. With every step, I'm overcome with a base urge to flee. I'm alone. I don't belong.

The narrow glares of some villagers run over my body, like red laser beams. I don't make eye contact. They're glaring . . . as if they hate me. Why shouldn't they hate me? I carry the guilt of two men's deaths.

We turn the corner to Straight Street—my old home. The wood-and-thatch houses are unchanged against the warped brick sidewalk and mud road. New shutters block the windows of the Newton house on the corner. Who lives there now? Do the new inhabitants know the Enforcers attempted to murder the Newtons?

Mrs. Newton and her surviving daughter are all alone in Ivanhoe. Will I ever see them again? Does she think I'm dead?

Has she been able to follow through on buying the safehouse mansion for the Radicals sent through the Wall?

A few doors down, my small thatch hut is as dead as Reid's body. My breath fogs in front of me. This place doesn't feel like home. It's a cold trap soon to house the living sister of two dead brothers.

Hawke raises his arm to knock and I clamp my lips against the impulse to scream, "No!"

Rap. Rap. Rap.

We stand on the doorstep of my so-called home, waiting to be let in. Does that make me a stranger?

The door opens and the real stranger stares at me: Tawny. The ten minutes we've had together were spent wailing over Reid's body. Not the best memory.

She holds my gaze with storm grey eyes outlined in black to cover the red sorrow. With a sharp tilt of her head, she transfers her gaze to Hawke. "Yes?"

It's this small movement—this terse response—that snaps me out of my timidity. I step from Hawke's grasp. "I'm back."

Before Tawny can say a word, I take Willow's shackled hand and we push past her into the three-room house. I'm slammed with the scent of woodstove and fresh coffee. It brings a wave of abrupt memories—early mornings preparing to vouch at a hearing, writing my autobiography, exchanging Good-byes with Mother, Father, Reid . . .

I stand in the squished entry beside the mirror and basket of scarves, facing the kitchen. Father sits at the table, staring at his hands. Mother stands to my left, having just exited her bedroom.

"Mother." I stumble forward and raise my arms, but the shackles prevent our hug. I turn back toward the entry—toward Hawke. Lifting my hand and stump, I say a quiet, "Please?"

Everyone is inside now and the door is closed. Hawke enters a code and unlocks the shackles. I fall into Mother's arms. One of us trembles. I can't tell which—maybe it's both of us.

"These girls are under indefinite patrol." Kaphtor drops my pack on the ground and removes Willow's bindings. "Enforcer Hawke and I will be on day watch. Neither of you are allowed to exit the house without permission and supervision. Any attempt to do so will be met with punishment and imprisonment in the containment center."

"Indefinite patrol?" Father rises from the table. How I've missed his deep, smooth voice.

Kaphtor nods. "Until we determine the route of action to take regarding Parvin Blackwater's illegal actions and Willow's invasion of the USE, they are under house arrest and are not allowed to contact anyone outside of those living in this . . . home." He looks around the room. "Is this understood?"

I nod, numb.

He maintains eye contact. "Do you agree to comply?"

Was my nod not enough? "You've made yourself clear, sir." It's the best answer I can think of without flat-out lying. I can't stay here while Elm is starving inside the Wall.

"Good." He turns on his heel, opens the door, and leaves.

"Tally ho." Hawke's gaze flicks to me and he pulls the door closed behind them.

Willow hugs herself with her thin pale arms and looks around the room. She squeezes her eyes closed. I kneel by her and take her hand. "Willow, I'm . . . I'm so sorry you are here."

Her face tilts to the ground and a tear drops on the floor. "I don't like this house. So many trees died."

Despite her encounters with other cultures, it must still be hard for her to stand in a wooden house after being a protector of nature. I stroke a single finger down her face. "I know. I'm sorry."

Mother interrupts our soft conversation with a bark. "Hungry?"

Food. How can anyone think to eat on the day we buried my brother? Mother, of all people? I shake my head. "No thanks."

"What have you eaten since your return?"

I sigh. "I don't know, Mother." And I truly don't. Only the day before yesterday I stood on the first stair step of death. Sustenance didn't even enter my mind as a concern. "Food from the containment center, I guess."

Did they feed me? I suppose I'd be dead if they hadn't, but maybe the medibot altered my level of starvation. Can it do that? Enforcers took away my Vitality suit almost immediately, so that doesn't factor in to my hunger.

Mother stokes the wood stove anyway. Father rounds the table and kisses my forehead. "Welcome home, sweetheart."

My chin quivers and I clamp my jaw, breathing in his scent of soap and sawdust. "Thank you, Father."

Home. The word doesn't connect with this place anymore. It was a home six months ago, but no longer. It's weird and I don't like feeling like a stranger. But . . . I am new. This place is old. We don't belong together.

"I'm going to the shop." Father walks past me to the line of coat pegs.

Wait . . . what? "You're leaving?"

He shrugs on his overcoat. "Still got Reid's tombplate to finish. You get some rest and we'll . . . catch up over supper."

I suppose everyone has his or her own way of mourning. Maybe Father needs space. Or maybe he's just afraid to be with me.

He walks out the door. In the brief moment before the door closes, I see Solomon Hawke standing rigid against the doorpost. He's doing his job well—so well, I almost don't believe it's him.

Willow cowers in the middle of the room, still staring at the floor. I can't bring myself to invite her to sit in one of our wooden chairs. I won't play ignorant, but I don't know what to do.

I can't tell her about Hawke's help until I have a plan to get to Elm.

Mother is silent. Tawny sits at the table as if Willow and I don't exist. The force of awkward avoidance inflates a balloon of tension in my chest. I can't stand here. I can't be here. None of this is how it should be.

I push through the fog of problems I can't solve, pick up my shoulder pack, and slam through my bedroom door. It shuts, encompassing me in a new type of silence, and I fight a blur of confusion.

My bed is against the opposite wall than it used to be—to my right, with a light summery bedspread I've never seen before. My antique sewing machine sits on the floor in the corner to my left beside a pile of material scraps. The desk it used to sit on now supports piles of photographs and wooden frames.

A trunk with the name *Tawny Blackwater* carved on its surface sits beneath the window across from me, open. Even from this distance I recognize Father's handiwork. Bright clothing spills from the trunk onto the floor—skirts, blouses, high heels, scarves, hats, leggings. Beside the trunk is a folded stack of men's clothes. Reid's clothes.

My knees shake and I place my right hand against the closet door for support. This is *my* room. I came here for reprieve and all I find is . . . Tawny. Fellow Radical, but stranger. Foreigner.

The conflicted emotions laugh at me. I won't call this place home anymore, yet I'm offended that it's changed? Such irony.

I straighten with a deep breath and sit on the bed, clutching the pack Reid gave me to my chest. It smells like dirt and pine. I sniff again. Ah, the West—the closest thing to home I have.

The Enforcers took Jude's pack from me. I'll probably never see it again, but he didn't carry much anyway.

Unsure of what might douse Tawny's nice bedspread if I dump the contents, I resort to rifling with my one hand. First out is Reid's journal—his last gift to me, which I ruined when I fell into the Dregs. Water stains still distort the soft cover. Why didn't I throw the whole thing into his grave and rid myself of guilt? But guilt isn't the only thing that hits me as I clutch the swollen book.

Tears burn my eyes and my nose grows stuffy. I sniff and shake my head.

No. I released enough sorrow on the floor of that containment center. Reid knew he would die. He *knew.* He was ready.

A tear splashes on the journal.

"He knew," I whisper.

But even though he knew . . . even though I'll see him in Heaven . . . even though he was ready, I still miss him. I guess tears are okay.

I set the journal on a new carved bed stand—probably a gift from Father to Tawny. Maybe she'll want Reid's journal. She is his wife—well, widow—after all.

My hand reenters the bag, but the floppy canvas keeps moving and tilting off balance. I finally pick up the pack by the bottom and pour the contents onto the floor. Nasty socks, underwear, and bunched clothing cushion the clunk of my NAB and sentra.

Father's dagger isn't here. Neither is the Vitality suit from Wilbur Sherrod. Of course the Enforcers would take the suit. It's the most valuable item I brought back from the West. That strangely enhanced article of clothing kept me alive against the assassin's toxin for nine days.

I dig through the socks until my fingers wrap around a thin length of wood. I lift Jude's whistle to my lips. It has six holes and sap stoppers the end of it. I blow softly. *Tweet.* My small smile quivers. "Oh Jude . . ."

See you soon, he said to me before he died. They would have been his last words if I hadn't demanded to know *why* he gave the enemy his invention of Clock-matching—an invention he'd protected with his life.

An invention he died for.

His last words then became, *ask Solomon.*

Talk about a loaded question.

But I can't talk to Hawke, not yet. Not while his Testimony Log is in. What I *can* do is launch a rescue mission to save Elm. For that, I'll need Willow on board.

Voices drift from the kitchen. I return to the room of discomfort only to enter an argument. "He said nothing meaningful about Reid at that funeral." Tawny's voice is more girlish than mine, but not as prissy as her appearance. "Some people here call themselves believers? Please."

"No one is calling themselves a believer, Tawny." Mother sits beside her. Willow is not in the kitchen.

Tawny folded her arms with a huff. "Don't *you* claim to be one?"

Mother says nothing.

"So where's Willow?" This phony wife thinks, now that she's a Blackwater, that she can challenge my mother? Think again, little blondie.

"Outhouse."

"Where will we be sleeping?"

"Well, *you're* sleeping in Tawny's room, with her." Mother touches her forehead, as if pressing back a headache. "Willow will be with your father and me."

I choke on indignation. *"Tawny's* room?"

Tawny stands and raises an eyebrow. "Trust me, the bed's big enough for two." She turns with a swirl of her white dress and walks into her—*my*—room.

I can't hold on to my affront. I just want to cry. Sinking into a chair across from Mother, we both sit there for a moment. It's so good to see her face again, to see those little frown wrinkles and the weathered skin.

She stares out the lattice window over the sink. Is she thinking of when I smashed the single pane that used to be there?

"Mother?" I reach across the table.

She looks back at me, but not into my eyes. She's staring a little to my left. "Yes?"

"Are . . . are you happy I'm . . . back?"

"Of course." Her answer comes too quick, too sharp. She doesn't take my hand.

I curl my fingers into a loose fist, resting my thumb on the band of my silver cross ring. "Do you . . . want to talk about anything that happened in the West?" I need to share it with someone. I need to know that it mattered . . . that my biography—and the tsunami-like aftermath—was worth it.

"Parvin, I didn't really know what was going on with you other than what Enforcer Hawke came and told us. I was busy living my life here, with your father and Reid . . . and Tawny."

"Oh." She doesn't know my story? "Didn't you read my X-book biography?"

She sighs and her voice turns harsh. "X-books don't exist in Unity Village or any Low City, Parvin. Have you forgotten already?"

"Hawke had one. I thought he told you things."

"Not much."

Oh yeah, his Testimony Log. "Well . . . do you want to know my story?"

We don't talk often, but this could be a chance to reconnect—to open up with each other and be authentic. So much happened in the past six months, like I lived a full life in a condensed amount of time.

I need her advice. Her support. Her wisdom. I need to be able to share with her.

Mother finally meets my eyes. I lean forward, relishing the connection, but under the pressure of her gaze comes the oil of insecurity. She looks through me, not at me. What is she thinking?

"Mother?"

"No." She stands from the table and walks to the door of her room. Before lifting the latch, she stares at the door with her back toward me. "I don't want to know your story, Parvin. No one does."

Mother doesn't want to know about me. She doesn't care that I survived. My gut clenches from the emotional slug.

It's because of Reid.

It's because of that biography. What started as my selfish desire to be remembered has turned into a storm cloud over my village. It didn't feel right from the start. Well . . .

I've certainly made myself memorable.

Why did I do it? Why did I allow that selfishness to drive me to write about my life and then get involved with Skelley Chase? Why did I challenge the government's Enforcer system and then desert my people?

Only now do I see what I've done.

I put Unity Village on the map. The government sees us now—more than ever. Maybe that's why God kept me on Earth. My purpose is to restore shalom . . . and safety . . . in my village. Fix the damage I caused.

Mother's door closes. I look around the kitchen, taking in the familiar red water pump beneath the window, the wood stove to the left of it and the warmth of the cooking fire at my back. The small room feels even more constricting than before, yet an abyss of silence separates me from everyone.

I'm truly alone.

My people hate me. My family hates me. Maybe that's how things need to be. Maybe, in order to trust God fully, I need to be utterly alone. That's when my focus on Him is the clearest.

"Parvin?"

I turn with a sharp inhale. Willow is in the back doorway. Enforcer Kaphtor stands guard outside. She closes the door and whispers in a fierce warrior voice, "We must rescue Elm."

There are so many things to fix. So many things I never intended to happen. "I know—"

"Now." She's no longer an alien in the USE. Her determination is back. "Two days are gone. We must rescue him. He is a hunter and can't hunt in the Wall. He will starve, Parvin!"

"Hush." If Kaphtor hears us—if even Hawke hears us—we might be right back in the containment center with no way to save Elm. "We will. Tonight."

There's nothing—no one—to hold me back. One thing I learned in the West is that everyone is meant to save lives.

"Will your Enforcer man help us?"

I shake my head. "No. We have to do this alone."

She gives me a small nudge toward the front door. "Ask him. He helped you when you were real sick. He looks at you nicely and carried you home."

"I know, but he's being watched. It's not safe for him." I swallow. "Willow, do you . . . do you know who he is?"

"Your friend."

I tug at the bandage around my left arm. Should I tell her? Who else knows? Would I endanger him by telling Willow? "He's . . . he's Jude's brother."

Her mouth drops open. "Jude-man?"

I nod.

"What's his name?"

"Hawke—uh, Solomon Hawke."

She grabs my hand with both of hers. "The Hawke will help us! Jude-man and Elm were friends." As if convincing herself, she looks at the ground and says in a harsh voice, "He *must* help."

With a curt nod, she releases my hand and plops into a chair, no longer flinching against its woodenness. If her skull was made of glass, I imagine I'd see all manner of brain cogs spinning and clunking on how to save Elm, but she has no idea what this will take. She's not from here. Her little sling and stones will do nothing against the cold metal Opening—and even those have been confiscated.

"Willow, he's already helped us." I have a code for the Enforcer cars. "We just need to wait until nightfall. Then we will save Elm."

The rest of the afternoon passes in silence. I pace the kitchen awhile and finally sit. Mother remains in her room, oblivious to the dangerous road my mental adventurer trudges. Tawny comes back into the kitchen to prepare supper, so I re-enter the foreign space I used to call my room.

The seclusion welcomes me with a stiff salute. "At ease." Not a pinch of ease follows.

Tawny's trunk is now closed and I see on the windowsill what was obscured before—Reid's empty wooden Clock. The one I believed so strongly was mine. All twelve zeroes shine with a sick, blood color.

000.000.00.00.00

Why is Tawny displaying this? Does she want to be reminded of her husband's untimely death? The zeroes remind me of my invisible Numbers. I'm a bona fide Radical now and . . . it's terrifying. The assurance I used to have in my set time is stripped from me. I feel out of control.

Averting my eyes from the Clock, I grab my dumped pack items from the ground and sit on the bed I *would* be sleeping on if I stayed here tonight. I'd rather break the law, try to save a life. The worst that can happen from this rescue attempt is my captivity. I'm already a captive.

The more I dwell on this fearlessness, the more reckless I become. What can stop me? *Is this the reason You kept me alive?* I stuff new belongings into my pack, including the small pouch of specie leftover from my Last Year Assessment. Who knows when I might have to bribe someone? *Is this where You're calling me?*

I have ideas on what to do—rescue Elm, try to stop the Council from using Jude's information, get Willow home—but how do I know if these are *my* ideas or *His?* I guess I'll have to do what I did in Ivanhoe, pursue what I believe is the best choice and commit it to God and to prayer.

I pick up the NAB, somewhat tempted to write a journal entry, to process my thoughts and emotions through words. But I can't. Skelley Chase gave me this NAB and who knows what he's been monitoring.

My sentra is the next best thing—a flat, camera-like object that, instead of taking photographs produces emotigraphs. Snapshots of emotions. I lift it and take an emotigraph of my changed bedroom. The thin emotigraph sheet is spit from the side of the sentra. I slip it into my pack. Hopefully it captures my mixed feelings, my plans of rescue, my loneliness.

Tawny opens the door. "Supper."

I don't even have time to look up before she closes the door.

I'm not hungry, but I need to eat if I plan to travel all night.

In the kitchen, Mother, Father, Willow, and Tawny sit around the table in the only four chairs. There's no space for me.

Tawny looks up with a raised eyebrow. She scans the table. "Oh, um." She rises. "You can sit here. We're not used to having five people in the house."

No, Tawny, *we're* not. It's always been four—Mother, Father, Reid, and me. "It's okay." I wave my hand. "I'm not hungry anyway." The smell of corn chowder urges my stomach to growl out in opposition. "Willow, come say good night before you go to sleep." I return to the bedroom, throwing her a wink.

After changing into dark pants and a grey shirt, I wait by the window. Too bad I don't have time for a bath. I was allowed a sprinkle of seconds to rinse when locked in the containment center—just enough to scrub Reid's blood off my hand.

I stuff Reid's Clock into my pack with trembling fingers, afraid Tawny might come in any moment and know what I'm doing. But what's it to her? This was my Clock just as long as it was Reid's. I have a right to it . . . especially if it helps me free Elm. When I went through six months ago, the Wallkeeper had to send a Clock into the black hole in the Wall in order to open the door. Reid's should work just fine.

If we get the Wall open, I could return to the West.

An empty hole in my heart sucks up my breath. The idea of the West without Jude feels as cold as this house. I can't go. I have too many things to do on this side.

Willow comes into the room an hour later wearing her old out-fit—a pale pink skirt, loose blouse, and thick coat. Only instead of bare feet she wears old boots. They might have belonged to me once.

"Let's go."

I open the shutters inch by inch, holding my breath against a creak. How many times have I crawled through this window to escape family arguments and feel adventurous?

Willow lands beside me with barely a sound. I peek around the front edge of the house. Hawke stands sentry at the front door, staring slightly to his right—away from us. I can only assume Kaphtor is at the back door.

This is when I really test which side Hawke is on.

I round the corner. We tiptoe down Straight Street, silent as creeping caterpillars. He knows we're here. I'm sure of it. He could turn his head if he wanted, but he doesn't. Only a few houses to go.

We turn onto Center Road.

Against the silent night, my heart thunders louder than a watchdog. Willow follows me up the road, glowing like a little ghost with her long white hair and pale skin.

"Are we going to the train?" she asks.

"It doesn't run from Unity Village at night." I jog as soft as possible and stop in a shadowed alley between two thatch houses. No one is out. Do we look too suspicious?

"Horses?"

I lean my head against the wood house siding. "No."

"Then we walk." She takes my hand. "Which way?"

My heart pounds so hard I might be sick. "We can't walk. The Opening is two hundred miles north."

She waits as if the solution just needs to be spoken.

I breathe out a small laugh. "Be patient, Willow, and follow me. I'm going to learn how to drive."

The courtyard of the county building is open and lit by street lamps. We crouch-run to where thick cords leash the two black beetle cars to the electric charging port. I tug on the first one.

The plug doesn't move, and a glowing code dial laughs at me with eight grinning zeroes. I'd laugh back if I didn't have to stay silent. The string of numbers on Hawke's note blink across my memory. I don't even need to check the paper.

Memorization has always been an odd, useless skill of mine. Now it feels like a superpower.

I enter the numbers. The screen flashes red and returns to the line of zeroes. I pull on the cord. Nothing.

"Maybe the other car?" Willow suggests, but before I crawl over to it, she inhales. "Parvin!"

On instinct, I drop to my hands and knees. She curls in a ball beside me, pulling her coat over her white hair. Just her pale finger pokes out, pointing toward the county building.

Hawke runs across the courtyard, up the steps, through the front doors. He and Kaphtor know we're gone. Or maybe he's turning us in.

I wipe my sweating palm on my pants and turn toward the second car. "Thanks for the warning."

"Welks," she whispers.

I enter the code into the second car, and . . . green! The code worked.

The shriek of an alarm startles the night. A light rises from the top of the beetle car, spinning and flashing, giving away our position.

"We need to go."

We sprint across the dirt back into the village. I weave through houses, avoiding the flickering candle streetlamps, and anticipate pursuit any moment. The code worked, but set off an alarm. Did Hawke know the car was rigged?

Willow tugs on my sleeve. "That has wheels like in Ivanhoe."

I follow her gesture to where a rickety blue-and-rust metal bike tied by rope leans against the knobby trunk of a mossy tree. "We'll be going over countryside more than anything, Willow. That won't be much faster than walking."

She stomps toward the tree. "It will be faster."

"This is *stealing*." But then I visualize myself tugging at the Enforcer charging port cord. I was okay with stealing then, why not now? Because the bike might belong to someone I know?

Willow wheels the bike over to me. The handles are almost as high as her head. The front tire is nearly flat and the bike creaks as if it hasn't been used since the week of Creation. That makes me feel better about stealing it, but the noise unnerves me.

"Okay, come on." I toss a handful of specie into the grass by the severed rope—not bothering to ask how Willow cut it—and pick up the bike by the frame with my right hand. I carry it only a few houses down before my forearm burns. I finally set it down on the walking path out of town. The path curves into a steady downhill, just wide enough for the bike.

"Get on." Willow holds the bike steady. "Then I get on in front of you."

"In front of me?" I squeak. "I've never ridden a bike, Willow." I straddle the seat and move to grab the handlebars. My muscles turn limp. "And I have only one hand."

She's unfazed. "We go downhill, just hold it tight. We do this for Elm."

I steady the bike while she climbs onto the handlebars, one pale hand on each handle. As she's climbing, she accidentally rings the small thumb bell. It chirps like a dying bird. Her shoulder pack hits my face "Go."

"Wait." I choke on my pounding pulse. "God, please . . . please get us to the Wall safely. Be with Elm—keep him alive. Do what You need to do with us, but . . . please save him."

I needed a verbal prayer. Mental prayer just didn't feel strong enough in this moment. A dash of peace rests upon me. God hears. He knows. He *wants* me to save lives.

Right now . . . I'm the only one who can.

"Okay, now go."

I push forward with my feet, already unstable. The front wheel settles into the worn path and gains speed as the downhill increases. I squint against the wind, half-blind to our path. When it's too fast to balance with my feet, I keep my legs spread out mid-jumping jack style.

The bike whooshes down the hill. A tree zips by. Wind hisses in my ear like a warning. My rear end bumps with every jolt and my stump slides against the handles. A scream builds in my throat. I hold my breath.

This was stupid.

Ahead, through the misty night, is a sharp right curve. My hand tightens on the grip and I press my left forearm into the metal. The bike emits rusty shrieks with each wheel rotation. We reach the curve and I jerk the handles. The tire spins too far and the bike bucks us off, headfirst, onto the stiff ground.

I tumble through a bush. Some part of Willow knocks me in the shoulder, a heel or elbow maybe. When I stop rolling, I'm on my back, my left arm trapped beneath me. Prickly sticks dig into my skin. Hot pain washes up and down my muscles, but I push myself into a sitting position.

Willow crashes through the bushes to my right. A rash mars her smooth cheek. She reaches toward me with her small fingers. "Parvin?"

"I'm fine." I lean over my knees and pray my body calms. "That was dumb."

"Still faster than walking."

I can't bring myself to laugh. She might not be joking. When it comes to Elm, her logic takes on a desperate tone.

I manage to get to my feet. My shoulder announces the start of a large bruise. We find the bike on its side beside the trail. It's still intact, creak and all. I pat the stiff frame as if to congratulate it on its durability.

For the next hour, we take turns pushing it along the path. I'm not sure why we bring it with us, maybe for the next downhill. I don't try to ride it again. Hopefully we'll reach another town by morning, where we can find a reliable means of transportation. I have a bag of specie after all. Someone's bound to offer a favor for a price.

We reach the base of the Wall within a few hours and start the two hundred mile trek north toward Opening Three. Beneath its looming, thousand-foot night shadow, I feel safer—closer to the West. My heart trips at the thought of reaching the Opening.

The longer we travel, the more I consider returning to the West. I could finish building the safe haven for Radicals sent through— the welcome shack filled with survival information. Have the supplies from Ivanhoe arrived at the Wall yet? I could build the bridge over the chasm to the plateau, help Radicals, and escape the rejection I've met from my own family in Unity Village.

"Parvin." Willow stops and looks back at me. "What is the light behind us?"

I turn. A tiny bulb of light bobs through the darkness a couple miles away. It's moving faster than someone walking with a lantern. My concern escalates. The light grows larger.

Someone is hunting us.

"We need to hide." I grab Willow's hand. "Leave the bike."

"They'll see it!"

"We can't conceal it, just run."

We stumble through the brush, between trees, over rocks and hidden holes. My pack slaps against my back. Willow pants behind me, but I don't slow. Something, anything, needs to hide us. The Wall is smooth stone with no cracks or coves, the bushes too low and thin to hide behind.

Willow's hand yanks out of mine. I skid to a stop and squint behind me. "Willow?"

A flash of her white foot catches my eye, disappearing up a maple tree. "Careful."

"I know how to climb without having to atone," she calls back.

That's not what I meant. I don't want her to fall, but she scales the branches like a tree frog. "Hurry, Parvin!"

"I can't." The bobbing light is closer now, and a high whine enters the night silence. An electric car. An Enforcer car. "I'll hide somewhere else."

I sprint away from the tree and Willow. At least if the headlight illuminates me, it won't see her. Why can't she seem to remember that I have only one hand? I can't climb. I'll never be able to climb anything again.

In a last minute effort, I crouch behind a larger bush at the base of a tree, pushing myself beneath the branches. I face outward to see if anyone approaches.

The whine grows louder like an approaching hornet. I squeeze my eyes tight, as if my tension will make me unseen. The car sounds practically on top of me when it finally stops. At least it didn't run me over.

Someone gets out, leaving the car running. Will this person kill me or just capture me?

"You get Blackwater. I'll get the albino."

Kaphtor's voice.

What will he do to us when we're out here alone in the dark? Beat us? Separate us? Threaten my family?

Footsteps slow, mere yards away. My heart thrums and I'm gripped by acute awareness of what it means to be a Radical. I don't have a Clock. I might die in the next five minutes. I don't know when my time is. I'll never know.

But Jude was right: I placed more faith in my Numbers than God. The Numbers don't matter.

Branches snap beneath a boot. My eyes fly open. How do the Enforcers know I'm here? It's almost as if they . . .

I gasp.

My tracker. I'm a registered Radical. So is Willow. They'll find us no matter where we hide.

The Enforcer nearby either heard me or has a tracking device in front of him, because the boots stop by my bush, inches from my face. If I had my dagger right now . . .

"Miss Parvin?"

My body propels me out of the bush before my mind can scream a protest. "Hawke?"

I practically collide with him as I stand. I can't decipher whether I'm happy to see him or terrified. Apprehensive seems the most accurate description. The beetle car is thirty yards away.

"Are you going to take us back?"

"You broke your word." His words are harsh, but sweat lines his forehead. His eyes are wide, like he's not sure what to do. "Good thing your sister-in-law respects the law."

"I never gave my *word*." What do I do? He's acting like a normal Enforcer. Curse that Testimony Log! "And . . . Tawny told you we were gone?" Maybe if we keep talking long enough, I'll think of some way to get out of this.

"Good thing, too, otherwise I wouldn't have reached you in time. Then we would have sent an army of Enforcers after you if you made it to the Wall. You don't want to deal with *that*."

I back against the tree trunk. A loud *thunk* comes from somewhere to my right, followed by the flop of something heavy—something human—on the ground.

Hawke doesn't turn, but his shoulders tense. "Now, are you going to come quietly or not, Miss Blackwater?"

"Um . . ."

Behind him, Willow appears, parting a black curtain of night. Running. Glaring at Hawke's back. She raises her arm behind her head, a stone in her hand. My brain sprints through sludge, trying to transfer a panicked thought into speech.

She executes a single skip, coiling her body for a throw.

I stretch out my hand. "Gently!"

Mid-throw, her startled gaze snaps to mine, and the stone flies through the air. It strikes the back of Hawke's head. His eyes glaze like when Jude died.

"Hawke."

He crumples to the ground. I try to catch him on his descent, but he's far too heavy for my single working arm. I manage to slip my hand between his head and the ground before it hits. The ring Reid gave me pinches my skin from the impact.

"Parvin!" Willow's face is tight and her purple eyes are narrowed. She clenches her tiny fists and looks down at Hawke. Her anger evaporates into arched eyebrows and an open mouth. "Oh, it's the Hawke." Her eyes slide to meet mine. "Sorry I almost killed him."

I look back at Hawke's unconscious form. His chest rises and falls with strength and his eyes are now closed. In this resting state, there are similarities between him and Jude. I feel the same urge to smooth back his hair and brush a single finger down his cheek.

But Solomon Hawke isn't Jude.

"Tawny betrayed us." Hawke and Kaphtor came after us, but it still worked out in our favor, almost as if Hawke planned it. I clench my hand into a fist. "He'll be okay. Let's go."

We pass the unconscious form of Kaphtor. "I only knocked out his mind. He's still breathing." Willow peers into the Enforcer car. "He was nice when he cut my arm for the chip."

"He was?" I can't imagine Kaphtor being nice.

I peek over her head into the car. A small bench seat lines the back of the squat car, wide enough for two people—one convict and one Enforcer. I close my eyes at the memory.

Willow climbs in the back, leaving the single front seat for me. I plop in the driver's seat, which is so far from the steering wheel that I have to hunch forward to reach it. A board of electric lights blinks—some with numbers and others with acronyms. On the ground are two pedals. I press my foot on the one on the right. We lurch forward so fast, the door slams shut.

I lift my foot to catch my breath against the startling movement, but it takes me only a moment to press it again. Hard. The car moves forward with a high whine that eventually disappears into an electronic hum. I'm taken back to the moment when Enforcers drove me to my hearing—the last time I rode in a car.

"We're moving!" Willow shrieks.

"Yes, we are." I clench the wheel and stare hard into the darkness. "And we have to be fast. Hawke said an army of Enforcers may be at the Wall."

There's no going back now. We've injured two Enforcers, stolen an Enforcer car, and we're fleeing our promise to remain captives.

I feel no remorse. Not even nervousness. I feel . . . empowered. This car used to deliver Radicals to their condemning hearings—it used to promote death and injustice. Now it is my tool.

We're going to save a life.

4

I wake from a pothole jolt and crush the wheel beneath my fingers. "Willow?"

"Hm?" Her soft sleep voice drifts from behind me.

"I fell asleep. I think we need to stop."

That wakes her up. "No stopping! I will drive. You sleep now."

"You're too small to drive." I widen my eyes against the drowsy pull of slumber.

"I'm not small for anything!" She's so fierce. "I will drive."

Only now do I realize how dangerous driving a car can be. We're going so fast. I blink and it seems to take a full minute before the blink ends. A tree pops into our path and I swerve. "Okay, you drive."

The idea of sleep sounds so glorious that it's not too difficult to entrust my life to Willow's hands. After all, if not for her, I would have died many times in the West.

We coast to a stop and she crawls forward. I point to the pedal on the right. "That one makes us go. There's a really light trail I've been following. It keeps us from the thick brush and trees."

She plops into the seat and it almost swallows her. I shove my shoulder pack toward her and she sits on it, leaning forward and pressing the pedal with the very tips of her toes. The car lurches onward and I tumble backward onto the bench seat.

Willow giggles. We go faster. She lets out a triumphant, "Ha!"

I smile and curl into a ball on the cramped seat. My right arm aches from doing all the steering. After a few more jolts and potholes, my awareness seeps into lethargic bliss. The rumble of uneven ground beneath us and whine of the car escort me into a dream like a lullaby.

Jude is beside me, but I can't seem to see his face. We sit side by side in a yellow locomotive—the *Ivanhoe Independent*. Most of our surroundings are a blur of fuzzy white. There is no sound, not even the sound of train tracks beneath us. He is on my left, his shock of dark brown hair covering his tanned forehead.

I have the strangest sensation that God brought us here—bringing Jude down and me up to a mysterious middle ground—to give me a chance to speak with him after his death. It's a dream, yet it's not. So many questions swirl in my mind.

"Were you surprised?" Somehow I know he understands my thoughts behind the question—was he surprised to wake up in heaven and realize life was over?

"Things were in order. Peace was in the process of being found."

I stare at him and everything in me tightens—my heart, my face. Tears creep from my very bones. I hurt for him and his shortened life. I hurt for his family—for Solomon Hawke to have lost him. I cry for things not being as they should.

"Why are you crying?" Jude looks at me for the first time. My gaze meets his raspberry-chocolate eyes. His voice is soft and confused.

In a dreamy sense, I realize he doesn't understand. He does not comfort me because he does not process sadness. Nothing in him hurts. He is free from it all.

My sorrow leaves with a long breath. I don't need to cry or hurt for his situation because he is in complete shalom.

I wake with tears on my face.

The car creeps along, slowing, until it stops. I sit up, still reeling from seeing Jude. A strange calm envelops me as I think of him.

Thank You. I am undeserving of such relief. I have hardly trusted God since Reid died. *I'm sorry. Thank you.* My prayer words come in short, sleepy bursts.

My tranquility feels nothing short of miraculous, and I still can't seem to get rid of the feeling that was more than just a dream.

"Is this it?" Willow asks.

I glance out the window on the left. Beside us is Opening Three, shrouded in darkness and moonlight. The door is black arched metal, set deep in the stone. To the right of it sits the rickety guardhouse with a wooden door and a four-paned window.

Reid died here. I half expect to see his body spread-eagled on the ground in front of the Opening.

My throat convulses and all tranquility scatters. "You drove right up?" Our car light illuminates the guardhouse. All I can think of are Hawke's words: *Enforcer army . . . Enforcer army . . . Enforcer army . . .*

As if catching on to the implications behind my question, Willow launches out of the car, something thin and shiny clamped tight in her little fist. A knife? Where did she get a knife? She heads for the guardhouse.

"Willow," I hiss, scrambling after her. I take my pack with me, Reid's expired Clock safely beneath the buckled flap. "Willow!"

She glances back at me then swerves to the side of the guardhouse and crouches beneath the window in the night shadows. I reach her just as candlelight grows from inside, spreading into the darkness from the single window. The front door opens and a man steps out. His silhouette is mere feet from me, illuminated by the candlelight.

He's very different from the Wallkeeper who sent me through the Wall six months ago. Though I only see his back from an angle, I can tell he is young and tall with a long face. His hair is neck-length, pushed behind his ears and his brown winter uniform looks freshly ironed. So fresh that I frown. He couldn't have been sleeping in it, otherwise it would be wrinkled. Why isn't he in pajamas? It's early morning. He couldn't have been expecting us already . . . could he?

Willow and I don't breathe as he stands on the threshold, holding a gun. His face turns toward the Enforcer car. I wish I could see his expression. I lower my head and squeeze deeper into the shadow of the house. By not looking at him, maybe I'll be invisible.

His footsteps crunch toward the car.

I open my eyes. The darkness is different than moments before. It's no longer fully black, but tinged with blue. Morning blue.

Sunrise is coming.

"Hello?" The wallkeeper glances back at the guardhouse. At us. But the shadows must be strong, because he turns again toward the car.

"How do we open the Wall?" Willow looks up at me.

I slide my hand under the flap and into my pack. My fingers find the cold worn wood of my—of *Reid's*—Clock. It will open the door for only fifteen seconds. That's all we need to run inside, grab Elm, and escape back to the West.

My thoughts skid to a stop.

Am I going back to the West? Or am I staying here? After what I've done to get us here, I ought to cross the Wall again. Otherwise, I'll probably be killed or at least imprisoned on this side.

But what about Solomon Hawke? He still doesn't know how Jude died. And Skelley Chase? Someone needs to convict him for Reid's murder. And the Council? They probably already have

Jude's Clock-matching invention information. They'll know how to Clock-match anyone. Jude said they would have far more power than they ought. They would have to be stopped, but can *I* do that?

Willow grabs my arm and yanks me out of my jumbled thoughts. "How do we open it?"

I dart a glance back at the Wallkeeper, then give Willow a slight nod. Maintaining a crouch, we slip around the back of the house. A small passage rests between the wood house and Wall. We tiptoe until I see the square hole for Reid's Clock.

Two crisscrossed metal bars are bolted into the stone, blocking the hole. I set down the Clock and pull against one of them. It's icy and doesn't budge. The Enforcers and the Council *did* intend Elm to die inside the Wall. They never meant to save him or allow him to live, otherwise why block the Clock hole?

Footsteps come back toward the house. "Who's there?" The Wallkeeper's voice is strong. Firm. Unafraid.

I wish he was afraid.

Willow holds her weapon aloft. Only now do I see it's a dovetail chisel—the type Father uses in his wood shop. She must have stolen it from his apron before he went to work. But what chance does a chisel have against a gun? Then again, she has excellent aim.

The footsteps come closer. Faster. Willow and I stumble backward, toward the back of the house. We turn to round the corner and a flash of light blinds us. Spots swim in front of my vision. I extend my hand to fend off whatever caused the flash. Another flash. I blink furiously, but before I regain my sight, hands clamp around my arms. Fingers turn to fists with handfuls of my clothes.

Willow shrieks. Someone—a man's voice—yells, "Look out, she's got a knife!"

I can't see. There are too many hands.

"Let me go!" I'm dragged out of the small alley. By now, the sky has lightened to pastel blue and a tinge of coral pink. My body generates my exhaustion and I feel abruptly weighted and tired.

Willow and I are yanked into the guardhouse. My eyes are almost fully adjusted. People fill the guardhouse, as if they've been hiding out on watch. My blur of vision clears and the first face my gaze rests upon won't meet my eyes.

Hawke.

He stares at his feet with a bandage around his head and a gun in his lap. How in time's name did he get here before us?

Willow and I are cuffed wrist-to-wrist and then shackled to the hanger bar in a small closet at the back corner. There's no door, so we can still see inside the one-room guardhouse. It looks like my kitchen at home, but longer, with a tiny cot against one wall. Four Enforcers currently sit on the cot, looking too close and uncomfortable. A wood stove is across from them. The Wallkeeper tosses two more small logs inside. Other Enforcers lean against spare bits of wall.

The rest of the house is fairly empty of furniture—wood floors, log walls with chipped caulk, and a steepled roof. Sachem, the Lead Enforcer from Unity Village, paces between the others with a NAB in his hands.

"A representative from the Council should be here soon." He looks up at me. "Then you'll be questioned."

The Council—the people who sent the assassin after Jude. Why does a representative need to come? What information can I give him?

I want to drift into ignorant optimism and hope all of this is a plan to let Elm out, but the Council murdered Jude. They're not about saving lives. Their assassin tried to kill me, too. Maybe the representative is coming to finish the job.

A reporter with a fancy camera sits on a stool beside the stove. He's scanning the screen on the back of his camera. He glances at me, then returns to the screen. So that's what the flash was. Did he take pictures of our capture?

Everyone here seemed to know we were coming.

Hawke meets my eyes and holds my gaze. His mouth forms a sad frown these days. I continue to stare at him, straining to interpret his emotions, but all I focus on is how his eyes are a darker teal this morning.

Kaphtor is here, too, standing with his back to us.

"Why do you want to kill Elm?" Willow shouts to the room.

All eyes turn to us. She pulls against the cuff keeping her in the closet. Her narrowed gaze flicks from one person to another. Challenging. Fiery.

"How many people did you let into the Wall?" Sachem looks back down at his NAB. "We can't open the Wall to an albino army."

"It's only Elm!" Then she gives a tilt of her head. "But he is like an army by himself. You *should* be afraid."

Hawke chuckles, but my heart sinks. Willow's not helping. "So, what are we waiting for?" I almost don't want to know what they plan to do—with me, with Willow, with Elm.

"We are waiting for the representative from the Council," Hawke says. "Then we will open the door."

Willow gasps.

"Hawke . . ." Sachem sounds weary.

"Yes sir?" Hawke's response is almost a challenge.

Sachem sighs and taps on his NAB. A light flashes past the window. All Enforcers stand and exit. No one bothers with me or Willow. I crane my neck to see through the window. Only lines of black Enforcer coats are visible.

The muscles in my neck and shoulders clench. It's just me and Willow with . . . countless Enforcers. We are the enemy. They could do anything to us and no one would know. They could kill us without a trial—shoot us and toss our bodies inside the Wall.

Hawke wouldn't let them do that.

"What do we do?" Willow tugs against the cuff, trying to wiggle her hand out.

Hawke reenters the guardhouse. I straighten. The air feels different with just us three in the room. I want to say something or ask him questions. How did he get here? Will he protect us or maintain his Enforcer façade?

He strides forward, holding a small key. When he unlocks Willow's wrist from the closet bar, we are close. In fact, we are touching. There's no way to avoid it and . . . I don't want to. Avoid it, that is. Even in the midst of this captivity and failed rescue, something about Hawke makes me breathe easier.

The cuff clinks and detaches from the bar. He turns his head and looks down at me. I open my mouth, but he squeezes my shoulder.

"Fear not, Miss Parvin." To Willow he says, "You have good aim."

"Will you save Elm?" she asks as he leads us out of the guardhouse.

He steers us toward the Opening. "I always strive to save lives, Miss Willow, no matter whether those lives are from the West or from the USE."

It's like hearing my own calling come from his mouth.

The morning sun illuminates the Wall like a lighthouse beacon. Around the Opening stand a line of Enforcers, all armed. Whoever arrived must have brought more. I look over my shoulder. Sure enough, four more Enforcer cars and one sleek white automobile sit in a line beside the guardhouse.

A middle-aged man speaks with Sachem in front of the white car. His hair is cut short like toothbrush bristles. It's pure grey—clearly dyed—matching his equally short mustache and beard.

His eyes are squinted, anger wrinkles stretching back to his temple. As he talks to Sachem, his mouth moves in terse bursts, like he's a moment away from shouting.

This must be the Council member. What will he say to me? Ask me? Maybe he'll want to know about Jude.

He wears a smooth black suit with grey cuffs and a grey tie. Blinding white shoes rest stark against the sparse grass tufts and brown dirt. He's a walking black-and-white photograph. Even his ashy skin fits the look.

Sachem waves a hand toward me. Mr. Black-and-White meets my gaze. His eyes narrow even more, if possible. I swallow and rub my right hand over the bandage covering the cut on my left.

They walk toward me. On impulse, I grip Hawke's sleeve and face the Opening, not daring to breath. I can't explain my fear, but every fiber in my quaking being wants to flee from this councilman.

Hawke glances at me a moment before Sachem's voice speaks close to my ear. "Miss Blackwater."

Mechanically, I turn, fighting to bring out my old mask of confidence. It doesn't surface. Instead, the lift of my chin just interrupts my eye contact, which is a good thing because Mr. Black-and-White's gaze could petrify the most jittery child if met head-on.

"This is Elan Brickbat, from the Citizen Welfare Development Council," Sachem says. "He'd like to speak with you privately."

I almost say, "No thanks," but my vocal cords are immobilized. I nod, barely registering the clink of chain leaving my wrist. When Brickbat turns toward the guardhouse, ice melts from my joints and my body follows against my will.

Did I think Willow and I could get away with this? Was I so fearless? Foolish? The Council is who almost killed me the first time. I've given them a second chance to do the job—something I thought I wanted a few days ago. Death doesn't sound quite as freeing anymore, not when it takes me away and leaves this icy photo of a man behind to "lead" the people I love.

The creak of the guardhouse door as Brickbat opens it sounds like a beckoning into a hall of horrors. I don't want to walk past him. That would mean putting my back to him. Vulnerability.

I gesture to the door. "Please, after you."

He smiles as a jack-in-the-box might—frightening, not friendly. Too wide. Too white. "I insist." His voice is hoarse and wet, like he needs to cough or clear his throat because he's shouted too long without swallowing.

On impulse, I clear my own throat and practically sprint through the door. The moment it closes behind me, I spin around and plop onto the cot against the wall, not waiting for an invitation to sit.

Brickbat remains standing. He looks at me like I'm a stray dog urinating on his flowerbed.

Instead of being intimidated, fire builds inside my chest. I welcome it and dread it at the same time. This is not the time for an outburst. He's one of the men who had orphans tortured to test out Jude's new Clock-matching invention—he and his Council hidden behind their High-City luxuries. Does he think I don't know this? I imagine his cold narrowed eyes staring at a child's pain-wracked body.

When Jude first told me the Council did this, I could hardly believe such evil could exist in a person. As I stare at Elan Brickbat, I believe. Something is broken inside him. Broken shalom. This man is not the way things should be.

I rise to my feet, which puts me only a few inches from his face towering above me. "You had questions?" He better get to them because I have my own questions. And I intend to ask them.

"Sit *down!*"

Startled, I plop back down, my boldness disrupted.

"I have no problem having you killed, Miss Blackwater."

Why did I let him rattle me so quickly? I meet his stare unblinking. "I have no problem dying."

"Good." He pulls a pistol from the inside of his coat and fires a bullet into the wood, inches from my cheek.

I flinch so hard, my head hits the wall and I fling my arms in front of my face. My body tenses, waiting for a second explosion, and my memory throws up a vision of Reid's bloodied features.

My ear is deafened and slivers burn in my cheek. Brickbat laughs. It sounds like he's drowning in his own throaty saliva. I try not to gag. A squint reveals he's returned the gun to his coat. "Don't lie again."

It wasn't a lie. I truly thought I had no problem dying, but now, as my heart pounds so hard it makes me nauseous, I'm enlightened. Peace would not come with my death. There are too many things left unsaid and unfixed—things only I know about.

"You're learning how to be defiant, Miss Blackwater. I've read your X-book. Defiance is a trait you should try to stifle. It's not attractive and it certainly won't free your little albino boy."

That biography truly was one of my worst ideas.

His voice grows louder as he speaks. "Now who else is in the Wall? If you lie, I will blow your head to bits, followed by that albino girl outside. Maybe even the Enforcer you seem to consider a friend—Jude's brother."

I can't swallow. I can't breathe.

"Yes, we know about them. The death of Solomon Hawke would affect only a handful of people whom no one even cares about."

Why is he threatening me? "No one else is in the Wall. Just Elm."

He leans inches from my face. "Part of me wants to open the door and shoot him. But to keep you *obedient*, I'm willing to get this over with. When the boy is free, he is under the care of the Council. So is your little Willow. We are allowing her to remain in Unity Village until other arrangements are made."

His hoarse wet breath hits my face. I close my eyes and attempt to calm my voice. "Can't you just let Willow and Elm go back to their home?"

"No."

"Why not?"

The door opens and I startle. Brickbat straightens slowly, no sign of surprise. Only annoyance.

I dare a glance to see who ventures to enter without knocking. Hawke closes the door behind himself. He strides to stand beside my cot. His face is set with hard lines—a mixture of the cold Enforcer persona and . . . is that anger? Whatever emotion swirls behind his countenance, it's akin to when he fought Sachem for my life only six months ago. He'd just found out about the death of the Newtons and he tried—oh, he tried—to save me from the Wall.

In hindsight, I'm glad Hawke didn't save me, but I *am* glad he fought for me.

"Message, Enforcer?" Brickbat barks.

Hawke gives a small bow. "No message, sir. Only on monitoring duty." His voice is cold.

"I prefer privacy." Brickbat turns back to me, dismissive.

Hawke doesn't flinch. Doesn't even seem to breathe. "Unfortunately, sir, Miss Blackwater is still assigned to the Enforcers of Unity Village. It is my duty to both protect and monitor her—a *registered* Radical."

Brickbat gives a guttural laugh. "If you defy the Council, Enforcer, you will *have* no duty."

"It is not in defiance that I stand here, sir, only concern for Miss Blackwater's safety."

Moments ago, Brickbat threatened to obliterate me, Willow, and Hawke. Doesn't Hawke realize that, despite his claim against defiance, he is defying this leader? The leader who killed his brother?

Maybe that's why Hawke is standing up to him. He's staring into the eyes of his brother's murderer.

The door opens again. It's Lead Enforcer Sachem. His face is pale and his eyes dart to each of us, resting on Hawke. "Enforcer Hawke, please resume your position by Miss Willow." His voice is low, cautious, and uncertain.

Hawke doesn't even turn his head. "I believe Council member Brickbat and Miss Blackwater are almost finished." He nods his head toward Brickbat. "Please continue, sir."

Brickbat waves his hand at Sachem and finally, *finally*, clears his throat. "This Enforcer is out of your hands, Sachem. For now, you may leave him here. He was right—I am finished."

Sachem leaves. Brickbat turns, but I risk another question. Just one more. I must. "The Council is for the citizen's welfare. Why do you allow men like the biographer Skelley Chase to kill innocent people like my brother? Why do you send assassins after brilliant inventors? Why aren't you protecting the *citizens?*"

His eyes narrow with a tiny flinch and he holds the glare. "You don't understand yet, Miss Blackwater, do you? We *are* protecting the citizens."

I frown.

"We are protecting them from Radicals." He heads toward the door and opens it. "Radicals—registered or unregistered—are not citizens. We are protecting the people from *you.*"

He leaves the guardhouse, closing the door behind him. I shut my mouth, only just realizing it hung open. Protecting the citizens from me? From Radicals?

Now I see the plan.

The Council never cared about saving Radicals—that much I already knew. But that's why they'll use Jude's Clock-matching invention. They'll Clock-match Radicals, even against our will.

I can't let that happen. It's exactly what Jude feared. And once we're all Clock-matched, the government will have complete control over us.

In theory, giving Radicals their own Clocks sounds good. Valiant, even—despite the fact that the Council will rob all of us of free choice. But I can't erase the knowledge of what the Council did to gain the ability to do what they want. They ruined the lives of innocent orphans. More than that . . . they tortured them.

Murdered them.

It can't be worth that. I can't support that, or the death of every Radical I've attempted to save in my short lifetime.

Brickbat's intentions are clear. If I resist the Council in any way he—*they*—will come after my Radicals. Me. Tawny. Willow. Jude's orphans.

He might do it anyway. The fate of every Radical in Unity Village may very well rest in my hands. I look down. My stump twitches. Even in metaphor, my hands are weak, maimed, and unable to carry the strength I need.

My list of people to protect just skyrocketed in number. It's not Willow and Elm anymore, now it includes Hawke, my family, and the Radicals in Unity Village.

Hawke touches my elbow. "You are safe."

I sigh and an unwelcome tear trails down my cheek. *God, I need Your help. We need to save lives. Work through my weakness.*

I stand. "Thank you, Hawke."

He releases my arm. "Please, if you can, call me Solomon."

I brush away the tear, and wipe my palm on my pants. "All right, Solomon. Let's go save Elm."

We walk outside and I take my place beside Willow. She grabs my hands. Her fingernails bite into my skin as we struggle to breathe against the silence. She strains against me, undoubtedly fighting the urge to run to the Opening. Enforcers surround us, but we have a clear view of the door.

The Wallkeeper tosses away the metal bars recently wrenched from the stone, so he can insert Reid's blank Clock into the square hole.

The Enforcers, including Hawke—I mean, *Solomon*—train their guns on the Opening. I hear the suction of the Clock entering the Wall, activating whatever mechanisms control the East and West doors.

The East door—our door—slides open with a hiss. Thirty Enforcer guns cock, but nothing comes out. No pale boy. No Elm.

Almost as one, we all step forward, peering into the black tunnel. That's when I see it. Judging by Willow's high scream, she sees it too.

A skeleton.

5

The skeleton is small, curled on the ground right by the door with a torn, scratched pack clutched in its arms. The eye patch is crooked with animal teeth marks in the leather. No one can mistake the cut slicing down the skull's face—his eye wound must have been deep to leave a mark on the bone.

Willow yanks from my grasp, but gets only three steps before the door zips shut.

Fifteen seconds are up. And Elm is dead—eaten by the creatures hiding inside the Wall.

Willow collapses into the grass, croaking out Elm's name between small broken gasps. Tears burn my eyes, but don't seem to fall. Maybe it's because I'm too hollow to tackle the haunting emotion of failure again. Maybe it's because I need to be strong for Willow. Maybe I'm just numb.

Elan Brickbat turns on the heel of his white shoes, throws me a firm glance, and then walks away. He passes a sealed envelope to Lead Enforcer, Sachem, then climbs into his sleek car. Trailed by three cars of Enforcers, he zips away as if this was all just another boring breakfast meeting.

Sachem opens the envelope and reads a portion of the paper inside. "Take them back, Hawke."

Hawke lowers his gun. "Yes, sir."

Why is Hawke taking us? Is it because of Brickbat's paper? The enemy *knows* I'm friends with Hawke, but they're acting as if they trust him to be on their side.

What game are they playing? Should I warn Hawke?

The other Enforcers return to their cars. The Wallkeeper hammers the bars back in place. I walk tentatively to Willow as she pushes herself to her feet. Her knees buckle, but Hawke catches her and lifts her into his arms.

He looks so tender and Willow so fragile. Is that what we looked like when he lifted me away from the horror of the Wall a few days ago? It's such a soft, yet broken, picture.

"Come, Miss Parvin." He holds Willow with one arm and stretches his free hand out to me.

It's a gesture he didn't need to make. I would have followed anyway. But the fact that he made this effort to provide me with comfort through the touch of our hands makes me want to cry again.

We climb into the back of an Enforcer car. Hawke slides into the driver's seat. Before starting, he pulls a small silver case from his pocket and removes what I can only assume are his Testimony Log contact lenses. I glance away as he pulls the thin man-made membrane from his eye.

Once the silver case is returned to his pocket, we start driving. A line of other Enforcer cars follows us. That eliminates any escape plan I might have had.

I want to ask Hawke if he'll get in trouble for taking out the contacts, but Willow's lapsed into a dead silence. She stares out the window with her neck craned too far for me to see her face. What do you say to someone who's just lost the person dearest to them?

When Jude died, I wanted no words. No comfort. There was nothing that *could* comfort. I wanted to lie in that forest until I slipped into heaven, which I practically did because of the toxin the assassin inserted into my veins. I'll never know if my hopelessness was sparked by the toxin or by my own sorrow.

I reach to take her hand, but think better of it and clench mine again in my lap. Anger burns my skin. If the Council and the Enforcers had allowed Elm through three days ago, he wouldn't have died.

I think back to how he carried me the last day before I returned to the East—how he and Willow were my pillars of strength and survival in those last hours. He was strong for a fourteen-year-old and proud of it. And he loved Willow. He loved her as much as a young teenager could love a girl.

They were grafting partners after all.

Will Willow now be alone the rest of her life? What does albino culture call for? Brickbat said she was under the care of the Council, which I wouldn't classify as *care* at all. If she grew reckless and desperate when she thought Elm was alive, what will she do now that the Council has caused his death?

She heaves a sigh and turns away from the window. I face her, ready to be what she needs.

"Elm is not dead." To my concern, she smiles.

"What do you mean?" I now take her hand without hesitation. *God, I don't know how to combat denial.*

She giggles. I can't even bring myself to smile. "Willow, please, you're scaring me."

"Elm wouldn't die like *that*." She points her thumb at the window. "He is free. It was a message. He is free and coming for me."

I don't know how she got that out of a disfigured child's skeleton with an eye patch. "How do you know?"

"He's my Elm. I know him. He's smart. He's strong. He survives."

"Yes, but *how* Willow? What else do you know?"

She slams her tiny fists in her lap. "He survives, Parvin! This is all we need to know."

I turn my head away and lean back against the bench seat. I want out of this car—somewhere my family doesn't hurt me, my friend doesn't shout at me, the Council doesn't threaten me. Somewhere my absence and my presence won't cause harm.

"Your reaction was pretty convincing, Miss Willow," Hawke says from the front in a low voice.

Willow speaks soft again, but I can't bring myself to look at her. "I was afraid of where Elm is. Afraid I won't go home. It was easy to pretend."

We remain silent after this. I ought to speak to Hawke. Say something about leaving him abandoned in the dark last night. How did he get to the Wall anyway? And Jude . . . we still haven't talked about Jude.

"Hawke—"

"I thought we'd established that I'm Solomon."

I clap my lips shut. *Solomon* sounds like a different person to me—not the Enforcer I came to trust while in the West. "Solomon is what Jude called you."

Hawke is silent. I hold my breath. Then he says in a low, almost contemplative, voice, "Yes, it is."

Should I tell him about my dream of Jude? Thinking of his death now isn't so painful. Something changed. That dream changed me.

"I don't think I can call you Solomon." I might as well admit it.

"Why not?"

I look out the window at the hills rising and dipping as we pass. "It's too familiar."

His hands squeak against the stiff steering wheel. "Aren't we . . . familiar?"

I'm on the roll of honesty, so I might as well get it all out. "Yes, but when I was in the West, I felt guilty communicating with you while with Jude. Interacting with you now is . . . hard." Plus, Elan Brickbat threatened to blow Hawke's head to bits.

I can't get too familiar. "You're not under surveillance anymore, are you?"

He shakes his head.

I gulp. "Then I need to talk to you about . . . Jude."

Seconds pass like stilted bell tolls. "I know you loved him."

That's *not* what I was going to talk about. I look away. How embarrassing. I can't discuss love. Not with Hawke, the only contender for my affections. I stopped contact with him in Ivanhoe because I thought I'd never see him again. It made sense to choose Jude. And yes . . . maybe I did love him.

"You don't have to explain, Miss Parvin. I don't want this to be uncomfortable for you."

Too late. "I'm not sure what to say." This is so awkward. "I actually wanted to talk about Jude's . . . death."

"Oh, okay."

How ironic that we both relax about the topic of murder and tense at the topic of love. "When I was in the Wall, you asked me how he died. You seemed confused that he died."

The car slows, whether from a rough road or Hawke's reaction, I don't know. "Yes."

Willow stares out the window with vacant eyes and no evidence of hearing a thing we're saying.

I try to strengthen my voice. "Well, the Council's assassin found us before we got to the Wall. He . . . put a syringe with a toxin in my neck, threatening to kill me unless Jude inserted a pirate chip into his brain." The raw harshness of each word scrapes against my throat. "So . . . Jude did it. He put in the pirate chip and it . . . terminated him."

If only I could see Hawke's face. He says nothing to this and his silence entraps me. "Just before Jude died, I asked him why he did it. He had only a few seconds left and . . . well, his last words to me . . . were *ask Solomon.* Then, at the Wall, you told me his death was a choice. What did you mean?"

He rubs a hand over his face. "Jude was always so cryptic. He believed faith could overcome Clocks. He never trusted his own Numbers. To tell you the truth, he fiddled with so many different Clocks, I'm not even sure what his real Numbers *were.*"

His voice is calm. He's not angry. He doesn't hate me. He doesn't blame me. "But if he thought that, why did he die? Shouldn't his faith have *protected* him from death?"

"I don't know."

"That doesn't make sense," I huff. "Why would he tell me to ask you about it if you don't know? Is there more information?"

"Yes." He knocks a knuckle against the car window. "I'm quite certain September twenty-fifth was *not* his zero-out date."

"But . . . that's when he died. How are you so sure?"

"Because that's my birthday. I would have remembered his Good-bye if it landed on my birthday. It doesn't make sense that he zeroed out on that day . . . unless he was right about being able to overcome our Numbers."

Jude died on Hawke's birthday. What can I say to that? Happy birthday, sorry your brother killed himself for my sake?

The car curves away from the Wall. "I wish I knew more, Miss Parvin, but Jude shared most of his secrets with our father."

These Hawke men and their secrets. "Is your father still alive?"

"Yes, he zeroes-out in April."

"Oh, Haw—Solomon, I'm sorry."

He shrugs. "We've all accepted it." From the tension in his voice, I don't think he likes this topic.

Willow falls asleep beside me, her face pressed against the glass, sticking just enough to keep her head from falling forward.

Maybe I should give Hawke a break. I've done what I wanted to—told him about Jude's death. There aren't any answers yet, but maybe time will help us figure things out. "It's strange talking to *Enforcer* Hawke."

"Enforcer Hawke—or, *Solomon*, which I think sounds much more appealing—is the same man who sought your freedom prior to your trial." A brief smile lines his voice. "The same man on the other side of your NAB sending you messages. The same man who asked Jude to protect you."

The car slows. "The same man who, three days ago, desperately prayed out of selfishness that you would live, even when he knew you wanted to die."

"Oh." It's all I can get out. Hawke asked Jude to protect me? Does he mean when the albinos first captured me or does he mean longer than that? I can't imagine independent Jude following me around at the order of his brother.

The automobile is crawling now, the closest thing to a stop. So is my heart—unsure how to pound.

He turns in his seat. "Parvin."

This is the first time he's ever said my name without a *Miss*. If I liked *Miss Parvin*, the way he says just *Parvin* leaves me leaning forward in my seat, my stomach fluttering. Parvin . . . what? What will he say?

"I'm on your side."

This statement, so simple—and to some, like Elan Brickbat, so obvious—cuts loose the film of emotions keeping my tears at bay. A sob escapes and I turn my face sharply away so he won't watch me. "I know, Hawke. I know you are."

I'm not alone. I don't need to be alone.

The car accelerates back to normal speed.

"So then, why are you still trying to keep your Enforcerhood?"

He breathes out a long, slow breath. "What you have come to know as an Enforcer and what I trained to be as an Enforcer are drastically different. After escorting the Newtons here, I stayed in Unity Village because of the injustice. I saw how the Enforcers chose not to register people without Clocks. I remain an Enforcer with the hopes of restoring rightness. To save lives. To make things the way they should be."

"Shalom," I say in a hushed rasp.

"Yes, shalom." His voice is smiling again. "Another reason you should call me Solomon."

I quirk my lips to one side. "Because of shalom?"

"The definition of my name, *Solomon*, is *shalom*. I guess you could say I've always felt that defined my purpose in life."

His name means shalom? Part of me is jealous. Another part wonders what this means—I can't give it up to coincidence. Coincidence is God's way of surprising us.

"I wish my name meant something purposeful. *Parvin* means a cluster of stars. It can't get more bland than that." I could stretch it to mean I'm a shining light or something, but that doesn't feel like *purpose*.

"No, no, look. You have to break it down. *Par* is Scandinavian for *Peter*, which means *rock*. And *Vin* is a Latin name meaning *conquering*. There you have it: conquering rock."

"So I went from a star to a rock."

He chuckles. "The more you think on it, the more you'll like it." Has *he* thought about my name like this?

We bump along in pensive silence. How does Hawke know so much about names? Scandinavian? Latin? Do people study these sorts of things?

"You should be warned, I won't be an Enforcer for long, Parvin."

"Why not?"

"I'm raising too many questions. Refuting too many laws."

"Can't you just talk to Sachem? He seems like he *could* be understanding."

61

He gives a humorless laugh. "Last night I appealed for Elm's release, but Sachem said it's out of his hands. Problems seem to be out of everyone's hands only because no one chooses to take them on. I've taken on enough problems to paint a target on my back."

I sit straighter. "What do you mean?"

"I'll be dismissed soon. Maybe even tonight. Taking out my Testimony Log is a pretty big flag."

"Because of me?" My voice comes out hollow.

"Because of me, Parvin. Because of who I choose to be. It doesn't fit the Enforcer standard in Unity Village. No matter how many times I argue with Sachem, he still allows all Radicals—registered and unregistered—to be sent across the Wall."

"But no one is being sent across the Wall right now." Should I tell him the Council is going to get rid of all Radicals?

"That is because of you."

"I hope it stays that way until I can find a way to make the crossing safe."

He says nothing to this, which worries me. How can I make the crossing safe if I'm stuck on this side of the Wall? What if the government starts sending people back through now that they know an albino army isn't lurking inside?

More lives lost to the cliff on the other side.

Where do I start to protect the Radicals inside my village? I can't very well tromp around demanding they read my X-book for knowledge about the West. It's ironic, really, that one reason I wrote my biography was to share my story and save Radicals—to reveal my worth to the people of my Village—yet Mother is proof that it made people hate me and endangered more lives.

According to Hawke and Skelley Chase, I'm quite popular in the High Cities—famous, even. Famous among the people who don't matter to me.

I don't feel popular. I feel like a criminal. "Hawke, do you see me as a criminal?"

He laughs—not loud or hard, but enough to convey at least a small amount of humor. That's a good sign, right? "No, Parvin."

I sigh.

"I'd classify you as an outlaw."

Both words still ostracize me from my village. "What's the difference?"

"A criminal moves *against* the law. An outlaw moves *beyond* the law."

"And that's . . . better?"

He turns off the small path and the road grows bumpier. We must be close to Unity. "I think so. Some said Jesus was an outlaw."

Jesus? Any reference to God is spoken so infrequently that it's strange to hear it in normal conversation. This isn't the first time Hawke has shown signs of sharing faith. After all, he understands shalom.

"I guess I'm okay being an outlaw." Especially if Hawke views it as a good thing. "You sure know a lot of . . . definitions. Your name, my name, criminal versus outlaw . . ."

He tilts his head. "Jude used to make fun of me. *Definitions* was the only cap I ever took in school."

"Cap? What's that?"

"I'll tell you later." He nods toward the windshield. We roll into the courtyard of the county building where two Enforcers wait.

Wait . . . we're here already? I don't recognize the Enforcers. Hawke returns his Testimony Log to his eyes and we climb out of the car.

"By order of the Council"—a short ruddy Enforcer pulls out wrist shackles—"Parvin Blackwater is to return to her family and the albino goes to the containment center."

"The *albino* has a name," I snap.

He doesn't look at me. Hawke doesn't argue. I want him to, but these other Enforcers can change nothing. They're just lousy messengers.

I don't want to go back to my family, where Tawny has taken the role of perfect daughter and Mother doesn't care about my story. I wasn't around Father enough to see if he has residual hatred of me.

"We'll take the albino." The short Enforcer takes her arm.

"No." My throat closes and I look to Hawke.

"I will escort Miss Blackwater home." Then in a quieter voice directed to me, "She'll be okay."

"Elm is coming for me, Parvin. Don't be scared." There it is again—Willow acting as the adult while I react in fear. We part ways.

"Can I still visit her?" Hawke and I walk on the side of the street.

"Probably."

"But Brickbat said she's under the care of the Council now. They're going to take her away."

"Not for a few days." His speech comes out clipped and careful. I hate that Testimony Log.

We round the corner onto Straight Street far too soon. His fingers squeeze my arm and he stops in front of the Newton's door, possibly to give me time to gather my strength. A few houses up, flickering light illuminates the lattice window of . . . dare I call it home?

"I live here, Parvin." Hawke pulls my gaze away from my house. He points at the old Newton house.

"You live . . . here?" My lungs squeeze my chest cavity into a tiny ball.

"In case you need me."

I can't take my eyes off the front door. Hawke moved into the Newton house, maybe to take care of it in their absence. It reveals something precious about him—a tiny corner of a deeper Hawke. I want to know this Hawke.

"I thought Enforcers lived in the county building."

He shrugs and urges me forward with a firm hand. "With a strong enough voice, there can be change."

We reach my door and he raises his fist to knock. I snatch his wrist. "Don't. Please don't knock." He lowers his arm and looks at me. The morning light flashes against his teal eyes. "It makes me feel even more like I don't belong."

"Don't strive to belong, Parvin. Your effort is much better placed elsewhere."

Semi-blinded by my nervousness and unsure of his meaning, I settle with, "Thanks."

"Welks."

I push the door open and enter as quietly as I can. The entry and kitchen are empty and silent other than the pop and crackle of the fire. I hang my coat on one of the loose pegs by the small mirror and walk into the kitchen.

All four chairs are pushed tight against the table. By the looks of the thin fire-eaten logs, someone tossed them on around sunrise. Whoever it was must have gone back to bed.

I set a few smaller sticks atop the charcoal pieces and then fill Mother's new kettle at the sink pump. It takes a few tries to set the kettle in the correct spot in the washtub so that the water flows into the hole. So many small things used to be easier with two hands. I plop in a bag of coffee grounds, return the kettle lid, and set it on the hook above the fire. A few drops of water fall onto the coals, hissing.

I sit at the table and pull *The Daily Hemisphere* electrosheet from my bag. I try not to think about Tawny, Elm, Willow, or Hawke. Right now, if I could, I would empty my memories and enter the day with fresh clarity.

I run my hand down the curled electrosheet and it springs apart, settling into a stiff rectangle. The headline blares from the front.

Will the Council Take Action Against Chase's Rash Behavior at the Wall?

So, Skelley Chase is in trouble with the people who killed Jude. As much as I hate the Council for torturing Jude's orphans and then hunting him down, I can't think of a better group to sic on the man who shot my brother.

I scan down the gaze-controlled screen to read the article, but then a new headline catches my eye.

Can We Control the Clocks? – An Interview with Skelley Chase.

I skip the intro and read just the interview between a newspaper correspondent named Gabbie Kenard and Skelley Chase.

> **Gabbie:** *Thank you for granting us an interview, Mr. Chase. We'll just jump right in, shall we? Many people were a little shaken up by your actions at the Wall, when you shot famous Radical, Parvin Blackwater's, brother. Tell me, why did you do this?*

Yes, why did you shoot Reid, Skelley Chase? What possessed you to insert a medibot inside my shoulder and then blow my brother's brains out?

> **SC:** *Many reasons, but the main was for the people. Miss Blackwater carried information regarding Clock-matching that is crucial for everyone's welfare.*
> **Gabbie:** *Ah yes, we've heard rumors of new Clock information. So, in a way, you chose to kill this man in order to let Parvin live and bring the information to the Council?*
> **SC:** *In a way, yes.*

Gabbie: This almost sounds as if you can control the Clocks. In fact, many people wonder if you did change the Blackwater Clock. Miss Blackwater appeared on schedule for zeroing out until you altered things with the medibot and her brother. Can you expound? Can we control the Clocks?

SC: Absolutely not. As we all know, the Numbers are never wrong. They are nothing more than a connection to unchangeable information regarding our deaths. I simply deduced—call it intuition, if you will—that the Clock belonged to Reid Blackwater. I've spent my life as a biographer and I've come to understand Clocks in a way many people might call supernatural. I made Reid Blackwater's Good-bye as painless as possible.

I stop reading. If *The Daily Hemisphere* were made of paper, I would crush it, tear it, and then burn it. I'd prefer to crush, tear, and burn Skelley Chase, but that's even less of an option.

His explanation for Reid's murder might make sense if it weren't a lie. I carried no knowledge regarding Clock-matching when I returned. The Council had already stolen Jude's invention using the assassin. Why is Skelley Chase lying? Why would the Council even let him take credit for all of this?

Maybe they're using his fame to help them, and he's doing it to keep from being punished for shooting Reid. I guess murderers stick together.

It's too much—too many lies for me to decipher, too many questions tumbling in my mind. I can do nothing about it. I'm just a dangerous Radical living in a Low City. Meanwhile, Skelley Chase is being interviewed like a celebrity instead of convicted for murder.

What a twisted world.

Does no one care that Reid's death destroyed my family? Then again, death has always meant more to me than to others because I never knew for sure when Reid or I would die. We weren't like the rest of the population. We weren't prepared. And others would scoff at us for that.

A crack of pain jolts me. I'd inadvertently clenched my nails into the wood of the table and one snapped backward. Blood lines the soft skin beneath it. I hiss in a breath.

"Back so soon?" Tawny stands in the doorway to my old room. Her arms are folded over a skimpy black lacy nightgown and her hair is messy in that I'm-a-perfect-model type of way. What startles me most are her eyes—red and puffy, but narrowed into slits, like an angry cat.

"You turned us in!" I'm staring at Skelley Chase in female form—she told Hawke and Kaphtor we'd left.

Her eyes narrow even more. "Of course. I'm a *Radical*, Parvin. Even though I was registered in a High City, your rashness brings the Enforcers' focus on *me!* No one's safe around you."

My jaw falls open.

"I can only assume you're here to give it back." Her voice cracks.

I press my bleeding finger against my leg to help the pain. "Give what back?"

She lifts an eyebrow. "Reid's Clock."

"Oh." I bite my lip. Drat. "I don't have it anymore."

Her glare wavers as if determined not to allow tears to interrupt, but I can see she's struggling to keep the rage hot.

"I'm sorry. I would give it back if I did."

She doesn't ask why I took it. She doesn't ask where it is. Her arms fall to her sides and she retreats back into her room.

Ugh. What was I to do? I needed a zeroed-out Clock to open the door for Elm. The Wallkeeper took it from me, probably to make sure I never try to breach the Wall again.

The kettle whistles. I pick up a thick towel and lift it from the fire, moving it to the top of the cold wood stove. I don't pour myself a cup. Instead, I lay my face against the smooth wood of the table and try not to think.

It's impossible.

The Council may be using Jude's Clock invention soon. I need to stop this, but how can one Radical go up against the leaders of an entire nation? I can't even stand tall among my own people.

Mother comes out of her bedroom, dressed and hair combed, but with hollow eyes. I lift my head off the table. She glances at me, then at the fire.

"The coffee's hot," I say. "May I pour you a cup?" Odd to be discussing coffee when I really want to release the pressure of my own story.

She snags a mug from the cupboard and pours it herself. "Where's Willow?"

Where's Willow? No, *Good morning, Parvin* or *How was your night?* Just *Where's Willow?* She doesn't even *know* Willow.

"In the containment center. The Council has custody over her."

"Oh." She sits at the table and stares at her coffee.

I don't know what to do or how to speak to her. I don't even feel like her daughter any more. "I'm not going to give up on her, Mother. I'll protect her in every way I can." But can I? Can I protect Willow?

Mother leans her chin on her hand, staring out the window. Maybe she's thinking about Reid. I always wondered if she loved him more. Now that she's a permanent mourner and stares through me, it's near impossible to convince myself otherwise.

I lean forward, interrupting her view of the window. Fighting a tremble, I take her hand. "Mother?" My voice is softer than a downy blanket. I suck in a breath. "Do you hate me?"

Something in her returns for a moment—the mask of hardness that often flares when I probe her emotions. Our gaze holds.

"No." She gives a brief shake of her head. "Not you."

"Who then?" But I think I know. While I hope it is Skelley Chase, I'm not surprised when she says, "Myself."

My fingers tighten around hers and my broken fingernail twinges. "None of this was your fault."

Her eyes narrow and she pulls her hand from mine. "Hush."

"It's true, Mom." Tawny steps into the kitchen, now wearing a brown knitted sweater with giant wood buttons and white leggings. "This wasn't your fault."

Mom? Tawny's been part of this family for six months . . . and the majority of those months she spent in Florida. Even *I* don't call Mother something so informal as *Mom.*

I play deaf to the hidden accusation in her words—it's not Mother's fault, it's *my* fault. I don't mind her blaming me as long as Mother doesn't blame herself.

Mother adds a teaspoon of sugar to her coffee. Perhaps, in her silence, she believes us. Should I tell her what Reid wrote in his journal? That he somehow knew he was going to die? That might set her at ease . . . or might crush her even more.

"So are you back for good or something?" Tawny pours herself some coffee.

I shrug. "I guess, but I'm still under house watch."

Tawny sits. "So the Enforcers will still be outside our house?"

"Yes."

She sighs and rolls her eyes. "You do know I'm a Radical, don't you?"

I rub my forehead. "Yeah, but you're registered."

"That doesn't mean anything here and you know that."

"The Wall is currently closed. There are no trials or Radical executions right now. You're safe."

A gust of wind slams into the window. It rattles and Mother grips her coffee mug tighter. "How do you know all that?"

"I went to the Wall last night to save Elm."

They both go silent. Tawny blows on her coffee, then takes a sip. "Mmm, Mom your coffee is always the best."

"Parvin made it this morning."

I use every iota of willpower to squish the urge to smirk.

Mother looks at me. "So did you save Elm, then?"

The desire to smirk dissipates with a single breath. "No." What else do I say? That the flesh-eating beasts hiding inside the Wall devoured him? "Willow says he escaped and is coming to rescue her. We don't really know what happened."

Silence. Coffee sips. Fire crackles. Never have I so greatly desired conversation. We're almost acting like a family—well, a cold, distant, semi-hateful family.

"Where's Father?"

"At the shop." Tawny's voice is tight. "Working on Reid's grave marker. It will be carved, since we can't afford stone."

"Oh." Trust me to somehow steer the conversation back to death. "That will be beautiful, and Father's woodwork is created to last." Hollow. Hollow. Hollow. *What do I say?*

Mother returns to her room with her mug. Tawny throws one glance at me, then retreats to her own room.

That night, while my family is in the kitchen, I change into a thin shirt and shorts and crawl beneath the covers of the bed Tawny and I will share. The fresh clothing is like a thousand kisses on my skin—the only comfort I've found since returning 'home.' I scoot to the very edge of the bed so Tawny will have plenty of room when she comes in.

She enters an hour later, smelling like soap. I lay on my side, my back to her. She lights a candle and crawls into bed. Her foot brushes mine and I move it. I don't want to touch her. We're not close. We'll never be close.

"I hadn't planned on sharing a room with you," she says, as if she knows I'm awake.

"I don't have to sleep here." I inch closer to the edge.

"But you want to be in your own bed, don't you?" She shifts her weight and it feels like she's trying to look at me.

I keep my eyes tightly shut. "I haven't been in my own bed for six months. I had a different idea of where I'd be sleeping when I returned east." Like in a grave.

She sucks in a breath. "Yes, so did I."

"What does that mean?"

"I didn't think you'd be sleeping at all. I thought you'd be *dead* and that *Reid* would be next to me."

At last, she's confirmed what I suspected. "Well, it's nice to have this out in the open."

"Good night, Parvin." She spits this out like a fly from her mouth.

"Mhmm."

She snuffs the candle. I'm thankful for her tartness. I'd much rather understand her anger than wonder if the surmounting silence among my family is my fault. Because now . . .

I know it is.

I wake at sunrise, lost.

Okay, God, my family hates me, Elm is dead (maybe), Solomon is probably in trouble, and I'm back in Unity Village. You said you were calling me. I need details, please. What am I supposed to do?

SPEAK.

I bolt upright. Finally! His voice! *Speak? How? When? To whom? What do I say?*

Silence.

Tawny is no longer in bed, but dishes clatter from the kitchen. My heart squeezes at the thought of her having *my* morning coffee time with Mother. Maybe this is where I need to start—creating peace with my family.

I try to change quickly into day clothes, but my stump hinders me. After much squirming and use of my teeth, I pull up some thick leggings and get a cream, wool long-sleeved shirt over my head.

I enter the kitchen with Reid's journal under my left arm and my NAB in hand. Mother's not here, but the kettle is over the cooking fire. Tawny stands at the sink washtub in a loose grey top and coal-blue jeans, scrubbing a wooden mug with a towel.

She sure has a lot of clothes. "Where's Mother?"

"Sleeping."

"She never sleeps this late."

Tawny sets the mug on a drying stick and turns to me. "You haven't been home. You don't know her anymore."

The punch of anger that hits my chest is squashed by regret. Tawny's right. I hate it . . . but she is. "Where's Father?"

"The Silent Man is at his store."

"Silent Man?"

She averts her eyes. "Oliver never speaks to me."

That doesn't seem like Father—he's all warmth and kindness wrapped up in human skin. I don't want to hear Tawny talk bad about him. "Are Hawke and Kaphtor still outside?" I sit at the table, setting Reid's water-puffed journal on top of my NAB.

"No, there are new Enforcers keeping watch." She moves the kettle from the cooking fire. "Coffee."

"Yes, please." Is Hawke in trouble?

"Well, it's ready. Help yourself." She turns back to the washtub even though there are no dishes in it. I close my eyes for a long moment, then get up. What did Reid see in her?

Snatching a dry mug from one of the pegs on the wall, I set it on the table, grab a cloth, and lift the kettle from the hook with my good hand. I pour carefully, trying not to tip over the mug with a slosh of coffee. The weight of the full kettle sparks a twinge in my wrist. I fill half the mug before the pain in my wrist is too much. I replace the kettle on the hook.

I lay my hand on the cover of Reid's journal, almost as a good-bye. Then I slide it across the table. "This is for you."

Tawny glances over her shoulder at the book. "I'm not much of a reader."

"It's Reid's journal." She stills and I surge forward. "That's how I found out you and he were married, from an emotigraph inside. The journal got ruined when I fell into the Dregs—uh, into a giant swamp canyon—but some of it is still readable."

I want to know her response. Will this instate peace between us? Allow us to actually be sisters? Move past our mourning?

Mother exits her room and sits at the table. Her eyes are red and heavy, sleep wrinkles line one side of her face, and she doesn't greet either of us.

"Good morning, Mom." Tawny pulls down a mug and fills it for her in a flash, saying nothing about Reid's journal. Ignoring me.

Well . . . I tried. I turn to Mother. "How did you sleep?"

She rubs a hand down her face and sits across from me. "Fine."

Tawny sits beside her with the sugar bowl. "Mom, I want to talk to you about the sleeping arrangement."

My head jerks up at this. What sleeping arrangement? *Ours?*

"I really don't think Parvin and I should share a room."

"What?" I shout and Mother jumps in her seat. I place my hand on her arm, surprised at her easy startle. "Sorry, Mother. I didn't mean to scare you." Turning back to Tawny, I unleash my harshest glare. "You and I could have talked about this. You don't have to burden Mother."

"No, no." Mother's voice is airy. "I understand."

Numb apprehension accosts my senses. "What do you mean?"

Mother doesn't seem like herself. I can't predict her response to something like this and that frightens me. She stirs a small spoonful of sugar into her coffee. "It wasn't fair to Tawny. We'll have to figure something out. Perhaps your father can bring the cot home from the shop. Then you can sleep in the kitchen."

Tears singe my eyes, hotter than the coffee in my mug. "The . . . kitchen?"

"Oh, I can sleep in the kitchen, Mom." Tawny's light voice is like blades scraping my nerves. "I get up so early anyway to prepare the household . . ."

Prepare the household? Oh please.

Mother shakes her head. "No, I thought about this last night. This became your new home, Tawny, and I'm not going to ask you to upheave your life again."

I can't seem to swallow. To speak. To breathe. Last night I thought I wanted to understand the tension among my family. Now I wish I didn't.

"This was my home once, too," I croak.

"Tawny lost her husband. She needs a place to herself."

I restrain the urge to shout. "I lost my brother."

"And I lost a son." Mother looks at me this time, her gaze fully connecting with mine. No looking through me. No looking past me. These words are intended for my heart and they hit like the blow of a silver axe.

"Okay." Leaving my coffee untouched, I stand and walk to the bedroom. "I'll get my stuff."

The next two days pass slower than clouds on a windless day. Father leaves to the woodshop so early I hardly see him during the days. The first night, I slept on the floor in the kitchen, using the skirt Mother made me as a blanket–despite Reid's bloodstains. I don't dare ask where my old bed blanket is. I can't shake the feeling that I have no right to be here, no right to ask for comfort.

At the same time, an indignant anger grows inside of me. No one sees me as a victim, but I suffered too. I pushed through the gates of death to return to my family. Don't they realize how much I needed them? Loved them even while in the West?

The rage will escape sooner or later. Best to hold my tongue while I can.

Father brings the cot home from the shop after that first evening and sets it in the entry. This leaves no room at all for walking, but I give him a long hug and a kiss on the cheek. He's the only one who still sees me with love. He doesn't even look at Tawny, let alone talk to her. Ever.

She was right.

Part of me is glad.

I'm trapped in this house. I can't leave thanks to the Enforcers and I don't know what to do for the Radicals in Unity Village.

Progress among my family is nonexistent. I sit through awkward silences and tense conversations of nothingness. Meanwhile, the Council gains more and more time with Jude's information.

I spend most of my time lying on my cot, trying not to miss Reid or Jude too much. Praying, since I have no Bible to read. *What are You calling me to? Show me! Give me more!*

SPEAK.

That's all I ever sense from Him, but maybe I'm making it up. I'm not the speaking type. Why would He ask me to do *that?* In fact, why should He listen to me? The more time that passes, the more I realize that my choice to write my story caused the horrors I'm now living through.

I'm sorry. It was wrong of me. How did I not see that it was wrong? I was pursuing *my own* glory. At the time, I didn't really know God. I didn't try to. Now that I do, the clarity of my mistakes is physically painful.

All the things I used to do when I lived in Unity no longer appeal to me—making new clothes, reading newspapers, daydreaming, wasting time. This place is used to the old Parvin. The new Parvin and Unity Village don't know how to coexist.

Hawke is not assigned to guard our house, but on Monday I clamber over my messy cot to answer a knock at the door and find him standing on our threshold.

"Good sunrise, Miss Parvin." He wears his Enforcer uniform and holds out a sealed envelope of thin paper. The other Enforcers are not at their posts.

Finally. Some news. Someone to talk to. I take the paper. "You didn't get fired?"

"Why would they fire me?"

I meet his eyes and he gestures to the envelope. On the back, over the seal, are scribbled words: *TL — I'm staying an Enforcer to monitor Willow while I can. No visitors allowed yet. Don't know why they didn't dismiss me.*

TL must mean *Testimony Log.* I'm glad he told me no visitors are allowed yet because seeing Willow is the first thing I want to do with my freedom. I have to trust him. I have to trust that he's watching over her while I can't.

I open the envelope carefully. I can use this paper for something later. Before I get a chance to read the typed note inside, Hawke summarizes it. "You're no longer under house lock."

I stare at the letter then look up at him. "I'm not?"

He grins. "No. You are an official registered Radical under the protection of the laws of the USE."

I plunk onto my cot. "Did you do this, Hawke?"

He points to himself. "It's Solomon, remember?"

"Oh yes, um, Solomon." I might as well start making the name adjustment if I want to keep my only friend.

"And no, I didn't do it." His smile wilts. "It was by order of the Council."

Early winter snow drifts into my veins. The Council. We both ponder in silence, me on my cot and Hawke—ahem, *Solomon*—in the doorway, allowing chilly October air to drift into the house.

I can't say anything—not if his Testimony Log is in. I scan the release paper. It's filled with boring jargon and official stamps.

He holds his hand out toward me. "Since you are free, care to take a walk?"

I eat up the word *free* as if it's a dessert. "Yes."

A walk. With Solomon Hawke. My stomach jump ropes with my nerves. Why does he want to go on a walk? Doesn't he have to work? Won't he get in trouble? And . . .

why did my stomach flip?

The last time it flipped, I was with Jude. My body's betraying me . . . Solomon needs to be a *friend*. Attraction just wouldn't be right. Jude died only a couple weeks ago. Has it been that long already?

I take his hand, trying to keep my fingers from trembling. He pulls me to a standing position. "I'm on duty in the square today."

Snatching my coat and pack from the loose peg, I step outside and close the door behind me. He helps me into my coat, not flinching when his hand brushes the stump of my left arm.

I've never been helped into my coat before, not even by Father. How pleasant.

I swing my pack over my shoulder and we head toward the square. The air is like fresh soap on my stained memories. Every breeze of cold and burst of autumn sun brings me back to the West. I lived outside for practically five months. Now, once again under the sky, I am free of the oppression that came from being cooped up in my house.

We reach Unity Village Square. It's market day. I try not to recoil from the throng of people. A few deep breaths allow me to survey the scene. For the first time in my life, it looks . . . alive.

The weathered wooden platform in the center of the square—mostly used for the Radical hearings—is empty and lit by the sun. Dogwood trees surround the border of the square, their leaves colored in gentle pastels and bright reds by autumn's paintbrush. Market booths fill every muddy square foot with small aisles between each one. Vendors shout to one another, someone tosses a peach to a little boy. Shoppers stroll in and out with woven bags over their shoulders.

I've never before seen this joy in Unity Village and I can attribute it to only one thing: the giant electronic post board hanging on the side of the county building, glowing over the few rows of houses between it and the square. Bold italic words line the top:

All hearings and Clock-checking currently postponed due to Wall closure.

My people are still safe. The beast of tension inside my chest releases me. No one's been sentenced to the Wall during my time at home. I can still protect them.

I'd forgotten about Hawke beside me until he whispers, "You did this, Parvin."

I stare at the lively people. A few fearful glances come our way, many of which rest on me. Some of the fear melts away into frowns and narrowed eyes. My throat tightens, trapping my breath.

How much do they know about my survival and Reid's death? Judging by the glares, they know enough to condemn my character.

I don't fear them. I fear *for* them. The Clock-matching will hit the Low Cities first—Unity Village. Then the Council will be able to control everyone according to their Numbers.

Despite the waves of dislike and anger lapping at my ankles, I allow Hawke's words to sink in. Yes, in a way, I did this. In a strange way, I protected my people by causing the Wall closure. They don't know it—they may never know it—but I care not for their recognition. My attempts to save lives have finally been successful, even if that success is temporary.

He squeezes my shoulder. "Care to browse? I want to buy a peach during my rounds."

No thanks. I don't really want to browse among the piranhas. But Hawke doesn't wait for an answer. We enter the bustle. The entire time I squeeze between booths and people, oxygen doesn't exist. I force short stilted breaths and try to look as if I'm shopping.

Harman, the master gardener, haggles with a customer over his vegetables. Another booth has racks and racks of leather shoulder packs—none as sturdy as the one Reid made, but still good quality. Some even have metal clasps instead of ties. I pass a pottery table of teapots and mugs and nearly run into a woman spinning wool on a wheel beside baskets of yarn and thread.

The food booths make my mouth water—wooden pallets of berries, pots of hot lamb stew, and baskets of cheese bread, apple muffins, and potato biscuits. Even the milkman has his slatted pushcart in the shade with precious glass bottles filled to the brim with goat milk. Two little nanny goats nibble the sparse grass nearby.

Why isn't Father here? He would sell so many goods. I notice again a few stares from vendors and shoppers. Their gazes rest mainly on my left arm. Maybe Father's embarrassed because of me and doesn't want the questions. Or maybe he doesn't want to be in public directly after the death of his son. He's a quiet man, after all.

"Found some peaches." Hawke returns to my side with a small hemp bag. "Had to pay for the bag, too."

The stares turn even bolder. What are they thinking? *Look, there's Parvin Blackwater, the one-handed girl who let her brother die and is now hanging around with an Enforcer.* The last thing they saw of me was the post board picture of me throwing up on the ground by the Wall.

I focus on what Hawke just said. "Don't you know to bring your own bag?"

"I do now." We amble to the hearing platform and Hawke pulls himself up, sitting on the edge. I hesitate. He pats the platform, then reaches down to hoist me up. "The people need to see you."

"Trust me . . . they see me."

SPEAK.

Now? No way!

"They're afraid. You've *done* something . . . and that's foreign to them. Your presence can change their fear."

I settle beside him and knock my boots together to dislodge the clinging mud. The last time I stood on this platform, my people encouraged the Enforcers to send me through the Wall.

I guess I'd rather sit in the rays of their anger than in the shadows of my family's despair.

"Peach?"

"No thanks."

He must hear the tension in my voice, but all he does is plop a peach in my lap.

We sit on the platform until the sun reaches the height of afternoon. Its rays combat the cold with the perfect intensity to keep us comfortable. After eating Hawke's peach—which tastes like heaven—I lean back on my elbows and fully breathe for the first time. The vendors and shoppers seem to have gotten used to my presence. They still glance at me, but I'm no longer suffocating.

When was the last time I sat somewhere and let calm flow in? It's different doing it with someone. Jude and I never did this. We didn't have much opportunity with all our traveling, fleeing, arguing, and injuries.

Hawke is quiet, like he's enjoying the calm, too. I sit upright with a sharp breath. "Hawke, you don't have a tune chip, do you?" I don't know why my heart suddenly pounds double speed. What if he's been in his own world of implanted music and I've really been alone this entire afternoon?

"No, *Solomon* does not have a tune chip."

"Oh." I exhale out embarrassment. Why can't I remember to call him Solomon? "Well, Jude had one."

"Tune chips are ingenious and music is wonderful, but Jude gravitated toward those sorts of inventions. I don't. The less metal in my head, the better it works. Besides,"—he scratches a spot on his knee through his black Enforcer pants—"it may sound sentimental, but I really love the sounds of, well, life."

"Me too."

He smiles. I smile. I think we're having a moment. One where we're not thinking about our dead brothers. But then, I guess now I *am* thinking about our dead brothers. Drat.

Should I tell Hawke—er, *Solomon*—that I dreamed about Jude? Or would that be too dangerous on the Testimony Log?

"I need to go report to Sachem. Sorry our stroll was short-lived."

If there was ever a way to ruin a calm moment, that was it. "All right." It comes out with a croak. I want him to walk me home, but I need to be strong. I need to be here with my people and show them I'm on their side.

"You should speak to them." He slides off the platform.

Okay, mind-reader. God's talking through *people* now? But . . . what would I say?

"Think about it."

"I will." Though the idea of standing up on this platform and yelling something down to my angry people doesn't seem like a great idea.

He walks away. I don't allow myself to watch him leave my sight. It feels . . . shallow. Like I've already forgotten Jude. Instead, I people watch.

Most shoppers and vendors have Clock-shaped bulges in their pockets. They all know how long they have. What will happen when the Council comes in to give them new Clocks? Will it *really* cause as much harm as Jude predicted?

I pull out my NAB. I'm not sure what I'm looking for. I wish I had my Bible—*a* Bible. No one sells them in Unity Village and they're not in the library. I'm sure there's a way to get it onto my NAB but I'm not tech-savvy enough. Maybe when Solomon's not bound by his Testimony Log, I can ask for his help.

I don't regret leaving my Bible with Ash and Black—my allies in the albino village—but, now that it's gone, I crave God's words more and more. He knows I need a new one. He'll find one for me. Why didn't I appreciate it while I had it?

What am I not appreciating right now that I might lose soon?

My finger slides into the grooved start button along the top of my NAB. The screen lightens to a familiar aqua blue with a tiny chime sound, but where there used to be only two communication bubbles in the center there are now three.

Skelley Chase
Unknown
The Daily Hemisphere Correspondent

Unknown belongs to Solomon. Only the last bubble blinks with a waiting message. I stare at it. A new correspondent? How did they contact me? The bubble pulses, enticing me. I tap it and a message unfolds in typewriter script.

> *Dear Miss Blackwater,*
>
> *My name is Gabbie Kenard and I am the senior editor of The Daily Hemisphere. We want to express our sorrow at the unexpected tragedies you faced upon your return. We understand you may be disinclined to continue your correspondence with Mr. Chase. However, you have many people in the world desiring to know updates on your life now that you are back.*
>
> *Would you consider continuing your journal entries through us? The Daily Hemisphere would print them and you would receive a small payment per entry, which, as I'm sure you know, is unusual for Radicals. Your story should not go unheard. I look forward to your response.*
>
> *~Sincerely, Gabbie Kenard*

The words blur together as I read them again and I'm reminded of who Parvin Brielle Blackwater is outside of Unity Village. Here, my people know only a part of my story and I'm still invisible, shunned because of my survival. I'm no one. But somewhere in the unknown—those places in the United States of the East to which I always hoped to travel—people know my name. They know my story.

But they've seen only what Skelley Chase let them see. They've watched, but what have they done? They allowed Willow to be captured. They allowed Elm to be locked inside the Wall to die. They allowed Skelley Chase to shoot Reid in the head and walk away.

No. Why should I empower them with my story? I'm not just an adventure book. I'm not just entertainment.

Dear Gabbie,
  Your offer is kind, but I'm not interested in being a zoo animal anymore.

After I send it, I pull out *The Daily Hemisphere*. It's curled in a stiff roll and it takes two tries to slide my hand down the electro-sheet correctly. It unfurls like a waking caterpillar. In the center of the screen, in full color, is Skelley Chase's face—bored smirk and all. Above his asparagus-green fedora runs a bold headline, but before I can read it, a shadow crosses over the screen.

Dusten Grunt, in all his hairy-knuckled glory, stands beside me. His dirty blond hair is swept to the side and even his breathing sounds nasal. His small mouth is pursed in a very female-ish way.

I frown. "Hi, Dusten." *Hi childhood bully.*

"Hey there Empty Numbers. Since you don't have any Numbers anymore, I guess that nickname's pretty accurate, eh?"

I inhale deep through my nose.

"Now that you're famous for vomiting in front of the cameras, you're hanging out on the platform? Gutsy."

I don't have the energy to deal with taunting. "Leave me alone."

"You *are* alone. Everyone feels awkward with you here."

I slap the electrosheet on the platform, barely keeping myself from hitting him across the face with it. "Is that why you're talking to me? You like being associated with the loner?"

"Naw, I'm here 'cause you're hurting business. Besides, you should be thankful. I'm the first person in our village to talk to you outside of the Enforcers." He slides one hip onto the platform, pushing aside my outstretched legs. "I'm curious about that stump you call an arm."

"Curiosity killed the jerk."

He's unfazed. "So, how are you dealing with being a *real* Radical?"

"What's it to you? You're not a Radical. As I recall, you have only ten months left. Is my freakish memory accurate?"

His pinched face turns into a nasty scowl. "Shut up. Not like you'd understand, Empty Numbers. You've never known when you'll zero-out."

"I don't *want* to know," I snarl, but he's already disappearing among the booths. I hit my fist on the platform.

Am I hurting business? Am I hurting my people? And do I *really* not want to know my Numbers? The assurance is tempting, but I know I'd start relying on it instead of God to direct my future.

I pick up *The Daily Hemisphere* electrosheet again and read the headline above Skelley Chase's face.

CWDC Conducts Testing of New Clocks

There it is. They're doing it already.

Below the headline is my name. I stare at it, trying to force my eyes to move on and read the article. Why is my name under a heading like this?

Parvin Blackwater, the lone survivor of the Wall as recorded in Skelley Chase's X-book, A Time to Die, *may have just altered the future of the USE. Per reports from the Citizen Welfare Development Council (CWDC), she returned from the West six days ago with astounding information about Clock-matching a person after conception.*

It is common knowledge this has been impossible and has caused many unnecessary Radicals—Parvin Blackwater being one of them. We can only hope this new information might change the future of Clock-matching. Details behind how she gained this information are still undisclosed. The Council is instituting testing procedures with the new Clock invention. Further information will be shared with the public soon.

A stone-cold chill turns my next inhale into shards of ice. They're testing the Clocks Jude invented . . . again. Are they using the orphans? Testing to see if they'll die before their Clocks?

I close my eyes.

Not only are they going forward with the plan Jude feared, but they're using me as imaginary support. They're using my fame. The Council is giving *me* credit for the information they stole from Jude. What will they do next, charge me with his murder?

They could.

They could accuse me and no one with power would argue. Maybe that's their plan. Maybe that's why Elan Brickbat didn't shoot me in the head. Maybe he's preparing a more public execution.

Or maybe, they're pinning it all on me so that if it goes awry, then they don't take the blame.

Why, oh why did Jude give the assassin his information?

It's the question I've loathed to ask myself all week because I'm afraid it will come down to one answer: *because of me.*

"*Stop, Jude,*" I'd said when the assassin threatened my life. "*Don't think about me.*"

"*I always think about you,*" he'd responded. And that's when I saw the decision in his eyes—the decision to give up all his protected information to the enemy.

Because of me . . . and because of something Solomon's supposed to know, but doesn't.

I clench my fist over my eyes. I never asked Jude to do that. I pleaded with him not to, but something in him must have thought the assassin could shorten my Clock. Something in him was willing to doom the world for the sake of my life.

Stupid, stupid, *stupid* Jude! Stupid Jude, whom I might have loved if he'd lived longer . . .

I force my fist away and stare up at the sun to distract me from these dark thoughts. I must not cry in front of my village, not in front of Dusten.

The post board on the side of the county building changes with a flicker, now revealing the headline I just read. My face is up there, too, next to Skelley Chase's. Some people stop their bustling in the market to read the new information. There's nothing I can do to stop them.

How will universal Clock-matching affect Unity? Registered Radicals come here because they like this style of life. Not everyone wants a Clock. *I* don't want one, now that I see how much of a faith-crutch it was.

"I think you should leave."

I startle at the low voice so near my ear. The milkman stands beside me, his hands tight around the handles of his pushcart. He has a heavy brow, thick eyebrows, and a droopy type of face. All his bottles are empty except three small ones. He wears a button-up shirt beneath a thick overcoat and his hair is nicely combed to the side.

"Leave?" I lower the electrosheet.

He doesn't look at my face, but I know his glare is directed toward me. "Get out of Unity Village. Leave us alone. You've brought only trouble and death." He speaks in undertones, deep in his throat.

I'm not sure what to say to the man I used to wave to in the mornings. "I-I didn't mean to cause any harm."

He drops the handles of his pushcart, grabs the shoulder of my coat and yanks me off the platform. I stumble into him, my pack swinging wildly on the crook of my bad arm.

"Leave!" He throws me into the mud.

I careen backward and land on my side. My pack flies off my arm, tumbling somewhere behind me, and sludge covers the right side of my face. The clamor of the market goes still. Everyone is looking at me lying in the grime with one hand and a tainted reputation.

The milkman kicks a splatter of mud at me. "Get out of here! Go on!"

I scramble to my feet. "I'm not a dog!" The words come out choked and teary. Oh no, there are tears.

"You might as well be!"

A tomato smashes into my temple, its cold pulp mixing with the mud. "Yeah, go away!" someone yells from behind a booth. Another tomato hits me in the chest. "We're not safe here anymore now that you've turned the government's eye on us."

I'm here to help *you!*

The milkman shoves me again. I stumble too slow, slam against the wood of the hearing platform, and fall again. I don't plan to get up this time. I'm sobbing so hard that words are too distant a thought to make it to my mouth.

"What is going on?" A new, familiar voice breaks into the clamor. It's angry and loud—louder than I've ever heard him before.

Heavy black leather boots step in between me and the milkman. I can't stop sobbing long enough to look higher than the boots, but I know who they belong to.

"Sure, protect her, Oliver," the milkman says. "But we saw you hide away when her story came out. Even *you* are frightened."

"Yes, I *am* frightened," Father shouts. "I am frightened by your disunity. If you think danger has come to our village, it is among ourselves, not from the government."

"Not *yet*." The milkman sneers.

Father's rough woodworking hands curl around my shoulders, lifting me out of the mud. "Come with me, sweetheart."

I cling to his coat with my mud-slicked hand, forcing my legs to support my crumpled form. Someone loops my pack over my other shoulder. I look up.

Solomon.

He is breathing hard and doesn't meet my eyes. That doesn't stop me from seeing the fire behind his—that same fire I once saw when he argued for my freedom six months ago. He finishes tying the flap of my pack closed and then wipes a thumb over my cheek. It comes away covered in mud.

Father leads me out of the square toward the woodshop.

"Don't expect milk on your doorstep anymore, Oliver!" the milkman hollers from behind us. "No matter how much you vow to pay me, I won't support this."

We round the corner. Finally, we reach the back of the woodshop where I release Father and slide to the ground, crying into my knees harder than my lungs will allow. Gasping. Choking. Shuddering breaths.

Father sits beside me, pulling my pack off and then cradling my head against his shoulder. "Shhh," he says in his deep whiskery voice. "Shhhh."

I don't quiet for a long time. All I feel is the suffocating blanket of my peoples' hatred. They hate me. They hate me, yet I love them and fear for them. Why?

Why do I not hate them?

"What have I done?" I can't fix this. I am nothing.

"You've done what they're too afraid to do."

I sniff. "What's that?"

His hand tightens around my shoulders and his voice comes out in a rasp. "Lived."

7

I don't tell Mother or Tawny what happened at the market, but for some reason they've become more cordial toward me—Mother being more human and Tawny being more like a sister than an evil witch. Did Father say something to them?

Reid's journal disappeared. I hope Tawny is reading it.

I avoid the market the next day, but I want to find Solomon. It will be an embarrassing and shameful encounter—especially after yesterday's incident—but I have to talk to him about the article in *The Daily Hemisphere*. The Council is using me to represent their corruption. My village thinks I'm on the government's side. Now that I'm free of house arrest, I need to do something about this.

I refuse to be used again, the way Skelley Chase used me. Not by anyone. I'm the only one who can fight for myself. I must be like Reid. After all, he's not here to be the example anymore.

The Wall closure is temporary. Soon there will be more Radical killings. Only I can help them, though I still haven't figured out how. So many problems and I seem to be the only one who sees them.

Solomon wants me to speak to the people, but after yesterday . . . I can't. I can't even think about it, despite my calling.

I'm supposed to protect and save them but . . . they don't *want* to be saved. So is that still my calling then? I shake the thoughts from my head. They hurt. They're heavy, and I'm too weak.

Maybe the strength will come tomorrow.

I visit the Newton's old house. Is Solomon home? Will he be able to talk or will he still be under the power of his Testimony Log? I need to move forward, and he is the key.

What will he say about yesterday? How much did he see?

I care that he saw. I wish he didn't. Does he think I gave the Council Jude's information? Does he think I'm bringing danger to my village with all this attention?

I stand on the doorstep a few minutes. Should I knock? Surely we're at a level of friendship where I can knock on his door. Surely.

Rap. Rap. Rap.

I almost flee, but instead force myself to stand and wait. I practice a few smiles. They all feel fake. The door doesn't open. I knock again. Nothing.

Maybe he's at the containment center. Maybe, now that I'm free, I can visit Willow.

The Lead Enforcer, Sachem, is behind the entry desk. He glances up from his NAB when I enter. "Get out of here."

I fold my arms. "I'm here to visit Willow."

He looks back down at his NAB. "Get out."

"Please, sir. She's the only friend I have and I promised to watch out for her." I need to know what the Council plans to do with her.

His chair squeaks as he leans back. "You're going to get your friends killed if you keep pushing your limits. Enforcer Hawke was a great resource for this town before he started up with you."

My mouth goes dry. "Was? H-He's still a great Enforcer."

"Not anymore." The way Sachem says this brings goose bumps to my arms.

"What do you mean?" Something's wrong. I start to shake and I can't place why.

Sachem pinches the bridge of his nose and then rubs his eyes. "He was stripped of his Enforcerhood yesterday for disloyalty and subversion."

"Parvin!" Willow shouts from down the cell hall. "Parvin, they hurt the Hawke!" Her voice is tiny, but might as well be a gong to my nerves.

"Where is he?" I growl at Sachem. He stands and rounds his desk, heat in his eyes. "Willow!" I back toward the exit. "I haven't forgotten you!"

Sachem reaches for my arm, but before he can touch me I hurtle out of the containment center. I fly through the market, ignoring the undecipherable shouts that follow me, and round the corner of Straight Street gasping for breath.

Solomon was stripped of his Enforcerhood? Was it my fault?

I pound on Solomon's door, forgetting even to be nervous about visiting him. "Hawke?"

What does it mean to have one's Enforcerhood stripped away? I pound again. "Solomon Hawke!" It comes out as a scream. This is Jude all over again—getting a concussion, having his arm amputated by the albinos, putting the assassin's pirate chip into his skull.

I'm helpless.

I wrestle with the door latch. It's locked or stuck. I slam into the door with my shoulder. Once. Twice. Three times. I am met by the crunch of breaking wood. Good thing it wasn't one of Father's latches—I never would have broken through.

The door swings open. I stumble through an entry, into the kitchen that is far wider than ours. The house is frigid, no warmer than outside. A plate of crusty day-old food sits on the table. The fork lies on the ground. Two chairs and a rough bench rest on their sides. Candlesticks are crushed and smeared into the wood floor, as if they were stepped on in a scuffle.

"Solomon?" My pulse batters every centimeter of my skin. Ringing inhibits my hearing. A stench reaches my nose—old blood. I gag.

A hallway in the back leads to three different doors. One is cracked open. I trip over a crooked chair on my way and fall through the first door on the right.

There he is, lying on a wooden cot with a thin cotton mattress. The lone blanket has fallen to the floor, revealing his body in nothing but a sleeveless white undershirt and thin shorts that are probably his underwear.

Both are soaked in blood.

I swear every bit of exposed skin is swollen with green, purple, and black bruises, many of which have cracked, leaving trails of dried blood down his body onto the floor.

The worst part is his face. It's turned toward me, but his eyes are so swollen they couldn't open even if he wanted to look at me. The entire left side of his face is covered in thick blood, dried enough that it's almost black. Pools of it lie in the corner of his eye, on his cheek, in his ear.

My knees buckle, but I grab the shadowed dresser beside me and pull my body back up. Trembling, I toss the blanket over his body before dashing out of his house, knocking chairs aside in my wake.

"Mother!" I'm screaming her name before I'm even in the house. "Mother! Tawny!"

They burst from their rooms just as I enter and bang my knee against my own cot.

"It's Hawke!" I feel my face crumpling. I mustn't let it. I need to hold it together long enough to talk. "He-he's been . . . a-and there's blood . . . everywhere." I'm losing it. "I-I don't know . . ." My gasping comes stronger, more desperate. "Help! Please, he's d-dying!" I can't say *dead*, even though that's what I fear.

Without waiting for a reply, I run back to Solomon's house.

God, please pull Tawny and Mother out of their grieving. I need their help. I need Your help.

When I'm back at his side, I light a candle found on his dresser. The moment the wick catches fire I wish I hadn't thought of light. It reveals the full extent of his injuries. He's paler than a full moon. His dark blond hair sticks to his forehead from sweat.

Sweat. He must be alive.

"Hawke." I clear my throat. "Solomon." I take his limp hand in mine. My fingers brush against rough skin. I turn over his hand and stare at his lacerated palm. His other hand is the same, as if someone repeatedly shoved him to the ground.

What do I do? *What do I do?*

This strong Enforcer is dying. The man who fought for me. The man who sent his brother to save me in the West.

I care for Solomon Hawke. Maybe not in the same way I cared for Jude . . . not yet, anyway. But I care enough that I will be crushed if he dies. I'll be alone. He's the only other one who shared my story with me. Everyone else is an outsider.

Mother enters the room, holding a cloth to her nose and another damp one in her hand. Tawny stands in the doorway, her eyes wide and her hands over her mouth. It takes me one glance to realize she'll be no help at all.

If only Willow were here. She and Mother would make a vicious healing team.

Mother seems to realize Tawny shouldn't be present. "Go fetch Oliver."

Tawny flees.

"What happened?" In this moment of trauma, Mother's as normal as she ever was before these six months of madness started.

My voice—*thank you, God*—comes out collected and determined. "The Lead Enforcer said Solomon was stripped of his Enforcerhood for disloyalty and . . . and something else. Subvi . . . sub . . . subversion, I think."

Her eyes widen and she presses the damp cloth to the left side of his face.

"Mother, how bad is it?"

She takes a deep breath, then seems to fight a gag. "It's good that you found him today." Her fingers turn red as the blood moistens and seeps through the cloth. "Did you locate his Clock?"

I choke on my own saliva. "No, I forgot." How could I forget? It's as if, now that I'm a Radical, I've completely overlooked the role of the Clocks and the information they can give.

It takes a moment to find what looks like a carrying satchel leaning against the wall by the fireplace. It's not the one that went with his Enforcer uniform, but I rummage inside.

First, I find his silver contacts case with the Testimony Log contacts inside, then his NAB, and then a thick leather strap that might be worn around one's wrist. I'm about to toss it aside when I see the Numbers clicking away—tiny, red, and digital, but not like ours. It *is* a wristband—a Clock band. Different forms of Clocks exist?

I'm staring at his Numbers, watching them change. I register them before I can decide to look away.

032.072.15.01.44

"Thirty-two years and seventy-two days, Mother."

"Gracious. He has good Numbers for a man with the type of path he's been walking."

I nod, though she can't see me. I know Solomon's Numbers. I'm not even sure how old he is—twenty?—but those Numbers take him at least into his fifties. Thirty-two years sound forever. What would I do if I knew I still had thirty-two years left?

Still, just because today is not the day of his death doesn't mean we can relax against his agony. "Can we get him to Nether Hospital?"

"They don't treat stripped Enforcers."

"How do you know?"

She pulls away the cloth, with it comes some chunks of dried blood. The wetness has dampened the crusting on his face. She wipes it gently. It smears. The backward black Enforcer *E* is gone, scraped off his left temple as if the person removing it was peeling a potato.

"The husband of midwife Bridget—the woman who delivered you, Reid, and William—was an Enforcer in his younger days. He was stripped of his Enforcerhood when they found out his wife was a Radical."

"What happened to them?"

"They moved to a Dead City when Enforcers started sending more Radicals across the Wall. You were ten years old." She hands me the bloody cloth. "Rinse this in the kitchen and bring it back to me. Then go home, put some water to boil, and prepare Tawny's bed for him."

"Are you sure we should move him?" He looks so fragile, but at least we are now confident that he's alive . . . and will stay that way.

"If the other Enforcers see us going between our houses to help him, they may restrict us. Tawny and you could both end up in trouble because you're Radicals. We need him where we are."

I curse my missing hand the entire ten minutes it takes to prepare Tawny's bed. But determination wins out. By the time Father and Mr. Contrast—the blacksmith—lay Solomon in my old bed, I've laid fresh sheets and filled two pitchers of boiling water.

By evening, Mother has cleaned and bandaged his face with strips of the extra cloth I used to use for sewing. She and Father shove me into the kitchen while they peel off the rest of his clothes and check his other wounds—not that I wanted to stay.

Tawny and I sit alone in the kitchen, hearing the muffled voices of Mother and Father on the other side of the door.

"You're lucky, you know," Tawny says.

I push the newly filled kettle over the fire again. "How in time's name am I lucky?"

"*He* didn't zero out."

I close my eyes for a long breath before turning back to her, but she stares at the table, her lashes dripping tears like icicles. I reach over and take her hand. "I'm sorry, Tawny. I wanted Reid to live. That was always my prayer."

"I guess his prayers were just stronger than yours." She pulls her hand away.

"What do you mean?"

She spits out her next words as if she's waited a long time to say them. "Before we married, Reid told me about your shared Clock. He told me he would be the one zeroing out. I never believed him, but he knew it as a solid, unarguable *fact.*"

"I know. He told me in his journal. But *how* did he know?"

"That's what I asked him, too. He always said, *Because I prayed for it.* He was so confident in the power of prayer that he knew the answer to the Clock." She sighs. "Yet, I still married him with only six months promised to us. It was easy to doubt when we stood outside that Wall, waiting for you to come back. Especially when you looked practically dead yourself. I'd hoped . . ."

"So did I."

"I begged him not to go to the Wall, but I also wanted to be with him every last second I could." She stares out the window into the dark street.

"I'm sorry."

"So was he."

"Did he ever tell Mother and Father?"

The kettle whistles and she jumps to retrieve it, even though I'm closer. "No. Please don't tell them."

I don't respond and she doesn't seem concerned that I agree not to. I can't keep this from Mother. She's still blaming herself for his death, though I don't know why.

"Thank you . . . for his journal." Her words disappear into the crackle of the fire, but I catch them. I can't justify saying *you're welcome*. The journal should have been hers in the first place. And I ruined it.

Mother and Father come out of the bedroom, carrying two bowls of bloody rags. "He's cleaned up," Mother says. "I doubt he's woken since. His head shows signs of a few nasty blows."

Tawny and I stare at her. I'm ready to sit by his bedside, as I did with Jude. I'll hold a mug of hot broth to feed him whenever he wakes. This is no different than when we each atoned in the albino village. Except we have no white pills for pain. The Enforcers took those out of my bag when they searched it upon my return.

But Mother doesn't say anything about watching him through the night. She strides over and gives me a long hug. "He'll be okay, Parvin."

I cling to her and my worry dissipates. All I can think in terms of thanks is *God* . . . The words "Thank You" can't form past my clog of emotion, but I guess this is where the Holy Spirit intervenes and translates my one word into a paragraph of undying gratitude.

Mother releases me. "Now you two get some sleep. I'll set some extra blankets out and you can turn the table on its side for more room. I'll check on Mr. Hawke every couple hours."

"No, Mother, let me."

"You may take over tomorrow, Parvin. For now, though, he needs a sharp eye."

I won't sleep a wink anyway, but his health is more important. I don't know enough about healing to help him the way he might need. "Okay."

As Tawny takes the cot, I have no problem curling on the floor by the fire beneath the kitchen table. I watch the flames flicker from yellow to orange, licking the air and logs like a famished animal.

Today was chaos and yet deep peace is all that surrounds me. Solomon will heal, Tawny opened up to me, and my family was unified with a purpose to save a life.

But the best part of all has to do with Mother. I don't know where to pin the blame—on Solomon's injuries, or my desperation, or maybe she was just tired of everything. All that matters is that today, on this very bloody Tuesday . . .

My mother returned.

"Miss Willow is gone. I'm sorry."

A cyclone of chills brings every hair on my body on end as I stare Enforcer Kaphtor in the eye. He sits in Sachem's usual spot in the containment center—a good thing for Sachem, because I came here to deliver a vicious tongue-lashing for Solomon's sake. I might even have resorted to a physical lashing if my temper got the better of me.

"What do you mean Willow is *gone?*" He can't mean dead. He can't.

"She was sent to Prime early this morning."

"Prime? The High City in New York?"

"Yes."

I grip the edge of his desk to keep myself up and to restrain my desire to shout for her. "Why?"

Kaphtor glances around the containment center for a moment. "The Council summoned her."

My spirit sinks lower and lower. "Why?"

He shrugs. "Questioning, I think."

I cover my face with my hand. What now? Willow is in the custody of the very people who are currently lying about me, manipulating the people, and using Jude's Clock-information.

What if they want to Clock-match her and then test her like the orphans, seeing if she'll die on time? My head snaps up so hard it pops my neck. "No! We can't let them take her."

I turn my back on Kaphtor and stride out of the containment center. In only two days, Solomon has been beaten senseless and Willow has been carted off to the enemy. *God, what in time's name are You thinking?*

I need to meet with the Council somehow. Either in person or through my NAB. I need to stand up to them and talk about Radicals, about Willow, and about Jude's Clock-matching invention before they start *using* it.

Willow may be my key to meeting with them.

Is this what You meant when asking me to speak? I enter my house, hyperventilating from a brew of thin winter air and emotions.

"He's awake." Mother stands in front of the bedroom door and wipes her hands with a cloth, then sets aside an empty bowl of broth. "And quite alert."

I drop my pack onto the table and enter my old room as softly as possible. Solomon sits upright in bed, wearing one of Reid's shirts. The blanket rests at his waist and a kitchen chair is situated at an angle by his bedside.

His right eye is open, but the other is swollen shut and lined with purple. The left side of his face is bandaged at an angle. Cuts and bloodstains cover the exposed skin. What hair is not trapped beneath the cloth strips sticks up in odd angles from his long days of unconsciousness.

I intended to walk in and say something soothing, maybe even witty, but my throat constricts and I blink in quick succession against the hot burn of tears.

"Oh now . . . don't b-b-b-at your eyes at mmme," he croaks with a small smile. "I already think you're p-p-p-retty."

He winces. Saying that small bit of speech seems to take every bit of facial muscle control he has.

His statement is so . . . Reid-like. And unexpected. And sweet. Tears push past the barricades of my eyelashes. So much for being strong.

I sit in the chair beside him and clasp my stump in my lap. "Oh Solomon, was it my fault?"

His non-bandaged eyebrow angles down. He opens his mouth as if to speak, then shakes his head *no*. Screwing up his face, he gets another sentence out, and even I can't mistake the pride in his beaten voice. "You sssmash muh door."

I laugh and then sniff hard against the tears. Thank heaven I'm not sobbing. That could get ugly. "Yes, well, your latch was poorly made. Have Father make a new one, otherwise anyone could get in."

"'Kay."

I look down at my hand and stump. I want to tell him about Willow, ask his advice. But should I bombard him the first moment he's awake? "Why did they do this?"

He lets out a long breath, then lifts a hand with effort and points to his eye.

"Because you took out your Testimony Logs?"

He nods, then waves his hand back and forth, indicating *sort-of*. This won't work. I can't rely on hand gestures for answers. He needs more time to heal and it's heartless of me to pepper him with more questions. "We'll talk again when you're a little better."

He gives a stiff, swollen smile.

"But you should know, they've sent Willow to the Council. In Prime." The words come out fast, as if spoken against my will. Solomon should know. He reaches a bandaged hand toward me.

"I'm going to go after her."

Solomon's eyes widen and his hand stills. "You . . . c-can't . . ."

I won't let him dissuade me, but I don't want him to think I'm impulsive. "I'll let you know my plans."

"Duh C-C-Council is dan'rous."

"I know! They're trying to convince people I'm on their side. They said *I* gave them Jude's Clock-matching information." I glance up sharply to meet his eyes. "I didn't, you know. They stole it. I didn't help the Council one bit."

"I know . . ."

"Good." My nod is curt. "I'm really going to think this through." I pat his shoulder. "I'm glad you're healing."

Back in the entry, I pull on my boots, loop my arms through my shoulder pack, and grab a scarf. "I'll be back soon."

Mother, who sits at the table, gives a solitary nod.

I walk outside beneath the grey clouds. We're halfway into October and the weather is biting. I shove my hand and stump in my pockets, having forgotten my gloves.

I probably shouldn't have run out on Solomon like that. But I couldn't bear to hear him tell me *not* to go after Willow. He'll be fine. He's on the mend.

Right now, my focus is on Willow . . . and the Council.

My steps pound the dirt as I propel myself to the square. The closer I get, the brighter an idea grows, as if inviting me to come snatch it off the hearing platform.

Today, I claim this location as my safe space.

This platform is such a morbid place, symbolic of death and hopelessness. But, like Solomon said, it's time to get the citizens of Unity Village used to my presence. If they're ever going to listen to me—if I plan to figure out this *SPEAK* thing God keeps pushing on me—they need to be able to tolerate looking at me.

The square is empty save the occasional passerby. No market today. I climb onto the platform and sit in the light of my idea. It's not what I thought it would be. It's not exactly . . . legal. But it has power.

I pull out *The Daily Hemisphere* and my NAB. Opening to the *Contact* section, I click on the bubble for Gabbie Kenard, the senior editor of *The Daily Hemisphere*.

Because no one is around, I speak aloud to the NAB, allowing the frustration and anger to flow out.

Gabbie,

I've changed my mind. I will provide further journal entries. I've been reading your current articles about the Council and Skelley Chase. I have many things to say on these topics—things the people ought to hear and know. You're right, my story should not go unheard, especially when it's being skewed by the leaders of our country.

I have one condition, however. You must provide me with the contact information and physical address of the Council.

Sincerely, Parvin

Perhaps it's impulse that pushes me to do this, but I owe it to Willow and to my village to *try*. I glance around the cold square. The restless dragon squirms inside me. Staying here and waiting isn't enough, not when I know I can do something more.

Not when I can blackmail the Council.

Two days pass before Gabbie writes me back. And now I'm biting my tongue, re-reading my blackmail message to the Council.

> *To the CWDC,*
>
> *I had the "pleasure" of meeting Elan Brickbat one week ago and his conduct revealed to me the quality of care the Council gives to the citizens of the USE.*
>
> *I would like to meet with you—the entire Council—as soon as possible. If you do not grant me a meeting, I will go to the press about your testing procedures on orphans. Since you've decided to lie to the public and paint me as a supporter of the Council, I have a feeling my words will carry quite a lot of impact when I make the front page of The Daily Hemisphere, revealing you as child murderers.*
>
> *I want Willow present during our meeting as well.*
>
> *I will be on the train to Prime the day after tomorrow.*
>
> *~Parvin*

I've never been threatening like this to anyone. Something about it feels good, which makes me wonder if it's bad.

I don't show the message to Solomon. I don't want to know if he approves or not. I'd rather just approach him and say, "I have a meeting with the Council."

I clutch my NAB in my hand and whisper, *"Send."*

The message bar fills up and disappears, sent into the void for a brief blink before entering the Council's contact box. Which member will read it? Elan Brickbat? I don't know any of the other members, though I think President Garraty is also on the Council. How many members are there? Three? Thirty?

I stop my train of thought before it leads me into regret.

The message is sent. Gabbie Kenard came through. Once again, I will be journaling my life. Maybe this time my family and village will read it.

Now . . . to tell Solomon my plans, as promised. I haven't talked with him since sharing my plan, but Mother says he's much more articulate now.

I enter the bedroom. Solomon turns his head toward me and attempts a smile. His swelling has lessened, replaced by a dark rainbow of bruises. Some of the bandages have been removed, but the one on his face is clean and white—freshly changed.

"How are you?" I ask.

"Better." His lips make almost normal movements, smoothing out the word. "Walked around today. On'y some cracked ribs."

I lower myself into the seat beside him and reach for his hand. "Why did they do this to you, Solomon? It can't have just been because of the Testimony Log."

"I'b surprised dey didn't do it earlier." He tilts his head to the side. "Lots o' rrreasons, Parvin. I took out mmmy lenses several times, you and I knew each od'er, I wasn't giving th-them . . . de feedback dey wanted about you or . . . J-Jude. And then there's my history. They ffffound out I helped Jude."

"What do you mean?" I straighten in my seat. "Didn't they know you were brothers?"

"W-w-when he first crossed duh Wall, they accessed my Enforcer Testimony Log and saw that I'd assisted him." He takes several deep breaths. "The Enforcers used my information as a t-t-tool to find Jude. Jude 'n I knew this would happen. Ssso we . . . acted out . . . false scenes. Using my Testimony Log, I convinced duh Enforcer Leaders and Council dat I'd recorded his actions to help them."

The wind batters the closed shutters and Solomon pulls the blanket tighter with his two bandaged hands. "When I transferred here to help the Newtons, I thought I'd be under less supervision. I started t-t-taking out my contacts to ssssend Jude messages of what I overheard—that an assassin was sent after him, that they were sssearching my Testimony Log, etcetera." He breathes deep. "That's all known now."

I stare at his bruises. There were so many more intricacies to Jude's quest and invention than I ever imagined. "What does it matter to them now, though? Jude is . . . gone."

"According to Enforcer standards, I was disloyal. And duh Council wanted to show y-y-you . . . their power."

"So they just beat you up and carved your face?" I'm cutting off the blood supply to my left wrist. It tingles and sharp phantom pain pulses in my nonexistent fingers.

Solomon leans back against the propped pillow. "Council's orders." His eyes droop. "So . . . have any plans yet?"

Ah yes . . . my blackmailing. "I'm waiting to hear back. I've requested a meeting with the Council." *Requested* is a bland way of putting it.

"I admire and . . . and envy your impulse." He wraps his fingers around mine. "Your call to action is an ir-ir-irreplaceable character trait, but b-be careful. We need to think it through."

This is the nicest way anyone's said, *You're being impulsive.* Coming from Solomon, it's probably a compliment. "So what do we do?"

He answers in a low voice. "I've learned the hard way that wwwe cannot fight the Council through force. Jude . . . learned this, too. Even if we sssave Willow, she has her tracker chip."

"We could take the tracker out of her, right? You know how to do that."

"Yes, but h-how far will an albino, a Radical, and an ex-Enforcer get undetected?"

He's right and I hate that. My hand strays to the cut in my left arm where my own tracker chip rests.

"It's shallow enough dat you c'n take it out." He gestures to where my fingers toy with the bandage. "When you need to."

Good to know. "So what else do we do?"

"Think. And . . . pray."

"I never know what to pray."

"It's a g-good thing there's not a right or wrong then."

I lean back, allowing deep breaths to punctuate the silence.

His pillow slips and I help him readjust it. "It's not dat easy to meet with the Council, Parvin. You need a really good reason—a reason for them to accept and schedule a meeting."

How about blackmail? "I'll think of something, Solomon."

He squeezes my hand. "When you do, I-I'll come with you."

I look him over and lift my eyebrows. "You will?"

The corner of his mouth turns up, squeezing his puffy eye closed even tighter. "I'm bruised and scarred, not b-broken. I need to return to Prime anyway. As a stripped Enforcer . . . I lose my High-City status. Still need to tie-up some things in Prime before settling here."

Settling here. He's going to stay.

I look out the window, allowing my mind to drift to another day—a future day of rescue and freedom. "Okay. We'll go together." I look back at Solomon, but his eyes are closed and his head rests heavy against the pillow.

• • •

I hand one of my two train tickets to Solomon the next day. Today he's in his own house, sitting in a chair by the window. The place doesn't smell anymore. Mother took care of the blood and I threw out the old food while he healed.

"Can you come?"

Solomon stares at the small slip of paper. The swelling beneath most of his bruises has disappeared, leaving behind giant stains of purple, yellow, and green on his skin. "You work fast."

A gush of air escapes me. Was I that nervous about his response? "Yeah, well, it's where I'm supposed to go."

"Of course I'll come. Have you told your family yet?"

I drop into the other chair by the table and it wobbles beneath me. He really needs to invest in Father's carpentry. "I'll tell them tonight."

"I'll get packing, then." He lifts the ticket. "Thanks for this. I'll pay you back."

"No need."

My feet are blocks of cement, taking me back to my house. What will everyone say? Are my reasons solid? Mother won't like that I blackmailed the Council. Or maybe she will . . .

Why am I nervous? Reid left home all the time. He got *married* without telling any of us. It shouldn't be a problem for me to go. Besides, I will not abandon Willow.

This is for shalom. The Council has stepped too far, and I get the sense this is only beginning.

"Hello Parvin." Mother sits at the kitchen table with a thin book resting beneath her hands. The cover is black with fluttering red dogwood petals.

"You're reading my biography?"

She reaches a hand toward me. "Come sit down."

I do, breathing past the suffocating thumps in my chest.

"I haven't started it yet, but I thought I should. I was wrong to ignore your story." Her shoulders rise and fall. "It is . . . painful for me."

"Why?"

"Because I know you've been hurt." She brushes her fingers over my stump.

If I had a hand, I'd clench it against her touch. "I've also been healed, Mother."

"Healed from what?"

How can I summarize everything I've learned? "Healed from myself—from my own stagnancy. From selfish desires. From misplaced faith. I'm finally following God instead of my own desires. In doing so, I've noticed how broken the world is—how broken I made it with my selfish sin. Not just that, but I can *fix* parts of it."

Occasionally I get a wellspring of vision—I imagine stopping the Council from condemning hundreds of Radicals. It halts my breath every time. So lofty . . . but could it be possible through me? "In fact, I have some news. I wanted to tell everyone at once, but maybe it's better to tell you now."

She slides my biography aside. "Yes?"

I pull my train ticket from my pocket and place it on the table. "I'm going to Prime, the High City. Tomorrow."

She stares at the ticket, not speaking. Maybe not even breathing. A good ten seconds pass and I wonder if I've crossed some sort of terrible line between keeping Mother normal and returning her to her cocoon of depression.

"Mother?" She looks up and I launch into more detail before she can zone out again. "When you read my biography, you'll see some small entries about a man named Jude. He's Solomon Hawke's brother and he saved my life multiple times when I was in the West. He invented something very important." I can't bear to tell her I might have loved him.

"Yes, the Hawke family line has always been filled with inventors."

My jaw drops open like a broken nutcracker's. "W-what?"

She straightens in her chair and speaks with poised strength. That's my mother. "Erfinder Hawke invented the projected Wall sixty years ago, didn't you know that?"

"I don't even know what a projected Wall is. I thought the whole thing was made of stone."

Mother laughs. "Not across the *oceans*. Stone doesn't float, Parvin." Her response sounds like something Tawny would say. Belittling.

"I know," I mumble. "I just thought the Wall went around the entire world."

"It does, in different formats. The projected Wall is just as impassable as the stone one. Wall building came to a standstill when they reached large bodies of water. Erfinder Hawke solved that problem only eleven years later with his invention of the projected Wall."

How did my attempt to share my story with Mother turn into a history lesson? Not my idea of success, although Jude and Solomon's family line *does* intrigue me. Does Solomon have inventor qualities in him?

"So, you're leaving. I didn't catch why."

Can't imagine how that happened. "To get Willow back and to challenge the Council about Jude's invention."

"Will you come back?"

If you want me to. There's no telling what the Council might do to me. I scoot to the edge of my chair. "I'll try." For the sake of all people who shouldn't have to be Clock-matched. For my village.

And for Jude.

• • •

Tawny rolls her eyes and shrugs when I tell her I'm leaving. Father gives a slow nod and a tight hug. "Be safe."

I pack my things and make sure to bring a toothbrush this time. Six months in the West without one left too great an impact for me to forget it now. For nostalgia's sake, I slip Jude's whistle into my pocket. I wear thick winter leggings, boots, and an old vest I haven't touched since before crossing the Wall.

I take the bandage that covers my tracking chip incision off my arm. The cut is now a pink line on my skin, like a faded scratch.

That healed fast. Maybe the chip was coated in some sort of healing fluid.

I lie on my back in front of the fire, thinking through every possible scenario of meeting with the Council. What if they don't receive my blackmail or refuse to meet? Well, then I'll stay in Prime until they agree.

What if they test the Clock invention on Willow? Then I'll announce it to the newspaper and try to rescue her.

What if they try to kill me? Maybe I ought to bring Solomon to the meeting with me.

What if they try to kill *Solomon?* Hmm . . .

I brainstorm and worry until the moon starts its descent. So much for getting rest. At last, I resort to the one conclusion I should have reached from the start: Do not worry about tomorrow.

Because You are beyond time. Not to mention You're all-powerful and can take down the Council with a flick of Your pinky.

The peace I wish would envelop me doesn't hit my heart, but my mind settles a little. Enough to let me sleep.

The first thing I check upon waking is my NAB. A new bubble, labeled *CWDC,* rests with the other three.

God, what have I done? All I can picture is Elan Brickbat's face after he almost shot me. I've put another target on my body for the Council—one to join the other hundred.

I tap the bubble.

~Thursday. 9:00am.

That's the whole message. No signature. It could have been from the president of the USE or a secretary.

But who cares? They didn't threaten me and I have a meeting. I have a meeting!

I burst out of my house, pack in hand, and run smack into Solomon. I hear his grunt before seeing the grimace on his bruised face. "Oh, sorry. I was coming over to . . . well . . . hi."

"Good sunrise."

I am immersed in his scent of blueberries and thatch. "We have an official meeting with the Council! Thursday at nine."

"Wow, they fit you in soon."

"I can be quite convincing."

He takes my pack and swings it over his shoulder. "Do you have your train ticket?"

"It's in my pocket." I reach for my pack. "You're injured. Give it back."

He grins. "Not doing. So you're ready to go?"

I glance back at my house. I bid good-bye to everyone last night and I can't bear the idea of doing it again. I slipped Mother a note in the cover of my biography. It says, *I love you.*

Will she believe me?

"I'm ready." It feels abrupt, but if I draw a good-bye out too long then it will feel too permanent. I don't want permanent. I want to come back to my village and my family—to protect them.

We walk to the train station, my heart pounding double to my footsteps. The carbon-fiber train arrives five minutes early, as if anxious to take me away from what I know.

"You a Radical?" the ticket man asks as I board.

Out of habit, I glance around for Enforcers who might capture me, but Solomon rests his hand on my shoulder. "She is a registered Radical with a purchased ticket."

The man looks Solomon up and down, maybe assessing whether his injuries are intimidating or incriminating. "All right, no harm meant. It's my job, you know."

We settle into our seats. Solomon lets me have the window and I stare over the thatched houses of Unity Village. I returned two weeks ago expecting to die in my brother's arms. Now I'm leaving to fight for my people's freedom.

Has it really only been two weeks? Everything is a blur.

The train moves forward, soundlessly. As it gains speed, my thoughts shift forward. Instead of dwelling on leaving, I lean back and contemplate my destination.

Prime. A High City—the highest class city in our country. Will it be anything like Ivanhoe? Drenched in technology and scrapbook architecture that captivates one's imagination?

I have no way of knowing. I've never seen a picture of Prime, but I'll be there in eight hours.

Eight hours.

Eight hours sitting next to Solomon.

I crane my neck. Our car is empty. It may not be for long, depending on what stops are ahead, but this is my opportunity to finally get some answers. I let a full five minutes pass before I dive in. "Solomon?"

He looks at me with his light teal eyes and I adopt a new favorite color. "Yes?"

I gulp. "You said that Jude shared most of his inventions with your father. Does your father live near Prime?"

Seconds tick by. "You want to visit him."

"Don't you?"

He scratches the back of his neck, then winces and taps his bandaged face. "I want answers just as much as you, but sometimes it's safer to wait."

Wait? This is perfect timing—we're going up to Prime, the Council hasn't released the new Clock-matching information yet, and I'm ready to do some digging. I refuse to waste more of my time by *waiting*. "Wait for what?"

Already, the train slows for its first stop. "Until we're no longer tracked, and until after you meet with the Council."

The way he says this raises my hackles. I straighten in my chair. "Why? Do you think I would *tell* them Jude's secrets? You think I would give anything up to *them?*"

He meets my eyes. It's strange looking directly into a man's eyes, especially when he doesn't break the gaze. "I know you would never give information to them, Parvin . . . not of your free will."

"They couldn't force anything out of me." My voice is fractured.

The train comes to a full stop. People climb into our car and Solomon lowers his voice. "Don't forget, they have Willow."

He lets that soak in. Then . . .

"And they will use her any way they want."

10

The beauty of a city built on the cornerstones of technology is eclipsed by my fear for Willow. The rest of the train ride passed in near silence since too many people surrounded us. I did manage to share my blackmail message with Solomon, but it only served to remind me . . .

This meeting is dangerous.

Solomon and I stand in the train station now, working the cement out of our joints. The station has a high ceiling with grey stone arches forming a square in the center. A fan of glass spreads on the opposite wall around a gold-embossed clock. Long regal steps lead up to shining doors beneath the glass.

The station alone would be enough to steal my breath, but in the center of the entry, projected up from one of the marble squares of flooring, is a glowing blue orb of our half of the earth. Lines circle it and cross, mixing vectors and routes. Words scroll around it with circles popping up and red pulsing dots.

"Route schedule," Solomon says as we pass it.

Other people walk through it. The projection doesn't waver. Above us, rectangle screens—are they screens or painted air?—advertise so many items and products I can't digest a single one.

No one is looking up.

Aren't they interested in what these screens show? I study their focused faces and the human beings around me bring new intrigue. They have screens on their bodies, like Jude's snake tattoo.

One woman, dressed in a blue pencil skirt and a white short-sleeved blouse, has a tattooed armband around her bicep. It's light green with colorful flashing pictures. A gentleman with a buzzed head and dark clothing connected by small chains has a tattoo over his entire scalp.

My face flashes across it. *Download your copy of* A Time to Die *today!* In the picture I'm pale, unsmiling, and looking up. When was that taken? By whom? "My face is on that man's head."

"What?" Solomon steers me around a crowd, but I twist my neck to watch the bald man.

"My face . . . it's on that guy's head."

When Solomon looks, the tattoo changes to an ad for hair products. "It's an ad. No one notices. He just has it to earn a little money."

"But . . . *my face.*" Prickles skim my spine. "Do people here . . . know me that well?"

"You *are* famous, Parvin."

That doesn't help. "So anyone could recognize me? Come after me?" Going from a life of invisibility to being an advertisement on a bald man's scalp is too much. "Let's go. Let's get out of here. There are too many people."

What am I afraid of? That they'll mob me? Ask me questions? Blame me for Reid's death like the people in Unity Village? Solomon's pace doesn't change.

"Come *on*, Hawke." I try to pull him forward, but he grips my arm.

"Parvin, wait."

Don't panic. Don't panic. Why in the world do I want to panic?

"It's going to be worse outside."

I stop and face him. "What?"

"This is a High City. There are people and advertisements *everywhere*. I think . . . you might get overwhelmed." He slides his hand halfway into mine, then he must think better of it because he returns his hand to my elbow.

We start forward again, now climbing the long steps toward the exit. "Where are we going?"

"Jude's apartment." The words come out heavy. "Someone has to organize his affairs now that he's gone."

I'd forgotten Jude came from Prime. I'm going to see where he lived. How will I feel? How will Solomon feel?

We step outside.

Crowds of people shuffle up and down the sidewalk, pushing past each other with brisk strides. Buildings tower around us, higher than the Ivanhoe Marble, higher than the county building—higher than any building I've ever seen in my life. Screens and advertisements line the sides of each one.

Weaving through the sunset sky are tiny electronic birds. They have four propellers and zip in a pattern so perfect and so fast I grow dizzy and fall against Solomon. He steadies me and pushes me along the wall of one of the buildings, up the sidewalk. Through the masses.

"Those are delivery quadcopters. They have their own flight patterns. Everyone calls them heralds."

Beside us is a type of road with cars gliding along—no, *over*—rails set in the ground. They float inches above each rail, speeding along. All the windows are tinted, so I can't tell if people are driving them.

We reach a line of identical black cars and climb into the first one. There's no steering wheel, four separate seats, and a screen for a dashboard. Solomon types in several words, then lifts a patch of skin off the underside of his wrist, revealing a square of lines with a short string of numbers.

He scans it into the dashboard screen and the car slides forward, easing into traffic with the others. He leans back in his seat and looks at me. "I know this is all new to you."

I gape at him. "You . . . have a fake wrist? Why did that screen scan your body? How does the car know where to take us?"

He grins. "Do you really want me to explain everything?"

I don't know. I'm not sure I like it. I look out the tinted window as we move along, studying the people who chose to walk. The best description for them is . . . decorated.

Some decorations are subtle, like makeup and tattoos. But one shirtless man has tiny rose thorns snaking in a line down his spine and then across what I can see of his shoulders. Another woman has blue swirls, like liquid metal, ornamenting her buzzed head. Someone else has feathers attached *in* her skin, fluttering with the evening breeze.

Some of it would be fun . . . if I were at a costume party. If I ever got a tattoo, what would it be of? And what would feathers feel like on my skin?

"Might be nice for a day, eh?"

I swear Solomon can read my thoughts. I let loose a small smile. "Yeah."

"Well, everything's temporary nowadays. If you want to buzz your head and paint it pink, you can do it for a day."

I laugh. "But what about my hair?"

"There's a growth parlor by Jude's apartment."

I think of the bald man in the train station with his advertisement for hair growth. "I could just plaster an ad of my own face on the back of my head."

He lifts his hands. "Double Parvin? I don't think I'd mind."

"Such a flatterer." Are we bantering? I think we are.

"Here we are." The floating car stops next to a skinny building that stretches so high into the sky that I can't see the top. It's dark now and lights blink from the windows not covered in advertise-ments. A colorful shine comes from around the corner. I catch a glimpse of glowing trees, but we don't go that way.

Glowing trees?

A special code and scan from Solomon opens a glass door that lets us into a cramped square room with an elevator. We take it to the seventh floor. The doors open to reveal another closed door, as if we're on the doorstep of a house. Solomon enters a code and then we step inside Jude's apartment.

The elevator leaves us behind. I stand on polished stone floor-ing, mixtures of tan and grey squares. A living room the size of my house is straight ahead, with a wall of windows. To the left is a curved wooden staircase with a railing of swirly metal vines.

I drift into the living room, not feeling my legs move. A square patch of wood marks the flooring beneath a wooden coffee table. A white couch, loveseat, and armchair surround the table, all angled toward a fireplace set in the marble wall behind me.

Above me hangs an electric chandelier. The second floor is open, revealing bookcases and more white walls in a wrap-around walkway.

"Jude lived here?" I'm surprised any sound comes out of my mouth.

"Not exactly what you're used to, is it?" Something in Solomon's tone tells me it's not something *he's* used to, either.

"It's just hard to believe that he'd waste so much money like this." I slide my hand over the white armrest of the couch.

Solomon sets my pack on a stone bench built into the wall by the fireplace. "It's not like that, Parvin. This was the cheapest Jude could find, and it came furnished. High Cities require this type of living."

"Why? How can they force people to spend money on such . . . luxuries?"

"Because High Cities are 'the best.' They want to keep it that way, perfect it. Jude lived here for the sake of research and inventions. He needed access to the best."

My room is upstairs. More windows and a flat, smooth bed with blankets made out of the finest material I've ever touched. I'm not sure it will keep me warm, though. Solomon returns downstairs. Maybe to give me a moment to swallow this world of expense I'm standing in.

High-City life . . . I'd never fit in here. But right now, I feel like a queen.

Along the wall opposite the bed is a suspended verse of cut metal: *For by me your days will be multiplied, and years will be added to your life. – Proverbs 9:11*

Further proof of Jude's insistence that Clocks don't run our lives. Who is that verse talking about? God?

I return to the living room and plop on a couch. It bounces me back off. "Wow, that's stiff." I lower myself again.

Solomon sits on the loveseat and looks up from his NAB. "Jude didn't stay here long enough to break them in."

"But long enough to hang a verse in my room. Isn't that . . . dangerous here? Don't High-City people hate believers?"

Solomon tilts his head. "They don't *hate* them, it's just against the Law to spread our beliefs unless someone asks about them. And it's illegal to share with people underage, even if they ask. If an Enforcer came in here, he'd make Jude remove the verse. But Jude didn't have many visitors. What verse was it?"

I see it floating in my mind, word for word. *"For by me your days will be multiplied, and years will be added to your life."*

"Ah, Jude's favorite."

Really? Why did he never share it with me? "Is it talking about God?"

Solomon shakes his head. "I think it's talking about wisdom.

123

But the verse before that one says the fear of the Lord is the beginning of wisdom. It all comes back to Him in the end."

So having wisdom means fearing the Lord? And He has the power to multiply my years. What a powerful thought. "What do we do now? My meeting with the Council isn't for another three days."

Solomon returns to his NAB. "How about something illegal?"

I start. What does *that* mean? "I'm coming here to blackmail the leaders of our country and you want me to do something illegal?"

"I think you'll like it." His tone is playful, like he knows the answer to a hidden joke.

"What is it?"

"An underground church meeting."

I arch my back against the stiff cushions and try to smoosh them down a bit. "I didn't know church was illegal, too."

"Religion is a lot more . . . controlled here. Churches have to register with the government and then teach only from a list of approved topics. There used to be different denominations, but they're all forced to meet in the same building, taking turns. Discussion of actual Scripture isn't allowed. Anyone who goes outside those rules is imprisoned or turned into a Radical."

Skelley Chase said something about religion being dangerous back when I thought he was on my side. "*That* makes me want to go." Despite my sarcasm, I love the idea of rebelling against the law for the sake of gathering with others who share my beliefs. Maybe they'll have a Bible I can borrow.

"We get together to be a family. To support each other and fellowship."

I've never been among a group of believers. It's like what Solomon said on our drive back from the Wall. We're outlaws going *beyond* the law. I tilt my head. "I'm in."

His lips spread in such a wide smile, it erases my hesitance. "Okay, bring me your NAB and I'll explain how this works."

I move beside him. "Are you sure it's safe to tell me these things before my meeting with the Council? You said they could force me to talk, remember?"

He takes my NAB from my hand and taps the screen so fast I can't keep track of where he's going or what he's programming. "They won't ask you about this. You're safe. There." He hands my NAB back to me. "Now if we get separated, you'll always know how to get back to people who will help you."

A new tiny bubble on my home page says, *Verse of the Week*. My stomach leaps. A Bible verse! I tap the bubble.

And through his faith, though he died, he still speaks. Hebrews 11:4

I look up. "Well, that's . . . random." Or maybe not. There's the word SPEAK again.

"It's a code that tells us when to meet." He points to the reference. "The name of the book tells the day of the week and the reference tells the time. It's always in the evening. This means Wednesday at eleven-forty."

"How does *Hebrews* mean Wednesday?"

"Matthew means Monday, Timothy means Tuesday, Hebrews means Wednesday—because it's one of the only books with a *W* in it—Thessalonians for Thursday, Philemon for Friday, Samuel for Saturday, and Song of Solomon for Sunday."

"I bet Sunday verses are fun."

He chuckles. "We've had some good ones come through."

"So my NAB will update the new verse every week?"

"Yes."

I look back at this week's verse. *And through his faith, though he died, he still speaks.* "Who is this verse talking about?"

"Abel, I think. The murdered son of Adam and Eve."

He still speaks . . . My throat constricts. "It's kind of like Reid and Jude. They still speak in their own ways, even though they're gone."

SPEAK.

Where? When? I need more!

"Yeah." Solomon folds his hands in his lap.

I force despondency out the window. Will my story be like Jude's and Reid's, continuing even after I'm gone? "We're going to honor their deaths, Solomon. I'll do everything I can to keep the Council from using Jude's invention."

"Don't do it for Jude, do it for everyone. Do it for God."

"I will."

Tuesday afternoon finds me drenched in sensory overload as I meander the streets of Prime. Solomon has gone to meet with someone who can put Jude's apartment up for sale. After hours of mulling over what I'll say to the Council, I opted to go shopping as a distraction.

Shopping. Me. I don't think I've ever gone *shopping*. Not unless I spent a month scrounging up specie for something specific, like a new sewing needle. Now I have my pouch of Last-Year funds from before I crossed the Wall. I don't know how expensive things are in Prime, but I'd like to get some new clothes—clothes I haven't made or haven't worn six hundred times over.

After all, I'm meeting friends of Jude's and Solomon's tomorrow night at the underground church. I want to make a good impression.

I find a long street with shops on both sides of the road. Cars float down the road at a crawl. Small bridges cross from one side of the street to the other every block or so. Several of the stores have clothing. I never considered my clothing unfashionable until

I saw these stores. People walk out with giant bags and boxes. What will they do with so much clothing?

The mannequins in the windows are clad in garments that won't last or keep me warm. Much of it is pretty and . . . fun. Not something I could wear in Unity Village unless I want to ostracize myself even more.

I didn't think it would be so hard to find something new that would be useful. I finally enter a store. I try not to be overwhelmed by the displays, but the floor is *carpeted*. In a store! I want to take off my boots and run my bare feet over it, but no. This is normal for a High City.

People live like this every day. What a different world.

I browse, avoiding the eyes of the two female workers whispering together in the back by the check-out table. Their stares burn my back. I know I'm rugged. I wear the black dress and thin boots that Wilbur Sherrod, my old employer, gave me in Ivanhoe. I'd much rather be in Mother's skirt, but Reid's blood is on it. They'd whisper a lot more if I wore *that*.

I stop at a rack of clothing colored in tans, blacks, and browns. At least they carry my colors. I wave my stump under a loose dusty-brown blouse. It's soft. Good quality. It is a V-neck with loose long sleeves. No buttons, no collar.

A tan dress catches my eye—sleeveless, ankle-length, and simple. Where would I wear it? The material is sturdy. It might look nice on me. What would Solomon think?

My hand rests among the cloth and I stare at it before laughing under my breath. Maybe *that's* why the employees watch me— because of my missing hand. I was more self-conscious about my clothing than about my stump. Weird.

"May I help you find something?"

Oh dear. I turn around, clutching the dress in my right hand. The woman is young, with flickering purple and green leaves tattooed down her neck. Her blond hair is up in a side do and curls come down across her other shoulder. She wears one earring—a giant dangling heart with small ticking Numbers on its face. Is that her Clock?

"Um . . . I'm just . . . how much is this dress?"

She looks under the neckline and a virtual price glows at the back of the neck. "Three hundred."

"Th-three . . . *hundred?* Specie?"

She drops her hand and purses her green lipsticked lips. "Yes."

"Oh." I turn away. I don't even have *one* hundred specie in my pouch. But . . . that doesn't make sense. One hundred specie in Unity Village lasts forever. How can a dress cost more than my entire Last Year funds?

"May I be of assistance?" a smoother, older voice asks from behind me.

Great, now the other one has come and I'll have to tell them both I don't even have enough coin for a sock.

I turn around. She has a black vest on under a white see-through blouse. The dark electronic word *Manager* is displayed below her left shoulder. The other employee looks at her feet. Maybe she's new.

"No, thanks, I—"

The manager gasps and her eyes fix on my stump.

This isn't awkward at all. "Yeah, kind of disturbing, huh? I can guarantee it's an interesting story." Though not one I'm willing to tell right now. So why did I say that?

"Are you Parvin Blackwater?" She's breathless.

The other worker jumps with a squeak. "She *is!*"

Drat. They know my name and face, and now they also know I can't afford a single dress.

"Parvin Blackwater's in my store." The manager isn't looking at me anymore. She's fixated on nothing, in awe. After a pro-longed moment of silence, during which I start to think this is turning humorous, her gaze returns to me. "You just go ahead and take that dress."

The younger employee snags the long-sleeved brown shirt I liked and thrusts it into my hands. "And this, too."

The manager glares at her. "Go man the register."

The girl hangs her head and slouches back toward a white standing desk in the back corner. I wish I could do something for her. I don't want to be like Skelley Chase, famous and above everyone else.

"Bee was right, though, you can have anything you like. This black skirt goes *perfectly* with that blouse. And you're so thin and dainty they'll look elegant on your frame."

I hold up my hand. "I can't allow you to give me these things for free." Besides, her comment about *thin* and *dainty* is clear flattery. I'm short with long legs and half a torso. "I was just about to get going, actually."

"Well, I hoped we could take a few emotigraphs with you . . . in the clothing."

"I really should—"

"Please." She grabs my left forearm and looks as though she's about to cry. Then she must realize she's clutching the arm with the stump and she lets go.

I relax. These women have read my X-book and they like me. They admire me. They want an emotigraph of me. "Oh, all right."

"Bee! Set up the sentra!" She shoves the clothes back into my arms. "Take these. I insist. As long as you let me blow up these pictures and hang them in my store."

Ah, a catch. So *this* is fame. But who cares? "Sure."

I'm holding a year's worth of Unity Village luxuries right now. Can I really take them for free? I imagine wearing the black skirt with the blouse and my calf-high boots. I might be pretty.

We take several pictures. Some of me in my new clothes, then me with the two workers, then me with the manager, and then me with Bee, who hugs me so tight I can't breathe.

They're all squeals, giggles, and unprofessionalism—and I love it. They fluff my hair, talk about their favorite parts in the X-book—when Jude tried to save me and when I tried on Wilbur Sherrod's suits—and wave me out the door just as a fresh batch of oblivious customers walk in.

I leave with a new dress, skirt, blouse, scarf, wrist bangles, and a shoulder bag that barely fits my folded NAB.

What a day.

As I walk down to another store that sells emotigraphs, I have to ask myself . . . is this prettiness for me? Do I just want to impress Solomon's friends or is this to impress Solomon?

I don't want to drift back into the selfishness that spurred on my biography.

And why did I go along with those workers? Why didn't I tell them about the Council's lies? About the *purpose* behind my actions?

I sigh and enter the emotigraph store. It's small and cramped, with polished wood flooring, wooden shelving on every wall, and a wooden register stand. A narrow man stands behind it with thick glasses and a pointed nose. He doesn't look up when I enter.

The shelves are covered in stacks of thin emotigraphs and organized according to mood. *Happiness, Encouragement, Anger, Motivation, Fear* . . . Why would anyone buy a fear emotigraph?

In the middle of the shop is a specialty stand with my X-book on display. It's surrounded by stacks of emotigraphs—the pictures I sent to Skelley Chase. There's the one I took when I was bleeding in the cave after the wolf attack. Grey with his wounded foot. My stitched-up leg. When I first saw Willow. A picture of Ivanhoe in three stacks.

A lurch hits my throat and I look away. Those weren't for entertainment.

But what *were* they for? Why did I take them? How are they affecting people now? I hope they motivate people into action, but I can't bring myself to believe it.

In the corner is a bookstand under a sign reading *Spiritual Wellness*. Odd among the many emotigraphs, but this store seems geared toward emotions and inner health. Some of the books have scuffed corners or broken spines. A post above the stand reads, *Trade-ins: 3 specie*. At the bottom of the spiritual wellness shelf is a single Bible, crammed between *Emotigraph Therapy* and *Calming Your Technological Spirit*.

A real Bible—leather and paper. I gasp and snatch it from the shelf. At last! The bottom corner displays the USE's seal—a Wall and Clock—over a small sentence: *Council approved*.

The door opens and two men walk in, browsing the romance section of emotigraphs. Yuck.

I walk up to pay for the Bible.

The clerk barely glances up from his NAB on the desk. "All trade-in books are three specie."

I'm glad he doesn't ask for some sort of identification. I hand him three of my precious coins. They're not a loss at all, but I'm a bit ashamed that this costs only three while the dress in the bag I carry cost three hundred.

He looks at the coins, then frowns. "You're from a Low City?"

The coins are stamped with the USE symbol. Nothing on them would reveal my city status. "So?"

He straightens and folds his arms. "I can't take your coins. Where's your wrist code?" That's when he meets my eyes. His mouth opens and closes like a suffocating guppy.

I struggle to maintain cool confidence. "Why can't you take my specie? I promise it's valid." Is he really so prejudiced against Low Cities? Maybe he'll give me the Bible for free, now that he recognizes me.

"I don't want to get mugged, Miss Blackwater." He speaks in an undertone. "Best you find a bank to transfer that to your wrist code before someone mugs *you*."

I stuff the coins back in my pocket. "It's *money!* You don't take money?"

He shrugs, but then his eyes alight on the Bible. "Where did you get this?"

"Your trade-in shelf."

He snatches it off the counter and tosses it into a bin behind him. "I don't sell Bibles. Someone snuck that on the shelf—not for the first time, mind you."

I half-reach for it. "Then just give it to me. I'll get rid of it for you." Please!

"No. I'll be burning it tonight."

"You can't! I'll give you as much specie as you want. You can't refuse *specie*."

"No one's carried the real thing in years." He eyes me. "And no store's accepted it for payment either. It keeps crime lower."

"Well, that's not how it works in my village. People there don't mug each other. We've got respect and order." My gaze rests on the Bible lying in the bin. "Is there any way I can purchase that? It says it's USE approved! I desperately need it. Can't *you* take the coins to your bank? Or . . . or—" my stomach churns at the very idea, but I spew it out anyway, "—I could sign some of your emotigraphs."

The shopkeeper shakes his head. "Sorry, lady."

He doesn't look sorry. He looks like he wants me out of his shop. The two men surveying the romance section shoot glances in my direction. I grip my bag of new clothing and stride out of the store, my chin held high but a burning in my eyes.

My ears alert to the light shutting of a door behind me. I glance to my left, pretending to look in a store window, and catch the reflection of the two men from the shop directly behind me. *Close* behind me.

I speed up.

They speed up.

"Leave me alone!" I break into a sprint, gripping the handle of my bag so tightly that my fingernails cut into the palm of my hand.

I don't hear running behind me. I enter the small square park at the base of Jude's apartment building, where people recline on benches or sit on the grass. Only once I'm in the sight of witnesses do I look behind me. The two men are gone. Maybe they were never there.

My heart hammers my eardrums. Am I paranoid? I catch my breath and then round the corner of the building to the entrance door. I enter the code Solomon told me this morning. The door unlocks and I step inside.

An inch before it latches, fingers slide into the crack and swing it open. The men from the emotigraph shop step in. I careen backward until I hit the wall. This room is too small. To go up, I need to enter the elevator code. To go out, I need to pass them.

"Good sunset," one says in a voice that conveys things are anything but good.

I shake my head, but my voice won't work.

"We don't want a fuss."

I press firmer against the wall. That's the only message he needs before he lunges forward and grabs my hair.

"What do you want?" I screech.

His friend hisses, "Hurry up."

The first man is yanking at the bag in my hands, but my money is in my pocket. I push at him and he slaps my hand away.

"No," I croak. "No, go away."

I'm weak. I'm pathetic. Why am I not fighting?

Fight.

I can't.

I must.

I drop the clothing bag and shove my hand in his face. He reels backward. *Escape. Escape. Escape.*

But he's got his feet under him again. I thrust my hand into my pocket and pull out the pouch of money. "Here!"

He stops.

"Here," I say again, calmer, holding it farther from my body. "I don't care about specie, but clearly you need it." My head spins. My vision is blurry. *Just take the bag, mister.*

He lifts an eyebrow and yanks it from my fingers.

My voice trembles, but I continue speaking, afraid that if I stop they'll attack me again—this time for something else. "I don't want it, I don't. All I wanted was that Bible in the emotigraph store."

He glances in the bag. "This is all ya got? I thought ya were famous."

I shrug. "I haven't seen a single coin from my biography. Skelley Chase kept it all for himself. Would you expect anything different? I'm Low-City scum."

They don't say anything else, but after one last queer look, they both exit at a run. I stand for a long minute, swaying against a headache and trying to convince myself to be strong again. My money is gone. I gave it away.

Why would I give it away? How will I buy a train ticket back to Unity Village? How will I *eat?*

What a mess.

Maybe it's good. Maybe it's just another step toward becoming weaker and relying on God's provision and strength. But why would He allow those guys to attack me?

I crush a wave of anger and then find myself praying. *That was . . . awful. Did You have a reason for that? Are those guys going to somehow turn to You now? Or maybe my little bit of money will get them on their feet.*

What else could I have said to those men? I could have told them I don't blame them. I could have said something spiritual, like . . . like a Scripture. Instead, I sounded desperate, like every other victim I'm sure they've mugged.

After three tries, I enter the elevator code and return to the apartment. I still have my new clothes. Let's see if I can cover whatever bruising is cropping up on my face from the scuffle and make myself pretty for tomorrow's illegal church hang-out.

I blink against the hot tears threatening to fall. Those men made me grovel. But . . .

I will *not* let them make me cry.

11

"Hey, it's Jude's girl!"

A chorus of "Heys" breaks out, mainly in male voices, and a group converges—slapping Solomon on the back and pulling me into so many rough man-hugs I'll never differentiate who gave which hug or whether or not I liked it.

I'm not sure how I feel being called *Jude's girl*, especially with Solomon next to me. I never thought of myself as Jude's girl, even after our awkward declaration of attraction.

I don't look at Solomon.

We're in the basement of an abandoned industrial factory of sorts. Cement pillars form a labyrinth design holding up different portions of wall or ceiling throughout the room. They must have been painted at some point because a thin membrane peels in places off the beams.

Two electronic screens have been slapped on opposite walls and programmed to send in what looks like real sunlight, even though it's almost midnight. The massive, high-ceilinged room is still fairly dark. I imagine people lurking in the shadowed corners.

Solomon and I arrived late. He said everyone tries to arrive at different times so we don't draw attention to the location. With the amount of creeping and sneaky hiding we did to get here, I doubt anyone even *saw* us let alone connected us with the other people arriving over the course of an hour.

I look around at the many faces. More men than women, but that might change by the time the meeting starts. I've never been around so many men my age—a pack of God-loving males who see me as famous. Who want to know me.

The man who called me Jude's girl comes up and puts his arm around my shoulder. "Gee, you're a pretty little thing."

Gee, *little* and *thing* aren't my favorite compliments. He has medium-length rust-colored hair held up in a spiked style by a thick belt cinched around his head. The belt shadows his eyes, but he leans close enough for me to see the playful smirk behind them.

"Hi," I say.

He's tall and smells incredibly manly. Baggy pants, a loose cut-off black shirt, and heavy boots. He'd do well in the West.

"Parvin"—I'm surprised to hear a smile in Solomon's voice— "this is Fight."

I rotate to look into Fight's face. "That's your name?"

He shrugs and folds his arms. "Yup."

"Well, nice to meet you." I almost offer my hand, but after he draped his muscular arm around me, I sense that a handshake will just make things awkward. What would fit nicely is coyness—a raise of my eyebrow, a sensual smile, a witty remark.

I settle for silence and inch closer to Solomon.

There's a strange mystery behind Fight's dominating personality . . . best viewed from afar, I think. Besides, I didn't come here to play. Or to be fickle.

A tall, thin girl with blond hair twisted back from her face strides into the building. "Hey all!"

A smeared tattoo on the left side of her face looks like smoke. Both her ears have at least seven piercings. She wears a loose black tank top that shows off her midriff, and studded black straps crisscross up one arm for no apparent reason other than fashion.

She wears rings and metal bolts for earrings, which match her necklace. Her tiny black skirt appears made up of woven belts.

What is it with belt fashion?

"You're late, Idris," Fight shouts.

She stops in front of him, resting the strapped arm on her hip. "Only 'cause I was savin' your hide, you lazy red-haired beacon."

"I've been here for two hours."

Her eyes narrow, revealing the dark eye makeup giving her such a fierce appearance. Or maybe she's just fierce. "Yeah, and I've just spent *two hours* chattin' with an Enforcer about complete *nonsense*, hoping he'd forget about the whole thing. He *saw* you, Fight. He saw you looking all cocky like you always are, and he followed you. I had to run into him like it was an accident, risking my *own* hide, and talk about the weather while dodging his kisses. You owe me some brain cells."

Fight laughs, pulls her tight against him, and plants a firm kiss right on her lips. "Done. They just transferred."

Her lips don't smile, but her eyes do. She leans back and slaps his arm. "Shut up."

"Besides"—he shrugs—"you had your Clock with you."

She pats the top belt of her skirt and I see the glowing Numbers lining the thick leather—small enough that I can't make them out, thank goodness. I don't want to know anyone's Numbers anymore.

What is it with High-City people and their decorative Clocks? I'd never seen Numbers displayed differently until I found Solomon's armband.

"You bet I had it. The best-looking Clock in all of Prime, thank you very much. But that wasn't the problem." She pounds a finger in Fight's chest. "*You* are. What if he'd followed you here? Where would we be?"

That's when she notices me and I suddenly wish I were taller, fiercer, and sexier. My black skirt and new top did exactly what

I'd hoped—made me look dainty and stylish. But now I want to match this girl. This . . . warrior who stands up to Enforcers.

"Hey, Enforcer." She gives Solomon a quick hug. "Sorry about Jude, but we all knew it was coming. How you holding up?" He doesn't even get a breath to answer before she says, "Never mind. Dumb question. And no, I'm not gonna ask about your face. But you look nicer without the tattoo. Is this Jude's girl?"

My name is Parvin, thank you very much. "Hey."

"I love all that shalom stuff." She hugs me, too, in a clash of belts and leather. I don't know what to say. I guess I expected a slug in the arm. "Heck, you're brave."

"Oh, um . . ." I curl my loose hair behind my ear. "Well, thanks." Can I be any wimpier?

"Keep eet down," someone hisses from behind the group. Everyone turns around. A teenage Hispanic boy sits against one of the cement pillars.

"New guy?" Idris looks to Fight.

"Yeah." Fight walks over to the boy. "It's nice and soundproof in here, man. We'll be fine."

"Well, don' be careless." The boy scowls. "Soun' like you been fine for a while. I was at Vault when Enforcers broke in. Got a bullet to the leg."

Fight kneels. "We'll be careful. As Idris said, my cockiness got in the way."

Everybody settles into a place on the floor against a wall or pillar. Solomon and I sit against the wall across from Idris and Fight. Those in the darker corners scoot closer.

"All right everyone," Fight says. "What's been happening in—"

"I want to hear from Parvin." This from Idris.

I jolt back against the concrete wall, as if to escape the request. The chill in the cement becomes one with my emotions. No. No thanks. I don't want to speak.

SPEAK.

No. Not now. Not yet. I'm going to speak in front of the Council tomorrow, isn't that enough?

I look to Solomon, but he doesn't say anything. Why should he? The silence mounts. I clear my throat. "Wh-what do you want me to say?"

"Well, what are you doing here? What's up with your connection to the Council? I mean, Solomon brought you, so you *must* be trustworthy, but I'm curious. What happened to Willow? What did you discover about God? Is there religious freedom in the West? How can we get there?"

Solomon holds up his hands. "Calm down, Idris. This is Parvin's first time gathering with fellow believers. How about we have a Q&A afterward?"

She folds her arms. "Fine."

No! How about instead Parvin gets to leave in peace after this? That's my vote.

"Okay"—Fight picks up where he got interrupted—"what's been happening in the last week?"

"I got caught."

I peer around Solomon to see the young woman who spoke. She's sitting on a pillow with an arm in a sling and heavy bruising on her face. Her voice is thick. "The Enforcers found me housing a Radical. She and I were reading through the Bible . . . she was fourteen."

"Oh no," Idris breathes.

The woman nods. "I know it was careless, with her being underage and all, but she was curious. I couldn't keep it from her. The Enforcers beat me and then took her away three days ago." She starts to cry. "I am so afraid for her. I haven't seen her since."

Light muttering surrounds her. Prayers, I realize. But before I can consider joining them, someone else starts.

"My aunt and her family were killed on Monday." Next to Fight, a middle-aged man with a high forehead and glasses closes his eyes as he speaks. "They lived in Neos, the Illinois High City, and had been sharing verses, talking about things that aren't on the approved sermon lists. The Enforcers made her and her two sons dig their own graves, then shot them. Their deaths matched their Clocks, so they were ready. But it doesn't make it much easier for me. At least it was for the Lord."

Fight lays his hand on the man's arm and starts praying, low and intent. Idris joins them, and then several others. My throat burns. I had no idea this happened in the USE. These people aren't even Radicals, they're just believers—and still they're attacked by the authorities. Even more so than Radicals.

"I became a Radical on Sunday." A woman beside us looks to be about Mother's age and a girl in her twenties sits beside her. Her daughter, maybe? "We were also at the Vault gathering with Evarado when the Enforcers found us. They ripped up the few Bibles that were brought because they weren't USE approved and then destroyed the Clocks of those who couldn't escape in time. Mine was one of them."

I gasp. The government is *making* Radicals and then labeling us a threat?

Solomon moves from beside me and kneels with the woman. I join him and allow him to pray. The daughter is praying as well, and their voices blend. The woman joins in and suddenly my self-consciousness disappears and I find myself praying.

My voice is light, soft. And I'm fully in God's presence. "God, You are greater than the Clocks. You *are*. You are showing us that it is better to trust in You than to have a Clock. It's scary. I'm scared. I'm sure this woman is scared, too. Give us the courage. Give us Your strength."

I'm breathing hard when I stop and I'm not sure why. Some of the praying voices drift off. While we prayed someone else had shared a personal story or struggle, but I didn't catch it. A circle of people prays around that person, too.

I hug the woman. She squeezes my hand. Solomon returns to my side and Fight starts speaking Scripture. I don't know where he's reciting from, but the words tumble from his mouth, smooth and easy. Verse after verse after verse. Everyone finishes praying, but he keeps going.

For an hour.

I close my eyes and lean my head back against the wall. Listening. Resting in the words.

When he finishes, a long calm—like a deep breath—rests among us. When others begin to move, breaking the silence with the shuffle of their clothing and feet against concrete, I address Fight. "How did you memorize all of that?"

I thought *my* memory was good, but Fight's is phenomenal. If *I* knew the entire Bible, then I wouldn't be in the predicament I am now—desperately craving His Word, but having no access to it.

Fight raises an eyebrow. "I got one of the last Bible caps."

Idris gasps and turns to him. "I didn't know that!"

He nods sagely. "Yup. My parents bought a canister at the first rumors of the government putting Bible caps on hold. They gave one to each of us kids, even though it was against the law."

I want to pretend I understand, that I know what they're talking about, but I don't. And I refuse to be left in the dark, even in prideful ignorance. "Um . . . what's a Bible cap?"

Solomon mentioned a *Definitions* cap when he drove me back to Unity Village. Is it similar to this?

They all stare at me and, for a millisecond, I feel foolish–but then Idris launches into an explanation without a second blink. "Caps are pills, only instead of medicine they contain information that you can consume. Once you've ingested it, all that info enters your bloodstream and travels up to the brain. The caps are programmed to know when the blood reaches the brain and then the information is deposited in the right places. Like a tattoo . . . on your grey matter."

Fight stares at her.

She shrugs. "What? Jude told me. You know he's the tech-head."

"So . . . people just *ingest* information?"

She folds her arms and looks at me. "Yeah! School's only a few weeks a year. But the government controls which caps you get and when. They're not sold in stores anymore. You need to apply for each cap."

"School in Unity Village is . . . different. I sat at a desk in a classroom." For hours. And hours. Withstanding the torment of bullies.

Fight leans forward and rests his elbows on his knees. "Really? I would kill to experience traditional schooling."

"Sounds boring and long to me." Idris grimaces.

"Shut-up, textbook-brain." Fight winks at her.

Ingested information. In Unity, we're forced to fight for a seat in the school and here people just . . . *swallow* information? It's not fair. Years of life could have been spared from sitting at a desk. Reid's life, my life, the lives of all the students in Unity.

"Any one stepping out?" Fight's voice breaks into my thoughts.

Stepping out? I look at Solomon. "You'll see," he whispers.

Evarado, the Hispanic boy, stands. "I am. On Sunday, I am travelin' back to my home. There is no gathering there and my *familia* is too afraid to start one. I think it is for me to start."

Several people around me nod.

"Need anything?" someone asks.

Evarado sits down. "I have enough specie. I need prayer the most. In my town are many Enforcers."

Fight sweeps a look over the group. "Any advice?"

"Be brave!" someone shouts. A few people laugh.

"I'm stepping out, too." Idris stands. "The Enforcer I met tonight . . . well, I think I left him before doing what God asks of us. I flirted to distract him, but I never told him about Jesus. I was too afraid." She pops her neck. "But I'm going to find him again."

Fight leaps to his feet. "Whoa, now, Idris. Don't be foolish. That's like walking up to the government and telling them to arrest you. What if they destroy your Clock?"

"Sit down, Fight."

He mutters in a low voice near her ear, "Don't you think we should talk about this first?"

"No. Boyfriend or not, God trumps you, and He's asking me to step out."

Fight slumps back to the ground and rests his arms on his knees, no longer leading the group. Pouting. I can understand a little of his hesitance. Idris is playing with fire. But I guess if it's God's fire, it's okay.

"So, stepping out means doing something dangerous?" I ask Solomon in an undertone.

"It's more like taking a step of faith that often makes us uncomfortable. We have to become uncomfortable in our lives to become comfortable in our faith."

I like this. I like hearing how other people are going to push themselves for God. It makes me want to share my story with these people. I stand up. "Um . . . I think I'm stepping out, too."

My body turns into a sheet of goosebumps, but I press on. "Tomorrow I'm meeting with the Citizen Welfare Development Council. You might have seen in the news that they're undergoing new Clock testing. It's Jude's invention and it will force all Radicals to be Clock-matched. It's dangerous. Jude died trying to keep this information from them."

As I talk I realize this is a lot more complicated to explain than I thought. I don't want to talk too long. I just want their support. "I'm trying to stop them. And I'm trying to rescue a friend."

"Willow?" Idris asks.

I nod.

Fight comes out of his pout. "Wait, but didn't *you* give the Council all this Clock-matching info?"

"No!" My shout reverberates off the stone.

"*Shhhh!*" Evarado hisses.

"They're spreading lies. I tried to *protect* Jude." I sit back down, hard, not wanting to defend myself any more than that.

"Do you need anything?" someone asks to my right.

Specie. I need specie because I got mugged today. But do I really *need* it? I shake my head. "No."

Solomon takes my hand and squeezes. My stomach lurches and the goosebumps return. "Any advice for her?"

Fight resumes his glare at the floor.

"They could kill you," Idris says.

"That's not advice, just common knowledge." I mean it as a joke, but it comes out hollow. "This is something I need to do. The threat is bigger than anyone understands."

"Clock-matching sounds *bueno* to me." Evarado scratches a spot on his knee.

"Me too." The new Radical woman on my left leans forward.

I look from one to the other. "The government is already forcing you to meet and fellowship in underground meetings. This invention is just another tool of control—another way to force you into something. Personally, I *like* being a Radical because it forces me to trust God with my time. I'm closer to Him because of it."

"It would make us all *igual* . . . you know, equal."

"You're *wrong.*" My face warms–my voice came out so loud Evarado jumped. But I need to make them understand. "It would give the government full control over all of us. Look what they do already! They persecute Radicals in the Low Cities, they don't let Radicals get jobs, train tickets, medical care, etc. What more will they do when being a Radical is no longer a voluntary choice? Forbid marriage between people with low Numbers? Take away food? Force you to join their military? Universal Clock-matching is the ultimate tool of control."

Everyone stays silent. I don't think it's because they agree.

"We will pray for you," Idris says.

I need to be strong. The response of these people reminds me of the ignorance the Council is creating. The High-City people really *don't* know what's going on. Not even here, in a safe meeting of shalom.

Can I possibly do this? What if the Council *does* kill me?

And through his faith, though he died, he still speaks. God can speak through me in any way. Even when I'm dead.

But . . .

I'd really prefer not to die.

12

"Don't come with me, Solomon."

We stand on the small balcony of Jude's apartment. The sun is at the end of its rising. I'll be before the Council in less than an hour.

The long hours from last night's Q&A still ring in my memory. My eyes are tired, my voice is tired, but my hope is wide-awake. It's funny how, in telling my own story to Idris, Fight, and the other believers, I saw God's hand through it all for the first time. I'd never seen the patterns before—rescue, purpose, shalom.

I'm more confident in my faith today than ever before. Good. I need it today more than ever.

Solomon stands close to me. So close. My face tilts up to meet his gaze and we stand like this for a long moment. He brushes his fingers up and down my arm lightly.

I shiver. "It's not safe for you." Elan Brickbat will be there. The Enforcers already carved up Solomon's face. Brickbat might kill him on the spot. And he's just one Council member. What might the others do?

To give the Council Willow *and* Solomon as leverage against me is like instant surrender.

"I don't care," he says. "You need me there."

I shake my head.

"Yes, you do. You don't need to be strong all by yourself. They'll be less likely to do anything to you if I'm by your side."

"They'll be *more* likely to use both you and Willow if you're there. Don't you understand, Solomon? Just wait for me and, when I return, we'll go visit your father and get more answers about Jude's invention."

"You can risk your own life, but won't allow me to risk mine?" His statement hits me, but he says it without passion. He knows as well as I do that he needs to stay.

"I'm sorry."

He closes his eyes for a long time and drops his hand. "God honored my prayers for your life two weeks ago. I'll ask Him to do it again today."

"I'm sorry." This time it comes out choked.

I turn and leave the balcony before he can open his eyes. Once I'm in the elevator, I look up as it closes. He's still out there. I remember the last time we separated in a similar situation. He was arguing against Sachem for my life. He held my hand until we were pulled apart.

This time, it's my doing and not Skelley Chase's.

The elevator descends. Solomon has gotten the worst side of everything. He fought for me and then lost me to the Wall. Then he risked his life to send Jude to protect me and he lost me to Jude. Now he may lose me to the Council—the very people who killed his brother.

His is a story of loss.

Someday, I want to change that. I want to give Solomon something he can keep. Maybe my heart will loosen enough to let that gift be me.

I exit the elevator and stumble over a brown paper-wrapped package on the ground. I pick it up and turn it over.

To: Parvin Blackwater is written on the paper in thick black ink.

Is this from Solomon? If so, why would he leave it on the ground out here? I lodge it against my body with my left arm so I can unwrap it with my hand. The wrapping is poorly done. When it falls away, I hold in my arms . . .

A Bible.

The same small USE-approved Bible from the emotigraph store. This isn't a gift from Solomon. It's a gift from those guys who mugged me . . . from God.

What a strange twist of a blessing.

I hug the Bible to my chest. *Thank you. Thank you!*

I AM WITH YOU.

Don't I know it.

After putting my Bible in my shoulder pack, I enter the small park at the base of the apartment complex. A wooden bench rests by a small path. As I walk the path, I find myself under dogwood trees—beautiful cream blossoms glimmering under the morning sun and reflecting advertisements from the buildings above.

Their flowers are wide and perfect. Petals flicker with a gust of wind. These trees have marked my journey. They surrounded the hearing platform in Unity Village when I was sentenced to the Wall. They covered the albino forest where I lost my hand and God taught me to sacrifice and be weak so He can be strong in me. Dogwoods decorated Ivanhoe, where I first developed the plan to create safe passage for Radicals sentenced to the West. And now they bend above me, each blossom like a resting butterfly, as I prepare to challenge the leaders of our country.

I reach up to pick a blossom, but the moment my fingers touch the stem I know something's wrong. It doesn't come off. The stem is too stiff, the petals too . . . smooth.

Wait . . . it's October. Dogwood trees don't bloom this time of year.

"What are you doing?" An old man with a grey mustache and a gardening advertisement tattoo on his forehead walks toward me from the apartment building. He wears a tool belt and gloves.

He examines the flower I almost picked. "These are fragile. I could write you up for destruction of property."

"I-I'm sorry, I thought they were real."

His brow scrunches. "*Real?* Why would I ever put real plants in a garden? Pollen, allergy risks, and wasted water alone would have my company shut down!"

My tranquility is gone. "But . . . dogwoods don't bloom in October."

He folds his arms. "I can't very well replace the tree every season, can I? People like blooms. Spring. No one likes bare branches in winter. Besides, the blossoms glow at night and save on street lamp costs."

So these are the glowing trees I saw when I first arrived. "But the whole beauty behind seasons is the fact that they're temporary."

"I've got gardening to do, girl." He bends down at the base of another dogwood tree and opens a door in the fake trunk. He pulls out a wrench and some wires.

Some gardener.

I continue on, trying to hold on to the beauty I felt when I saw the dogwood trees and not the discouragement now weighing on me. Why is everything fake here? Even the people seem fake, covered in paint and masks and tattoos. They live off artificial emotions from emotigraph stores. They believe lies from their leaders and don't seem to mind. They treat Clocks like fashion statements.

I tug the sleeve of my coat over my stump. Solomon helped me remove my tracker this morning, just in case things go wrong and I have to flee. He'd put it in my left arm so I'd be able to take it out on my own if I had to. Now it's bandaged to my upper arm. My stump doesn't tingle as much as it used to when I think about my hand. The old stitching scars are smooth and healed. It's become so normal to me now.

I reach the address of the Council and stop. The building is a sleek silver oval and . . . it's floating. It's at least twenty feet off the ground, with a long, arched walkway from the ground to the door. Beneath the building is a thick slab of what looks like black metal.

What is the purpose of a floating building? *How* does it float? If Jude were here, I bet he'd know. Maybe Solomon knows.

Here I go. Please . . . guide me, God. I take the arched path up to the double-door entrance. Inside, a line of Enforcers stand on each side of the entrance. Between them are different colored films floating in the air.

"Please proceed through the safety detectors," the Enforcer on my right says.

Walk through that pink screen? It could do anything to me. I reach out and stick my fingers through. Nothing happens.

"Please proceed through the safety detectors."

I fill my chest with nervous air and step forward. Nothing happens. I walk through a light green film and then a blue one.

"You may continue," a different Enforcer says, so I enter the rest of the building. Signs lead me to an elevator up to the third floor. It opens into a lobby with grey carpeting and chairs that look like little white eggs with a hole in them. A petite woman sits behind a tall white desk that curves around her. Only the top of her head pokes out.

"Um . . . I have a nine o'clock appointment with the Council. My name's Parvin Blackwater."

She doesn't look up. "Yes, Miss Blackwater, it is only eight fifty-four. Please take a seat until your appointment."

I sink into an egg chair. It's not comfortable at all, but I stay seated. Six minutes before I stand before them. What will I say? How will I start? Will they honor my demand that Willow be present?

I reach my hand into my pocket and take an emotigraph with my sentra. Then I pull *The Daily Hemisphere* from my pack and reread the articles about the Council claiming I helped them. I skim a few articles about Skelley Chase, too. I'll be asking the Council what their connection is with him. They let him get away with Reid's murder. I can't let that go.

Lastly, I read my blackmail message. It seems so amateur now.

My nerves stretch tight. *Calm down.* People are praying for me right now. At least, I hope they are. Idris, Solomon, and Fight. I'm not alone.

I think back to their call to *step out.* I like the idea of sacrificing for God. It'd be nice to have that much zeal. Is that what I'm doing right now?

Not really. I'm a sheep walking in to slaughter, but who else do the Radicals have to fight for them? No one.

And that's worth dying for.

"The Council will see you now." The receptionist points to a heavy metal door on my left.

I feel mildly like I'm at the county building on Assessment Day again, but this is worse. Much worse.

"Thank you," I rasp.

I step up to the door. It has no handle, but slides open when I'm an inch away from touching it. Inside is dark, almost black, but I step forward anyway. Before my eyes adjust to the dim lighting, I'm assaulted by a strong, heart-stopping scent—a tangy sour smell that brings to mind a bored smile and a warbled voice.

Lemon.

My eyes adjust and the first thing I see is a green fedora on the opposite side of the room.

Skelley Chase smiles. "Come in, Parvin."

13

My first impulse is to cry.

I don't.

This awful surprise—on top of my fears—obliterates my anxiety and turns me to stone. Even if all is lost, I will do what I must, because I am up against all odds. That's when God thrives.

The door zips shut behind me.

"I should have known you were part of the Council." My voice is strong. In command.

Skelley Chase leans back in his chair. "Yes, you should have."

It makes so much sense. His involvement in my story—how else could he have published such a rebellious biography?—his demands that I journal about every person I met in the West, his lack of punishment for shooting Reid.

I cannot let this distract me.

The room is a circle and I am at the edge. Five black chairs line the walls of the room, each with a person in it. Skelley Chase is directly across from me. To his right is Elan Brickbat in a suit so white it glows.

Closest to me, on my left, is man I don't recognize. To my right sits a woman with smooth hair that curls at the base of her neck. I can't tell what color it is in this dark lighting, but no matter. It's her curious face with raised eyebrows that gives me hope. She might be one to listen.

Last, to Skelley Chase's left, is the president of the USE, Ethan L. Garraty. His face is easily the kindest in the room, though he doesn't look very aware or involved in the situation.

I stand tall. "Where's Willow?"

"Not dead," Brickbat says in his wet, throaty voice. "Yet."

"She was supposed to be here. Those were my terms."

"You have no leverage to make any terms." Skelley Chase examines his fingernails. A thin metal cord encircles his wrist, not decorative enough to be a bracelet.

He's speaking to me. The murderer. The betrayer. "Why did you shoot Reid?" The question is out of my mouth before logic can reel it back. I look only at Skelley Chase. My voice breaks. "Why? I did what you asked."

For the first time since meeting him, I see something other than arrogance and boredom. It's a flinch, a tiny twitch by his left eye. It almost looks like regret. Then it's gone.

From my sight, but not from my mind.

My hand and sentra still in my pocket, I snap an emotigraph. He trained me well.

"Irrelevant."

I'm back in *Faveurs* with him, being "completely open" as he demanded I once be. He can't wave this question away. Not now. "It's completely relevant. Why did you shoot him?"

"We needed your face, Parvin. The public respects you."

"So you could use me as your poster child? Tack me up with lies? Not good enough, Mr. Chase."

He leans forward in his chair. "I gave you a second chance. Your brother was ready to die. You weren't."

My fist clenches. "Yes, I was. Still not good enough, Mr. Chase."

He looks away. "I have no reason to provide you with an explanation—"

"You have *every* reason!" He owes this to me. And he knows it. That eye flinch gave him away. "Tell me!"

His gaze snaps back to mine. "The Council needs you—"

"—Not good enough!"

"The public needed you—"

"—Still not good enough, *Skelley!*"

He leaps from his seat. *"I needed you to live!"*

There it is. I broke him. Sweat glimmers beneath the brim of his hat and the single light in the ceiling. There's my answer.

He needed me to live.

No, that can't be right. That sounds personal, like he cares about me. That's impossible. He shot my brother. People who care about others don't shoot innocent people.

Skelley sinks back to his chair and clears his throat. "I needed you to live, for the Council's reasons."

Nice save, but it's not working. President Garraty stares at Skelley, eyes wide, as if he's never seen him lose his cool. I broke him within five minutes of being in the room.

How?

"Why did you need me to live?"

Brickbat cracks a thumb knuckle. "We have jobs for you."

I let loose a defiant laugh. "No thanks."

"Let me remind you, Miss Blackwater, just how easy it would be for us to dispose of you."

"No reminder needed, thank you."

"You don't understand. By *you* I mean *Radicals.* You threaten to blackmail us, but your . . . *boldness,* shall we call it? . . . has bumped your precious village up on our list. We have something special planned for your little Low Cities. I think you ought to listen to us."

He's tearing through my wall of courage. What does he plan to do to Unity? "You don't control me."

Skelley leans forward and steeples his fingers. "You still don't get it, Parvin. You've been our tool from the start. This is no new thing. You've played along, obeyed, and delivered information whenever we wanted it."

155

His confidence is back. Maybe he's trying to scare me because I cracked him for a moment. "I've never been your tool."

He smiles. "Oh really? Let me enlighten you. I came to Unity Village to find out more about Jude Hawke from his brother, Solomon. I believe you know him? Well, through . . . *providential* circumstances, I met you—an inconsequential Last Year teenager with desires to save and discover the world. As a side interest, I took on your project to monitor your rebellion. I knew that if I didn't monitor it, you might connect with that troublemaking Enforcer and his brother."

A trickle of dread worms its way down my spine.

"When Solomon Hawke fought for your freedom, it was the perfect window. I sent him to 'inspect' your nano-book. I knew full well he'd gather your information for contact later."

Skelley stands. "Then, when in the West, the two of you led us straight to Jude. Every journal entry you sent me was forwarded straight to our sniper. To him, following you was like tracking an elephant."

With every sentence, he moves a step closer. "Jude gave us the information we wanted . . . all because of you. Don't you see?" I'm backed against the wall now. "Your quest for shalom, your pursuit of rightness, has accomplished everything *we* wanted. You . . . are controllable."

I stare at him, my inner horror freezing my limbs. He's delivered the ultimate insult and he knows it. Controllable—everything I don't want to be.

It was my fault. All of it.

Skelley sits back down, his smirk plastered on his face.

Brickbat yawns and picks up where he left off. "If you don't cooperate with us, we will kill Miss Willow."

Solomon was right, they're using her as leverage. "You can't kill her." My voice comes out small. "You can't control anyone's Numbers."

Brickbat's face turns red. "Says the girl who watched us control her *brother's* Numbers."

"Reid knew he was going to die. He was ready. He *chose* to die." These words sound very similar to when Solomon said Jude chose *his* death.

"Do you really want us to *try* to kill your little albino?" Brickbat speaks just short of a shout, his voice suffocating beneath the gurgle in his throat. He needs anger management. "We're all curious how this new Clock will work on her."

"You have no right to her. She's not a citizen of this country."

Brickbat smiles. Skelley doesn't have his smirk on anymore. President Garraty stares at his shoes.

"She's an illegal trespasser"–the woman's voice is low and smooth–"with no parents or guardians. She is under our care for investigation. She is considered an orphan."

"*I* am her guardian! And she has parents in the West."

"An eighteen-year-old cannot have charge of a child," Skelley says. "Parvin, you need to cooperate."

"Why, so I can be *controllable?*" I throw my arms up. "You *can't* use Jude's invention. You stole it from him, murdered him, and tortured orphans. If you kill Willow, if you use Jude's invention, I will spread *all* of that information across the press."

I'm threatening them back. It's my only defense. Otherwise Willow will be doomed. *God, what do I do?*

Everyone is silent for a moment. I stare into each of their eyes, except President Garraty's, because he's looking at the floor. "Mr. President?"

He looks up at me.

"You are the leader of our country, don't you have anything to say?"

His eyes dart between the other Council members. Skelley folds his hands in his lap. "President Garraty is the *voice* to our country. Presidents are chosen from a seat on the Council, but all decisions are made by the Council as a whole."

By *whole,* he means by him or Brickbat, because President Garraty doesn't look like the type of person to stand up or argue for anything. More deceit. More lies.

"Does the public know that?"

"Of course it does." Brickbat spits the words at me. "How do you think we received positions on the Council? The public also senses that this new Clock-matching will tremendously help our nation."

"By *help* you mean eradicate all Radicals."

"Of course." Skelley stops Brickbat from what was sure to be a scream of frustration. "Radicals weaken the system. They deplete our resources. It's because of *them* that we even need Openings in the Wall. Once everyone is Clock-matched we can fill in Opening Three. No one need ever go through it again."

He fixes me with a firm stare. "It's what you wanted all along, Parvin."

My throat closes. Fill in Opening Three? That's my gateway to freedom! If the Council closes passage through the Wall, we'll be trapped in the USE forever. I'll never get back to Ivanhoe, Willow will never get home, and believers like Idris and Fight will always have to hide to worship God.

I shake my head. "What I want is unity between Radicals and Clocked people. I want unity between the USE and the West side of the Wall. I want the barriers torn down!"

"We're giving the people freedom."

I stand straighter, my arms stiff at my side. "No, you're taking away our choice!"

Brickbat shouts so loud, I jump. "You're forgetting your little albino girl! Shut up and cooperate or she's dead. And so is your Enforcer friend."

"You're forgetting that I'll go public." My voice is weak, the threat feeble. I can't leave Willow to Brickbat's whims.

Skelley chuckles. "Parvin, I think you'll find it a little hard to get the press to listen to you."

They don't know about my offer from Gabbie Kenard. I can write anything. They don't know the power I have. "You'd be surprised, Mr. Chase."

Hands grip my arms and I startle. Enforcers are on either side of me—the largest, tallest, strongest Enforcers I've ever seen. They melted out of the shadows. Have they been here the whole time? Their hands squeeze, tighter, bruising.

"Surprised?" Skelley smirks.

They rummage in my bag, jostling me. "Stop! You have no right to touch my things!"

"You're a Radical, Parvin. We have whatever rights we want."

"I'm a *registered* Radical! I'm completely legal and protected by the law."

"Radicals—registered or unregistered—have no rights any longer. The world is changing . . . all thanks to you."

An Enforcer hand emerges with my NAB. He flings it across the room and Skelley catches it with one hand. "Besides, *I* bought this for you. It's always been on lend. Now I want it returned."

"Give that back!" My connection . . . my only connection to Gabbie Kenard and to fulfilling my blackmail threats, is in his hands. All the messages I ever wrote to Solomon, all my journal entries written in private anguish on the West side, are now his.

Brickbat clears his throat. "Gabbie Kenard no longer works with *The Daily Hemisphere*."

Did he read my thoughts?

"In fact, you might not ever hear from her again. Same with your little Willow."

I sag and the Enforcers hold me up with their hands of steel.

Giving in to the bruises is the least of my worries now. What was I thinking?

"What do you want?" My voice is empty.

Skelley seems to be done talking. He opens my NAB and the blue glow lights up his bored face. Brickbat rubs an eyebrow with his forefinger and crosses his legs. "First, tell us about the man who made your Vitality suit—Wilbur Sherrod."

I didn't expect *this*. Wilbur Sherrod is an old memory. I can't even remember the names of all the suits I tried. "That's all I know about him—he made the suit."

"What other suits did he make?"

I try to jerk a shoulder out of the Enforcer's grasp. It doesn't work. "I won't give you any information unless you promise not to use Jude's Clocks and to set Willow free."

But their promise would mean nothing to me. Perhaps they know that, because they don't give it.

"Next, we want you to be the first privileged citizen to be Clock-matched with our new invention—"

"You're not listening!" I bite the inside of my cheek, but panic simmers on my skin. Clock-matched? Me? I'm too weak in my faith to have Numbers again. I can't have a Clock or I'll start trusting God less. I can't give in.

But they have everything—my NAB, Willow, Jude's invention.

God is stronger than Clocks. I don't have to let it change me. Do I even have a choice?

YES.

I sigh. I *do* have a choice and I know what it is. I can't give Willow up because of my own weak faith. I have to cooperate . . . and I'll have to trust that God has a reason for this.

"If I cooperate, will you send Willow back across the Wall?"

Brickbat sneers. "No."

"Why not? You're going to close up Opening Three anyway!"

"If you cooperate, she'll return to the government-run orphanage we've chosen for her."

Which means she'll remain under their power. They'll still use her to blackmail me. But I've gained one thing from this: she's at an orphanage. Now I'll know where to start looking when I start my rescue mission.

"Okay." It comes out as little more than a croak.

Brickbat gives a single nod and the Enforcers haul me out of the room. Before the door zips shut, his voice echoes with a parting sentence: "I'll say hello to Willow for you. Personally."

14

I sit in a fake doctor's office with a helmet of needles next to me.

I'm on a film set that looks like a sterile yet welcoming High-City hospital room. Workers set up filming equipment. Enforcers pour in and take their positions near every entry and exit.

The frenzy frightens me, so I close my eyes "I didn't know this would be filmed."

"Of course."

I open my eyes to see Skelley standing there. I want to smack the nasty grin off his face.

"Your story needs to be told, remember?"

"You'll say nothing," Brickbat growls.

Skelley shrugs. "It doesn't matter if she does. This isn't being filmed live. We can cut out anything we don't like."

It's happening too fast.

Breathe deep. I'm not alone, but I'd be lying if I said I wasn't scared. Even terrified.

Brickbat sets a thin metal cord on a tray beside the strange wiry helmet mechanism. The cord is like the one around his own wrist, around Skelley's wrist. I'm trembling. *Stop it. Stop looking at that freaky helmet.*

The only thing that keeps me in my seat is the thought of Willow. This isn't a big deal, being Clock-matched. It's just information. But the filming . . . the filming will convince the world I'm on the Council's side.

What have I achieved? What did I think would happen? That I could walk in and blackmail the Council into relinquishing the information they are willing to kill for?

All that's happened is I told them every bit of information I knew about Wilbur's suits. Oh, and I succumbed to their Clock-matching.

Willow is safe.

Not for long.

I know about the plan to fill in Opening Three.

That's true. That's something. Maybe this isn't all lost.

I meet Skelley's gaze. He presses a button on one of the cameras. I try very hard not to pant. Panic shrinks my lung capacity for a moment. But I finally manage to speak. "Go ahead."

Skelley sits in a cushy chair next to me. I move my legs so they don't touch any part of him. Filth. That's what he is.

His face transforms into his charming half-bored, half-confident smile and he looks at the camera. "Today, Parvin Blackwater will be the first USE citizen to be Clock-matched with the new invention she brought to us."

"Hey! I didn't bring it to you. You know that."

He rolls his eyes. "What's the point of speaking, Parvin, when your voice will be cut out of the video?"

"Because it's truth!" I turn my head to the Enforcers lining the walls, standing behind the cameras, guarding the other Council members. "The Council *stole* this information from Jude. They almost killed me in the process! I *never* brought it to them."

Skelley yawns. "Let's get to the Clock-matching shall we?"

Brickbat comes behind the couch and places the helmet on my head. Tiny pricks enter my skull, but the pain is brief. Skelley almost puts the thin bracelet on my left wrist then, after a moment's hesitation, moves it to my right arm, then back to my left. He snaps the two ends together and they tighten until there's no way the bracelet would slide over my swollen stump. He connects a wire from it to the helmet.

I close my eyes and focus on breathing. This is the Clock-matching. It's not torture. The portions of the helmet connected to my head grow tight. *Just breathe.* Tighter. *Breathe.* Numerous sharp pricks.

Then it stops. The helmet is removed.

I glance at my wrist. I don't want to know my Numbers, but they're projected into the air—red Numbers on a blue screen.

031.035.18.32.12
Parvin Brielle Blackwater

Thirty-one years. That's what it says, but it's wrong. It can't control me.

"Cut!" Skelley shoots me a glare. "Okay, take her back."

The Enforcers converge on me, but I can't tear my eyes away from the red blinking symbol of government control. I have a Clock. For the first time in my life, I have my own Clock.

And I hate it.

The Enforcers don't let go of my arms the entire eight-hour train ride back to Unity Village. All I can think for eight straight hours is *Willow, Solomon, Willow, Solomon, Clocks . . .*

We finally arrive, and the Enforcers shove me out of the train doors. I stumble onto the Unity train platform. When I look back, one throws my pack through the air. It hits me in the face and I fall. The Enforcers close the door and watch me until the *Lower Missouri Transit* leaves again.

I'm home.

And I'm alone.

Is Solomon still in Prime? Does he think I'm dead? He might think I'm captured. Without my NAB, I can't tell him anything. But once the Council releases that Clock-matching video, Solomon will know they got me. *If* he's alive and safe.

This is the second time I've left a man behind by getting on a train. Only this time, it wasn't my choice. And this time . . . I want that man to come after me.

I scramble to the ticket counter, but know before even asking that I'll never be able to purchase a ticket out of Unity Village again.

I've been marked.

Still, I have to try.

The ticket clerk—a fat man with a brown toothbrush mustache—pricks my finger on a small needle connected to the in-desk screen. Red messages flash. All I see is the word *DENIED* before he shoves my hand away.

"But I'm . . . I have a Clock."

He shakes his head. "Doesn't matter. I gotta obey the messages."

Even if it wasn't denied, I have no specie to pay for it. I plunk onto a wooden bench and stare up at the rickety roof that never stops the rain. Was I right to give in to the Council? Will Brickbat really send Willow to the orphanage? What will they do to my people here?

At least they sent me back instead of imprisoning me in Prime.

They have Unity Village in their sights—all because of me. It was hard to think on the train, while seated between two beefy Enforcers who wouldn't let me speak or even move, but now that my back is against the rusty wood of home, clarity drifts in.

I'm sorry, Solomon. I have to focus on my people. I can't go back to Prime yet. I must warn Unity that the Council is going to target Radicals and Low Cities . . . because of me. Jude saw this coming, but I still don't understand all the potential repercussions.

The only way I can warn people is to speak . . . like Solomon suggested. Like God's been telling me to do ever since I returned.

So far, speaking has brought only trouble. But I have a feeling it will make a difference now. I *must* do it, despite my fears and insecurities. Like those in the underground church in Prime—I'm stepping out. The Bible says that in faith Abel died, but he still speaks. I will still speak.

I'll start tomorrow. Friday. The market will be active. People may throw tomatoes again, they may refuse to listen, but this is part of my calling.

I imagine myself strong, standing atop the hearing platform. When they panic or feel the first tinges of fear, I must be strong for them. I can do this.

As for Willow . . . her life has never been in my hands. God knows I want to rescue her, but He's redirected my focus. I have to trust He'll keep her safe or, at least, keep her where He wants her for now.

Please guard her until I can find her.

With a grunt, I push myself to my feet and pick up my pack. It's lighter. I already miss my NAB. A quick glance tells me my Bible is still in there. Ha, they left the thing of *true* value behind.

By the time I reach the house, it's dark. A candle flickers in the window. Mother, Father, and Tawny sit at the table eating something out of wooden bowls. I allow myself three seconds to watch them through the window, then push open the front door.

The cot is gone and the house is back to normal.

"You're back." Mother exhales.

I try a smile. "I'm back."

Tawny sets down her spoon. "So what'd they do to Willow?"

I sit down beside her. "They said she's an orphan under the care of the government."

"Is she safe?" Mother passes me a bowl of lamb stew.

Safe . . . what a drifting word. We use it so flippantly, but when's the last time any of us has been safe? What does safe mean? "I hope so."

I relay as much of the small journey as I can without losing control. I don't tell them about my plan to speak tomorrow. I don't think I could withstand Mother's disapproval. "Unity Village is in danger because of me. The Council is going to force us all to Clock-match."

Tawny's knuckles turn white around her spoon. "Really?" Her eyes are round. Hopeful.

"It's not a good thing, Tawny."

Father folds his hands and meets my eyes. "This could be a logical step toward political peace."

I stir the stew. "Political peace?" The Council's lies have reached my family. "What about freedom? Freedom to choose not to have a Clock."

"That's not freedom." Tawny flips her hair. "Why would anyone not want a Clock?"

"*I* don't want a Clock." I make sure my sleeve covers my new wrist Clock. I don't want them to know. They'll think I'm a hypocrite.

She rolls her eyes. "Yes, well . . . I wouldn't be a Radical anymore and I could finally plan out my life without uncertainty."

"Why not start *living* your life now?" As the words exit my mouth, I catch myself. Tawny's a little bit like I was before my Last Year. I had waited and waited, too uncertain about my life to try anything.

"And what would I do?"

"Well, what do you *want* to do?" I take a bite of stew, ignoring the sensation that I'm acting like a Mentor. *What are your Last-Year desires?* Does she have any?

She sets the spoon down in the bowl. "I think I'm finished." Her voice is so quiet, I barely hear her. She gets up and walks into her room.

I'm an idiot. She's been a widow for barely two weeks and now I ask what her dreams are? They all probably died with Reid. Maybe she wanted to settle down, build a family, and be a homemaker.

"I'll go get the cot." Father stands from the table.

I rise with him. "No need, Father. I'm going to stay in Solomon's house. I'll clean it up a bit for his return. Besides, I need to know when he gets here." *If* he gets here. If the Council hasn't hunted him down and killed him.

Mother gathers the bowls and scrapes the leftovers back into the pot on the wood stovetop. "I don't think that's wise, Parvin."

"Why not?"

"Staying in a single man's home? What would people think?"

My face warms. "He's not even here, Mother."

"It doesn't matter. People know you've been spending time with Mr. Hawke—you traveled to a High City with him . . . alone. And those who know he lives in the old Newton house might get the wrong impression if they see you there."

"What, that I'm *sleeping* with him or something? That's what you're implying, isn't it?" My voice crescendos. "Yes, because *that's* what I should be worrying about—whether or not people think I'm a . . . a . . . tramp. Even though they already attacked me and threw tomatoes at me, they judge me for Reid's death, for putting Unity Village at the top of the Council's hit list, and for pretending to have a Clock my whole life."

"Calm down, Parvin."

Father walks into their bedroom. My gaze follows him. I want him to stay and take my side—take *any* side, just so I know where he stands.

"Mother, I can't control whether or not people want to judge me."

"You can remain above reproach."

I put on my coat and grab my pack. "That's not a lesson you taught when you told Reid and me to hide the fact that we had only one Clock. It is in *this* house that I feel the most judgment. The only reproach I need to stay above is God's, and He knows my motives."

I open the front door. "I cannot sleep here again. I lose sight of my vision in this house."

I leave her standing in the center of the kitchen, a dishcloth in one hand and a dirty bowl in the other. That is the picture that is imprinted on my mind as I try to fall asleep in one of the extra bedrooms of Solomon's house. A week ago, I celebrated having Mother back. Now I've left her.

She's not my strong point any more. I don't know when that changed or if *I* just changed, but now I'm more alone than ever. No Willow, no Solomon, no Mother. *Can I still do this with only You, God?*

I guess we'll see tomorrow.

The day is dark with heavy wind and grey clouds. My new sturdy boots scrape against the rough hearing platform wood. Father gave them to me this morning.

I take the stairs this time. The market is full. I can't breathe.

I stand in the middle of the platform, wearing the new tan dress I got in Prime with my tattered coat. I want to clasp my hands together, but can't.

I clear my throat. No one looks. I glance back at the post board over the rooftops, lining the side of the county building.

Parvin Blackwater Visits the Council

Below that is a picture of me standing before the floating Council building in Prime. I don't know who took the picture or how, but they captured it perfectly so that it looks like I'm hesitating in excited awe. My hair is blowing around me and I have a content look on my face. They probably caught me in the middle of a prayer, when I surrendered my fear to God. But to everyone else, the photo looks like I'm meeting the president for tea and crumpets . . . whatever crumpets are.

More deceit. More lies. More attempts to make me look like the Council's puppet. The only *good* thing on the post board is that the Wall is still closed. Soon, though, there will be an announcement that I have the first new Clock.

I tried everything to get the Clock band off last night—hacking with one of Father's chisels, warming it over the fire, sawing it with clippers. But there's not much one can do without a left hand.

I return my focus to my people, milling in the market below me. How in time's name do I start? The longer I stand here, the faster my heart beats.

I can't do this.

YOU MUST.

God, I can't do this!

YOU MUST.

Before I overthink and talk myself out of it, I force words through my lips. Any words. "Um . . . hi everyone."

Not a single head turns. I try again, louder, over the din of shoppers. "I'd like to say something!"

A few browsers stop. Their gazes are as friendly as a rabid dog's.

God . . . help!

Someone points at my left arm and whispers to the person next to them. I don't hide my stump. It makes more people look at me. That's what I need.

Where do I start? My visions of firm voice, and strong posture are gone. I'm an inconsequential whisper speaking to shadowed minds. "I just came back from a High City where I met with the Citizen Welfare Development Council. I'm sure some of you have heard about the new Clock-matching testing going on."

I pause for affirmation but no one nods. A few go back to their shopping.

"They're going to force everyone to have a Clock. They stole an invention from my friend—murdered him for it, actually."

No one's looking at me anymore. The peaches, stew, and shoulder packs are all more interesting. Panic swells. Don't they get it? Don't they see the looming tornado about to hit?

"I know you hate me!"

Movement stops. Sound stops. Life stops.

Then they turn. To me.

"I know you hate me." I meet their gazes. "I get it. I messed up. My selfishness put Unity Village on the map and now the government is cracking down on us." I ignore the Enforcers who inch closer to the platform.

"Because of me, the Council now has an invention that can Clock-match a person at any age. They're bringing it to Unity Village and no one will have a choice to be a Radical."

I have their attention now. "The government is trying to get rid of Radicals, no matter their innocence or if they're registered. If you know of any Radicals, please tell them they're in danger."

"Danger?" the milkman sneers. "You think Clock-matching is danger? I know ten Radicals who would kill for a Clock. This is the answer to our problems."

Several shoppers nod. "Is it true? They really have a Clock that matches after conception?" The basket weaver's eyes are excited, hopeful.

I'm hesitant to answer. "Yes."

She clasps her hands in front of her. "Time be blessed!" Another woman hugs her and that's when I see how skewed their view is. They *want* the Clock-matching.

People laugh and a, "Hurray!" rises above the celebration.

They see this as an answer to prayer. I'm the only one who sees it as a threat. Am I wrong? Is this a good thing? I imagine

Brickbat's face when he said, *"We have something special planned for your little Low Cities."*

No, this is not good.

"You don't understand! The Council despises Radicals and Low Cities and everything we are!" No one's listening. They're all hugging and shouting and spending their specie on food to celebrate.

"Do you *want* to be stripped of your freedom? How many more laws do you think will come, dictating your life because of your Numbers?"

I'm invisible.

I spoke . . .

And all it did was stir them the wrong way.

I sit on the platform the rest of the day, and the next, and the next . . . hoping people will ask more questions or will come to me for help. None do. Their faces are brighter, they check the post board every morning, and hope is evident in their every action. Everyone in this town knows a secret Radical.

I read *The Daily Hemisphere*—something the Council didn't take from me—waiting for more news. It comes Monday morning.

Parvin Blackwater is the First to Receive a New Clock

Beneath it is a photo from when I was matched. My eyes are closed and my fist clenched on my lap. I'm pleased to see that I don't look happy. Thankfully, my Numbers are blurred out. The article shares that the matching will come first to the Low Cities, in honor of my bringing the invention to the Council.

High City Enforcers will arrive at each Low City over the next several days to set up a matching station. All USE citizens are required to show up for matching.

The Council is using Jude's invention already. Why are they in such a hurry?

"I'm going to be the first," Dusten Grunt hollers to anyone who will listen. "First in line! First with a new Clock!"

First to die. He's dooming himself.

The first person to call me a hypocrite is the milkman. Next is some woman I don't know, and then Dusten.

A day passes and all I can bring myself to do is lean my head back against the restraining post and pray. I've never prayed quite so hard for anything and my prayers all sound the same. *God, save my people. Open their eyes. Show me what to do.*

It's fascinating watching my love grow more and more for these people who seem to hate and reject me. It goes against everything I know myself to be—angry, impulsive, bitter.

I'm a little frightened. I cannot explain this strange love and that means I cannot control it. I fear it may disappear any day, but something like this—when out of my control—just confirms it's not of me.

The Enforcers arrive on Wednesday on an old boxcar train instead of the carbon-fiber one. A few people stand on the train platform and cheer. *Cheer.* For Enforcers.

What is happening to this village?

My people are *choosing* this. How can I save them?

I watch each tattooed face step off the train. I wait until the doors close and the train heads up to Nether Town, taking my tearful heart with it.

Solomon didn't come.

Where *is* he? What happened to him? It's been almost a week. Did the Council get to him or did he go visit his father for answers?

I killed Jude. Have I killed Solomon, too? I shouldn't have gotten attached to him.

All I can do is sit in my deceived village and wait. Hope. Pray. I'm trapped, worrying about Willow, Solomon, and my people.

"A Clock-matching station will be set up tomorrow morning at sunrise," Sachem announces as the Enforcers stand in straight lines behind him. There are so many. Why are there so many for a single matching station?

"All residents of Unity Village are required to report for the new Clock-matching. Any unregistered or registered Radicals are under the protection of the government until the Clock-matching is completed. You may come out of hiding for matching without fear of punishment."

Muttering starts. I can't make out any specific words, but I bet they're doubting. Radicals have never been safe in this town.

Sachem holds up his hands. "Please understand that, under the new system, *all* residents are required to be matched with a new Clock."

He doesn't tell us the *or else*, but no one seems to mind. No one except me. I guess I'll find out what the *or else* is.

What will they do to those of us who refuse to be matched?

I wake the next morning and stare at the ceiling. The ceiling of Solomon's house is much nicer than my parents' house. It feels safe, until I remember what's happening today.

People are giving in to forced government control.

My people.

Picketing would be pointless. Arguing will do no good. I can't attack the Enforcers. There's only one thing to do: sit and wait until the government starts enacting its control, and then be here for my people when they need me.

A knock startles me out of bed. I slip on my boots and coat and walk down the hallway to the front door. When I open it, Tawny, Mother, and Father stand in a small huddle.

"Come on," Tawny says.

"I'm not going."

"I knew you'd say that." She turns to Mother. "She's already matched. Let's just go."

Mother grabs her arm and holds her in place. "No. We'll do this as a family. You heard the Enforcer, *everyone* must come."

"I'll come"—I slide my pack over my shoulders—"but I'll wait on the hearing platform while you go in."

Tawny shrugs. "Okay, then, *come on*." She takes long strides. Bouncy strides, as if she can't get there fast enough.

I don't want to know her Numbers. I already know that Mother will die in twenty-one years and Father in nineteen. It's an awful feeling, knowing how long or how little time I have to prepare for the death of someone I cherish. Then again, I don't cherish Tawny. Still, she's family and maybe someday I *will* cherish her . . .

Like when a miracle happens.

We reach the town square. Mother grips Father's hand so tightly that both their fingers are white. Tawny leads the way. The line to the registration booth winds out into the square. Dusten Grunt is first.

I settle in my usual spot on the platform.

The line moves forward slowly, like cattle stepping forward to be slaughtered. Tawny cranes her neck to peer ahead. Father glances back at me for a second.

Enforcers keep people in order. Their rifles aren't strapped on their backs anymore. Now they hold the weapons, as if waiting for someone to step out or make a fuss.

Around midday, the line has only grown. Dusten Grunt hops up on the platform. "Well, I'm registered. Get my new Clock tomorrow."

"Good for you." I continue staring at the *Daily Hemisphere*.

"What are your new Numbers?"

I shake my head, feeling only sorrow for the bully across from me. "They're private and they don't matter. They're invisible to me."

"Gee, you're set against this thing."

"Yup."

He scoots closer. "Why?" His sneering tone is still there, but beneath it is genuine curiosity.

"The Council tortured and killed orphans to test the Clock you're going to get tomorrow. They murdered the man I might have loved to get you a Clock tomorrow. They captured a little girl who only wanted to go home, all for the sake of blackmailing me into supporting the Clock you're going to get tomorrow." I meet his eyes. "So, maybe you can see why I hate them. It's another leash the Council is putting around our necks."

"Whatever." He slides off the platform.

"What does it matter to you anyway, Dusten?" I shout. "You already had a Clock—won't your Numbers be the same?"

I hit a tender point. His face turns a fierce scarlet. "Shut it, Empty Numbers."

"What did they do with your old Clock?"

He shrugs a shoulder. "Destroyed it."

The Daily Hemisphere slips from my grasp and tumbles off the platform. "They *destroyed* it? And haven't given you a new one yet?"

"So what?"

My pulse pounds a nerve in my throat so hard I can't get a word out. Dusten rolls his eyes and leaves.

They're destroying Clocks and saying the new ones will be assigned tomorrow. Can't my people *see?* Are they so blind they'd allow a stranger to smash their Clocks with an empty promise of a new one?

A heavyset woman and a tall slim blond walk past me. Madame and Frenchie, from the coffee shop *Faveurs*. "I don't understand why zey burned your Clock, Madame." Frenchie wraps a shawl around her shoulders.

"Because they're replacing all Clocks with a universal style."

"But zey deedn't give us new ones."

"Tomorrow, Angelique." She holds up two slips of paper. "We get our new Clocks tomorrow. See? Here's your approval slip and here's mine. We present these any time tomorrow and we'll have our new Clocks."

Frenchie squeals and grips Madame's arm. "I will 'ardly be able to sleep!" Even though I now know her name is Angelique, I can't break my mental habit. She'll always be Frenchie to me.

I jump up on the platform and face the line. "Stop! Don't let them destroy your Clocks!" A few faces turn back to look at me. "There's no guarantee they'll give you a new one tomorrow. Don't give in!"

Enforcers step out of line, but I said what I wanted to say. I hop off the platform, pick up my electrosheet, and trudge back to Solomon's house. My feet smash clods of dried mud, leaving my footprint behind. It's nice to know I can cause change, even if it's the minimal adjustment of a dirt lump. No one else can step on it and leave the exact print I can.

If only I could channel that change into my people. I don't want my life to be marked simply by footprints. If they don't lead anywhere, it means nothing.

I eat a short and lonely lunch of corn crackers and goat cheese. Mother, Father, and Tawny must be back by now. I walk past the few doors up Straight Street and enter my old home without knocking . Tawny is at the sink and Father sits at the table with a little dish of ashes and a few gears in front of him. He stares at the fire.

"Father?"

"They burned it." His fingers scoot under the ash of his Clock and lift a tiny handful. They flutter back into the dish. "They demanded my Clock and then burned it."

I rest my hand on his.

"You will get a new one tomorrow." Tawny fiddles with her paper voucher.

I swallow hard. Will he? Or will the Enforcers leave on the train, making everyone a Radical? What would the Council do to us? "Maybe Tawny's right, Father."

"But . . . I've had this one my whole life. I don't understand the need to destroy it, at least not until *after* I get the new one."

"I don't understand either."

He looks up then, and I see something new in his eyes. What is it . . .?

"You may be right, Parvin. This may not be the good move it seems to be."

And then I know what is in my father's eyes.

Fear.

The square is in complete chaos.

It's day two of the Clock-matching and masses of people push into each other, smashing groups into walls as they surge toward the county building. I elbow through, trying to find the source. Someone knocks me over. I fall into the cold mud and a boot heel smashes my hand. I yelp and scramble back to my feet.

"What's going on?" I call to no one in particular, but everyone is too busy yelling and pushing.

A gun goes off, and the screaming stops. I get to the front and meet a line of Enforcers, three men deep, all with guns pointed at us.

"Everyone will remain calm!" Sachem steps in front of the line. "You have two days to meet the required terms. That should be plenty of time for everyone."

"We can't!" a man screams. "You know that. These terms should have been clear *before* you destroyed our Clocks!"

Fists punch the air. A clod of mud hits Sachem in the face. People roar and I can't make a single clear sentence. But listening becomes a lesser concern when I spot a form on the ground, curled up against the wall of a house. His arms cover most of his dusty blond hair and, by the harsh lurches of his shoulders I can tell he's crying. Sobbing, more like it.

I kneel beside him and lean close enough so he'll hear my voice in his ear. "Dusten?"

He looks up. His entire face is wet, his nose is running, and his eyes are so scrunched I'm not sure he's even looking at me. His sobs come out heavy, from deep in his chest.

Someone runs past and sprays mud up in our faces. I lean forward and wrap my arms around Dusten's shoulders. It's instinct and, before I can withdraw my awkward show of compassion, he buries his face in the crook of my neck and his tears smear against my skin.

I don't understand the details of what's wrong, but it's exactly what I expected. Betrayal from the government.

Dusten clings to my coat, a little boy in my eyes . . . or a broken man. The madness doesn't cool. It increases. Feet pound by us. I'm knocked against Dusten. Our position is dangerous. We need to move or we'll get trampled. I pull him to his feet and half drag him away from the mob. We go to the hearing platform. He climbs up and collapses on his side, covering his face with his hands.

I don't know what to do. "Dusten, it's okay. It's going to be okay." Why do empty words come out when I need meaningful ones?

He shakes his head against the wood flooring of the platform. With a shuddering breath, he stops the sobs and flops on his back. "I'm a Radical."

"Why can't you get your new Clock?"

He points up to the county building post board. "They cost one hundred specie."

"One *hundred?*"

"Per person."

I fall back against the restraining post. No one here has that amount saved up! In smaller writing on the post board is a warning: *Those who do not conform to the new Clock-matching policies will be considered illegal, unregistered Radicals and will be sent across the Wall.*

"See what they did?" Thick saliva gathers in his mouth. "They turned us all into Radicals and now they're giving Clocks only to the rich."

"There are no rich in Unity."

"We're all going to *die*, Parvin."

It's the first time he hasn't called me Empty Numbers. He's desperate. I take his hand. It's calloused and rough, but I squeeze it anyway.

"No, we're not." I raise my eyes to see the crowd in the roads leading to the county building. Some people still yell, but others have sunk to the ground like Dusten. Only a handful are in line to get a Clock. Other people throw mud at them.

"But I'll be sent across the Wall!"

"I know." My grip on his hand is so tight I'm sure it's cutting off his circulation. He doesn't complain. "But you won't go alone. I've been there. I will go with you."

I'm finally starting to understand. "And I will help you survive."

15

By nightfall, the people of Unity Village turn into monsters.

Happy Halloween, let's celebrate with an uprising. But there's nothing happy about it. On a normal Halloween, children in grotesque costumes made of cheap material and faces painted with dyed cornstarch and honey stroll around the market booths for treats.

This year the holiday is marked not by fun . . . but by desperation.

All night, screams wake me and sounds of breaking glass come nearer and nearer. I blow out all the candles and sit at Solomon's dining room table, waiting for the chaos to hit Straight Street.

Are people attacking the Enforcers or each other?

Around midnight, something slams against the door. I bolt upright, a string of drool stretching from the corner of my mouth to the kitchen table. When did I drift off?

I wipe away the drool and stand.

Slam!

Someone kicks the door. Father's latch will hold . . . won't it? Is it Solomon?

The person does it again and smashes into the room. I scream and grab a candlestick, the closest thing to my hand. A tall figure walks in, wearing an awful grim reaper costume with a painted face and a scythe in hand.

I'm going to be sliced to ribbons.

"Stop! Get out! What do you want?" I brandish the candlestick, but it's too lightweight. It will do nothing.

"Parvin?" The voice is stuffed up and nasal.

I lower the candlestick. "Dusten?"

He picks up a match from the windowsill, strikes it, and lights the candle in my fist. Then he stares at the ground and I stare at his face. Beneath the gaudy paint is the receding chin that quivered with sorrow this past sunrise.

He falls into one of the chairs at the table and covers his face with his hands.

My breathing slows. *"What* are you *doing?* I . . . I . . . you scared hours out of me!"

"I didn't know you were staying here," he mumbles through his fingers. "I thought it was abandoned while your favorite Enforcer was gone."

The fear that blossomed only moments ago shrivels into a lump of burning coal. I'm shaking. "So that's reason to break into someone's house?"

He shrugs.

"No. It's not. I didn't think you'd be part of the Halloween traps and tricks. At least not this year, with everything that's happening."

"Shut up, Empty Numbers."

The old Dusten is back. What did I expect? That crying into my arms during a mob and the collapse of his lifestyle might *change* him? Silly me.

I sit across from him and tame my tone. "So, what *were* you doing?"

"I figured an Enforcer would have lots of specie."

"Still trying to get a Clock?"

"Either that, or hide from the Enforcers." He leans his scythe against the wall. It's a strange feeling, being a counselor to the grim reaper. "Well, what do *you* think I should do?"

"Just because the government is taking away your Clock doesn't mean your life span is any different."

He smashes his knuckles on the table. "Don't you *get* it? I *want* it to be different! I thought maybe these new Clocks . . . maybe they'd . . ."

". . . give you longer?" I supply.

He rolls his eyes and looks out the window into the blackness. "I told you I'd go with you across the Wall."

He stands and grabs the scythe. "Yeah, well I don't want to cross the Wall. People are fighting . . . I might as well join. See ya."

My voice is a hollow whisper as he steps through the broken door. "Bye."

Halloween passes and twenty-three people were killed, four of whom were Enforcers. I can't help wondering if their Clocks— now smashed—would have revealed that. Maybe they were Radicals and never knew their Numbers. No matter. The new day is gloomy. Dark. Tainted with blood and greed.

Father's store was broken into, but he'd had the sense to gather the till and bring it home. He, Mother, and I sit at the kitchen table. Tawny isn't here. I don't ask where she's gone. This is another blow to her smashed dreams.

"I'm going into the square today." I hold my hand and stump toward the cooking fire. "When it's time, I'm going across the Wall with the other Radicals. I want people to know that I'll help them survive."

"No." Father runs his fingers along a rough patch in the table. "We are leaving as a family."

Mother shakes her head. "The Enforcers caught others fleeing last night and killed most of them. The perimeter is now watched. We can't leave."

I can't desert the people, anyway. My own safety is no longer my priority.

"We will hide in Unity until the Enforcers leave." Father's firm. I've never seen him so determined.

"No—" Mother protests again.

"Others are doing this. We'll go down in the cellar of the shop—"

"—They'll know—"

"—No they won't."

Mother grips his hand. "They'll find us!"

I turn my back on them and speak low. "I can't hide. I'm going with the people across the Wall."

"Sweetheart . . ." Father's chair scrapes the floor and soon he's behind me, turning me to look at him. "You already have a Clock and we have enough specie for two more. You don't have to go back there."

That still leaves one of us four without a Clock. "I want to go."

My chest suddenly swells. I get to go back! I get to save people, show them how to survive over there! It's all my prayers answered. I asked to save Radicals. This is the clearest calling and answer I've ever received from God.

Saving them was never in my power—only in God's. And to save these people, I have to lead them through the fire.

"We'll wait until Tawny returns to decide who gets the Clocks." Mother stands and peers out the window.

I reach across my body and grab Father's coat as he moves to sit back down. "I don't think any of us should get a Clock." Even now, it's hard to say something of which I know they'll disapprove. The words taste like sand coming out and my parents react to them as I'd expect they'd react to a sandstorm.

"We don't share your views, Parvin." Mother folds her arms. "You can't change an entire government system just because of your personal stance."

Has she not read my biography yet? "Maybe not, but don't you see this opportunity? This is a moment of change. This is the time where we can step in and push that change in the right direction."

It's moments like these, when I'm speaking with passion, that I imagine Reid sitting beside me, chewing on my ideas and forming his opinions.

What I'd give to have his smiling voice share his thoughts right now.

The door blows open and, for a wild moment, I half expect to see Reid walk in. It's Tawny. She's beaming, wearing a black button up coat and a red scarf. She sees us and her brightness fades a bit. Veins pulse in her neck.

She takes a deep breath and closes the door behind her. "I got one."

"One what?" I rasp, but I know to what she's referring.

She holds out her left arm. "A new Clock." Around her wrist is a thin fragile-looking piece of wire, identical to mine. "All I have to do is press my thumb and forefinger here and—"

A small screen pops out of the metal ring, shining a line of numbers a few inches above her wrist. I look away so fast it pops my neck, but Tawny makes the announcement anyway. "Fifty-seven years! That's an eternity! I have fifty-seven years to live and do whatever I want!"

"How did you pay for this?" Father studies her.

Tawny gasps. "The Silent Man is speaking to me? My oh my, this *is* a special day."

"Don't be rude." I push her glowing Numbers away from my face. Father watches her, void of external emotion. Waiting.

She looks to Mother. "Well, I took some of it from the shop till and the rest from Reid's and my savings."

How *dare* she? "You had no right—"

"It's fine, sweetheart." Father pulls out a chair for Tawny. "We would have given her a Clock anyway."

Of the two we can afford, Tawny never would have let us deny her a Clock. She sits and has the grace to look ashamed.

"So, who gets the other Clock?" I look at my parents.

Mother kisses Father's cheek. "You do, dear. I will go with Parvin."

My heart snaps like a wafer crisp. My parents can't split. They're meant to be together. "I don't want to tear you two apart."

"You're not." Mother speaks with firmness. "Your Father and I talked about what we'd do if we chose not to take a new Clock. He can provide for Tawny. I can help protect you."

"You don't need to protect me. I know how to handle what's over there."

"I cannot say Good-bye to you again, Parvin."

Tawny retracts her Numbers back into her wristband. "But Mom . . . I need you!"

"Let's all go across." Father's whiskers muffle his hesitant statement.

"No!" Tawny shrieks. "I'm not crossing that Wall! I . . . can't!"

Mother tilts her chin up. "Then you will stay here and Oliver will take care of you. You'll find new dreams and follow them. We'll all figure out how to be reunited as soon as possible."

Father nods. He and Mother *have* talked about this, but I can't bear leaving him again.

I must, for the sake of Radicals.

"Now, Parvin, go with your Father to the town square. He will get his Clock and you can sit on the platform like you'd planned."

"This isn't fair!" Tawny slams both her palms on the table. "They can't just kick you across the Wall because you don't have enough specie, Mom! We can earn more, can't we? Enough to get you a Clock?"

"I already had a Clock. I know my Numbers. And either way, I want to go with Parvin, even if we had enough money."

I almost sprint out of the house. I can't listen any more or I'll break. My family is being torn apart again by the Clocks. Tawny was right—it isn't fair. But I will do everything in my power to protect Mother on the other side of the Wall.

Father catches up to me.

"I'll come back for you." I speak without looking at him. "And Tawny . . . if she wants."

He rests a hand on my shoulder and I stop walking, tears burning my eyes. He smiles. "I'll be on this side until you come for us. I'll keep an eye on things."

With a sniff, I nod. "My inside man."

He laughs and we continue. My family is on my side this time—they see my vision and are joining me in it.

At last . . . there is a taste of unity.

The town square is filled with market booths, but this time everyone is selling and no one is buying. Hysteria floats along the waves of bidding. "Flour! Real flour! Only three specie!"

Three specie for flour—a precious and rare food that is never sold in Unity Village. It's going for the price of a newspaper. Father shakes his head and turns toward the Clock-matching station.

"Socks and scarves! One specie each!"

"All fruit is free! Donation only!"

My people are so desperate, they're getting rid of everything they have if only to afford a Clock.

Someone grabs at another person's coin pouch. A fight breaks out. I climb up the platform. No Enforcers are in the square. From my raised position, I see them lining the border of town. None of us can flee anymore. Everyone must either pay, hide, be killed, or surrender to the Wall.

I didn't want the Clocks to take over, but I also wanted people to have a choice.

I watch the chaos for a long moment. A booth gets knocked over. A woman has a young girl by the hair. Several people scream and I find myself not wanting to speak. Not wanting to bring their attention to me.

Will they blame me for letting the Council get Jude's information? Or for putting Unity Village in the government's sights? If they turn against me, I'll have no chance. They'll kill me.

God? Will You protect me?

No magical calm enters me. No insight to His plan for my life. But I remember the verse Mother told me before any of the mayhem started six months ago—God will complete the good work He's started in me.

I shout over the commotion. "Hey! Everyone!"

A few people stop to send glares my way.

I try again. "I know you are panicking and trying to get your new Clocks."

"Shut up!" The milkman throws a jar of milk at me. I block it with my right forearm, but the impact sends a shoot of pain up to my elbow. It clatters to the platform.

"*You* shut up," someone else yells. "She's got answers, ya know? She's friends with the Council."

"I'm not a friend of the Council." I want to rub my arm, but can't because of my missing hand. It throbs. "They are my enemy. They stole this Clock information from me and they are trying to rid the USE of Radicals and of Low City citizens."

I shrug my pack off my shoulders and let it drop to the platform beside the milk bottle. "I'm going through the Wall with anyone who can't afford a Clock. I've been there. I know how to survive. If you have any questions or want to know how to prepare, I'll be here—on the hearing platform—every day until we're sent away."

My words instill more panic. Those who stood close, flee from the platform. Others resume their fighting over specie. The milkman walks up, snatches his milk bottle, and stomps away.

They'll calm down once they've given up all hope. Then they'll come to me and, if God is on my side, I will be able to give them new hope.

I pack the next day.

I'm not ready to be a leader. I don't know when we'll be sent across the Wall, but I need to be prepared—more prepared than last time.

I coat the bottom of my pack with as many pairs of socks and underwear as possible. I wasn't in the West during winter, but if it's anything like Missouri winter I'll need warmth. I can wear layers and leave the extra room in my pack for other things.

Matches, toothbrush, baking soda for toothpaste and cleaning, needle and thread, bandages, healing salve, Jude's whistle, *The Daily Hemisphere*, a bar of soap, and one blanket.

I'll tie Mother's old kettle to my pack and fill it with corn kernels and dried meat for a soup. She'll have a better idea of what food to pack. If I can get the other Radicals to pack accordingly, we should be okay once we cross the Wall. It's only a few days' walk to the *Ivanhoe Independent* stop. We'll take the train to Ivanhoe and I'll work for Wilbur to pay off as many train debts as possible. The Radicals can stay with Mrs. Newton if she's set up her new mansion by now.

All that's left is to say good-bye.

Solomon has two flasks of Mother's blueberry ink in his house. He must have purchased it from her. What did he write? Who did he write to?

Well, now it's my turn.

Dear Solomon,

I did not leave you in Prime by choice. The Council took my NAB, Clock-matched me, and forced me onto a train with two Enforcers.

But now I must leave you by choice. The Council is sending most of my people across the Wall. I am going to help them. They are so afraid and I'm the only one who can do anything. Otherwise they will die in the West.

The Council still has Willow somewhere—Brickbat mentioned an orphanage. If you're alive, if you return, if you read this . . . you must save her and send her back to the West. I can't.

I will try to take my people to Mrs. Newton's safe house in Ivanhoe. After you save Willow, if you want to, come find me.

-Parvin

I fold the note and seal it with a smear of the candle wax. The scent of the blueberry ink hovers in the air. It brings back memories of writing my biography.

I lay the note in the center of the kitchen table. Two fingers of flame squeeze my throat shut. Tears burst forth before I can halt them.

Solomon's house is spotless. I've been releasing my frustration in the only way I know how—by acting like Mother and cleaning. It took a long time with one hand, but he's not here to see it. With every day that passes, I'm convinced the Council killed him.

Yet . . . he had thirty-two years left according to his Clock. *Could* they have killed him?

I don't know. I don't know how to think anymore. I step outside. "Good-bye, Solomon."

The air is made of ice today, as if to match my soul's sorrow. I stop by the house to grab a scarf and thicker mittens, then make my way to the hearing platform. This time, no one is there. No booths, no mayhem, no people. I climb onto the weathered wood. Its chill creeps through my trousers within seconds.

Everyone's given up on earning—or stealing—money for a new Clock. Maybe they've realized that, even if Unity Village pooled everyone's resources together, it still wouldn't get everyone a Clock.

Enforcers surround the village. Is this happening at other Low Cities or just to us? An hour passes and no one comes. How are my people handling the idea of crossing the Wall—the terror that's hovered over their village all their lives?

When I first found out I'd have to cross, I thought for sure I would die. I gave up all hope. All I could think about was saying good-bye to life.

But I lived. I became someone new—someone weak, but wrapped in God's strength. Now I want to go back. Will my people change, too? For the better? Or will I be alone in my change?

My ears perk to a new sound, shutting off my waves of thought. Mutters. Footsteps. No, not mutters . . . growling. And the footsteps are more like stomps. A lot of stomping. I stand up on the platform.

A blanket of heads bobs and marches, pouring out of the side streets. Toward me. An organized mob, carrying clubs and knives, glass bottles filled with rocks and nail-ridden boards.

The milkman and Frenchie are at the front. Jaws set, hands clamped around weapons, and tendrils of hatred preceding their marching.

Dear God . . .

They're coming for me.

16

They reach the platform and I stumble back, but the mob parts around it as if I'm a boulder interrupting the river flow. No one acknowledges me. The low hum of anger thrumming from their countenances implants deeper fear in my heart.

If they're not here to kill me, then they must be planning to attack—I turn on my heel—the Enforcers.

The Enforcers stand guard at the train station and along the border of the village. Some tighten their hands around their rifles. Others withdraw long, black clubs. All of them press something on the chest of their suits and screen shields pop up.

"No." I stumble off the platform into the midst of the mob. I land on a few people. They fall to their knees, but shove me off them. Marching. Marching. Humming rage.

I scramble to my feet and shove forward. They don't move for me. "Stop!" I try to scream it, but it comes out as a breathless whisper. I grab at someone's arm.

They're going to get killed.

If they attack the Enforcers, who knows how many people will be beaten beyond sense? This is playing right into the Council's plan—Brickbat wants the Low Cities to fight so he can obliterate us.

"Stop! Stop!" I squeeze between weapons and shoulders. Something scrapes my arm, but I keep going. I must get to the front. "You can't fight them!"

Someone slams a rock against my head. I crumple to the ground.

They march.

Heels and feet crush my hand, my arm, my feet, my legs. Someone kicks me in the face. Everything's blurry. I taste blood.

I'm going to be trampled.

A hard boot crushes my arm stump. If I don't move, I'll die. No one is here to save me. I am the only one who can save anyone right now.

I push myself to my knees, straining against the moving bodies. I grab someone's wrist with my bleeding hand and pull with all my might. It is beyond me. I can't. I'm weak, but I must pull or I'll die.

The man yanks his arm away and the momentum pulls me up, just enough to get my knees locked. A gun goes off. It is the gong that breaks the monotonous marching.

People freeze physically, but still shout. This is my chance. While they're stopped, I push forward. No one seems to notice. I shove through bodies, sliding past weapons, until I'm on the front line. A forty-foot gap lies between us and the line of Enforcers. Everyone on my side raises a weapon and screams what I can only label as a war cry.

I bolt forward shoving through the last line of people until I fall free and slam into the mud between the Enforcers and my people. I don't know what I'll do. They never listened to me before, why should they now?

I launch to my feet and hold my arms out—the stump toward the Enforcers and the hand toward my people. "Stop!" My chest heaves. I can't breathe.

It starts to rain.

The war cries continue. The Enforcers step forward as one. The gap between the Enforcers and my people shrinks.

"Don't do this!" Who am I addressing, the Enforcers or my villagers?

Someone needs to stop.

My voice is weak. The gap gets smaller as the Enforcers press forward again. More Enforcers from different sectors of the city join them, cocking their guns. Some of my people flee toward the gaps the Enforcers have left in the town perimeter.

I can't move. I won't move.

I drop to my knees and press my hand into the icy mud. "God! God, don't let them die. Do something. Do something. Do something . . ." I lean forward until my head hits the dirt. My pleas turn into a whisper. *"Do something. Do something. Do something."*

I stay between the two hordes and pray, tense and waiting for the bullet that will find me. Screaming increases around me and I know . . . this is the moment I will die.

"Get them onto the train!" an Enforcer commands. "Clock or no Clock, rioters will be sent to the Wall."

The hordes swarm together, around me, clubs on flesh, zaps of electric shields. Screams. Blood. Agony.

They're going to put my people on the boxcar train—send them to the Wall. I haven't fully packed. I need food and rope.

And Mother.

We must go together. I can't protect her if we're separated.

A body falls beside me. It's a woman with a gash in her head. Two Enforcers grab her body, and drag her toward the train platform. I manage to crawl my way back to the surface of the churning sea of madness, ducking a club swung at my head.

The Enforcers throw the bleeding lady into a boxcar. They club someone else and toss him in after her.

I dash out of the square, ignoring the splashes of blood that sprinkle my face and the weapons that bruise my body in their frantic swinging. I break free, past the platform, until I careen onto Straight Street. I enter the house with an explosive, "Mother! We have to go!"

She's in her room, digging through the safe in her closet. She looks up and then jumps to her feet. "Parvin? What's going on? There's blood on your—"

"We have to go! Get your pack." I ransack the kitchen, grabbing bits of food from the cupboards. "Do we have rope?"

"It's at the shop." She throws on her coat and shawl. "What's happening?"

"People started to mob the Enforcers. They're putting everyone on the train *now* to send them to the Wall." I remove anything that's not absolutely necessary—the bar of soap, an extra pair of socks—and replace the space with more bandages.

"No one's supposed to be sent until tomorrow."

I stuff more gloves into my coat pocket, pull on the blood-stained skirt Mother made me, throw Father's coat on over my own, and tie one of Tawny's thicker sweaters around my waist. "I know! I know! *No* one's prepared. And some of them are wounded."

I run out of the house and take the route to Father's shop. I glance over my shoulder. Mother's running full sprint with a shoulder pack flapping against her back.

"Parvin, wait."

I slow.

She reaches me and rests a hand on each shoulder. "We *could* stay here, hidden. The Enforcers might not send us."

I squeeze her elbow. "I can't, Mother. I'm all they have. I can't abandon them."

She gives a harsh nod and we continue into Father's shop. He's there, alone. No customers and very little product, thanks to the havoc of the past three days.

I throw myself into his arms, ignoring the poke of chisels sticking out of his apron. "Father, we have to go." I choke and release him. "I will come back for you. I'll be at the Wall for you on New Year's Eve. No matter what."

"Sweetheart—"

"No matter *what*, Father. I'll be there." That's two months from now. I'll come back for him. We need the hope. We need to be together.

His face is all crumples and tears. Surprise and sorrow. I snatch a few of his chisels and pocket them. Weapons are good in the West.

Mother steps up, but doesn't hug him yet.

My heart is screaming, *Let's go! Go! Go!* But I cannot rush them. Father smooths back the strands of her hair that stick to her cheek in the autumn wetness.

She covers her mouth with a hand and shakes her head.

I've never seen Mother cry and I turn away before it happens. I step out the door of the store, but not before I hear the rustle of their clothing meet in an embrace and Father's harsh, whiskery whisper. "I love you. I love you. I *love* you . . ."

The sound of these words will echo in my heart forever.

We reach the train station and the battle is over.

Blood covers the wood like an unfinished paint job. Enforcers and villagers alike lay in two heaps in the mud. Some people in the heaps groan, but the rest are dead or unconscious.

Does no one care that they're stacking bodies of living people?

"Close 'em up!" Sachem yells from the train platform.

The train looks old with lines of boxcars—some stacked two-high. Three Enforcers start sliding the boxcar door closed. The boxcar is a rusty red color and inside the dark, shadowed interior are lumps of people.

"Wait." I step forward, but the door closes with a heavy clang and the Enforcers lower a metal latch with a screech. I approach Sachem. "I'm going with them."

He looks at me and laughs. It's so out of place among the dying bodies surrounding us that I slap him.

My hand leaves a bloody print on his cheek and his laugh comes to a fierce halt.

Mother yanks my arm. "Parvin!"

I shouldn't have done that.

Sachem stares at me for a long time. There was a moment when I thought he could be a good man—a Lead Enforcer with a heart. But I don't see that now. He buried his potential for goodness.

He gestures to the Enforcers by the door. They unlatch it and crack it open. "You think you're going to save these people, Miss Blackwater? Such lofty heroism. Climb in."

I don't want to step into the boxcar graveyard.

But I do it anyway.

I don't want to weave my way around the ragdoll bodies bleeding into the thin straw covering the floor.

But I do it anyway.

I don't want Mother to have to sit in this black space that smells of blood and trauma.

But she does it anyway, and I sit beside her . . . because strength is a choice.

The door closes with a screech. A sliver of light comes from a barred window and a hole the size of a dessert plate in the back corner of the car.

Here we are. Mother and daughter . . . the only two with packs of supplies to take care of this mob of beaten humans. My bandages aren't enough for more than a single person. It's too dark to see who's here or what injuries they have.

All we have are our ears.

And all our ears have are the raspy breaths of people choking on blood or spit. The slow breathing of those sleeping from bashed skulls. The air of pain and defeat breathed out for us to take in.

We wait. The train doesn't move. Some breathing turns into groans. I rub my hand over the forehead of whoever lies beside me. Judging from the length of hair, it's a girl.

"How can we help them?" I try to see mother's face.

"Pray. And wait for them to wake."

I shake my head. "Can't we treat their wounds?"

"Not in the dark."

An hour later, the stench of drying blood, sweat, and rebreathed air is filling my lungs and I want to hold my breath until it clears. But it never will.

I must do something to distract me from the tragedy scourging my people. Even with the several bodies in here, Mother and I are alone. We'll be traveling together, surviving together. I have things I want to ask her—things I must know. Perhaps now, as we're locked away like cattle, she'll tell me things.

"Did you read my biography?"

She breathes out through her nose. "Yes. And . . . I've learned a lot. I'm . . . sorry, Parvin."

She knows me. She knows my story. That's all I wanted. "Mother . . . remember when Skelley Chase first turned me in to the Enforcers?"

"Of course."

I adjust Tawny's sweater around my waist. "You said you didn't come to my hearing because you were doing . . . other things." The memory of her eyes flicking to Skelley burns in my mind. "What were you doing?"

I hate the idea that she and Skelley might have had secret communication.

Her voice comes out low, as if trying to keep her words from the ears of the conscious. "I can't tell you that, Parvin."

"Because you don't trust me?"

"No, I just . . . can't." Her voice breaks. "I can't bear for you to know."

My stomach plummets. What was she doing? What were *they* doing? "Please tell me. You can trust me. Nothing can be worse than what my imagination dreams up."

She gives me nothing. Not a word. Perhaps sitting in a black boxcar having bid farewell to Father isn't the time, but at least now she knows that she can tell me. She *must* tell me. Someday.

More hours pass and the wounded stir.

"Where am I?"

I turn my head toward the voice. "Inside a boxcar,"

The question is repeated with every awakening, sometimes more than once from those who have head wounds. Those with mobility scoot away from those bleeding out. I hear their fabric rub against the straw. I hear their weight rest against the walls of the boxcar.

"In a boxcar?" one man repeats my answer. "But I have a new Clock. I spent a hundred specie on this! They can't send me across the Wall!"

"What if they're not going to send us across the Wall?" A woman's voice quakes into the darkness. "What if . . . they're going to leave us in here until we die?"

I hadn't thought of that. By the silence, no one else had either.

"Or," a man adds, "what if they're about to shoot us all? We're fish in a barrel here!"

The cries start. Some people shouting about their Clocks and the safety of their Numbers, others shouting for freedom, some just crying.

I say nothing.

I was so sure the government would send us across the Wall. Now . . .

I don't know what they will do to us.

Another hour passes and the door opens a crack. That's when I see our companions again, clearer than when I first entered. Men and women I've grown up seeing but never meeting look up at the beam of light.

The milkman sits by the door, awake, but with a neck wound and glazed eyes. He pushes himself to his knees, maybe to get out of the boxcar, but instead more people come in. A line of them, some bleeding, supported by friends. Others look healthy and reel back when they enter.

"Hurry it up!" A black rifle butt knocks the knees out of the older man trying to enter. He falls, but crawls over an unconscious person and sits against the narrow wall of the boxcar.

More enter. More. Too many to fit. They squeeze around the ones on the floor. The milkman remains by the door, as if waiting for the line to stop so he can jump out. The line doesn't stop. "We can't fit any more!"

But new Radicals keep coming—Harman, the master gardener . . . the town seamstress . . . Frenchie. We scoot limp bodies out of the way, into a tight line. Dusten Grunt is one of them and I pull him toward Mother and me. I place his head in my lap under the pretense of making more room for the others, but in reality I need to feel as if I'm helping someone.

He's unconscious and, thanks to the darkness, may never know it's my lap in which he rests. Two giant lumps interrupt the smooth flow of his hairline when I brush my hand over it.

The boxcar door closes before the milkman can get out. He pounds the door and screams, but it doesn't open again.

"Mommy, I have to go potty," a little girl says from the other side.

"Hold it," the milkman snaps. "We don't want to smell your waste."

"There's a hole in the back corner of the boxcar," I say. "I think it's for restroom use."

The little girl and her mother crawl across the boxcar, inciting grunts—and a growl from the milkman. They must reach the corner because the little girl starts crying. "I don't want to go! They're watching!"

"Shhh, it's fine," the mother says. "It's too dark for anyone to see. Here, I'll help you with your pants."

"No! No!"

"Just go already!" the milkman shouts.

She cries again and then the mother lets out a huff. "*Now* look what you've done." The girl's cries turn into a wail. "We don't have a change of clothes, honey." The smell of urine reaches my nose.

I lean my head back and close my eyes. How long will we sit here like this? Is this punishment for the mob?

Mother searches for my hand with hers, but finds my stump. Her fingers hesitate for a moment, then squeeze my wrist. "Parvin, you have to be a leader." Her words are a whispered foghorn to my emotions.

"What do you mean?" Does she expect me to do something about this?

"You have to prepare yourself. When everyone calms down, they will look to you. Are you ready for that?"

Who could possibly be ready for that? "I'm only eighteen, Mother. They hate me."

"Even those hating you will look to you. You are all we have."

I would have preferred her to combat my statement with, "No one hates you, Parvin." But the fact that she doesn't deny this shows me again Mother's fearlessness in addressing truth.

"How do you expect me to prepare myself?"

The murmuring and crying in the dark is almost too loud to hear Mother's reply. "They will be angry. You must be calm. They will have questions. You must be honest. They will all watch you. You must be confident."

It sounds like a motto. Maybe it's Mother's motto. She's always calm, confident, and honest—brutally so. But I can't be Mother. We are too different and ever since I crossed the Wall we've become near-strangers. But . . .

I can be me, I guess. And, in my heart, I know she's right. But how . . . how can I prepare myself to be such a different version of Parvin? A confident, leader version? Are those qualities even in me?

I AM IN YOU.

Even better.

Sounds outside with metal screeches and more wails imply that they're putting more people in the boxcars next to ours. How many citizens of Unity are they sending across the Wall? Are Father and Tawny being forced into one, despite their Clocks?

Tawny . . . I didn't say good-bye. Even though we don't get along, this still feels like I'm abandoning her.

The next time our door opens, it's dark outside, but the darkness is like a bright light to us. I see stars over the heads of people as they're shoved inside. The stars . . . they're stunning. I want to memorize their patterns so when the door closes again I will still have them in my mind to look at.

"Let me out!" The milkman pounds on the door. "I have specie to pay for a Clock."

An Enforcer angles a look at him. "Let me see it."

The milkman pulls out a pouch of coins before I can shout a warning. The Enforcer snatches it from his hands. "Don't got no specie anymore now, do ya?"

"Hey!" The milkman reaches for the pouch again, but the Enforcer pulls his gun out. The milkman stills.

Enforcers push so many new villagers inside our boxcar that those of us without injuries have to stand to make room. I try not to move because of Dusten, but I eventually slide his head out of my lap and stand next to Mother. Bodies squish against mine. My pack is sideways and my shoulders rub into the metal ridges of the boxcar.

"Please!" The milkman keeps shouting. "I have goats I need to take care of."

The Enforcer nearest the door gives a malicious grin. "Then I know what I'm having for dinner, don't I?"

The door closes, but I barely hear it over the milkman's pleading. Others wail. The train starts moving.

Thank you, God.

After this long day in the boxcar, the West will seem like a luxury to everyone. That will make everything easier for me.

Only three or four hours and we'll be at Opening Three. We can manage that. Then I'll be in my element.

I lurch against the sway of the train, but I don't mind standing. I'm going home. And this time . . .

I'm going as a leader.

17

It's been too long.

We should be there, but the train is still going full speed. I've fallen asleep on my feet at least twice. My lower back aches and my pack pulls on my shoulder. I try to squat, but my knees hit someone and they shove me away. No one wants to touch, but we're all smashed against each other, breathing one another's air, sweat, and fear.

Another hour passes. The stench of urine and feces join the mix of suffocation. It grows harder and harder to breathe, though I don't know if it's from our cramped space or the hysteria rising beneath my sternum.

Why aren't we at Opening Three?

Finally, the train screeches to a halt. This is the fourth time it's stopped and no one loses balance anymore. We're stopped long enough to hear the creak of other boxcar doors open, then the cries of people outside muffled by metal. More Low-City Radicals joining our journey.

When I decided to lead people across the Wall, I imagined villagers from Unity, not Radicals from *all* Low Cities. No matter how I work it in my mind, I can't figure out a way to get everyone on the cliff safely. If there's even a whisper of panic, people might shove others off the edge, down to the wolves.

We start moving again and my knees threaten to buckle. I allow a tendril of black fear to enter my mind . . .

What if we're *not* going to Opening Three?

The Enforcers could have lied. Besides, the Council said they'd fill in the passageway at Opening Three. Have they done this already?

I lose track of the hours and finally collapse to the boxcar floor. I land on someone's leg. They try to shove me off, but I don't move. I have to sit. People squeeze together and we make it work. Mother sits, too.

"Mommy, I'm hungry." The little girl's quiet plea barely makes it over the rhythmic *clack-clack* of the train.

My pack is in my lap. I could give her some of the small food ration I have, but something holds me back. This is only the beginning. The early twinges of hunger are nothing compared to when we cross the ridge into starvation. All I have to do is remember when Jude, Willow, and I ate plant bark.

Oh Jude, did he know giving his Clock-matching information to the Council would lead to a string of boxcars transporting Radicals to an unknown doom? Did he know it would land me among them?

What is Solomon thinking as he watches this happen? Does he even *know* it's happening? Is he alive? Is Willow in a boxcar somewhere? If Solomon returns to Unity Village he'll find my note. Then he will rescue Willow and get her back across the Wall. But if I'm not going to Opening Three . . . I missed my chance with him. I felt too guilty over Jude to let myself consider more than a friendship with Solomon—not that it would have done me any good.

Still . . . I feel as though I lost a friend.

Will the church people in Prime—Fight, Idris, Evarado, everyone else—continue praying for me? Are the High Cities aware of what's happening in the Low Cities?

I close my eyes and rest my head on the shoulder next to me. It smells like oatmeal and cinnamon. Mother. I nestle close, trying to block out the stench and clear my thoughts. Pure exhaustion ushers me into the arms of slumber.

Dreams of darkness and cliff edges dent my mind. Bloodied bodies fall around me, beaten by the Enforcers and thrown down to the wolves.

I wake to a scream, but not my own.

I'm tilted sideways, outside the control of balance. Outer light sneaks through the barred window and the waste hole. A swooping motion makes my stomach lurch. I grip the person closest to me and another hand snags my ankle.

More screams.

The little bit of sky through the barred window tilts and swirls. Our boxcar is in the air.

Deafening grinding precedes another swoop. Then we drop a couple feet. I scream now. Mother is silent beside me. The jerky drops meld into a smooth descent like the elevator in the county building, creeping down and testing my stomach's durability.

We land hard—metal scraping metal. From the outside of our boxcar I hear clips and belts being pulled off the outer edges. A brief breeze makes it through the window. The air is heavy, brackish.

Not Missouri air.

The day passes with metal clangs, grinds, and bursts of machinery. From what I've gathered, all the boxcars from the train are being stacked at this location. One is even stacked atop our own.

Another one is lowered beside us, its light blue metal blocking the light that had streamed into our window. There's still a gap between our boxcars, but their window faces ours.

"Where are they taking us?" Dusten's voice is a croak from my left. "Where's Parvin? Did they do this to her when they sent her across the Wall?"

"I'm here, Dusten." My voice is loud to my ears and the silence is heavy with expectation. What do I tell them? Can I admit I don't know what's going to happen?

I am supposed to be their leader.

"Well?" The milkman. Demanding.

I have to be honest, like Mother said, but before I can speak a man's loud voice comes from outside of our boxcar. "These two are Unity Village."

Something blunt pounds the outside of our door and another man with a low almost monstrous voice speaks. "Is Parvin Blackwater in there?"

I gasp and Mother clutches me to her. What do they want with me?

No one says anything. *Slam.* Monster Voice hits the metal again. "Hey!"

"Yeah, she's here."

Thanks, Milkman.

"You can have her if you let us out for some air and give us food."

The milkman's offer gets the rest of my people alert.

"Yes," someone else chimes in. "Food and air!"

"My tummy hurts, Mommy."

"Open the door!"

"Can you please let us out, just for a moment?"

Do they *want* him to kill me?

Slam. "Everyone quiet! We'll open the door long enough to let Parvin Blackwater out. You'll get food later today."

"He's lying."

I ignore the milkman's snarl and stand, but Mother grabs the edge of my coat.

"Parvin, no."

"He'll come for me anyway. I'll be fine, Mother." I hope.

It's impossible to cross the car without stepping on body parts. I trip twice before I reach the door and knock. "I'm here."

"We've got Enforcers if anyone else tries to come out," Monster Voice says.

I don't guarantee that no one will try. The milkman doesn't seem like the complying sort.

The door creaks open. Even without a breeze, the light alone brings in a fresh breath. My vision blackens, as if it can't handle the illumination. I take several squinty blinks before stepping down.

My knees buckle and one of the Enforcers steadies me.

"Holy zeroes." Monster Voice peers into the boxcar. I connect my gaze with his face. It's a smashed visage with small sunken eyes and an overbite. "Did you all get in a fight?"

"Enforcers did this." My voice exits my chest with venom. "They beat up these people and threw them in the boxcar. Some of us even have Clocks."

He stares for a long moment, then shuts the door.

"Hey!" I can barely hear the milkman's voice.

I'm led through stacks and stacks of boxcars—four or five cars high in some places. Are these all filled with *people?*

When I exit our row, it gets worse. I'm on a giant cargo ship.

Our row is just the first of fifteen. That's a lot of Radicals loaded like cattle. "Why are we on a ship?"

We walk to the back, across a deck made up of solar panels. My joints pop and tremble, but it's nice to stretch out. The ship is at a huge loading dock. The dock is covered in even more boxcars of all colors. Thousands.

I suck in a breath. "Are there people in all of those?"

"No, no." Monster Voice stops at the railing near the walkway to the dock. "The next shipment will come in a couple weeks. The shipping containers on the dock will go back on the trains to collect more Radicals."

My head swims and I grip the railing. I need food. "Where are you taking us? Why are we on a ship?"

"Well, *you* don't have to go anywhere. The Council is releasing you." He smiles, which shoves his eyes even further into the hollows of his eyes. "Aren't you lucky?"

Men on the dock unwind giant ropes from cleats and deck hands haul them up. The Council would let me leave? "Why?"

Monster Voice shrugs and gestures to two Enforcers next to the walkway. "All you gotta do is say yes and they'll take you where the Council wants."

Where the Council wants. He means they'll take me to the Council . . . to join them in their Clock propaganda. *Controllable.*

I swing my arm toward the boxcars on board. "I'm not leaving these people. Where are you taking them?"

"Get off while you can."

I stomp my foot, which is a bad idea because it reminds me that every muscle is a lump of jelly. "Not unless you release every Radical, too."

But part of me wants to flee. No one in the boxcar—or *shipping container*, as he called it—would know what happened to me. They might think the Enforcers killed me. I shake my head.

I can't leave Mother.

I can't leave any of them.

"The Council said they'll leave your village alone if you get off. They'll make sure your family has plenty of food and specie for the rest of your life. You can't say no to *that*."

He's wrong. I *can* say no . . . but it's not easy. "The people of Unity Village *are* my family. And they're in boxcars. The Council will have to release all of them, too." I can't abandon everyone. That would be turning my back on my desire to save lives, to bring shalom. "Now, where are you taking us?"

"Opening Four."

The blunt, cold way he delivers this information hits me like a jackhammer. I fall to my knees and no one helps me up this time. My speech comes out in a gasping whisper. "But that's . . . that's in Antarctica!"

"The ship's leaving. This is your last chance."

Antarctica. Antarctica. *Antarctica.*

We can't go there! There's no rescue from ice. People don't live there for a reason. We won't escape. We will *never* escape.

The last two ropes are thrown off the dock cleats. With a shuddering crank of noise, the cargo ship pulls away from the dock. I stay on my knees, watching the dock slide past, inch by inch. We're going slow, but far too fast for my despairing thoughts.

We're all going to die.

Antarctica, God? I thought You made my calling clear—to lead everyone to the West. Now they're following me to death.

We pass the end of the dock and head to open water.

"Lost your chance." Monster Voice hauls me up, but a shout from the dock scorches my nerves.

"Parvin!"

I snap my head around, scanning the pier.

"Parvin!" It'd be hard to miss the figure sprinting down the pier, past piled shipping containers and shoving workers aside. He's tall and still wears a black Enforcer coat, despite the scar on his face.

Solomon.

18

Solomon Hawke runs down the line of the dock toward us, but we've already left the slip. A gap of water separates us.

I break free of Monster Voice and sprint toward the stern, already gasping from memories of running to the back of the *Ivanhoe Independent* as it left Willow behind.

Not again.

Not again.

I can't bear to watch someone dear to me shrink out of my sight.

"Solomon!" I reach the end and maybe some of the deck hands think I'm going to jump overboard because they grab me—my coat, my hair, my arms. "Solomon!"

He's alive.

The water gap between the boat and the dock grows. His running form is already growing smaller. In a moment, he'll skid to a halt and realize he's too late.

But he reaches the end of the pier . . .

. . . and launches off the edge. He curves his body so he enters the water headfirst with his hands forward to break the impact. Everything about the action is perfect.

He's coming after me. *Me.* Even though he knows—he *must* know—this ship is carrying me to death.

Solomon breaks the surface, swimming with ferocious might, but the ship is too fast.

"Turn back! Don't come! You'll only die!" Maybe he doesn't hear me. Or maybe he doesn't care. I want him to come, but I don't want him to. What is he doing here? He's supposed to be saving Willow.

"Throw him a rope if we have one long enough," Monster Voice says from behind me. "If he wants a taste of Antarctica, so be it."

A deck hand picks up a coil. "I don't think we have one long enough, sir."

"No!" I spin around so we're face-to-face. "Don't bring him aboard."

Monster Voice points at an Enforcer. "You, put this girl back in the Unity Village container."

Before I can see if they throw a rope to Solomon, an Enforcer hauls me away from the stern of the ship. I struggle, but my puny form is no match. He opens the shipping container door, throws me inside, and bolts it behind me.

I burst into tears. Lying atop other bodies back in the stench, all I can bring myself to do is cry. Is it hope or despair?

I don't know.

But Solomon came after me.

Curse him, he *came!* Does he know that, if they pull him aboard, he's bound for Antarctica?

I sigh. He came.

He's alive.

"What did you find out?" The milkman glares at me.

"Did zey 'urt you?" It's the first time Frenchie has spoken. What was her real name again? Angelique? She was so excited to get her Clock. Now she's here. My heart aches.

I shake my head, even though it's too dark for them to see me. A battalion of sobs marches up my chest to my throat, needing an escape, but I force a deep breath. My people are turning to me for an answer, for some sort of leadership. Just like Mother said.

She said be honest.

I don't know how to be a leader, but I owe it to them to reveal where we're headed.

"*Well?*"

I sit up, wipe the tears from my eyes, and hug my stump to my chest. How do I say this? "I don't have good news."

"Get on with it!" The milkman seriously needs a lesson in tact.

I let several seconds of breath holding pass. "We're on a cargo ship en route to Opening Four."

I can almost hear the dread sink in.

"Antarctica?" Dusten shrieks. Those who hadn't connected it already, gasp at the word.

"Yes. They fooled us."

"No, *you* fooled us!" the milkman shouts. "You convinced us we could survive on the other side. You convinced us to trust you!"

If he finds comfort in blaming me, so be it. "I'm sorry you feel you were given false confidence. I still plan to help you survive."

"Oh you do, do you? Are you an expert in igloo-building?"

Several sniffs join the discussion.

"What did they want with you anyway?"

I don't want to tell them. It would sound too . . . martyr-like to say, "They offered me freedom and I didn't take it." But part of me *wants* everyone to know this—to know that I sacrificed my freedom and possibly my very life to accompany them to the Antarctic wasteland.

"Wait, wait," Dusten says. "Why are we all freaking out? We still remember our Numbers don't we? I have over nine months left. The Numbers are never wrong . . . right?"

Six months ago, I would've agreed, but Jude's death shook my beliefs. As did my own survival. But this wire cord around my wrist . . . it says thirty-one years. Should I believe it?

A dull blue glow stands out in the darkness across the boxcar, next to my mother. Dusten holds his wrist aloft and his projected Numbers blink red against in the blue-highlighted gloom.

Dusten R. Grunt

"See? Does anyone else remember their Numbers?"

Looks like he ended up stealing enough specie after all. Not that it did him much good.

"We are all Radicals now," Frenchie says. "But I remember my Numbers before zey were destroyed in ze fire. I 'ave thirteen years."

"You see?" His optimism—something I've never witnessed in this school bully—reinstates a modicum of calm. "That means you'll survive all this and probably escape Antarctica." Even as he says it, a choked sadness coats his voice. I know what he's thinking. *He'll* never escape. Not with nine months left.

The milkman snorts from by the door. "Or it could mean she'll learn how to scrape by in a winter wasteland for thirteen miserable years."

"Hush up." Mother directs a hard look at him from beside Dusten. While I have light from Dusten's illuminated Numbers, I scoot my way over the bodies, back toward her. I've done my duty. I informed everyone of our doom. Now, while they panic and worry . . .

I must plan.

I thought riding the train for an unknown amount of time was bad, but the cargo ship is far worse. Worse than wolves, worse than Wilbur Sherrod's nightmare simulations, worse even than having my hand chopped from my body.

Day one, they throw in a bag of potatoes and hand us two buckets of water.

"Did you guys pull that Enforcer out of the water?" I call, but the worker slams the boxcar door shut.

"What Enforcer?"

I ignore the milkman and he doesn't press the matter. I'm guessing he's more interested in food.

The potato bag makes it around the boxcar, but by the time it reaches my side the burlap bag is empty. The milkman blames some people for being greedy, Dusten blames the Enforcers for being stingy, but I just want a potato. I still avoid taking any food out of my pack. At least I get a sip of water.

Day two, I get a potato. It's raw and heavy in my hand. The skin is leathery. I try to smell it, but all that reaches my nose is the reeking boxcar air. I'm hungry, but uncooked potato isn't too tempting.

Still, I must eat.

I bite into the tip. It crunches like an apple, but tastes like dirt. Every chew releases another burst of earth-flavor. I chew against my gag reflex, trying to ignore the crunches. It's foul. I shouldn't have chewed. I should have just swallowed a chunk.

A pulse hits my throat. I drop the potato and close my eyes. *Don't be sick. Don't be sick.* I lick my lips—they're dusty with potato residue. The sea has grown wild and, while the rocking is subtle, I can't keep my stomach under control without a horizon on which to fix my eyes.

I vomit, probably on to someone's legs. There's a shout. Someone else follows suit. I grip my bitten potato and shove it in my bag. Maybe later I'll be hungry enough to eat it.

I still have no word about Solomon. I hope he had the sense to turn back to the dock, or that the sailors didn't have a long enough rope. Even though I saw his Numbers, I can't bring myself to be selfish enough to wish for his company. Willow needs him.

Day three, according to the little bit of light that makes its way through the barred window, some people recover from the seasickness enough to eat a little. Not me. We receive the same amount of potatoes, but the very thought of food sends me scrambling for the waste hole. Not everyone makes it and our shipping container is suffocated with vomit stench.

I try to read my Bible from the light of the window, but the nausea is too much.

Day four, we realize several people in our container are dead. We don't know how long they've been dead. I suppose the other fetor muffled their smells. The milkman stands by the window almost all day long, clinging to the bars and sucking in clean air. No matter how many people tug on his pant leg or shout at him to sit down so *we* can get some air, he doesn't move.

"I wonder what their Numbers were," someone whispers. "They must have known they were going to die, right?"

The milkman pounds against the metal of the container for a good hour before anyone comes.

"What is it?"

"There are dead people in here. You have to get them out or we'll all get sick!"

A couple hours pass before Enforcers come and take away some of the bodies. I don't look, despite some gasps and screams when the light reveals the faces. I don't want to know who died here.

I stop trying to figure out who took what—who took my freedom, who took my food, who took away my space or my hopes or my encouragement. It doesn't matter, because it's gone. Everything is outside of my power . . .

Everything except my thoughts.

Enforcers, distance, not even the Council can take my ability to think. I am human. I am living. I can plan, pray, imagine, dream, hope, and strengthen with only my thoughts.

The darkness impresses upon me a fabricated sensation of loneliness, but I am not alone. These people are in my charge and when we reach Antarctica, they will look to me. Despite the fact that they feel led to their doom.

They will look to me.

The only way to prepare is to compose my mind. I must not let my despair take hold of my intentionality. I start with Scripture. I haven't read much of it during my short life of frail faith. Only bits and pieces from this last year fasten to my memory.

My relationship with God has been stale and one-sided. During my time in the West I grew in my faith—I discovered a bit more about God and how He desires rightness and completeness in this world. I discovered my calling to save lives, to continue living regardless of tragedy. But recently I've plateaued.

I know *about* God. I know about shalom. I know that I am weak, but can be strong in Him. I know I sinned through selfishness, waste, and pride and He forgave me. But it's mostly in my head. Shouldn't my heart be involved somehow? Shouldn't something in me yearn for Him or connect to His voice?

My thread of spiritual connection is crusty and brittle. If my mind got destroyed and only my heart remained, would I still be in love with God?

The first verse that comes to mind is the section of Hebrews used as a code for the underground church. *"And through his faith, though he died, he still speaks."*

If I die on this trip to Antarctica, will I still speak? *God, is my faith strong enough that my voice will still be heard proclaiming You?* Oh how I hope so. But for now I need to focus on speaking during life. To my people.

Funny, how much harder that sounds.

My prayers feel flat, only a whisper in my mind against the creak of rocking shipping containers. How do I love God more? Is it okay to *ask* Him for that, or is that . . . cheating? Hesitant, I open my heart and mind and try to block out the stench of vomit.

God . . . I hope this is okay, but . . . will You help me love you more? I want to love You rightly because I've already seen a glimpse of what You'll do with my life. I asked you, so long ago, to take my life

*somewhere and You did. So . . . please somehow grow me and show
me what You are calling me for.*

I'm okay asking Him for this. Doesn't He command us to
love Him? So, in asking Him for more love, am I not pursuing
His will?

I let out a long breath and shift my thoughts.

Toward survival.

How does one survive on a continent of ice? That's how I've
always imagined Antarctica. Ice, snow, maybe a polar bear or two.

"Hey, Parvin girl." The milkman's words remind me of
Willow's funny speech and how she called me Parvin-girl. But
she says it with sweet endearment. The milkman spits it out like
tobacco chew.

"What?"

He turns from the window. "There's a note for you."

"What?" Who would write a note? Who has paper? Who
wants to . . .

Oh.

The crinkle of paper grows closer, as it passes from hand to
hand. I hold out mine and someone presses it into my palm. I
unroll it and hold it up to my face. It's too dark. I try to angle
toward the window.

"Who is it from?" Mother speaks in my ear.

With the dip of the ship, a glance of sunlight comes through
just enough for me to scan the note.

*I know you didn't want me aboard. But . . . you should
know by now that I tend to disobey commands. I'm with
you, Parvin.*
—Solomon.

19

He's with me. How can I be upset with a note like this in my hands?

"So your boyfriend's here?" The milkman moves away from the window.

I tuck the note into my bag. "You read it?"

"How was I to know it was for you if I didn't read it?"

Mother's hand startles me as it touches my shoulder. "Hush, Caprine. Your sour attitude causes more sickness in this boxcar than the sea."

Several people chuckle—myself included—and the milkman goes silent.

"Your name is *Caprine?*" Dusten is almost crowing.

"No." The milkman grunts. "It's *Cap.*"

"But that's short for Caprine, isn't it?"

"Mind your manners, young man."

Dusten gives a hollow laugh. "My Numbers are too short to be worried about manners."

I've seen the milkman on the corner of Straight Street as long I can remember and am hearing his name for the first time. How many people have I labeled in my lifetime, but never stopped to know?

If only I had a pen or pencil to return Solomon's note. He must be in the shipping container next to ours. So, they pulled him aboard and sentenced him like a Radical. Will he survive? Is Dusten right, that our Numbers mean we'll escape Antarctica? I envy the people in Solomon's container. His kindness and calm probably brings a light to them much brighter than what squeezes through their window.

We must be approaching land because bird cries join the whip of wind and clunks of ship machinery. Our boxcar grows too hot. The air is muggy, even when it's nighttime. The warmth starts to cook the filth coating the floor of our car.

I breathe through my mouth with my sleeve over my face.

It doesn't help.

Soon it doesn't feel like we're moving anymore. No rocking.

"Are we zere?" Frenchie whispers, as if speaking it too loud might jinx us.

"No, stupid," Cap snaps. "It's *hot* here. You think Antarctica's going to be *hot?*"

Another sack of raw potatoes and two buckets of water are given to us to pass around. Hot sea air blows into our container during the brief opening of the door.

Morning comes with a fist pounding our metal door. "I'm here for Parvin Blackwater." Monster Voice.

Again?

"What do you want with her?" Mother clings to me.

"Send her out and you'll get an extra bag of potatoes tonight."

I'm ripped out of Mother's hands. Yanked. Pushed. I trip over bodies and clang against the metal door. It opens a crack and Monster Voice pulls me out.

The sun blinds me and I fling my hand over my eyes. As he pulls me along the solar-paneled deck, my blurry vision clears.

We're at a giant metal dock with enormous, blue cranes overhead. I barely keep my feet under me.

Thousands of shipping containers cover the docks around me. One crane hovers over our boat, and operators lower it toward the end pile of containers. In the distance is jungle. Thick brush with tall grass, and trees that seem to fish for clouds with their fingertips.

"What's going on?" The air is thick and I cough . . . but it's air. I suck in deep breaths.

"You have a meeting."

I frown at Monster-Voice. "With who? Where are we?" Behind me is the sea dotted with cargo ships, sailboats, yachts, and all other forms of boats I could imagine. My gaze travels up the shore to where two canals lead toward enormous black gates.

"Panama."

I've heard that name before, but I couldn't place it on a map. Somewhere south of Unity Village—*way* south. I suddenly feel stupid, like I should know where this is. Reid would know. If I'd been raised with knowledge caps like the people in High Cities, I would know.

A man walks around the corner of a stack of shipping containers and I reel backward. The Enforcers yank me toward him.

Skelley Chase.

"What are *you* doing here?" I spit out. He's going to take me away. I know it. I won't let him.

"Walk with me," he says in his bored warble. A thin metal disc floats a few inches above his green fedora.

"No thanks."

He starts walking and the Enforcers lug me after him. He waves them off. "Release her." They obey.

I could run, but I don't. Every word from Skelley's mouth is a clue to the Council's motives. "What made you fly all the way down to Panama?"

"Oh, I didn't fly here." He gestures to the disc above him. "I'm a projection. I can do you no harm."

The Enforcers walk a few steps behind us now, giving off the impression of privacy, but I'm sure they can hear everything we say.

"Why do you want to go to Antarctica?"

I laugh. "I don't! You and your *Council* are the ones sending us."

"But you don't have to go."

I peer at him. "You're right. I don't *have* to go. Instead, I could join you as your *controllable* puppet, spreading televised lies to the entire nation."

"We'd let you return to Unity Village at times."

I roll my eyes. "Hurray. I can return to a place void of all the people I love."

He stops and faces me, a threat in his voice. "Your father and sister-in-law are still in Unity Village. Don't you miss them?"

My hand shoots out to grab the collar of his jacket, but passes right through the projection. "What have you done to them?"

"Nothing."

"What have you done to Willow?"

He shakes his head. "You don't get it yet, do you? *Nothing.* As long as you return and *cooperate* with us, nothing will happen to them."

"Why? Why am I so important to you?" All this effort, all these bribes, for what?

He raises an eyebrow. "You don't have the luxury of knowing the *whys.* All you need to know is what I'm about to offer you."

I prepare myself. Skelley knows my weaknesses. The offer will be tempting, but I must not give in. I can be strong, despite my hunger, fear, weakness, and desires. I'm suddenly reminded of Jesus being tempted by the devil when he was hungry and vulnerable. *Lord, give me Your strength.*

He waves a hand as if shooing a mosquito. "Just say the word and these two Enforcers will fly you back to Prime today. You never have to step on this ship again."

"I'm not going back. Not unless you free all of the Radicals and refuse to spread Jude's Clock invention." The crane above lifts a container from our stacks and backs up toward the dock. "What . . . what are they doing?"

Skelley rests a hand on my arm. I don't feel it, but I jerk away anyway. Not even his *virtual* skin is allowed to make contact with mine. "Listen, Parvin, I'll free all the captives from Unity Village. We'll send you all home—together. The Council will leave your village alone as long as you come visit us in Prime once a month to shoot a video. To be our spokeswoman. We'll provide your village with Clocks—free of charge—and make sure you live comfortably."

So they want my face. My voice. My cooperation. I must be more powerful than I thought. "And would you update our school system so we can learn with knowledge caps just like the kids in High Cities?"

He quirks an eyebrow. "You've been studying up on the High-City language. Sure. Anything else?"

"Will you leave Opening Three intact—*always* open—so that people can cross through if they wish? Safely?"

"I'd have to talk to my fellow Council members, but I'm sure something can be arranged."

That's the tipping point of the scale—the sign that this is too good to be true. He's lying. They're desperate. They don't stand for shalom. And I'm not controllable anymore.

"It's not just Unity people." My voice is deadly quiet. "I care about every Radical and Low-City citizen the Council is condemning. Unless you revoke the Clock-matching, unless you allow Radicals and Clocked people to live side-by-side with the same rights, unless you free *all* of us *today*, I'm not coming with you."

"So be it." He tips his fedora. "Enjoy the trip." His projection disappears and the disc falls to the ground. One of the Enforcers picks it up and puts it in his pocket.

I left my container worried. I return encouraged. The Council wants me . . . badly. This tells me I'm the strongest face and voice they can present to the people in the USE. This tells me I have power and they fear it. They want it.

I can tell the people anything and they'll listen to me more than to the president.

If You get us off Antarctica, I will use this power You've given me.

"What are they doing with that container?" I gesture to the one in the sky.

Monster Voice steers me down my row of shipping containers. "Selling them."

I frown. "The container?" We reach mine.

"No, the Radicals."

I grab his hand before it can open the boxcar door. "What? Why? To who?" Selling . . . people?

He throws me off him and yanks the door open. "As slaves . . . to anyone who wants them."

Then I'm back in the darkness.

We get no potatoes that night. No extra bag. No normal bag. Monster Voice lied. I tell no one about my meeting with Skelley, despite the many questions. If they find out I had a chance to free some of them and didn't take it, they won't understand.

I *do* tell them about other containers of Radicals being sold as slaves. They don't take it well, but they don't take it how I expected.

"Why aren't *we* being sold as slaves?" Cap asks. "Why do we have to go to Antarctica?"

"Maybe you will get lucky and zey will sell you later," Frenchie suggests.

"Why are there slaves at all?" Mother shakes her head. "There was never slavery in the USE before."

"We're not *in* the USE, Mother."

Her arm tenses against mine. "But still . . . how does the USE know *where* to sell people? Is that why they're doing this? To make money off the Radicals and get us out of their system?"

Sounds right up their alley.

The next day, our door is opened.

"Everyone out!" Monster Voice shoves Cap out first. We follow, stumbling along. Another container—not Solomon's—is released with us. We're led to the edge of the ship.

All around us are jungle islands. Deep green trees so thick I can't even see a shore or ground. Pelicans swoop overhead, mixing with black-and-white seagulls.

"Draw water." Monster Voice draws our attention to coils of ropes resting on the edge of the deck, one end tied to a cleat and the other to a metal bucket. "We'll be crossing Lake Gatun for about five hours. It's your job to get water to every shipping container. That's the only water they'll get over the next three days. Their deaths be on your heads. *Your* container gets no water until you're finished."

"That's ridiculous." Cap folds his arms. "Why do *we* have to do this? We're weak just like everyone else."

Monster Voice takes three long strides and knocks Cap in the head with his rifle butt. Cap falls, but remains conscious. "Your famous little Blackwater earned you guys this privilege. Now get to work."

He jerks a thumb at us and a group of Enforcers space themselves, monitoring our work. "Oh, and don't think about jumping overboard. *If* you survived the jump, there are alligators. Not to mention the panthers, snakes, and disease-carrying insects on the islands."

It's hard work, drawing the water in the ninety-degree heat. All of us sneak sips here and there to maintain our stamina. We get kicked if caught. The good thing is, a whole row of shipping containers are gone from the ship. The bad thing is . . . all those people are being sold as slaves.

My right arm burns after the first bucket. I have to pull up the rope with one hand, then tie the slack around the cleat until it's firm enough for me to grab another hand of rope. My left arm keeps inching toward the rope as if I have fingers to help. But I don't.

I work anyhow.

By the end of the five hours, my hand bleeds from blisters and I'm dehydrated despite the stolen sips. I don't know if we watered every container, but I've been given a better idea of how many Radicals are here.

Too many.

We're put back in our shipping container with a single bucket of water. We pass it around and share sips. Then we collapse, able to really sleep for the first time as the boat enters more locks that will eventually deposit us into the ocean again.

As days pass, I slip one potato a day into my pack. There won't be any food in Antarctica. We'll need all we can get and I can't bear wasting mine on seasickness. Mother does the same and, when we're not sick, we split the potatoes we choose to eat so neither of us goes hungry.

Solomon sends me another note.

I hope your potato tasted better than mine.

I smile and hug the paper to my chest. It's a tiny treat—a note with absolutely no takeaway content other than that he wanted to make me smile.

A few minutes later, Cap reaches through the bars and pulls in another scrap of paper. He holds it for a while with his back to us and then lets out a *"Hmph!"*

It's passed to me in a matter of seconds.

I'm going off of faith that you're receiving my notes, Parvin. Your window man doesn't boost my confidence. Window man, if you're reading this, give it to the pretty girl who's stealing my heart. This is boxcar love, dear sir, and you should be wary of hindering it. – Solomon.

Boxcar love? I read it in a playful manner, but what did Solomon really mean? Would he call our relationship . . . love?

Is it okay to . . . start loving him? Solomon and I are a team now. We've always been a team. I think Jude's okay with it. I try to move near the window so I can accept Solomon's notes instead of Cap, but people won't budge. The window is where the fresher air is.

I remain near Mother, accepting more notes as they're passed. They're always short and funny. Cap gets grouchier and grouchier with each one he has to pass. I'm certain he reads them, but how can he stay so grouchy when he's reading what I'm reading?

I lose track of the passing days. Every now and then, I catch Monster Voice pounding on a nearby container, dragging the cap-

tives out and putting them to work. From what I overhear, they
spend time pounding rust off railings or re-painting sections of the
ship.

After a while, I start to think *we* got the lighter work by drawing water.

I thought maybe after a few days of vomiting that I would grow
used to it—used to the sway and lurch, used to the burning in my
muscles from maintaining what balance I can, used to the overall
sensation of being trapped. Every time my skin tingles and my ears
ring with the threat of seasickness, I force myself to brave it. If I get
sick, I just have to be sick. If there's a storm, I have to brave it. I still
need to eat. I still need to drink.

Otherwise I *will* die.

I didn't think it possible, but another week passes. At least, I think
it's a week. It might be more, it might be less. Cranes have come
and gone, taking containers of slaves with them. How many of us
are left?

All I want is a bar—no, a *flake*—of soap. I close my eyes at the
idea of washing my hands. I allow a waterfall to flow from my imagination through my dirty, sticky, fingers. Clean, pink skin. When I
rub my palm over my face, it will be smooth. Fresh. Calming.

I open my eyes again to darkness. Our container lurches with
the tilt of the ship. No one screams anymore. No one apologizes for
bumping. My shoulder digs into Mother's side. She doesn't flinch. I
wait until the ship rights itself, only to lurch the other way.

With the movement, my thoughts inadvertently drift to my
fragile stomach. It pulses in greeting. I jerk my thoughts away, but
not before my nose detects the memory of vomit.

"Hungry?" Mother asks.

"No," I choke, too quickly. The odor of stomach acid drifts past—real this time. Will I ever want food again? It's so much more comfortable dry-heaving than having to worry about retching on another person in the darkness. Without rags to clean it. Without soap.

I take an emotigraph at the peak of my discomfort. Someday, I will release it to the High-City world and they'll see what the Council has done to us.

Seven more people die and, after we strip them of most of their clothing, Enforcers toss their bodies into the sea. I can't blame it on the Enforcer beatings anymore. I think a lot of it has to do with the suffocation of our container. Of hopelessness. The air has grown colder—too cold. We all huddle together now, squished as tight as possible for the sake of body heat, sharing the clothing of the dead. I'm one of the few with a coat. I hand off the sweater I tied around my waist and give someone else Father's coat.

We rotate every couple hours so no one is pressed against the metal container sides for too long. I feel the urge to keep Mother warm and safe—so she never touches the walls. It's a strange protectiveness since she's always been the collected, strong one in our family. But this isn't her territory. There are no soapsuds or dishes to turn to when things get too hard.

This is new territory to me, too, but I'm more prepared to fight for my life.

The door creaks open and the bag of potatoes is thrown in. The bucket of water is frozen around the rim.

"Shut the door!" Cap hollers at the Enforcer feeding us. "It's cold!"

The Enforcer levels a gaze at our smooshed group and then slides the metal door softly, dangerously shut.

"You fool, Caprine."

I don't know what Mother thinks the Enforcer might do to us, but Frenchie's cry distracts me from despairing.

"Ze potatoes are cooked!"

Everyone reaches for the bag. Now that so many have died, we all get a potato every time. The bag reaches Mother and me. I pass Mother her potato and then take one in my hand. It's still warm. I clutch it to my chest, willing it to warm my core. The earthy dirt-smell doesn't make my stomach roil this time—not when it's accompanied by heat. The little girl in our car gets two potatoes.

I take a bite. It's soft and hot, burning my mouth. I let it.

We get no potatoes or water the next day, even when Cap pounds on the door. No one comes.

"This is your fault." Dusten's accusation comes out in a puff of frozen breath. "You insulted the Enforcer."

Cap just returns to the huddle and pushes himself into the warm middle, right next to the little girl. People protest, but no one uncurls or pushes him away. It's too cold.

We get another two bags of potatoes after a day. They're raw again. Thanks, Cap. Everyone is shivering. I tuck my right hand under my armpit to keep my fingers warm. I keep my scarf wrapped around both Mother's and my face so our breath can rebound and warm us. We take it down only to eat the potatoes.

Raw potatoes become the least of my worries when loud clunks hit the outside of the ship. First one, then two. They don't sound intentional.

"I th-th-think it's the ice." Mother's teeth chatter. "W-w-we must be c-c-close."

My potato hits my stomach like a rock. We're almost to Antarctica and I still don't have a plan for survival. Soon we'll be out and we'll be even colder, with only ice to eat.

Right now, though, anything sounds better than this frigid metal shipping container. My feeble plan to save potatoes now sounds pathetic. How many do I have? Seven? Eight?

The cracking gets louder. Hours pass. I can't sleep. I'm so cold.

Three people have their limbs wrapped around the little girl in the middle, pouring all their body heat into her. It's like she's our symbol of survival. If *she* makes it, then we certainly can.

God, I'm not ready for people to turn to me. I don't know what to tell them. I don't know how to lead them.

Amidst my worry, I'm glad I'm not alone. God's with me, He sees me, and I exhale anxiety. Let the peace come in. I will do what I can.

The ship stops moving. Some shouts and noise come from the men on deck. The square of sky I glimpse through the window is dark and star-speckled. It's not until early sunrise—which comes much sooner than I expected—that the dreaded creak of our door reveals a group of Enforcers led by Monster Voice.

"Everyone up and out." His eyebrows have tiny clumps of ice in them. "We're here."

I can't remember how to walk.

It's been only a couple weeks—at my best reckoning—since I was on deck, hauling up buckets of water. Why can't I walk straight?

We step in between the two stacks of shipping containers and a gust of icy wind makes the container seem like a sauna. A hand slips through the window of the blue one to my left. "Parvin."

Solomon.

I reach for him and our fingers barely touch. His are icy and stiff. Even that movement—lifting my arm away from my body—causes a bone-wracking shiver. I tuck my elbows close to my core again.

The boat tilts and I stumble into an Enforcer. He pushes me away and Frenchie steadies me. "Keep your feet wider"—she demonstrates—"like zees. I came to America on a boat like zees one. Not een a boxcar, of course. I learned to balance."

I knew she was French, but never imagined she actually sailed to the USE from France. "Thank you." I look back at the container window, but Solomon's hand is gone.

My knees threaten to buckle. Two potatoes a day didn't cut it. The morning light burns my eyes. I squint against the reflection off the ship's surface. The rest of the Unity Village crew still huddles together. At least eighty of us. No wonder so many died in that cramped container. If the other containers were as full as ours, there must be at least a thousand of us.

Our breath fogs out, forming a mixed cloud of chill. Dusten Grunt's eyes are sunken and his cheeks seem more hollow. Frenchie—a model to begin with—looks like an emaciated Dead-City Radical. Mother's face sags as if she's aged ten years, but she grips my hand tight in a commanding way.

"Follow me." Monster Voice walks us through the rows. One container freed and doomed at a time, I guess. When will I be reunited with Solomon? How will he look once he steps into sunlight? I almost don't want to see the change. I like imagining him strong and in control.

A man carries the little girl from our container. She stares at the mountains of snow with a nutcracker jaw. "It's like a wonderland."

If only it were.

Several of us stumble, but Monster Voice doesn't slow. Thankfully, everyone is in pants, boots, and long-sleeved shirts, since the cold had just arrived in Unity Village.

I glance back at the stern-end of the boat. The sea stretches away from us, endless, dotted with enormous flat chunks of ice. But what claims my gaze is the Wall.

It stretches a thousand feet high a mile from the ship's starboard side. It rests atop the sea, bobbing in sections as if hinges keep it more flexible. It is smooth and grey, polished. It looks so real, but I remember Mother's degrading laugh: *"Stone doesn't float, Parvin."*

She said all parts of the Wall over water were *projected*— invented by Solomon's great-grandfather or something like that. Apparently it's just as impassable as a stone wall. Well, it *looks* like a legitimate stone wall from this distance. I guess, in a few hours, I'll see it up close.

As I stare, a part of the projected Wall flickers. Just for a moment.

A metal step-ramp lowers at an angle down to rubber motorboats, each holding a handful of armed Enforcers. Monster Voice points. "Down you go."

"We can't all fit in one boat," Cap says. "We'll sink!"

"Get going."

Cap folds his arms. Monster Voice steps toward him, but I lurch forward, dragging Mother after me. "I'll go down first."

"Sure, go brown-nose the Enforcers," Dusten says.

I roll my eyes. "Then *you* go."

He shoves me aside and I fall into Mother. I don't mind one bit. Climbing into a dinghy filled with enemies doesn't appeal to me. As he inches over the side, I notice he's trembling. Cold or nervous? Or both?

We watch him, but before he reaches the bottom, Monster Voice shoves me forward. Mother's tight grip on my hand is all that keeps me from falling down the stairs.

"Get going. We've got at least twenty more shipping containers to unload."

Twenty more, each with eighty or so people in them. I'm no Moses, I can't lead all of them. What do I do?

But it's fewer than I expected. How many people were sold as slaves?

"Climb down, Parvin," Mother says.

I make certain my pack is tight over my shoulders and start my descent, gripping the iced metal railing tight. My right hand burns. Some parts of it, like my warm palm, stick to the bar. Skin rips off as I slide my hand down. My blood makes my hand stick all the more. I wince.

Wind whips my hair around my face, but I don't dare use my hand to move it out of my eyes. My nose is already numb. How can we possibly survive?

I reach the bottom of the ramp. The rubber motorboat bobs. I need a hand for balance, but Dusten's not offering. Here goes.

I take a wild leap and my foot slips. I manage a single gasp before I land on my back against a seating slat in the boat. Something sharp from inside my pack digs into my spine. Tiny bursts of breath return the oxygen to my lungs. Dusten sits by, staring out over the ocean.

Thanks for the help.

"Parvin?" Mother's a few steps up.

"I'm fine," I croak.

I clamber to my feet as she reaches the bottom. I offer my bloody hand, but she steps into the boat like she's done it a hundred times and sits on a slat. We sit together—away from the Enforcers—as the other members of Unity Village come down.

Aside from Frenchie, Dusten, Cap, and Mother, I recognize Kaphtor, the black Enforcer who originally sentenced me to the Wall. The backward *E* is still on his temple, but he doesn't look like an escort. He's emaciated and covered in sick just like the rest of us.

Dusten leans toward Cap and me, whispering, "Shouldn't we fight back or something? We can't just let them strand us here."

"Didn't you see what happened in Unity?" Cap snaps.

"Well, yeah, but there are fewer Enforcers here." Dusten jerks his thumb toward the deck. "We could take out a few and open some of the boxcar doors—"

"And what would we do if we *did* take over the ship?" Cap looks around. "Anyone know how to refuel that thing or even drive it?"

One Enforcer in the boat knocks the butt of his rifle against Cap's knee. "We can hear everything you're saying. You want a bullet in that knee?"

Cap rubs his bristly chin and turns away.

Fighting back never crossed my mind—maybe because the beatings in Unity are still fresh in my memory. I focused more on survival, but *should* we fight back?

"We can't overpower them." Kaphtor's low voice sounds old and torn. He coughs. "We're all half-starved and weak."

"What are you even doing here?" Cap glares at him. "You're an Enforcer."

Monster Voice screams down at us. "Get *going!*"

One Enforcer revs the motor and we shoot toward shore. White mountains rise from the ground like sculpted icebergs. Clouds hang low, pinkish grey against the stark white of the snow peaks.

We reach shore in a matter of minutes. Once we're all shoved out by gunpoint, the Enforcers turn the dinghy around and return to the ship. Four of them stay with us.

"Aren't you gonna show us where to go or something?" Dusten claps his arms against his chest several times. Flakes of who-knows-what fly off his clothing. The Enforcers stay silent.

How long will they make us stand out here? Where is the Opening?

I look down at my own pants, boots, and coat and almost vomit. Instead of clapping the dried crud off the fabric, I stomp my feet and jump up and down a few times.

The ground is covered in small rocks and shells—thousands of shells, piled inches deep. I don't get a chance to pick any up because we're swarmed by a rookery of penguins. They waddle toward us with funny sounds and a stench worse than the boxcars.

"Gah!" Dusten backs away from them. "It's a stampede!"

Mother and Frenchie stare at the Wall. "Eet eez so big."

The smooth Wall connects with land and almost blends in to the snow. Drifts of white and ice slide up to meet the base. The projected Wall looks too perfect, with no snow on it at all.

"Get going." Just as another dinghy reaches shore, the Enforcers prod us forward.

Cap hisses like a snake. "This is madness. We're walking *toward* the Wall? We're like pigs heading to slaughter!"

"Only one of us here is a pig, Caprine." Dusten kicks a clump of snow and walks faster.

"Stop, fools!"

A dark line covers the crest of a snow hill far ahead of us. Enforcers. We all slow, but continue walking. What else can we do? Run? Get shot?

"So much for escaping," Cap grumbles. "Don't blame me."

More Radicals catch up to us. Now that guns are trained on us, we go where we're steered—toward the Antarctica Enforcers.

We don't walk long before a tower comes into view. The core of the tower rests close to the Wall. It is made of enormous stone blocks. Pop-outs of rooms are held up by metal scaffolding connected to the stone. It's all greys, blues, and sea greens—a product of the environment, not a paint job. A long elevated tunnel runs from the tower straight into the Wall.

That's our entrance. Is it warm in there? Even a blink of heat would be welcome.

Frenchie is whiter than bleached cotton with nothing but a shawl over a long-sleeved fall dress. I should give her my coat.

But I'm already so cold.

I should give it to her.

She won't know if I don't. One of the *men* should give her their coat. They're men after all, isn't that what gentlemen do? Solomon would do it if he were here.

I grit my teeth. Sometimes I really don't like myself. I slide my left arm out of my coat, twist it off my shoulder, and awkwardly drape it over Frenchie's.

"Oh no—"

"Hush." My harsh demand reminds me of Mother. "You'll freeze in that shawl."

"You will freeze in zat shirt."

A harsh gust of wind confirms her statement, ripping right through my thin, long-sleeved pullover and vest. "I'll be fine."

Mother helps Frenchie's stiff arms into the sleeves. "Accept it, Angelique."

Frenchie smiles at me. "Thank you."

I dip my head, still guilty over the turmoil it took to sacrifice my warmth. Now that it's gone, I'm glad I did it.

By the time we reach the Enforcer hill, snow has slipped into my boots and melted against my already chilled feet. I sniff every other breath to keep my nose from running.

"Here we go," Cap mutters.

The movement has warmed us enough so our teeth aren't chattering. I might even feel some sweat beneath my vest. Even though my very bones shiver, it's not as cold here as I expected it to be.

"What are you doing with these ones?" One of our Enforcers nods at us.

An Antarctica Enforcer grunts. "Sendin' 'em through for survival testing. Those still alive after a week get hard labor."

Survival testing? Hard labor? So that's the Council's plan— more experiments on humans. What will they have us build?

The Antarctica Enforcer uniforms are thicker than the ones in Unity. Each Enforcer wears a strange face wrapping with goggles. They lead us to the tower, forming us into a line by marching so close we can't do anything but comply. I end up somewhere in the middle. I can't see who's first. *I* need to be first.

"Ugh, they're so disgusting." The Enforcer to my left is talking to the Enforcer in front of him.

"They're Radicals, what do you expect? They have no hygiene."

I want to scream, *We've been stuck in a shipping container for weeks, you idiots!*

"I'm glad the government is finally using them for something worthwhile. That whole relocation thing was such a joke."

Their conversation grows louder. It stirs something up in the rest of the Enforcers—a disgust, as if every negative comment convinces them more and more that we're livestock, not people.

A rifle butt jabs my side. "Hurry up!"

I don't change my pace—a small act of defiance that settles the fury in my chest.

We file into the tower. The door is made of three parallel chunks of stone elevated off the ground, bound with metal wrapping. I climb icy stone stairs to go through it. When we're inside, it closes behind us. We walk through a small tunnel that's no warmer than the outside and to another door. We crunch into the space in a disorganized mass, seeking body heat from fellow Radicals. There's no single-file now.

An Enforcer stands in front of the second door. "When I open this, you will run through. And I mean *run*. We ain't wasting any heat because of your laziness. Got it?"

We all nod. Everyone seems to stand a little taller at the word *heat*.

He opens the door and we sprint as well as a mob of starved, frozen, weak Radicals can. Someone falls, but we somehow get him to his feet and pile through. As promised, the door is closed behind us.

We're in a giant round room painted with warm colors. A curved bench runs along the wall with spaced coat hooks a few feet higher. Enforcer uniforms hang from several of the hooks, with boots shoved beneath the benches. The heat covers me in a suit of goosebumps that almost feel colder than outside, but I welcome them. If only I could urge my body to warm up quicker.

"Through here." The Enforcer opens a door to the right. "Hurry up! Ugh! I can smell you through my mask."

I don't smell anything, either because my nose is too cold or because I got used to it in the container. I'm closest to the door and take this chance to claim the lead. I step after the Enforcer.

Mother is directly behind me. *"Parvin."*

I shake my head. Someone has to go first and it ought to be me.

Inside is a grated metal staircase curving out of sight. The Enforcer leads, leaving his mask on.

My feet are anvils, crashing onto one step after the other. I clutch the handrail on my right and drag myself up. After only ten steps my muscles spasm, firing pleas for rest. Mother nudges me from behind and I force myself forward. If only I had my Vitality suit.

We climb past closed doors, both on the left and right, always circling. Circling. Circling up. The air is thin and cold in this stairway. I suck in gasps.

Just keep going. Keep going.

Why?

Keep going.

Why am I submitting so easily to these Enforcers? Is Cap right? Are we acting like pigs heading to slaughter? *Should* we fight?

The Enforcer finally stops on a landing and opens a door to the left. I look back. The rest of the group isn't even in sight around the curved corner yet. I don't have time to worry for them. Instead, I brush a stray clump of hair from my face and look at the Enforcer.

"Can't you let us go? It's not right to send us through the Wall."

He looks at me. "You're Parvin Blackwater, aren't you?"

I nod.

His hand shoots out, grabs my hair, and throws me into the room.

Okay, so negotiation won't work.

Five more Enforcers are inside this room. Three slouch against the wall, another fiddles with his gun, and the fifth yawns loudly. A taller man in normal clothing—if you can call a parka, goggles, bright orange gloves, and a woolen hat with earflaps *normal*—jumps to his feet when I tumble in.

"Sir."

"Not now, Reece." The Lead Enforcer who threw me steps over my crumpled form and pulls an Enforcer off the wall. "Go check in with maintenance. We had a flicker. I want a report."

"'Kay." The Enforcer walks into the stairwell.

I scramble back onto my shaky legs and that's when I see the entrance. The door is already open and a long, white tunnel stretches out in front of me, curving out of sight into darkness. The ceiling before the stone is a peak with curved glass panels as a roof, letting in cold light. Icicles and snow chunks coat each supporting beam. Lumpy sheets of snow cover the inside walls. Even the floor is icy with snow built up on each side. A long thick rope swoops through a line of cold metal rings, sagging from the weight of absorbed snow, a sad excuse for a railing.

A harsh wind blows up the tunnel. My hair flies away from my face and my cheeks burn. We'll all have frostbite by the end of the day . . . if we don't have it already.

"Why is there even an Opening here?" I blurt.

"Sir." The tall man in mix-and-matched clothing steps closer.

"Shut *up*, Reece." The Lead Enforcer closes the door to the stairwell, keeping any other Radicals from entering. Then he turns to a screen in the wall, taps a few things, and pulls me in front of it. "This is for you."

Before I can ask, before I can close my gaping jaw to swallow, before I can even think, a screen comes up with Elan Brickbat in the center of it. It's not a video, it's a real-life connection.

He glances around for a moment, then his eyes settle on me. "You look disgusting."

He linked in to Antarctica to tell me *this?* "I'm not changing my mind."

"You liked the journey that much?" Already, a vein in his temple pulses.

I turn my back on him. "No matter what you offer me, it won't be good enough, not unless you agree to bring everyone back home."

"Oh, I'm not here to offer you anything." His wet voice prompts me to clear my own throat.

I turn. "Then why are you here?"

"I'm here to take things away from you." His eyebrows come together in a sharp *V*. "Skelley Chase should have skipped the bribes. If you don't return, we'll hunt down your father and your sister-in-law. Then we'll burn Unity Village to the ground. We'll send every Dead City and Low City citizen to Antarctica—Clocked or not. And . . . we'll bring Willow in for testing."

"You're the one who sent me away!" I scream. "I was there, *in your Council room,* and you had your Enforcers haul me back to Unity Village."

"Those are the terms."

My veins shriek *No!* It's the dreaded one-or-the-other option. Willow, Father, and Tawny . . . or every Radical here.

Can I do any good here? Do I really need to be here? Solomon's here. Solomon could lead them.

STAY.

Oh gosh. Really? *Really? You want me to stay?*

I AM HERE.

But Willow! Father! Tawny!

I AM THERE.

"This is your last chance, Parvin Blackwater."

Did I hear right? God wants me to . . . stay. But how can I–? No, wait.

I take a deep breath. Listen again. Yes, He wants me to stay. So . . .

How can I not?

The Council has taken their power too far. They don't own us. They don't own me. God is stronger.

"Good-bye, Brickbat." I turn my back on him and face the tunnel. The Lead Enforcer shuts down the computer and a whoosh of air leaves my chest. He opens the door to the stairwell again and my weary people tumble inside.

Who knows how much they heard.

"Sir." The parka-and-earflaps man—Reece—gives a salute. "I'd like to speak with you."

"Reece, get back to your books and antifreeze creatures."

Reece scrambles forward, shoving aside an Enforcer much taller than him. "You can't send all these Radicals through the Wall!"

I perk up. Someone willing to fight for us? Someone on our side?

"It's not your call, Reece."

"This land is precious." Reece rips off his earflap hat, as if to provide the Lead Enforcer with a better view of his determination. A few hairs, combed to one side, top his bald head, "Thrusting a thousand worthless Radical corpses through will *ruin* it!"

So much for an ally. He cares more about . . . *wasteland* than human lives?

"Your precious endangered penguins can go nest somewhere else."

"Did you know that it used to be illegal for anyone to even *relieve* themselves on this continent? Now we're talking about thousands of dead bodies!"

"We'll see how many die before we put them to work. Council's orders. It's the start of summer, they'll last a while. The work these Radicals will do here is for the good of the *world*. Besides, you have *this* side of Antarctica, Reece."

Reece crumples his earflap hat in his two fists. "How can this be allowed—?"

"Stations from other countries approved this. President Garraty wouldn't be able to send ship after ship of Radicals through this

Wall if he hadn't passed it through the United Assembly. Just get back to your research."

"While we destroy Antarctica from the other side?"

"The other side doesn't matter!" The Lead Enforcer gestures to another Enforcer. "Get him out of here, will ya?" Then he nudges my shoulder with his rifle. "Get going."

Mother is behind me. The rest of Unity crunches tighter into the room. Did she overhear what Brickbat said? Did she hear that they're going after Father and Tawny?

Then again, Brickbat said *hunt them down.* He doesn't know where they are.

"Get going!" The Lead Enforcer shoves me.

"Wait, can't you—"

He kicks me and I stumble forward. "You gave your answer to Council member Brickbat. You heard him—no changing your mind." He grabs a thin gun, presses it against Mother's arm, and presses the trigger.

I scream too late.

"Calm down!" the Lead shouts. "Everyone gets a tracking chip."

"Why?" I notice he doesn't give me one.

He thrusts Mother after me and the rest of the Unity group gets the idea. "To monitor your deaths, why else? Council said you already got one. Now *go.*"

Before I can respond, another Enforcer shoves me into the tunnel. I regain my balance and focus my attention forward. I step lightly down the tunnel, keeping my hand wrapped around the strap of my pack. What do I have in here? One rope. That's all that could possibly help us right now. What if the other side's a cliff like Opening Three?

Am I doing the right thing?

The walkway turns into carved stone and the light above ends in the dark. We're in the Wall. The rope railing continues and I run my fingers along it.

I walk ahead—first in the line of Radical sacrifice. Everyone follows. I imagine them looking to me for an answer, for life, for guidance.

What can I give them?

Dusten mutters from behind. "Eight months. Eight months. Eight months."

Is that right? Is his Clock his assurance to survival? Jude's voice in my head wars with my lifelong beliefs that the Clocks are never wrong. But just before Jude died—just before he inserted the pirate chip into his skull to save me from a toxined death—he said, *"I don't have faith in your Clock like you do. And I can't risk your life . . ."*

Then he died. Solomon said it's because Jude *let* the pirate chip terminate him.

So who's right?

Who's right?

Darker. Darker. I walk forward, oddly comfortable with the black mystery ahead. Despite the chill, this is familiar.

We reach the end and the exit door is closed. The rope railing is tied in a now-frozen knot to the last metal ring. I place my palm on the door and ice shoots through my nerves. We will freeze before we can even argue about survival.

The door slides open and I step back, away from the shine of light. After several blinks I make out the exit. Just like Opening Three, it's a long drop to the white winter earth below. Only instead of the door opening to an earthen cliff, this door is placed somewhere in the mid-range of the Wall. The drop is at least five hundred feet. Below are piles of trash, gunk, wood scraps, and tossed waste.

The rope in my pack is like a hair-ribbon compared to what we need to survive such a height. Mother's harsh breathing quickens, hitting the back of my neck. "W-what do we do?"

That is the question. What do we do before the Enforcers start shoving us out?

"It's easy," Cap growls. "We jump out and die until the pile of bodies is large enough to soften the fall for everyone else."

"You're sick," Dusten says.

Cap may be sick, but his comment is the most probable outcome unless we think of something fast. "We need to hurry. Anyone have an idea?"

Silence. I look up, and their faces petrify my heart. Every expression is one of frostbitten fear—pale and blank, with wide eyes. It is up to me.

"Wait here." I shove past them back toward the entrance of the tunnel.

"Wait here?" Cap screams from behind me. "For what? Our doom? Where are you going?"

I pull one of Father's chisels from a side pocket in my pack while sliding between the crowd of Unity villagers and the cold tunnel wall. I enter the lighted tunnel and get as close to the Enforcer room as possible. Six people stand between me and the Lead Enforcer. Kaphtor is one of them.

"Kaphtor," I breathe. I don't know why he's here, but I have to trust it's because he's on our side. His eyes slide from the heads in front of him to my face. I hold up the chisel. "Block me from view."

His brow corrugates, but I step to the rope railing, turn around as if I'm in line, and pick at the rope with minute movements. This rope is long. If I can free it from the first ring, I can slide it through the rest of the rings and we can use it to climb down.

Kaphtor steps close behind me so he's between me and the other Enforcers. The chisel just rebounds off the chunks of ice. The Lead Enforcer's voice echoes down the tunnel. "You have one day to build shelters for yourselves. Then we put you to work!"

My hand trembles and my fingers are cold. I find a new spot—a softer spot of rope.

"What's taking them so long?" an Enforcer asks from the entrance room.

The Lead laughs. "You've dumped enough waste there to know what's ahead of them. They're staring at their deaths right now. Give them a minute to accept it."

I chip through a piece of ice and a few threads come apart. *Faster. Faster.* Even if I finish it in time, the rope still may not be long enough.

"Sir, I beg your pardon but . . . they *stink*, can't we start pushing them through? The next load will be here soon anyway."

Oh God, no! Please! I pick at the strands, making little progress. It's frozen all the way through. Why oh *why* do I have only one hand?

"You've got a thirst for zeroes, don't you, Enforcer?" The Lead laughs again. "All right, go ahead."

21

Kaphtor yanks the chisel from my hand and hacks at the rope without a shred of secrecy. He has a rhythm: power and force. It takes him only a few strikes before the rope detaches from the frozen knot on the first ring.

"Hey, what are you doing?" an Enforcer yells.

A gunshot boxes my ears. Kaphtor drops the chisel and stumbles against the wall. Blood splashes the ice. Splashes me.

"Kaphtor!" He'd never been a friend until he started hacking the rope for me, but I don't want him to die.

The rope.

I grab the frayed end, shove it through the ring, and then run up the tunnel to the exit, pushing past frightened people. *God, please protect Kaphtor. Protect us all.* I reach the next ring and pull the rope through this time. It's getting heavy for a one-handed girl.

"Help me!"

No one does a thing. They just trample each other.

I approach the exit, dragging the rope along. It's looped over my arms, my neck, my shoulders. Freezing into my skin. It *must* be long enough.

The mob surges forward and several screams sever my control. The screams start loud and grow distant, until they're cut off.

"Stop shoving!" Dusten stands at the very edge, holding his hands out toward everyone. "You'll kill us all!"

But everyone's wide eyes tell me no one can control it. The Enforcers are doing it.

"Dusten," I gasp.

He doesn't look at me. I take the rope and toss it over the edge. It's knotted to the last and largest metal rung in the wall. *Please let it hold. Please let it be long enough.*

The rope yanks against the rung and then rests. "Okay, go!" I point to the rope, but don't push anyone in case someone else falls.

Cap shoves through those at the edge and grabs the rope. "Is it long enough?"

"Climb down and check."

He folds his arms. "Hmph!"

"For time's sake! If you won't save your own life, let someone else go!"

His glare would incinerate Wilbur Sherrod's Fire suit, but he climbs down anyway. Harman goes down a minute after him. People seem to process what we're doing and they fight for the rope, screaming. Another gunshot echoes down the tunnel and Frenchie jumps off the edge in a panic.

"No!" I reach for her, but she flails, managing to grab the rope mid-fall. She slams into Harman who's partway down. From far below, Cap screams. And I mean, *screams.*

I dare a glance. He's a twisted crumpled form on the pile of Antarctic rubbish below. He screams again. Good, he's alive.

"Harman, Angelique, help him." I don't wait to see if they heard. I can only hope Cap doesn't have a fatal injury. I catch my breath, then urge Mother and Dusten toward the edge. "Go. *Go!*"

The rope crackles and chunks of ice fly off. Dusten reels back. "It won't hold all of us!" The bodies press harder. Soon Dusten won't have a choice. Any minute he might be the one hurtling toward the icy ground. The crackles from the rope instill deeper mayhem.

"It's breaking!"

Frenchie and Harman scream.

Dusten clutches my shoulders. "It won't hold! What do we do?"

This is getting out of control. I shrug off his hands and give him the hardest stare I can muster. "It will hold." *It must hold.* "Now, climb down."

He faces the drop-off, pale. Trembling. It's amazing how easily he follows my command in this weakness of fear. I want to shriek at him to hurry, but am I any less terrified? He inches over the edge, sliding like a child and reaching for some sort of hold with his toes.

A loud pop comes from the rope.

"Parvin!" Dusten's screech is high and frantic. I'm struck by the weight of his reliance. Any ounce of logic would tell him I can do nothing to help, but he's looking to me. And I have only one option to which I can turn.

I place my hand on the knot—which is, more accurately, a bowling ball of ice—around the last metal rung and do the only thing that makes sense.

I pray over a nasty, frayed, frozen rope.

It stops making noise. The climbers stop screaming and resume their descent. I take my hand away and breathe a thank you to God.

Pop. A cord snaps, unfurling near the knot. I clutch it again. Deep breath. Okay. *I won't stop until all these people are down safe.*

Saying it to myself—or rather *praying* it—gives me a purpose. Direction. It feels right and freeing, like I'm passing the baton to God.

People swarm the rope faster than ants on a carcass. My hand tingles against the frozen grains. Stings. Burns.

The second container of people arrives with shouts and gunshots. Voices of alarm bounce among the tunnel. The Lead

Enforcer's command echoes a second time. "You have one day to build shelter! Then we put you to work!"

As they crowd me, I'm shoved against the icy wall. My hand almost slips off the knot and I almost let it. It's cold.

But I can't.

Something in me knows that, if I remove my hand and prayers, the rope won't hold. Isn't there a story in the Bible about some guy holding up his arms so people would win a battle? Maybe this is my turn.

Person after person descends the rope. After a while, I can't watch them anymore. I feel only the burning in my hand. I squeeze my eyes tight and pray with earnest. *Protect them all. Keep this rope together. Save Your people. Help Kaphtor.*

The hysteria lessens as climbers find a rhythm of survival. The Enforcers must be satisfied because no more gunshots reach my ears.

I lose track of how many groups of people pass me. My hand is numb. I dare not look at it, for fear of blue fingers and frostbite. Don't think about it. Think only of God. Think only of prayer.

God . . . I don't care if I have to lose my other hand. For the sake of these people, for the sake of shalom, I will sacrifice. Just use this to save them, to protect them, to show them You.

He's using me.

It's incredible. Powerful.

I drop to my knees, numb and spiritually depleted. No one pays me mind. They don't know what I am doing. It doesn't matter.

Sounds turn to distant humming. I'm here, but I'm not present. Voices, tromping, movement, and urgency—all a voided shadow to my mind. Deeper I crawl, closer to God. My soul heaves, overwhelmed with nearness. I'm too near to Him. I'm not near enough.

Is this what real faith looks like?

PARVIN.

I am here!

"Parvin."

I am here.

"Parvin?"

I lift my head, groaning at the pain the motion brings. A hundred blinks pass. A thousand blinks. Finally the darkness, the fuzz, the mist clears. Solomon kneels before me, Kaphtor draped over his shoulders. Solomon's hand rests atop mine. I don't feel it.

"I'll take it from here."

I shake my head and it seems to slosh. *No. I must do this.* I meant to say the words aloud. I lick my lips. My tongue barely works against the prolonged chill. "No. Help everyone until I can get there."

He nods, stands up, and takes the next spot in the jumbled, teeming line.

Solomon listened. He trusted me.

I return to my place of prayer with a mental flash. I don't try to speak. What can I say to my Creator that He doesn't know or hasn't already heard? No, I just rest in his presence—frozen before Him with strange, foreign peace.

I think hours pass. A flick to my forehead wakes me. I blink and try to swallow.

"She's alive!" The voice is muffled. A black coat swims before me. An Enforcer. The tunnel is empty.

"Well, send her down, then!" Whoever shouts this is at the entrance of the tunnel. "Then we can close the door and get back to the warmth."

The Enforcer beside me hauls me to my feet. My hand rips from the frozen knot, leaving a thick layer of skin behind. I cry out. I'm about to turn my eyes away from the blood now washing over the rope knot, when I see my hand imprint. Not only is there an imprint deep in the ice above the knot, but there's a burn *in* the knot...in the shape of my hand, as if my hand were made of fire and melted away half of the knot.

The Enforcer sees it too. "What . . . what did you do?"

I press my bleeding hand against my pant leg, but it meets ice. "Prayed."

He shoves me to the edge. Maybe the word makes him uncomfortable. "Climb down, Radical. And shut your mouth."

I don't know why his command and actions don't bother me. I find myself smiling. Does he have any idea what I just experienced?

I slip over the edge and grab the rope with my bloody hand. It doesn't sting right now, probably because it's frozen. I'll have only a few minutes before the pain and blood cause *some* sort of problem.

I hold the Enforcer's gaze for a breath. "I'm praying for you." Then I slide down several feet.

I was wrong. I don't have a few minutes before the pain gets to me. The pain is here. Now. Icy and hot all at the same time.

My descent smears blood along the top of the rope.

Don't look down. Just climb. Why was it so easy to sacrifice my hand and comfort for my people, but now that my own life depends on it I'm hesitant?

Climb down!

The rope rotates and groans. I slide another few feet. The grains—now worn from over a thousand Radicals climbing down it—cut into my raw palm. Slide. Wince. Slide. Groan. Slide. Scream.

I can't do it.

One of the cords snaps and drops down onto my head, hitting my ear. I almost let go.

"You're halfway, Parvin!" Solomon's voice sounds so far away. Halfway is still a death-drop.

"God." I grind the plea through my teeth. The rope turns again and the thick strands loosen. It rotates. They loosen more. I try sliding, but scream through my teeth. I have to try something else.

I wrap my left arm twice around in the rope. If only I had fingers on the end! *He is strong in my weakness.* No use bemoaning my missing hand right now. Or ever.

I wrap more rope around my leg, then use the other foot as a cinch to stop me from falling. When I think there's enough slack, I release my foot and slide again. This is too much for the rope. It groans just as the door above slides shut. In a moment of panic, I take my foot off and slide—no, *fall*—down the rope.

It snaps and I plummet.

Solomon catches me.

It's as simple as that . . . except that I flatten him. But when you're screaming, bleeding, and about to become bug guts on Antarctica's flyswatter, no amount of elbows, knees, or head-knocks will bother you.

We both lie on the ice and detritus—me on top of him, and his arms under my knees and back. My shoulder pack hangs off one of my arms. I can't get up yet—not until I can breathe.

His arms squeeze me. Tight. So very tight. He sits up and then kisses my forehead. "You're okay."

"You're okay, too?"

"Yes, but I can't say the same for everyone else here."

I climb off him and press my hand into the snow. It leaves a bloody print behind. Then I look up.

Chaos is a tame word compared to what's going on.

The different cities have gathered in their own groups, each one trying to make their own plan. Already, a few hundred people head away from the wall, following a beefy giant who's a foot taller than the rest. Snow mountains dot the white horizon. Is that where they're headed?

I stumble after them. "Wait!"

The leader stops and I catch up to him, Solomon trailing behind.

"You can't leave. You'll die!"

The man is almost seven feet tall, with a brown beard that reaches his belly. Despite our weeks of boxcar confinement, he still has a large gut. The people stand behind him, ready to follow him into the treacherous Antarctica wasteland.

"This place ain't any better," he says. "The Wall keeps us in shadow. Besides, we're not gonna wait to see if we survive long enough to be slaves. If we leave, we can find better shelter—maybe some caves—and possibly food. There are penguins here somewhere. Come with us."

"What if we find some way to escape? How would we notify you?" We *will* escape. I was in God's presence only minutes ago—there is a fire inside me now, one of unquenchable faith in His plan for our survival.

The hulk folds his arms, trapping his beard between his giant forearms. "Staying is madness." He looks me over. "And no teenage girl is gonna convince me otherwise."

"But . . . but I'm Parvin Blackwater."

He raises an eyebrow. "And I'm Rufus McTavish." He shrugs. "Now we're leaving. You're welcome to follow."

He doesn't know me. He doesn't trust me. I'm a nobody again.

McTavish walks away and his people follow. They grow smaller against the white backdrop. How can they leave? How can they think being apart is better?

"Let's return to those who need us." Solomon steers me back to the Wall. Desperate Radicals attempt to climb it. One man already fifty feet high loses his grip. He falls, and his scream splits the frigid air. Other people pile dead bodies up against the Wall, using them as steppingstones to get more height on the climbing attempts.

Some people argue in a huddle, others scrape together snow forts mixed with broken planks of wood and metal scraps from the piles beneath the Opening. The worst are those who have given up already, curled on the freezing ground, sobbing. The little girl from our boxcar tugs on her mom's arm, trying to get her to sit up.

Frenchie stands near a heap of rubble, toe-to-toe with Madame—the owner of *Faveurs.* "What are you *doing* 'ere?"

"I came after you, Angelique—"

Frenchie shoves Madame. "*Non!* I joined ze riot to *escape* you!"

"I joined that riot to *protect* you, Angelique, and look where it's gotten me."

"I am not your servant anymore. No one owns anyone in zis wasteland!" She turns on her heel and stomps away.

I thought Madame and Frenchie were a team, like a mother and daughter. I guess I was wrong.

"Come together!" I'm here now, we'll work something out. I will lead, even though I don't have a plan. "Let's figure out a plan!" God has one. All is not lost.

Some people from our boxcar group turn to me, but they don't approach. I frown. "I don't understand. Why won't they come together?"

Solomon's voice is gentle. "Many of these people have their own leaders. They don't know you yet. They're afraid. Just lead those whom you can, Parvin."

So much for being the leader. Even after I prepared myself because of Mother's advi—

I jerk my gaze to Solomon. "Where's Mother?"

He turns my face toward the Wall. A mixture of snow and wood forms a snow stable of sorts. The ground is covered in rotted planks from the debris pile and clothing stripped from the dead bodies. Wounded people lay atop it all. I must have been praying for several hours for them to have time to build this. Mother kneels beside two wounded at the end—one with Enforcer boots on, and the other screaming profanities as he clutches his leg.

"Cap broke his shin when he fell, and Kaphtor was shot in the thigh." Solomon lifts my bloodied hand to his face. "We'll get this wrapped up, too."

My injury pales against theirs, but we head toward Mother anyway.

It's quite different seeing our prison from the ground than from inside the Wall. The Wall is enormous—maybe even larger than the portion at Opening Three. Matted ice crystals protrude from the stone like spiky cement. I get the feeling that they don't melt during Antarctica's summer.

Beyond the people, after a long stretch of Wall, rests the ocean. The change from stone wall to projected Wall is distinct. The stone projection is smooth like paint. Unnatural. No crystals stick to it. I want to get closer and see how it works with the water.

We reach the makeshift infirmary, where Mother finishes tying a splint to Cap's leg. She glances up at us. "I'll need the blanket in your pack, Parvin, and your bandages."

No *hello* or *you survived?* That's Mother.

Solomon helps me get the blanket and extra bandages from my pack and hands them to her.

I study her face. "Are you okay?"

She throws a glance at Kaphtor, who's pale, bloody, and not fully conscious. "He has a tough wound. It's high on his thigh."

"He saved our lives."

Her lips tighten to a white line. "I'm doing my best."

"I know you are. But Mother . . . are *you* okay?"

Cap's head jerks up off Mother's wadded shawl. "Is *she* okay? My leg is broken! How can I escape now? You'll all have to carry me."

"One of the physicians set your leg," Mother says with force. "You'll be fine."

"Mother?"

"I'm fine." She doesn't look at me. Just lays the blanket over Kaphtor.

Cap eyes the blanket. "What about me?"

"You can scoot closer to Kaphtor and *share* his," Mother snaps. "He's an Enforcer."

"Who became a Radical and saved your life!" I almost kick his broken leg. Almost.

Cap uses his elbows to slide a few inches closer to Kaphtor.

Mother moves his broken leg for him, and he howls. She looks from Cap to Kaphtor. "The body heat will be good for the both of you."

She tosses a rolled-up bandage at me. Solomon's hand strikes out and catches it.

"This blanket smells weird." Cap turns his nose away.

Mother turns to me again. "I love you. Be strong."

It's hard to swallow. "Okay."

We walk out and Solomon scoops up snow. I hold my palm out, dreading the chill that will touch my skin. Now that my adrenaline rush is gone, the cold washes back in. Solomon presses the snow together in his bare hands. Some of it melts from his body heat—how does he have body heat right now?—and drips onto my torn skin.

"It's warmer here than I expected it to be." Still frigid, but not instant death.

Solomon cleans the wounds as best he can. "It's Antarctica's summer. I'd say we'll experience low thirties temperature-wise for a while. And since it probably won't get dark…it's the best we could have asked for."

I glance around. "Do you think…we'll freeze?"

He unrolls the bandages. His movements are kind and careful. I hope he takes his time. "I think if the people calm down and get to work, keeping their body heat up, we have a decent chance to keep warm long enough to escape."

Before he gets the bandage on, people from Unity besiege us.

Dusten gets to me first. "What do we do?" He shakes me by the shoulders. "How do we survive?"

"Hey!" Solomon knocks Dusten's hands away. "Stop that."

People surround me—Madame, Dusten, Frenchie. Looking at me. Glaring. Waiting. What in the world do I tell them? Why do they think I have any idea on how to survive?

"I think it's time you told us why you keep getting special treatment." Madame folds her arms tight around her body. "Who were you talking to with the Lead Enforcer before we all came in?"

I close my eyes and suck in a breath through my nose. It sticks to my nose hairs. "The Council has been trying to get me to return to the USE." There. Now they know.

"So you *are* on the Council's side!"

I start. "No! I didn't ask for any of this."

Madame takes a step closer, but Solomon holds a hand out—my personal bodyguard. It doesn't faze her. "They want you to survive. You're their pet, which makes you our enemy."

"I'm not their pet!" How can they understand that the Council has used me falsely to represent them? Curse Skelley Chase. Curse Brickbat.

"We're watching you, Parvin Blackwater."

"Watch away, Madame," I snap. "Maybe my actions will finally show you I *am* on your side."

She rolls her eyes. I shouldn't have lost my temper. Mother said I'd need to be patient as a leader, but don't leaders have to be firm, too?

The rest of the crowd hangs around, maybe waiting for some amount of direction "Look," I say. "I've never been to Antarctica either, but we can't just mope around. We'll all freeze—"

"No we won't." Madame gives a disdainful sniff. "I had a Clock before the government smashed it. It had thirty-one more years on it. I'm not gonna freeze."

"Neither am I," someone pipes up.

"Or me! I have thirteen years."

"Sixty-two!"

"Nine."

I don't want to talk about their Clocks and whether or not they should trust them.

"Are you really willing to bet your *survival* on your old Clocks?"

The little girl inches toward the front of the crowd with her mother behind her. Their lips are blue and the girl is trembling. I remove my bleeding hand from Solomon's grip, take off my scarf using two fingers, and hand it to her.

"*I'm* not willing to bet your survival on your Clocks. I want us to live, so we need to think of how we'll escape."

The little girl wraps the scarf twice around her face. Her mother seems more attentive to my words.

"We need to build shelters, like the Enforcer guy said." Dusten glances at my hand. Blood drips off my white, frostbitten fingers to the ground. He gags.

We don't have time for shelters. I'm about to say so, but Solomon chimes in. "I agree. The movement will keep you warm while we brainstorm."

"But other people are leaving!" Frenchie says. "Shouldn't we go with zem?"

"We should stay together." This is the only thing I'm certain about.

"For now, focus on the shelters." Solomon's voice is commanding, like a Lead Enforcer's. It doesn't frighten me. It calms. Tangible guidance and plans are what we need. "Cram as many people into a shelter as possible. Body heat is your main source of warmth. The Enforcers are probably monitoring us and if it looks like we're cooperating, they won't make things harder. Think of how to escape while you work."

They have a mission and they jump at it. "I 'ave a layered dress," Frenchie says. "We can cut ze layers into strips to tie pieces of wood together."

"I've got a knife in my pack." Harman lifts his pack off his shoulders. "Bring the cloth to me."

"Here." I toss them a few of Father's chisels to help cut material.

"We should get the rest of the clothing from the people who died." Dusten says it quietly, as though concerned about our reactions.

I nod. "Warmth and survival are our main concerns. Dusten's right." My observers scatter to start their work. I breathe easier.

Solomon tugs me away from them. "Let's get you bandaged." Careful not to touch the wound, he brings my fingers to his lips and breathes on them. I barely feel a difference, but the action warms my core for a blink.

"It's so cold." It's a dumb statement, like saying the sky is blue or the Council is evil.

"I know. We don't have long."

Now freed from the crowd, from the Wall, and from the boxcar, my mind returns to other thoughts. More pleasant thoughts, almost as an escape. "I liked your notes."

Solomon grins. The cheer doesn't fit the situation, but it shows me his strength. He can cling to joy. I wish I could do that.

"Solomon . . . how did you—what happened?" It's been over four weeks since we were in Prime together. I thought the Council had found him and locked him away. Did he learn anything from his father?

"I ought to make *you* tell me what happened. You walked out that apartment door and never came back. Next thing I knew, you were being Clock-matched on every X-book, post board, and video screen around."

I turn my face toward the workers where people are toiling together on a few shelters. Some wandering Radicals from other villages join in. "I know. I'm sorry."

I gave in. I gave in to the Council and he saw it.

His hand moves up to my forearm and squeezes. "I don't blame you. I just thought, maybe you'd . . . maybe the Council had . . ." He pulls the bandage a little too tight and I flinch. "Sorry."

He loosens the tie. "Anyway, I managed to trail you and the Enforcers leading you to the train station, but lost you once they took you on board. Since Willow wasn't with you, I assumed the Council still had her. I had to hope you were being taken home."

He meets my eyes in earnest. "You have to know, I would have checked but . . . I knew you were worried about Willow, so I went after her instead."

"Thank heavens. Did you find her?"

He ties off the bandage and I wiggle my fingers. It stings and aches up my entire arm, but my body relaxes against the pain now that it's wrapped and somewhat clean.

"I found out which orphanage they've taken her to—the one Jude got involved with." His voice recedes into a guttural growl.

"That's where the Council tested his Clock invention on the orphans." I choke. "Brickbat threatened to kill Willow if I didn't get Clock-matched."

Solomon rubs the back of his neck with one hand. "That orphanage is in northern New York, near where my father lives. It took me a while to travel up there. Dad and I visited the orphanage from afar. Enforcers surround it now, and the Council will be sending Clock-matchers there soon. I don't know if they'll experiment."

"I'd assume not, since they've already released the new Clocks to the public." It's odd talking to him—watching him grow upset. I want him to feel like we're on the same team.

"Dad's watching over the orphanage and Willow. I traveled back to Unity Village, finally managing a train ticket. When I arrived, most of the town people were gone. Oliver—excuse me, your *father*—and Tawny told me what you and your mother did. This is all very brave of you, Parvin."

Heat rises in my chest and my cheeks—a combination of embarrassment and growing anger. This isn't about bravery, it's about being *forced* by the Council. "So I'm brave for joining a bunch of doomed people to come to a wasteland. But what about *you*, Solomon? I told you not to come. What can you do now? Who's there for Willow?"

Brickbat's going after her! He's going to test her until her brain turns to mush!

I AM THERE.

The reminder soothes me. Of course God's there, just like He is here so tangibly.

"My dad is. And you will be, too when we escape." He glances up at the sky. "I left my NAB with Oliver."

"Father?" I almost laugh. "He doesn't know how to use a NAB!" And there go our chances of trying to contact someone on the other side—like Solomon's dad—to alert them about the Council's threats.

Solomon gives a half smile. "Neither did you at one time. I showed him the basics. Now he can contact Fight or Idris if he needs help. And, if we find someone here with a NAB, we can send him updates."

He rests his hands on my shoulders and stands there for a moment. I try to calm down. God is going to get us out of here. He'll free us.

"Now we need to save these people."

That's all. Just save an entire social class of people who don't even view me as a leader. Can I blame them? "Solomon, do you think they can die? Or do you believe what Jude did—that the Clocks can't control our deaths?"

He looks around, then lowers his voice. "I found something else out."

My pulse doubles. "What?"

"Jude was working on a . . . a glitch in the new Clocks. Dad told me. Apparently, after the Council tested his original Clock-matching on the orphans, Jude created a *new* Clock. One that . . . added something."

My mouth goes dry. "Added what?"

Solomon shakes his head, and I want to grab him by the shoulders, but that's all he knows. He'd tell me if he knew more . . . wouldn't he?

"Whatever it is, I think it's how he died. He used his new Clock as one final test to see if his invention worked."

As he says this, a memory surfaces of that fateful evening with the assassin. "Jude said something." I grab his arm. "When the assassin gave him the pirate chip, Jude said, *'You'll get your information . . . and I'll get mine.'* Do you think that's what he meant? That he was testing his new Clock?"

"He could have."

If only Solomon knew more! "But if Jude *knew* about this glitch, wouldn't the Council know too, since they stole information from his brain with the pirate chip?"

A shiver runs through Solomon's body, but it has nothing to do with the conversation. We've been standing still too long. "Dad talked to a fellow physician and discovered that Jude had a procedure done just before going through the Wall. He had a brain surgeon destroy the parts of his brain that harbored the new Clock glitch. It couldn't have been stolen no matter *what* the pirate chip downloaded."

"So all the Clocks being distributed to the citizens of the USE have this glitch . . . whatever it is?"

"I think so. We'll figure it out, Parvin."

A humorless laugh escapes. "We better. And we better escape before those Enforcers put us to work. Who knows *how* they'll use us."

No wood. No fire. No food.

No time.

That is our supply list. It's been a few hours and a handful of shelters are completed in a circle. The completed igloo huts—wonky and asymmetrical—are packed with people. They huddle with their backs to the walls, breathing their body heat into the communal air. No one builds anymore.

We're too cold.

How do I lead, God? What am I supposed to do? The sun cycle is different here. Will it get dark at all? If not, then we may keep our body heat a little longer. But without fire, food, or decent shelter . . . everyone's Clocks will be sorely tested.

I can't feel my nose, ears, toes, or fingers anymore, even beneath the hand bandage. Every breath pinches my lungs.

"We've all brainstormed and come up with nothing." Mother blows into her hands. "We need to escape. The shelters are a good idea, but they'll only last for so long."

She's right. "Let's find Solomon."

Solomon scoops snow from inside a half-finished dome. I kneel beside him and peer in. It's almost completely hollow. "Hey."

He looks up. A small white line mars the skin above his cheeks. "Good sunset, Parvin."

"You have frostbite on your cheeks."

One of his hands—wrapped in a sock—lifts to tap his cheeks. "So do you. And everyone else."

Cheeks aren't the only victims. Mother has some frostbite on her fingers and everyone's noses are turning redder and redder. "Why aren't you using the wood for a shelter?"

"Because snow will do just as well and wood may serve better as a fire for people to warm at."

Could there be enough wood to burn? "Any ideas on escape?"

He leans back on his heels. "I think we need to return to the cargo ship."

I cup my hand over my mouth and breathe twice, letting the warmth rebound on my face. "How?"

"I have an ice pick in my bag."

"For . . . climbing?"

He chuckles. "That's generally what they're used for. I tried to pack in preparation for Antarctica, but only the ice pick made sense. All the extra clothing I packed for warmth got soaked when I jumped into the ocean. It never really dried and now it's frozen."

"So . . . escape. Do you plan to climb up the Wall? Smash through the door, maybe?" I've already seen people trying to climb that beast. I loathe the idea of him trying . . .

And falling.

"It'd be hard with only one pick, but I'll do what I must."

Does he even think he *can?*

A gust of wind blows snow dust in a cyclone around each igloo. I tuck my head into my arms and suck in air through my teeth. That's cold. Too cold. Deathly cold.

Mother nudges us. "Let's go inside and talk for now."

"Okay." My voice comes out muffled through my arms.

Mother, Solomon, and I crawl into the hollowed dome. It's not dark, as I suspected it would be. Light shines through in a pale, icy blue. A torn tarp covers most of the floor. It's still cold, but no longer wet. The snow walls block the wind.

Mother pulls her shawl up over her head and wraps it tight around her face, leaving only her eyes uncovered. Her voice is muffled, but still understandable. "Some men talked of going to the ocean—to the projected Wall—to see if we can get through there."

Solomon shakes his head. "You can't."

"Well, your great-grandfather or something i-invented it." I tuck my stump and hand under my armpits. "D-Don't you know how it works or how to get past it?"

"I don't know much about it, Parvin, only that it's programmed against human DNAs. Everything else can go through, but a human would be killed."

"We have to try."

"Trying could mean someone's death."

I lean against the igloo wall, then recoil from its chill. "So could *not* trying. It's not that far away. Besides, the movement will keep us warmer. *And* there might be penguins there to . . . eat."

He rests his forearms on his knees. "The Enforcers are probably watching us. They'll have cameras."

"They didn't stop McTavish from leaving." Maybe they think he'll return. Or die. "I don't think the Enforcers care about us. They don't think escape is possible."

He sighs. "The projected Wall is impassable."

"I saw it flicker." Only as I say it do I remember this. "It flickered while I stared at it from the cargo ship." Not long enough for me to see through it or for a person to pass through but . . . maybe it means something. "Is it supposed to flicker?"

Solomon is silent for a breath. "No. It's not."

I sit straight, releasing my back from the frozen wall. "It's not? So maybe something's wrong with it!"

"Don't tell people. Don't give them false hope. At least, not yet."

It's too late. I've already given myself hope. "I'm going."

"You should rest first. Even the healthiest of us can't trek to the ocean and back without some recuperation."

"Rest?" Is he not as cold as the rest of us? "I'll freeze! I'll never fall asleep."

"Just wait until you close your eyes. The prolonged daylight is tricking your body into thinking it has stamina. You must rest, Parvin."

A yawn gives me away. "No."

"Ten minutes."

"No!" People are freezing out there. "I need to move around."

Mother places a hand on my arm "Just ten minutes, Parvin."

I sigh. "Fine." I need them on my side and, in truth, I trust these two people more than anyone else in the world. If they think I should sleep, then I will.

But . . . didn't Mother want me to lead? To take charge? How will sleeping accomplish that?

"Don't sleep alone, Parvin." Solomon buttons the top button on his coat. "It would be much too cold for you."

My stomach flip-flops. He's not suggesting that *we*—

"I'll go find others to join you and your mother."

"Okay," I squeak. What's wrong with my brain? Of course Solomon wouldn't suggest that we sleep together. And I wouldn't want it. Well, I *would* . . . wait, would I? Not unless we were, like, married. *Okay, stop.*

I take a deep breath to tie up my thought strings. Solomon was right—I'm definitely tired.

Frenchie and Madame join Mother and me in the small igloo hut. Frenchie glares daggers at Madame the entire time, but we squish together anyway, all curled up and tucking our faces and hands into each other's coats. Solomon stays outside to finish packing in the entrance hole.

This is ridiculous. We have *one day* before the Enforcers start putting us to work. I'm too cold to rest. To think. To sleep.

The icy ground sends its chill through the tarp and my thin garments in minutes. I wiggle closer to Mother. I manage to drift away from this nightmare for what seems like seconds before Solomon nudges my shoulder.

Ten minutes are up, and I feel half dead, both from cold and exhaustion.

"I'll meet you by the infirmary," he whispers, then ducks out.

Mother, Frenchie, and Madame still sleep. I don't want to move for fear of waking them, but I'm so cold. Stiff. Everything is numb, but I'm not dead.

I sit up slower than a waking flower. As I detach from the imprint I left against Mother's side a chill air rushes into the space. I shiver. Something inside me flutters, panicky. A quick scan of the three bodies resting with me reveals puffs of breath above each head.

Good.

But even with them breathing, if they're anywhere near as cold as I am, I ought to wake them soon and get them moving. Blood flow and food—our two lifelines.

Food.

If I don't eat the potatoes in my bag soon, they'll go old and I will have wasted them. I have only a handful, but I need to share them. We need to eat. I can't pick and choose who should eat and who shouldn't. Instead, I go with those in front of me. My new Antarctica family.

I leave a potato next to each of them and eat half of one myself. I put the other in my pocket for Solomon. Before I leave, Mother's croak comes from the ground. "Two hours."

I smile. "Two hours." Then I crawl out of the hut. It's silly giving the familiar valediction when neither of us relies on the Clocks anymore. Old habits die hard, I guess. At least she's counting on my return.

I hope we're gone only two hours.

As I head to the infirmary, I try wiggling my toes, but they feel thick and sausagey, sending painful zings into my foot. On my way, I find Dusten digging through one of the giant trash heaps.

"Hey, Dusten."

He starts. "Oh, hi."

"Why are you out here alone? Aren't you cold?"

"I'm getting wood for a fire. Your Enforcer guy said we'd build a fire and then head to the projected Wall."

I pull the collar of my shirt up over my nose with my bandaged hand. "You're coming?" He nods. "I was about to do some jumping jacks to help me warm up for the walk. Want to join me?"

"That's weird."

I could take offense, but instead I laugh. "It'll keep us warm."

"Whatever."

I do a few jumping jacks. It feels a little silly, especially since I'm winded after ten of them. "Come on."

He rolls his eyes and joins in. We do some more jumping jacks, facing each other. I can't help watching him do them. He watches me for an awkward jump or two, then laughs. I laugh.

We both stop jumping and laugh, avoiding each other's eyes. I'm sure our humor is based on hysteria, but who cares? On impulse, I pull the half a potato from my pocket and hand it to him. "Here, have breakfast . . . dinner . . . whatever." The sky is still bright. What time *is* it?

"Oh, thanks."

We stand there a moment, staring at the stretch of Wall. "Maybe while we're by the sea, we'll get some penguins to eat. Or even a polar bear."

"Idiot. Polar bears exist only at the *North* Pole."

"Oh." I look at my feet.

He swallows a chunk of potato with a grimace. "Besides, I don't want to stay here long enough to cook a single meal. We need to get out of here." His voice is fierce. "I need to do something. I know I'm going to die soon but . . . I can't die here. Not here."

I set my wrapped hand on his arm. "We'll escape."

He nods and takes another bite of potato. He chews for a very long time before managing what looks like a forced swallow. "Is Angelique coming?"

"I don't know. Maybe. I'll ask her."

"Where is she?" Dusten seems so hopeless. Even when he laughed, it came out hollow.

I gesture to the snow domes. "Sleeping in my hut with Madame and my mother."

Solomon walks up and tilts his head at Dusten. "Jumping jacks were a good idea. We ought to do have everyone do those to keep them warm."

Dusten shrugs. "Yeah."

"Let's stack another armful of wood chunks in the center of that hut circle, then we'll go."

I hold my arms out. "Load me up."

Solomon stacks icy planks on my forearms until they reach my chin. We take our wood to a giant pile in the center of the ring of completed huts. Solomon uses the matches from my pack, but the wood doesn't catch. It's too frozen.

He strips away smaller pieces, using them for kindling. Still, the fire doesn't catch. We spend the next ten minutes gathering lint from clothing and small sticks from the debris pile. Finally, after fifteen minutes and half my matches, the fire catches. We add wood to it carefully until it's a bonfire. I expect people to argue, to blame him for using good material.

Instead, everyone gathers around the warmth. Some people cry.

I almost cry.

Solomon straightens and speaks to those around the fire. "Don't let this go out."

My nose thaws and my toes tingle so fiercely I'm sure they're cracking to pieces.

"The group is already down there." Solomon points to the sea in the distance. "You sure you want to go? I don't think we'll find anything out."

The heat is too nice. Too soothing. *Do* I want to go?

Dusten starts jogging toward the ocean. "Come on, already."

"I'll catch up," Solomon tells me, then heads toward Mother's hut.

I'm too cold to protest, so I jog after Dusten. Muscles in my feet pinch at the impact. I run lightly on my tiptoes until the discomfort lessens, then I increase my speed to join him.

Solomon catches up soon, Frenchie and Madame in tow. Frenchie runs with her arms around her torso, trying to combat the wind our own movement causes.

It doesn't take long before we slow to a walk. I take deep breaths, but they're so cold they hurt my lungs. I put my hand over my mouth and breathe in the warm, rebounded air. "Mother didn't want to come?"

"She's staying with the wounded, specifically Caprine and Kaphtor. There is a thick blanket covering two men no one likes. She could not leave them alone."

The ocean looks no closer, but when I glance back, our makeshift Radical village is barely visible. It takes us ten minutes to reach the sea and my toes are completely numb by the time we approach.

We crawl over boulders of ice, following the Wall down an incline toward the ocean. There is no shore when the Wall turns into the projection, just a drop-off of ice into ocean water. Penguins speckle the blue sheen like dropped crumbs.

The connection of stone Wall to projected Wall is seamless. No gap. The projected Wall travels from one giant pole to another. Each pole floats on a buoy, spaced several hundred feet apart. The line of them disappears out to the horizon. I count only three or four before the ocean mist blocks them from view.

We join the group on the edge of the ice, a few feet higher than the ocean. The projected Wall is mere yards away. The group of people who came here earlier is smaller than I thought. One man turns to us. "There're no gaps between the projection and the stone."

"I knew it," Solomon mutters.

Out of the corner of my eye, I see Frenchie take Dusten's hand. His knuckles turn red as he squeezes hers. Madame plants her hands on her hips. "Now what?"

"Should we touch the projection?" Dusten asks.

"It's the one thing we haven't tried," someone says.

"No!" Solomon holds his arms out as if to keep us from rushing toward it. "It's programmed against human DNA."

Dusten picks up a snowball. "How do you know that?"

"He's a Hawke." I recall the little bit of Hawke family history Mother told me.

"I don't see no wings." Dusten laughs at his own joke.

I sigh. "His great-grandfather invented the projected Wall. Inventions run in the Hawke family line."

Solomon closes his eyes for a moment, almost as if I said something I shouldn't have. Dusten hurls his snowball at the projection. It sails through and disappears. No one moves. I don't even blink. What did I expect? That it would smash into it like snow against real stone?

"Um . . ." Dusten licks his lips. "You sure a human can't go through?"

"Give it a try," Madame says. "It's the word of an Enforcer against us. He might still be on their side. After all, he wasn't captured with us. He volunteered."

That's not fair. Solomon wants to save everyone as much as I do. "Solomon Hawke is a respectable man. He was stripped of his Enforcerhood trying to help us."

"Yeah, but"–Dusten waves to me—"you're his girlfriend. That's the whole reason he came. It doesn't mean he's on *our* side."

My jaw drops. "No, I'm—"

"It doesn't matter." Solomon opens his eyes. "Unless you're willing to die, no one should touch the projection."

"So . . . what's *under* the projection?" Dusten pulls Frenchie's hand to his chest. "How far down does it go?"

I take a careful step to the edge and peer into the water. Solomon's hand wraps around my arm, firm and safe. The icy water is at rest, but no Wall or projection is visible. "I don't see anything."

"Me either," Dusten says. "Wait, look! That fish just swam away through the Wall!"

Fish? "Can fish live in this water? Isn't it too cold?"

"I know I saw it."

Solomon pulls me back. "It doesn't matter. Let's stop talking about crossing the projection and instead look for kinks between it and the stone Wall."

"We already looked," a group member says.

"Can we break down the projection somehow?" I stare at the wall. "I *did* see it flicker." But the flicker was like lightning—too fast for anyone to take advantage of.

Madame raises an eyebrow and appraises Solomon. "I think he's keeping something from us. Why don't you want us to test it, Mr. Hawke?"

His hand squeezes my arm. "Because I don't want anyone to die."

"You're an Enforcer. Death's never bothered you before."

Solomon's face grows red.

I step toward Madame and he releases me. "You don't know anything about Solomon. He came to Unity Village to try and *fix* the unjust Enforcer problem."

Dusten sniggers. "Told you she was his girlfriend." To my horror, he throws his coat on the ground, then kneels down to unlace his boots.

"Dusten"–I swallow hard—"what are you doing?"

"What do you think, Empty Numbers? I'm gonna swim under that projection. I'm gonna be the first one to escape." Frenchie stands next to him, twisting her fingers together. Her lips are tight.

I kneel next to Dusten and press my bandaged hand to stop his trembling fingers from messing with his bootlaces. "Dusten." My voice is quiet. I hope only he hears me. "I know you pride yourself in being the first. You were the first to register for a new Clock, the first to join all the school sports, and the first to come talk to me when I returned. But . . . do you really want to be the first of our group to die?"

He stares at me, colorless and shivering. His wide gaze darts back and forth, searching my eyes. Can he see my concern for him? Will he let pride lead him to his death? *Please, God, let him trust Solomon's judgment.*

"I wish I *could* die, but I'm trapped here until this thing runs out." He presses his thumb and forefinger to his Clock band until the Numbers glow in the air above his name. "I'm tired . . . tired of waiting for my zeroes." He pushes my hand away and the thin metal Clock band—thinner than even a spider's strand—catches a glint of the sun.

Fire claws the back of my throat and I don't try to stop the pressure of tears. In fact, I urge them to drop, to show Dusten I mean what I'm saying. "Jude changed something about these Clocks—I don't know what it is but . . . what if you die?"

His voice comes out hoarse and broken. "I can't zero out over here, Parvin. I can't. Not on this side. Not without trying to escape."

Now my tears fall, but it's too late. I'm the only one stopping him. Everyone else's curiosity is too strong—they're willing to let him die.

Dusten slips off his boots.

"No, wait." My bandaged fingers fumble for his. "Do you . . . do you know what will happen to you, if you die? Do you . . ." For time's sake, why is this so hard? "Do you have any faith in . . . God?"

His lower lip trembles. "I'll be fine. I . . . I read your biography and . . . I saw you pray over that rope." Then, as if realizing he's being transparent and vulnerable, he shoots to his feet. "All righty, step aside, boys."

Solomon blocks his way. "Don't do this."

"Move, Enforcer."

"No."

"I'll take you into the water with me, if you want."

What should I do? Why is no one else doing anything? "Dusten could die." I hold Frenchie's gaze. "Don't you care?"

"*Move*, Enforcer!"

Maybe if Solomon and I tackle him at the same time . . .

"Fine." Solomon brushes past Dusten, hands in tight fists, and strides away . . . from all of us.

No, he can't go. He's the only sense left. "Solomon." I hiss his name in a reprimand, as if no one else will hear me.

He keeps walking. This departure is so unlike what I've come to know about him that I just stand and watch him leave. Chills zoom up and down my skin, skidding to a halt when a giant splash breaks the tension.

I spin around. All that's left of Dusten is a pile of clothes on the snow. "Solomon, come back!" I scream over my shoulder and run to the edge of the ice with Frenchie, Madame, and the others.

Dusten heads straight down, his feet kicking madly. He must be freezing. Even if he resurfaces, how will we get him warm again before he dies? Can we get him back to the fire in time?

I squint against the ripples. He stops kicking and releases a gale of bubbles. I can't see him clearly, it's deep and dark blue down there. Just a ripple of skin here and there.

He's moving. Swimming toward the Wall?

The projection flickers with a loud buzz and a shock runs through me. Every hair stands on end. I look up and see through to the other side for a moment—the cargo ship still floats with its motorboats on the shore. Then the Wall projection returns. Solid.

The water is smooth like glass, all except a small wavelet close to the Wall. A dark form moves beneath the blue glass. Closer. Clearer. Floating up to us.

Dusten's body breaks the surface . . .

. . . charred and black like coal.

24

He's dead.

He's dead and it's my fault. *Our* fault. Solomon's fault.

I don't collapse—not like when Jude or Reid died. I'm in a strange zone of disconnection. We fish Dusten from the water, two men doing most of the pulling. I don't bother to see if Solomon's returned.

He left us.

Frenchie doesn't watch, doesn't help, and doesn't seem to care.

We lay Dusten on his coat. It feels cruel to let his skin—blackened as it is—rest against something so harsh as the ice. I try to resuscitate him. My mouth against his. Breathe out, pump his chest, breathe out, pump his chest. Why won't my muscles work like they should? Too cold.

I did this to Jude once and he vomited on me.

What I would give to have Dusten react the same way. *Come back.* He didn't want to die here. "It's not fair!"

I don't understand, God. Why would You let him die like this?

I breathe again into his lungs and my disconnection evaporates. Maybe it's impossible to stay disconnected when skin touches skin. I cry and pump his chest with my stump and bandaged hand. I loathe those watching me. Why don't *they* try?

Ten minutes pass and I'm soaking wet and shivering by the end of it—both from tears and the salt water clinging to his thin layer of clothing. He doesn't even look like Dusten when I sit back on my heels and stare at his face. Black veins crawl all over his crinkled, charred skin. It's not black like the dark, creamy black of Kaphtor's complexion. It's like nighttime, death—harsh and unforgiving. Out of place.

"We have to take him back," I say.

"Absurd," Madame says.

"*You* urged him to do this, Madame! We *will* take him back. When we escape, we will take him with us and bury him in freedom on the other side."

Frenchie's eyes don't leave Dusten's face as she speaks. "What does zis mean?" She crouches by Dusten and lifts his Clock hand.

The blue projected Clock illuminates the air, his Numbers red and counting with his name beneath them.

Counting.

000.256.02.10.09
000.256.02.10.08
000.256.02.10.07

But beneath them is a new word in all capitals: *OVERRIDDEN*.

Frenchie drops his hands and looks up at me. "What does zis *mean?*"

I check his pulse one last time. Overridden. I try to swallow and my throat makes a funny pop sound. "It . . . it means he's dead . . . and the new Clocks can be . . . overridden." Jude's invention worked. The Clocks aren't foolproof anymore.

"Zat can't be right. Ze Clocks are never wrong."

"His is wrong."

Madame shouts. "It *can't* be wrong! Don't you understand? The Wall projection did something to him. It confused his Clock or . . . something."

So it begins. "He's dead. Trust me. I've seen dead. Let's carry him back."

"You're wrong." Two men kneel beside Dusten, neither of whom are from Unity Village. They hoist Dusten up between them. His limp body folds and contorts as they figure out a less-awkward way to carry him. I look away.

Dusten is dead before the end of his Clock. What does this mean for the rest of the world? Solomon was right. Jude tricked the Council.

Is the Council refitting everyone with faulty Clocks?

We trudge back. Solomon's nowhere in sight. A few others travel up the shore with some of my chisels and come back with dead penguins tied together at the feet. Their blood leaves a trail in the snow.

I hate death. Not the aftermath—the hope of heaven or the peaceful departure from the world—I simply hate the fact that death happens in harsh ways. Bloody ways. Suffocating ways.

The snow-hut village comes into view, with lines of people doing jumping jacks, facing the fire. It blazes even hotter. People seem cheered.

I don't see Solomon. A surge of anger drowns me. How could he leave? How could he move aside and allow Dusten to kill himself? Did his . . . *pride* get in the way?

He didn't come back when I called to him.

This is his fault more than anyone's.

We arrive back at the clump of snow huts, sweating. I'm sweating, yet I'm still freezing. Trembling. Hardly able to catch a breath against the cold. Strands of my hair are frozen from the salt water it gathered when trying to resuscitate Dusten.

The two men carrying Dusten drop to their knees. Dusten flops off their shoulders into the snow. The clump of penguins is tossed into the center of the ring of huts. One by one, people emerge and I want to be anywhere but here.

Frenchie strides to the center of the growing circle of people, standing between the fire and Dusten's body. She activates Dusten's Clock. "Look! He still 'as time left, but he eez *dead!*"

So much for breaking the news gently and avoiding panic. Where is Mother? Where is Solomon? I need their help to combat what is about to happen.

"What does this mean?" someone asks.

The circle of confusion grows. I force myself to meet people's eyes, but they're not looking at me yet. They stare at Dusten's Numbers, projected into the air—red Numbers against a blue transparent backdrop.

OVERRIDDEN.

"Are you sure he's dead?" Mother stands across from me, holding her shawl tight around her shoulders. I breathe easier with her presence and give a curt nod.

"That must not be his Clock," a man from the crowd mumbles.

"But eet has 'is name on eet!"

The murmuring grows. With the escalating sound, gazes rise—leaving Dusten's black corpse and fixing on . . . me.

"What does this mean?" asks the mother of the little girl in our container. "You brought the new Clocks to the Council. How can Dusten be dead?"

Um, God? Aren't you going to infuse me with inspired words? There is no inspiration. There is no Solomon to speak for me. Where is he? There is no sound except my heartbeat slamming in my ears so hard I get a headache.

I must speak.

Again.

"I didn't give the Council the new Clock information. They stole it from a man I met in the West. His name was Jude." I choke on his name. "He invented the new Clocks and, when the Council tested them by torturing orphans, Jude took his invention and fled across the Wall."

I take a deep breath and shudder more from emotion than from cold. "That's when I met him. He told me that our faith shouldn't be in the Clocks, that we should trust God with our lives. He is greater than the Clocks."

"Get to the point." Cap, his leg splinted, joins the group, supported by Harman. "How did Dusten die?"

"Should we believe any of this?" Madame whispers to him. "Remember, she worked with the Council."

I turn my back on them and face those circled behind me. "The Council found Jude in the West. Jude *gave* them his Clock invention information, but I think . . . I think he changed the Clocks—"

Where is Solomon? He would have so many more answers!

"—changed them so they can be overridden . . . by us."

How much of this is fact and how much is speculation? Jude gave the assassin the Clock information to save my life, but there had to be something else to it—and Dusten's death confirms that. Jude wouldn't sacrifice the lives of thousands of Radicals all for me.

Jude and Dusten have proven that there's something faulty in the Clocks.

"Overridden?" Cap lowers himself onto a chunk of ice at the edge of the circle, holding the single blanket tight around his shoulders. "So any of us could die at any moment? Even if we had a Clock once? Or is it just the new Clocks?"

"I don't have all the answers. But I can tell you this: life isn't about the day we die. Our focus should be on *right now*."

"Shut up." He throws a chunk of ice at me. "You act so above us, as if you're exempt from death."

I square my shoulders. "I'm not exempt. I could die *any minute*, but I've finally learned how to live. And it has nothing to do with knowledge of Numbers or death."

That's as far as I get before people ignore me completely. The foundations of their lives rest on the concept of Clocks. I'm ripping that foundation to unrecognizable pieces. I can't expect them to absorb what I'm saying just like that.

The last time I crossed the Wall, I thought I'd die, but I didn't. God wanted me to survive for something more. How can I fear death *now?* Mine *or* my people's? I must be strong. I must have faith.

"We are all going to die!" Cap buries his head in his arms. Frenchie sinks to her knees and a few others slump to the ground.

"He *can't* be dead." Madame nudges Dusten with his boot. "She's wrong."

Mother's face is in her hands. This visual overwhelms my control. I turn on my heel and stride toward the Wall. I push through the people as easily as parting curtains.

Their worlds are crashing, and I'm the last one standing.

It's lonely.

I find myself at the little infirmary snow hut. Kaphtor lies alone with no blanket. The rest of the healing hut is filled with unconscious invalids. Some no longer look alive. A physician examines someone at the other end of the hut. I stand over Kaphtor for a moment. Two Kaphtors exist in my mind—the one who sentenced me to the Wall and squeezed my arm so hard it left bruises and then the Kaphtor who took the chisel from my hand, hacked at the rope that would save everyone's lives, and took a bullet for it.

Yet the people hate him because of the backward *E* on his left temple. Unfamiliar tenderness brushes my heart. I crouch down and rest my palm on his forehead. My unbandaged fingertips touch his skin.

God, please heal Kaphtor. Keep him alive. I'm finally getting to see his goodness and his character. Raise him up to change hearts for You. Please . . . help us survive.

I lean back and stare at him for a moment. If only I had another coat with which to cover him. For now, I'll have to trust that God will protect him.

A deafening crash shakes the snow hut. I lurch outside as another snow chunk falls from the Wall. The spiky ice caked to the stone Wall looks as firm as usual . . . except for a dark spot halfway up the Wall, just past the Opening.

Climbing higher, with the broken escape rope looped around his body, is Solomon. He clings with both hands to an ice pick lodged in the Wall and scrabbles for a foothold.

"Solomon!" I clap my hand over my mouth as his name pops out.

He's trying to escape. Alone. I'm sure he has a plan to come back for the rest of us—for me—but . . . he left Dusten. And now he's climbing a thousand-foot Wall with a single ice pick.

He could lose his footing and die, or get over the Wall and die, or encounter Enforcers and die. But he didn't bother letting me know.

Are Enforcers seeing him do this right now? Will they show up and shoot him off the Wall?

Solomon wedges his feet in some of the ice and continues the climb. It's slow going, and I refuse to watch. I look at the ground and see a splash of blood. Did Solomon injure himself? A glint catches my eye. I squat to look closer. A small square rests among the blood and snow, so tiny I'm surprised my eye caught it. A tracker chip. Solomon's.

If he took his out, then I'm taking mine out too. I slip it from the rotten-smelling bandage on my upper left arm and throw it on the ground to join his.

"What's *he* doing?" Cap stands behind me with one arm draped over Harman's shoulders.

I ignore him and gesture to the blanket around Cap's shoulders. "Give that back to Kaphtor. He'll get hypothermia without it."

"So what?"

A vindictive part of me rejoices at Cap's broken leg. "You want to be responsible for the death of the man who helped save your life?"

"He won't die—he has a long Clock. And he didn't save my life."

"He took a bullet to get that rope for us to climb down."

Cap sniffs. "Then it's his fault I fell and broke my leg, 'cause of that dumb rope."

Harman takes the blanket off Cap's shoulders and tosses it to me. Without Harman's support, Cap teeters on his good leg and gropes for a hold. He snatches Harman's shoulder and grimaces. "That was rude. Now help me lie down."

I lay the blanket over Kaphtor, then stride away from them, my chest heaving with a brew of emotions. Why do I care about those no one else cares about? I care about Radicals—the government hates them. I care about Solomon and Kaphtor—all my Radicals hate *them*. Does anyone care about *me*? Does anyone see that I care?

I hover around the wounded for a while, not allowing myself to watch Solomon climb. When I finally look again, he's almost to the top of the Wall. I hold back the temptation of relief. I cannot hope yet. Not until he is safe. What is his plan?

Escape?

Mother steps up beside me. "He is brave. And he is a fool."

"A brave fool," I mutter. "He and Jude are so similar in completely different ways."

She shakes her head. "Parvin, let me change your hand bandage. It looks like you bled through."

The bandage is dark. "It's dried now. None of that blood is new."

"We should change it anyway."

"All right."

Mother takes my hand and picks at the knotted bandage. "I read about what happened during your first trip through the Wall. I know it was hard, but you were strong. Now you must be strong for everyone."

It wasn't my strength—can't she see? "I can't be strong, Mother. They all hate me."

She shakes her head. "They hate you because they are not sure where else to direct their hate yet."

I laugh through the tightness in my chest. "So . . . I'm right. They hate me."

She's silent. So much for the pep talk. "I'm afraid, Parvin."

"No you're not." I respond without thinking. "You're never afraid."

She peels layer after layer of bandage from the crusted blood. "What does Dusten's death mean?" She meets my eyes.

Why does everyone keep asking me this? "It means we can't put our faith in the Clocks."

"But how did he override his Numbers? Is it only Dusten's Clock or is it the new Clocks that the government gives out? It must not have been his Clock."

"It was his. It had his *name* on it. I don't have all the answers, but you need to start pushing yourself to believe that maybe the Clocks aren't always right."

She returns to my hand wound. The conversation is over. I hope she's pondering what I said instead of dismissing it.

Her sharp intake of breath cuts into my thoughts.

I look down–and jerk my hand from her grasp.

"What . . . happened?" Mother's voice is hushed.

I lift my hand, turning it in front of my eyes. Aside from mild redness, the skin on my palm is smooth, fresh, and completely healed.

25

I flex my fingers and rotate my wrist. "My hand is . . . new."

"How?" Mother is pale. "Did Solomon put something special on it?"

I shake my head. No salve, no paste, no medicine. Is this a miracle? Did God heal my hand because I wounded it through praying? I'd like that.

I tap my palm. "It doesn't hurt at all."

Mother takes a step back. "I . . . I'll go scrub this bandage with snow. You don't need it anymore." But she doesn't leave. She doesn't take her eyes off my hand.

"It's okay, Mother. It's just . . . healed. Maybe God did it." It feels like a normal hand, chilling in the exposed air, begging to be hidden in a warm pocket.

What in time's name happened?

My mind cartwheels through options. *Did* God heal it? Did Solomon do something to it when he wrapped it? Or . . . "Mother! It's the medibot."

The tense lines in her face relax. "From Skelley Chase?"

"It must be." I liked the miracle idea better. Then again, why can't God use a medibot for a miracle?

She exhales and nods. "Good."

Something falls from the Wall with a *thunk*. I jump and suppress a scream. It's not Solomon. He is at the top and threw the rope so it hangs down the Wall. It seems like multiple ropes are tied together.

A dot of sound comes from above. I can't make out Solomon's words, but he's moving. Waving? Something. "Does he want me to climb?"

Mother shakes her head. "I don't know. That doesn't seem like him—he wouldn't put you in danger."

He's on a rescue mission, to save the people. I won't be left behind. "I'm going to climb. I'm going to help him."

"Parvin."

I have a new hand. He can't stop me. The people are looking to me to rescue them and I have the most Clock knowledge here. Besides, the Council didn't want me dead. If we get over the Wall to the Enforcers in the station, maybe I can use that as leverage.

"I'm going." I drop my pack on the ground, but keep my sentra in my pocket.

"How will you climb? This is careless."

I grab the rope with my good hand and wrap my leg in the slack curled on the ground. "Tell the people what Solomon and I are doing."

"What *are* you doing?"

"We're going to get everyone out of here." I pull myself up with my arm and scoot my feet up the rope. They're wrapped tight enough that, if I clench the rope between them, I have enough leverage to push myself up a few inches at a time.

"Parvin!" Mother peers up at me, only a foot or two below my own face. She holds out her coat. It takes me a full minute of maneuvering to get my arms through.

She slips two potatoes into the coat pockets and puts a glove on my right hand. "Come back to me."

"I will." Whether dead or alive, though, I'm not sure.

I continue my climb, using my elbows to keep me from scraping the snow-sharded Wall as much as possible. My arms tremble and, after the first ten minutes I realize this won't work.

Solomon keeps shouting something, but I can't make it out. Maybe he's trying to say he doesn't want me to come with him.

Sweat slips down my temple. Good. Warmth. Body heat. I lodge myself in the rope to rest. I tuck my hand into Mother's coat sleeve, but that doesn't stop the freezing. It can barely grip the rope as it is.

A glance up shows the Wall top no closer than before. I glance down and groan. I'm barely ten yards high. I'll never make it to the top at this rate with my limited stamina and one hand.

Maybe I shouldn't have been so rash.

The rope jerks and I clench my fingers around it. Is it breaking? It jerks again and I'm lifted a foot. Then again. Then again.

Solomon's hoisting me up.

What is he thinking? He can't possibly keep this going. What if he drops me? I grip the rope tighter, muscles tense against the anticipated fall. But he doesn't drop me. Higher and higher I go. After several long minutes, the rope returns to a resting state. He must have tied it off somehow.

I look down. *Now* it's too late to go back.

My breath quickens and I look away. A group of people clumps beneath me, staring up. No one can reach the rope now that Solomon's gathered some of it.

"They're escaping without us!" Oh Cap, why is he so suspicious and skeptical?

"No, we're not!" My yell is futile. Even if they can hear me, they won't believe me. I hope Mother's standing up for us.

I resume my awkward scoot-climb. It's colder the higher I get. Windy. And clouds block the sun. Ice from the Wall scrapes my arms, my chest, my face. I can't do this. My arm trembles and the glove on my right hand bunches and messes with my grip. I yank it off with my teeth and let it drop. My stump is covered in the tied-off sleeve of Mother's coat. I wrap my arm around the rope, bringing my hand to my mouth, where I breathe on it.

The Opening is directly to my left. I'm halfway to the top. If only we could get through the Opening door somehow. A black orb sticks out of the archway by the door. A camera? Does it see me?

Up again I climb, ignoring the numbness. My feet grow weak and I need to switch them so one isn't taking the majority of my weight. I can't. I'm too high. I'm too vulnerable.

The ground sways in my blurred vision. It's so far.

This was foolish.

The rope jerks again as Solomon hauls me. This time I hold on and close my eyes. I must trust him, just as I ask the people to trust me.

Despite his actions regarding Dusten, I need Solomon. I need to see him atop this Wall, safe and solid. I need to know his plans. I mustn't allow the strain of deaths and decimated hopes to create anger.

My face scrapes against the ice. This pattern repeats. I inch up while my muscles still work, then Solomon hauls me while *his* work. Back and forth. Teamwork. The wind buffets me against the side of the stone, but I remain as still as possible while he pulls.

My right hand is icy, my fingertips dotted with white. Frostbite. Up one more foot. Another. My arm trembles. I'm so cold.

"Up you go."

My eyes fly open and there's Solomon a few feet above me, bending over the Wall edge and drenched in sweat. I scoot the last several feet until his outstretched hand is within reach. I stretch my left arm and his fingers wrap around my stump.

He hauls me over the edge, icicles scrape my stomach. I lie face-down for a moment. Wind howls, erasing any warmth I had from expended energy.

"I told you not to climb up." He moves hair away from my face. Does he mean when he called down at me from one thousand feet high?

My breath returns and I sit up, wrapping my right hand in the hem of Mother's coat.

"Here." He pulls my hand back out, sandwiches it between his two, and blows on my fingers. A chill encompasses me, but I'm warm for a moment. Emotionally, at least.

He doesn't release my hand, but frowns at it. "It's . . . healed."

"The m-m-medibot Skelley put in me must have f-f-fixed it." I slip it out of his grasp.

The top of the Wall is a bumpy white snow desert, stretching beyond us into misty cloud. Grains of snow swirl and spin with each blast of wind. Beside me, Solomon's ice pick is lodged in the top of the Wall with the rope knotted around it. It doesn't look sturdy enough to have held my weight.

"We need to go." Staying in a crouch, he wiggles the ice pick back and forth until it comes free.

I don't see him the same. His features look less soft. I suspect hidden things—hidden emotions and hatred and attitude—behind this man I thought I knew.

"You left us." My words come out accusing. "You left us a-a-and Dusten *died*. Y-you let him die!" Solomon did something I didn't like . . . and I don't know how to swallow it.

He stops fiddling with the ice pick and closes his eyes.

"You knew what the projected Wall would d-d-do to him. I called for your h-help and y-you *left* me. I tried to resuscitate him—*alone*. No response. N-no help. N-nothing."

"I'm sorry."

"I needed you." Tears singe my eyes. They're warm. I needed him, maybe that's why I'm so upset. He doesn't understand. He doesn't know what he did. A simple sorry isn't going to fix *anything*.

"Parvin." He takes my hand and I glance up, not wanting to meet his eyes but needing to hope I'll see something in them that brings me peace. "Forgive me. Please forgive me for walking away, for ignoring your call, and for not . . . bringing shalom. I have reasons and excuses for my actions, but none of them are right. I . . . messed up and I hurt you. Please forgive me."

So that's what an apology on a golden platter sounds like. His every word is sincere. Desperate. "I n-needed you." He needs to *know*. To really understand how deserted I felt. "Why did you leave?"

He doesn't meet my eyes. "I was afraid of my own anger. I feel it rise up inside me when people don't see logic. When someone's being foolish. I . . . couldn't stay, or else I would have done something regrettable."

Jude had anger issues, too, only he didn't control them very well. He hit me once—knocked me to the ground. Eventually, I forgave him. Solomon dealt with his anger by . . . running from it. Abandoning us.

It's not right, but I can't hold it against him. "I f-forgive you."

I do . . . I think. What exactly is forgiveness? Does that mean I ignore the hurt that still smolders beneath the surface? Or does it mean that I will *try* to forget it? Until I figure out the exact meaning of forgiveness, I'll try my hardest to move on and not harbor bitterness. That, at least, is what I know to be right.

"Why d-did you climb up here? There was a c-camera by the O-Opening."

He coils some of the rope, then helps me to my feet. "And it was focused on the Opening, not me. I know it sounds backward, but this was the least monitored spot."

"Okay, so what's your p-plan?" The wind intensifies and steals my speech. We need to get moving. I can barely talk against the ice water in my bones.

We head to the other side, angling toward the ocean. "I'm going to steer the cargo ship through the projected Wall."

"What?"

He repeats himself, but I understood the first time. Solomon plans to overtake the cargo ship *by himself* and then steer it through the projected Wall *by himself*? "You'll die! That Wall singed Dusten to a crisp!"

Poor Dusten.

"I'm going to set it to coast through. The Wall will only destroy human DNA, so the ship should get through fine without damage. I'll jump off before it goes through and then climb back over the solid Wall. We can then board it from our side. It would be great shelter, it has food, blankets, heat . . . and maybe we could figure out how to get out of here."

He stops walking. "You'll have to stay up here on the Wall until I come back."

As if! "If you d-didn't want me to come with, why did you throw down the rope?"

He loops more of the rope slack around his shoulders and neck so it doesn't trail behind as far. "I needed you to tell me if it was long enough to reach the ground."

I roll my eyes and pick up some of the slack, coiling it around my own body. "You were a thousand feet up! I couldn't hear you."

Solomon smiles and leans close to my ear. "I'm glad you're with me." His breath puffs heat against my skin.

My face warms—a blessing at this crisp height. I gather the last few feet of rope and we resume our pace. "Why don't we just destroy the projection?"

"How?"

"I think there's a control room." My throat grates against the dry wintery air. "I overheard the Lead Enforcer telling another Enforcer to go check with maintenance about the Wall flicker. There's got to be a control room."

I need to tear down this Wall. As a symbol for the people. For hope.

I try to gauge his reaction. His brow forms a tiny thoughtful frown. He looks up, as if into a cloud of thoughts. "You might be right, but we can't bank on that."

"We can't bank on the fact that you'll get off that cargo ship before it goes through the projection and kills you. We can't even bank on the fact that you'll *get* to the cargo ship!"

"Thanks for the vote of confidence." His joke falls flat.

Great. Nice job, me. Way to ruin his confidence. But I have to be straight with him. This plan can easily fail before we even try.

The ferocity of the wind lessens for a moment. I take advantage and relax my vocal cords into regular raised speech. "We could go for the control room first. Then if that fails, we'll go to the cargo ship."

A cloud of breath reveals his sigh. "No. One of us should go for the control room while the other goes for the ship."

"Split up?"

"I'll go for the ship. If I fail, then at least you're working on the projection so the people can come through to the East side. I'd also be a good distraction for you."

"Yeah, but if I succeed and stop the projection, you'll have to wait for me to join you on the ship, otherwise I'll be stuck in a tower full of Enforcers!"

His frown deepens. "Dress like an Enforcer just in case. The Antarctica uniforms have masks."

"I'm way too short to pass as an Enforcer."

"I doubt they'd notice."

"Trust me . . . they'd notice."

His lips turn up and the wind's temper recommences. "So whoever takes out the control room—if there *is* a control room— is a sitting duck."

"Quack." I can't help it. Why does the idea of death, failure, and destruction make me lose all sense?

Solomon laughs and I join him. It's short lived because the wind slips right through our curled lips and between the skin of our bones.

I nod. "I'll try for the control room. There's no way I can man a cargo ship. And I'll just have to find a way to get to the ship before you sail it through."

"I'm not sure I can man the ship either."

I roll my shoulder so my coils of rope settle better. "Yes, but you're a man. *And* you're a Hawke. Inventions and machinery are in your blood. At least if we get the projected Wall down, the people can come over to this side and help us."

We reach the edge of the Wall—the East edge—and Solomon peers over. We're in between the cargo ship and the Enforcer tower. "Too far to be seen, but close enough to our target points."

He kneels down and thrusts the pick into the icy rock. When he tugs on it, it comes out easily with a chunk of snow. We try another spot. Then another. Then he walks away from the edge and tries again.

It finally sticks, but my trust in its firmness is shaken. He knots the rope around it, tugs, then looks at me. "That's the best we'll get."

"That's heartening."

"I'll go first and you come right after me. That way if you slip, I can catch you."

The defiance in me wants to say, "I won't slip," but he's right. The half-starved handless girl with zero muscle *will* slip.

As if bidding us a somber farewell, the wind settles into silence. "Parvin, before we go, you should know that . . . I'm not actually a Hawke. Not through blood, anyway."

I stop fiddling with Mother's coat and meet his gaze. "What do you mean? You *are* Jude's brother, right?"

He stares out toward the gelid ocean. "The Hawke family adopted me."

"Adopted?" Why does this seem so strange? *Adopted* sounds . . . fragile. I picture Solomon as a little boy in ragged clothes, covered in dirt, and hunched against a cold wall with a dwindling bowl of porridge.

"Why do you think Jude was so concerned about that specific orphanage?"

My hand flies to my mouth. "Is that where you're from? His orphanage?" The orphanage where Willow is.

"He picked me out for a brother."

I shouldn't ask. I should hold my tongue. I should . . . "What happened to your birth parents?" *Please don't shut me out. Please.*

"We weren't compatible. I was seven."

Jude would have shut me out. He was similar to Mother— didn't like getting too deep. But Solomon is letting me *know* him. I cherish his vulnerability. If he lets me know him . . . maybe that means he wants to know *me*. "Weren't . . . compatible?"

"Nope."

You've got to give me more, Solomon. "What does *that* mean?"

He flaps his arms against his coat to warm up. "I guess it's a little different in Low Cities. Do you know what divorce is?"

I snort. "I'm not *that* cut off from the world. Divorce is as common as marriage in Unity Village."

"Just checking. Well, when couples decide they aren't compatible after a few years of marriage, they divorce. It's the same with parenting—at least it is in High Cities. If a parent or parents decide they're not compatible with their child, then the government gets custody over the kid. Over me."

That doesn't seem right. "So your parents are still out there?"

"The people who caused my existence through unrestrained 'acts of love' are still out there, yes. But they're not my parents."

Oookay. Did I say something wrong?

"My *parents* are the same as Jude's parents. Even though we don't share blood, they're my parents. I just wanted you to know some of my history because . . . you keep telling everyone I have inventions in my blood. Well, I don't." His voice sinks.

I sit on the edge of the Wall. "I'm sorry I said that. I didn't know."

"Shall we get going?" He pulls on the rope as one last test. His expression is soft and the tension spiraled in my chest relaxes. He's not angry.

He doesn't mind my questions or my mistakes. He's calm and open. I nearly hug him for it. Instead, I hand him one of the potatoes in my pocket. "Let's eat and go over our plan one last time."

"I have something better." He gives me an energy bar from his pack. He unwraps it for me and it tastes like Eden. "We'll climb down the rope, you go to the Enforcer tower and steal a uniform. Then you find the control room for the projected Wall and shut it down. Meanwhile, I head to the cargo ship, sneak on, and steer it through the Wall."

I liberate the deep breath trapped in my lungs. It comes out slowly, but not slowly enough for me to accept our plan without a nasty twinge of anxiety.

"Ready?"

No way! "I guess."

He pulls out a lump of cloth strips. Without asking, he wraps my left arm three times, focusing on my inner elbow and bicep, then binds it off. Next he wraps my right hand so it's in a bandage mitten. "We'll be sliding down. It's much faster and we don't have the strength to climb."

He wraps his own hands and binds them off with his teeth. I offer help with my one good hand but we both know it's a futile suggestion. He grips the rope and scoots over the edge. I come directly after him. Upon first grip, my forearms squeal out their weakness.

"Let's go." Easy for *him* to say.

"'Let's slide a thousand feet to our death,' would be more accurate."

The last thing I hear before his body zips down the stiff rope is his laughter. I wrap my left arm around the rope, grip with my right, and slide. It's fast. Thrilling. Good thing I'm not afraid of heights.

The Wall scrapes against my outer arms, but I turn my face away and let my body tear past the resistance. I bump over the knot between ropes and tighten my grip. The wind whistles around me. I hate it. Rotten icy warmth-sucker.

The bandage on my elbow bunches, but I keep going. A shout reaches my ears over the hiss of my own descent. I squeeze the rope and jerk to a stop. When I look down, the ground is only a few feet below me. Solomon steadies me at my waist and sets me gently in the snow. It's heavy and reaches my knees. Thankfully it's drier than Missouri snow and doesn't immediately soak through my clothes.

We're here. We're on the other side! I take a moment to register what we just did. We climbed over the thousand-foot Wall . . . and didn't die.

The top of the tower station is visible over a snow crest. In there . . . is warmth. Solomon turns toward the sea. His Enforcer coat will shield his identity from afar. Will it get him aboard?

Solomon takes my face in his hands. I meet his light teal eyes. I could describe them as deep and mysterious, but the very act of looking intently into another person's eyes is so rare I expect that it's always deep and mysterious.

"I'm not going to tell you to be careful." His eyes crease, but his mouth doesn't release a smile. "Be brave."

"Please survive." I hope he senses my mixture of feelings—the care, the confusion, and the maybe-love—because I'd never be able to express them with words.

"I can't promise."

"I know." But it needed to be said.

He stares at me, intense. My gaze drops to his lips before I can stop it. My lips have only touched those of dead men, both times in an attempt to save their lives. What does a kiss feel like when it's alive, warm, and from someone who whisks my insides into cream?

But . . . I don't want Solomon to kiss me. Not like this, when we're about to part ways into our separate forms of suicidal sacrifice. No good-bye kisses.

"If you survive all this, maybe I'll kiss you." There, I said it.

He pulls me into a hug. "If we survive all this, I hope to do much more than just kiss you."

I lean back. *"What?"*

He grimaces. "That came out wrong."

I laugh. "Uh . . . yeah."

"Well, don't take it the wrong way." He winks and then closes his eyes. "God, we do this for You—for Your people. Bless our attempts, that we may save lives and bring Your shalom back. Give Parvin the eyes and ears to find the control room. Make us invisible. Let it be."

"Amen."

He kisses my forehead, then breaks into a jog toward the ocean. I watch him for half a breath.

We just talked about kissing. And I didn't feel guilty.

I smile and then creep in the opposite direction. To the station. Already, the worry in my mind has been replaced by a thirst for heat and shelter. I run through the plan in my head.

Get to the station undetected. *Yeah, right.*

Sneak in. *Knock, knock . . .*

Steal an Enforcer uniform. *Preferably from a peg on the wall, not from a body.*

Get *into* the Enforcer uniform. *Hurray for having only one hand.*

Find the maintenance room. *Anyone have a map?*

With any luck, it will control the projected Wall. *Riiiiight.*
Destroy it. *Should've brought a hammer.*

No big deal, right? A shadow cuts off the sun's warmth. I'm here.

There's the stone-carved entrance I walked through only yesterday—before Dusten died, before Kaphtor was shot, and before I was made a leader whom everyone hates. There are no guards outside, but I'm not surprised. It would be foolish to station them out here.

God, help me figure You out. Do with me what You will, please give me food, keep me safe, and forgive me for whatever I've done wrong. My muscles relax. It's been a while since I prayed my own version of the Lord's Prayer. It reminds me of all the times I entered danger, and all the times God got me out of it with a deeper purpose.

Despite the fact that He let me lose a hand and make mistakes, I trust Him. *I trust You.*

I hunch against the Wall for several minutes and use my teeth to remove the wrappings on my hand. The tower station has no windows, but I still feel watched. Deep breath. No . . . don't breathe. Just go.

I run.

Four steps toward it, I crash to the ground. The heavy snow and my numb legs defeat my determined sprint. I push myself up and run again. Carefully. Like a secret agent, I plaster my back to the wall next to the entry steps.

It's so cold!

Now or never. I climb the steps, lift the latch ,and stride in. *Be brave.* Oh, Solomon . . .

This hallway seemed chilly the first time I entered it, but now it's a shelter . . . especially because it's empty. *Thank You!*

The door slams shut behind me, latching with a deep boom. Drat. Now anyone in the next room—the uniform room—will know someone's here. I dart to the other side and tuck myself in the corner by the door hinges. If someone comes in to check, they won't see me easily. I could even . . . attack them. Maybe.

The door doesn't open and it's too thick for me to hear through. I wait long enough for my breathing to slow. This is working so far. I'm in! Now . . . to get the Enforcer uniform.

God, I know I've only been asking for things lately but . . . please give me an empty room. Please!

I grip the latch with my perfect hand. He healed me. He kept the rope from breaking. He can do this for me if He wants. And if He doesn't want to, then He has a reason.

Creak!

The door screams out my presence as I move it. I thrust it open all the way and poise on the threshold to flee if need be.

The room is warm and . . . empty. Not a single Enforcer.

But neither is there a single uniform hanging on the wall. The pegs are bare and I stand exposed.

Footfalls clang down the stairs to my right.

26

I have a handful of seconds before I'm caught.

Across the room to my left is a wooden door, but bursting through an unknown door is just as bad as bursting into the stairwell to meet my enemies.

Eep!

May God translate that into a coherent prayer.

I tiptoe-run to the wooden door and slip through just as the voices enter the circular entry room behind me. Quiet as a cougar, I ease the door closed behind me. It rests against the frame and I don't let it latch—they might hear it.

Once I release the handle and remember to breathe, I turn around to face whatever I've walked into.

It's another hallway. The walls and floor are grey stone and plaster. Muted yellow light flickers from long tube bulbs in the ceiling. The coloring of this hall makes me shiver, but the temperature is equal to the entry room. My toes prickle inside my soaked boots, unused to the warmth.

Four doors—each with a glass window—lead off the hallway, two on each wall. They look like they might lead to offices. Are people *in* those offices?

I press against the corner so that if someone walks through the wooden door, the door will shield me from view. I need to search for the control room, but the voices from the entry creep through the cracked door.

"It is irresponsible, sir." I heard that voice before going through the Wall. It's not the Lead Enforcer. Who is it?

"It's not my call, Reece." Ah, *there's* the Lead Enforcer's voice.

"Didn't you see the Radical groups dispersing? They might kill penguins to survive! Even *touching* a penguin used to be illegal."

Reece—the old guy who looked like a bookworm. The guy more concerned about the environment than about human lives. But maybe that's the problem—he doesn't see us as humans.

The Lead Enforcer sighs. "It's just a small portion of Antarctica."

"Small portion?" Reece chokes on his own outrage. "This coastal region is one of the richest, survival-friendly habitats for Antarctic life. Where will they go if the Radicals ruin it?"

"They'll come to *our* side of the Wall, where you can examine, draw, and study them to your heart's content." The silence following the Lead Enforcer's statement says it all. Reece is mollified. What a fickle environmentalist.

Now, if only this fickle environmentalist would somehow drop a clue to where the control room is.

"So, are you going to visit that cute navigation officer from the cargo ship?" the Lead Enforcer asks.

"I don't like blondes."

"You do if it's a Macaroni penguin."

Reece snorts. "Penguin or woman, there's not exactly a date-friendly location here."

Oh please, they're talking about *dating?*

"Does a female navigation officer seem like the type of lady who needs a date-friendly location?"

How about taking her on a date to the control room? And letting me tag along?

"I'll see you later, sir."

"Whoa, hang on, Reece." The Lead Enforcer's voice is louder—close to my door. "I'm coming, too. Gotta check on that flicker."

Flicker. Does he mean the projected Wall?

The wooden door opens with a bang and rebounds off the toes of my boots. I wince, but bite my tongue. Reece and the Lead Enforcer are halfway down the hall before the door closes and I can see them again.

My heart didn't even have time to panic.

They push through the door at the end of the hallway. I run after them, praying I don't alert anyone in the offices. I slow the closing of the door with my palm and slip through before it latches.

Another hallway slopes in a curve to the right. This hallway has picture windows on the inside, with beach scenes, mountain views, and a cityscape.

I inch around the curve, straining my ears for footsteps. Faster, slower, faster I walk. A door on my right is closing. I sneak up and peek. A spiral metal staircase twirls down, down, down. Reece and the Lead Enforcer descend into shadows. I hurry after them, so that my footsteps can get lost among theirs.

Someone is going to come after me, or hear me, or come up toward me. I know it.

They disappear and the pounding steps on metal ceases. I come to a halt and tiptoe like a ninja down the rest. I reach the bottom of the stairs and face an open doorway. Inside the dark room, Reece and the Lead Enforcer sit in plush swivel chairs in front of a long set of screens. Their backs are to me.

Neither speaks, they just tap on screens and projected key-boards. On one screen, a scene pops up—Radicals cowering in snow huts, two groups of people facing off and shouting, a third group of Radicals doing jumping jacks, more people tossing wood onto the fire.

My people.

Solomon was right, they do have cameras on us. They've been watching us starve, freeze, and die. *But . . .* they haven't been watching us the whole time.

"Look!" Reece shrieks, jamming his finger against the screen. "They've already destroyed wildlife. Murderers!" A group of people—the ones led by Rufus McTavish—has returned with a pile of dead penguins.

The Lead Enforcer ignores Reece's panic. "Can't wait to get them building the projection towers tomorrow. The sooner we get to work, the sooner we get that pay bonus."

Projection towers?

I can't just stand here and hope they talk about the Wall. I can't wait for them to pull up the controls to the projected Wall, not while Solomon is risking his life taking over the cargo ship. But the Lead Enforcer said something about checking the flicker. Surely . . . *surely* this dark room full of controls, screens, and technology, is the room I need.

If only I had some sort of weapon. *Don't do anything stupid!* I reach into my pocket for one of Father's chisels, but there's nothing there. I had three! Where did they go?

My brain pieces together the mystery. I gave one to Kaphtor and then one each to Harman and Frenchie. Drat. What does this dark room have for me? Wires, boxes, electronics . . . nothing weapon-worthy. The Lead Enforcer has a gun and is my biggest threat. How can I get rid of him?

To my left, against the wall, is a cabinet with glass doors. Liquor bottles rest inside—clear, amber, and dark liquid. One bottle sits on top of the short cabinet, with two empty shot glasses upside down beside it.

I'm going to hurt someone. Admitting it to myself helps me take the breath of courage I need. *Be brave. This is for the people of Unity—for the Radicals.*

I step inside the room and grab the bottle with my right hand. Neither of the men turn around, but a mere flick of the eye will give me away. I jump at the Lead Enforcer with a scream—*why* do I scream? He turns around and I see his eyes pop and his mouth open.

Smash!

Blood, glass, and liquor spray the desk and screens. He slumps in his chair, then his body weight pulls him to the ground with a loud flop.

I scream again. I'm not proud of it, but that's what comes out after I obliterate another human's consciousness. My fist clings to the neck of the shattered liquor bottle. To grab the Lead's gun, I need to set down the glass, but if I do that Reece might attack me. Curse my missing hand!

Reece stares at me through his glasses like a bat under torch-light. His knuckles are bright white, clenching the arms of his chair.

"How do I control the projected Wall?" I do my best to elimi-nate the trembling from my voice.

He doesn't move. Doesn't seem to breathe. I don't have time for this. I level the sharp bottleneck at him. *"How do I control the projected Wall?"*

"Th-through the computers!"

"Get me to the controls."

His eyes flit from the glass bottle and up to my face, and his shoulders relax a little. His death-grip on the chair loosens, but he doesn't turn toward the screens. It's as if he's figured out I can't hurt him much with a bottle.

I steady my voice. Calm it. "Listen, I don't want to be on Antarctica any more than you want me—or any of the other Radicals—here."

"There's nothing you can do, miss."

I round his chair and shove the jagged bottleneck against his back, but not hard enough to pierce skin. "I can slice open your spine, that's what I can do. Then you'll be paralyzed for the rest of your Numbers."

Ick . . . it sounds so violent. I repress a shudder. There's no way I'll cut this man, but he doesn't have to know that.

Reece taps away at the computer screen. He doesn't seem nervous anymore. Why not? What am I missing?

Someone behind me yanks me back by the hair. I screech and crash to the ground. The Lead Enforcer jerks me to my feet, his hand still tangled in my hair.

Oh.

How is he conscious already?

He wrenches the bottleneck from my hand and throws it on the ground. Blood pulses from his head wound into one of his eyes. "How did you get here?"

My feet barely touch the ground and every hair attached to my scalp pulls against my skin as if attached with micro fingernails. I hear them snapping, ripping from my cranium.

"Let me *go!*" I kick out and connect with his shin.

He rams me against the wall and his other hand wraps around my throat, pinning me. *"How did you get here?"*

His hand grows tighter. Tighter.

Black spots flash across my vision. I can't see. I can't breathe. *Oh God, I can't breathe!* I'll answer the Enforcer. I'll tell him everything. I'll go back across the Wall. Just . . . give me air!

His fingers squeeze and my lungs spasm. I attempt a struggle, but my muscles turn limp. My eyes burn, wanting to cry, but I don't have the breath to release a sob.

Okay God, if this is how You want me to go then . . . okay.

Noise surrounds me—a din coming from the stairwell. It's drowned out only by the deafening screams in my mind. I'm dying.

I open and close my lips like a suffocating fish. Air. Please.

Air.

Please.

God . . .

People spill into the control room. Black coats everywhere. Through the blur of tears, I notice one coat isn't quite as pristine as the rest.

Solomon.

He's been caught.

27

Solomon has to watch me die.

His eyes scan the room, then land on me. *"No!"* His voice is distant. Fading.

He thrashes against the Enforcers holding him at gunpoint, growing more and more blurry as my brain shuts off.

My vision cuts out. All that's left is my hearing.

At least I'm warm.

"No. Parvin! No! Let her go! *Please!*"

I'm sorry, Solomon. Keep trying . . . Good-bye.

"Sir, she's the only one with the answers. She's our leader. You won't get any answers if you kill her."

Something changes. The fleshy anvil leaves my windpipe. I crumple to the floor. The Lead Enforcer released me, but I still can't breathe. I strain. Nothing. No air.

He crushed my trachea—that must be it. Am I broken? I don't want to die broken.

My vision blinks on, blurred and out of focus. I can't move, can't bring in a breath. I try. Oh, I try, but the airway is blocked. Smashed. Hopeless.

Solomon lurches forward, dropping to his knees by my side. Then his mouth is on mine, blowing air into my lungs. Once. *Air.* Twice. *Air!*

I've never been on this end of the saving. My lungs expand and something in my neck pops. I cough and Solomon leans back. I throw up. He pulls me against his chest. I'm coughing, he's trembling, Enforcers are watching.

His hand strokes my hair and he's making noise, but it's not coherent. They pull him away from me and that's when I see his smeared tears. He was crying . . . for me.

They haul him to his feet and his head hangs. One sob comes out of him, ending in a groan. My heart shatters. *I'm so sorry.*

As I suck air down my raw, grainy throat, I stare at the man trying to regain his composure. I stare at that dark blond hair stuck to his forehead from sweat and the clump of scars on his temple showing his rebellion against the government. That light skin, those red-rimmed teal eyes, and those gentle hands trembling at his sides.

Solomon Hawke . . . I love you.

There's no room in my heart for questions about what love is, or if I ever loved Jude, or if love even matters at a time like this. All I know is . . . I love Solomon. Right now. Probably forever.

And I know he loves me. He's loved me much longer, he's just been waiting for me to catch up.

"All right then, how did you get here?" The Lead Enforcer has his gun trained on me.

Oh yeah, we need to survive. And Solomon told them I was the leader so they wouldn't strangle me. Time to come up with an answer.

I clear my throat, but it comes out as a wheeze. I hold up a finger so he knows I'm trying. After all, it's *his* fault I can't speak right now. How did we get here? What do I say? I want to lie . . . but I shouldn't. Should I? When is it okay to lie?

If he's asking, that means he doesn't know about the rope still hanging against this side of the Wall as our escape.

"The projected Wall"–I rasp–"It flickered."

He turns to one of the Enforcers holding Solomon. "I thought I sent you to *fix* that?"

The Enforcer lowers his gun. "I-I did."

"Well, check it!" The Lead Enforcer thrusts him toward the open seat.

Solomon and I watch the Enforcer tap the screen and navigate the controls. Solomon has a better view, but I have a better memory—I'll need to remember how to get there in case we return to the control room.

I struggle to my feet and watch the Enforcer's actions. That screen, a blue box, that little tower symbol, one swipe to the left, a glowing triangle . . . the process goes on and the Enforcer whips through them so fast even *my* excellent memory has trouble following.

"Sir . . ." Reece reaches for the Lead Enforcer, but the man brushes his hand away.

"Get out of here, Reece."

Reece's eyes narrow and he glances at me. "I have some information I think you'd like, sir."

"There's a lot of information you think I'd like, Reece, but I never do. Now get out! This is government business."

Reece raises his eyebrows, rises serenely, and leaves the control room. Ah, the beauty of offended pride.

The Enforcer at the screen reaches what looks like the last hurdle—a screen that says *VERIFICATION*. The Lead Enforcer steps forward and presses his thumb into a depression by the screen. Blood from his head wound drips onto the desk, but he doesn't seem to care.

Once his thumb is pricked, controls flicker onto the screen, one after the other, filled with acronyms, measuring bars, and flashing percentages. "It looks fine, sir."

The Lead Enforcer rounds on me.

I shrug. "I said it *flickered*. I didn't say it broke." My voice is a shredded whisper against my damaged vocal cords.

"What made it flicker?"

I fold my arms, but the very movement drains my energy. "Now that you ask, you ought to know that one of our Clock-matched people—meaning he's *not* a Radical—tried to cross the projected Wall and got burnt to a crisp *before* his Clock zeroed out. He's dead right now and his Numbers are still counting down."

"Liar."

I gesture to one of the screens. "Check your cameras. You've been watching us, haven't you? You'll see us return with his body and you'll see the people panic. Now his Clock says *overridden*."

The Lead Enforcer leans toward the camera screen. Solomon leans, too, but his feet inch forward. The Enforcers flanking him are curious, too. It takes only a few minutes before they're all crowded around the screens, watching the replay of Dusten being brought into our snow camp.

I don't dare move. We've already seen that my plans fail.

"Look, Parvin, the group that left has come back." Solomon points at the screen, but his eyes look at the projected Wall controls. Reading them. Darting from one to the other.

Find it. Find the one that turns it off.

As he points with one hand, he runs a bunched bandage across the desk face with the other, wiping up the Lead Enforcer's blood. In one swift movement, he taps three buttons on the projected Wall controls and then presses the bloodied bandage into the finger depression.

The computer accepts the blood verification.

Before the Lead notices what happened, a giant red alert flashes over the screen:

SHUT-DOWN WALL PROJECTION? PLEASE CONFIRM.

"What are you—?" The Lead reaches for Solomon.

Solomon smashes his palm against the *confirm* button and an electric current runs through all of us.

Impulse more than logic moves me to action. I rip the gun off the shoulder of the nearest Enforcer, prop it on my stump, and aim at the screens.

Solomon leaps toward me, hits a button on the gun, and then ducks. I let the bullets fly. The Enforcers drop to the ground, but I'm not aiming at them. Electronics and sparks flash into the darkness as I cut their life source. I shut my eyes, scream, and don't release the trigger until the bullets stop.

At that point, Solomon grabs my wrist then hurtles up the spiral staircase, dragging me after him. The gun flies from my hands. We're halfway up before the Enforcers are after us. Their bullets ricochet off the metal stairs.

We burst through the top door, run up the curved hall, through the office hallways, and into the entry room.

No one is here.

We break free of the tower and sprint out into the wild of Antarctica. I'm slapped by the cold and lose my breath. No. I can't bear to be so cold again. We *have* to get the cargo ship!

"Next gun you steal, be sure to turn off the safety." Solomon's voice reflects a smile. I grin, wild and exhilarated by our success.

We round the tower just as the door flies open behind us. A bullet tears through the air next to my ear. Before I can shriek, we're on the other side of the tower and Solomon runs to a stone shed. The door is a metal sheet that he lifts upward into the ceiling.

I don't know why it's not locked. Maybe they're not used to outlaws running around.

Inside are machines—strange snow bikes with tracks on the back and skis in the front. The one closest to us has a sleek wedge enclosure painted white and black on top of two skis and a tri-angle track in the back.

Solomon hoists it open to reveal two black leather seats side-by-side. I climb in before he says anything. He hops in next to me as a bullet ricochets off the thick plastic windshield.

Bulletproof? Or luck?

He pulls the hatch closed, rams his thumb onto a red button, and the engine rumbles to life—a mixture of whines and grumbling. It has attitude.

The steering wheel is two handles with a thumb pedal. The moment Solomon presses it down, we lurch forward. One Enforcer makes the foolish choice to stand in front of us. We run into his knees and knock him sideways.

Then we're in the open. Bullets bid us farewell and we leave them in a cloud of snowdust.

We're free.

The projected Wall is down . . . for now.

We're both alive.

"Woo*hoo!*" I rest my head against the headrest, allowing a brief moment of celebration before addressing the next list of questions. "And you said you didn't have the inventive Hawke blood in you."

"I *was* rather awesome on the computer, wasn't I?"

While I laugh, Solomon presses two buttons and my seat grows warm.

"I don't know how long this will run, Parvin. It seems gasoline-controlled, since electric wouldn't be efficient in such cold. These are old models."

He dodges an ice boulder and we slide sideways. On instinct, I lean. He leans. We don't tip.

"Where are we going now?"

"I'll go for the ship and you can take this to warn the others. I'll try to bring the boats across."

"Solomon, we're being *chased!* Shouldn't we both get on the ship? They'll follow me to the people."

We approach the ocean, where seven empty motorboats rest on the shore. "The Enforcers will follow me, not you. And I can't risk you being on the ship in case the projected Wall goes up again."

We skid to a stop. He lifts the latch and jumps out. A clump of penguins waddle toward him. I slide into his seat as he gives me a quick primer on how to work the machine.

"This thumb lever is the gas. This one on the left is the brake."

He doesn't comment on my missing hand. He trusts I'll figure something out. It's like he believes I can be strong.

He's about to run to the boats, but I grab his hand. "Wait, you should know, I . . . I love you." At least, I want to call it love.

He stares at me for a stunned moment, long enough for me to rethink my confession. Then a smile commandeers his expression. He brushes his thumb down my cheek, swallows, and whispers, "I loved you first, Miss Blackwater."

He closes the hatch. I press down the thumb lever and shoot toward the Wall. My last view is Solomon pushing all the motor-boats out into the water, wrapping their tie-down ropes in one hand, leaping into one, and heading out to sea.

My heart is full.

It takes me less than a minute before I'm at the edge of the stone Wall, where the ocean meets land and the projected Wall *should* meet the stone. But it's gone. All that's left are the bobbing towers that connected one screen to the other—*projection towers,* I think the Lead Enforcer called them.

Wasn't that what they were going to have us build? Why?

A small ledge of ice runs along the stone section of Wall, poised over the ocean, to the other side. Will this snow machine fit? Just in case, I lift the hatch so I can get out if it falls into the water.

I inch toward the ledge, hugging the Wall. Don't think of the projection. It's gone. I'm not going to get roasted like Dusten did. I'm safe. We shut it down.

I'm lined up for the ledge, but it's thinner than it looked before. I adjust my grip on the handle, then gun it. Faster. Faster. The whine of the machine matches the loudness of the wind around my zooming capsule. I reach the ledge and shoot across it. The snow machine tilts toward the ocean, but I lean left.

"Come on!"

Faster. Faster. The stone Wall hurtles past on my left, ocean on my right. I'm so close that the left ski scrapes against the Wall.

Then I see Frenchie and Madame ahead, walking on the small ledge to this side. Frenchie's stomping away from Madame, and Madame follows, hollering after her.

I'm going to run them over if they stay there. "Move!"

But they're deer in my headlights. Not having a hand to press the brake, I jerk right and launch off a snowberm, over open ocean, inches from where they stand.

They both scream. I twist in my seat, while flying through the air only to see the ice shelf crumbling, and the two of them topple into the sea.

Then I land. My chin knocks against some part of the machine. Water consumes me.

I've never been submerged in a mixture of fire, ice, and death . . . until now. It's akin to having your skin scraped off with one of Father's wood chisels, though I haven't experienced that either.

The snow machine bobs once and then sinks. I flail through the water and just catch Madame's cry. "Help me!"

She's not that far from me and she's pulling on Frenchie's arm. Frenchie's unconscious, blood pouring from her mouth. It looks like she bit through her lip.

"An ice chunk landed on her head."

I swim over as best I can in my soaked skirt and boots. "G-Get h-her t-to shore." Each hair on my body freezes as I kick. I've never been so cold. The salt water makes everything worse—in my eyes, in my mouth, in my wounds.

We swim parallel to the Wall, dragging Frenchie between us.

One good thing has come from this: the snow ledge is broken and impassable. The Enforcers can't come to our side now. But there's no time to laugh in victory. We're about to get hypothermia.

"Wait!" Madame veers toward the open water. "A dinghy!"

Solomon has loosed one of the motorboats a few yards from us. He lets the others loose closer to shore before veering back toward the cargo ship. Someone still would have had to swim for the motorboats. That makes me feel a little better about the submersion. "Y-You go for the d-dinghy and I-I'll bring Angelique."

Madame doesn't protest, but splashes toward the boat.

We're freezing fast. The back of my neck aches. I can't do this.

I pull Frenchie after her, but given my skinniness, my missing hand, and the weight of my clothing, I'm of little use. I've never been a strong swimmer.

Madame reaches the dinghy and hauls herself onto the edge. Her portly form flails, finally getting a leg over the edge. Frenchie comes to as we reach the boat. "We deedn't die?"

"N-No, b-but the snow b-b-bike did."

She reaches her hand up for Madame, but does nothing more than that. No squirming, no effort. I try to boost her up, but my limbs grow stiff. She steps in the crook of my elbow for leverage and I'm shoved underwater. I choke on salt water and scream against the cold, but it comes out in a stream of bubbles. I claw for the surface. What if Frenchie doesn't let me up soon enough? But then she's in the dinghy and I'm above water again, panting.

My turn.

Madame grabs my hand, Frenchie gets my stump, her hand bloody from touching her lip. I abandon all dignity. I convulse like a fish, wiggling over the edge and flopping into the bottom. My body doesn't obey. I'm a rubber human, freezing over. The back of my head hits a set of wooden oars strapped inside.

I don't ask why Madame and Frenchie were standing like two statues on the small ledge. I don't ask where they thought they'd go. I don't care. "W-We need t-to g-get warm."

On the shore stands a mass of people. Mother's at the front, shouting commands I can't hear. She believed in us. She got everyone ready.

"Let's get those other loose boats to shore."

Madame pulls the motor cord and it roars to life. Frenchie wipes the sleeve of my borrowed coat across her bloodied face. Thanks a lot. "Ah. Ow." She shoves Madame aside. "I drive."

I twist in my seat to look for the cargo ship. As if my gaze is the magic touch, the ship releases a mighty belch and starts moving toward us. A few Enforcers line the shore, stranded and staring. Then they turn and sprint back toward the tower.

"He did it! Solomon took over the ship!"

The words have barely left my mouth when a lightning zap singes my skin. The projected Wall flickers back into view. All but the stern of the ship was already through. The rest follows within seconds.

A cold wave, one that has nothing to do with the water, washes over me. "Solomon."

Madame scoots toward the bench seat beside me and Frenchie grabs the handle, zooming toward the cargo ship.

"Where are you g-going?" I gasp. The coating of water on my body numbs my lips.

"Eef your—" she stops and holds the sleeve of my coat to her bleeding lip, then shakes her head.

Madame answers instead. "If your Enforcer just burnt up, we have to steer the ship."

Burnt up. My Enforcer. My Solomon.

No . . .

I don't know where the control room is, but surely he was already through. I force a deep breath. *Solomon is in your hands, God. Please . . . spare his life.* "W-w-we have to g-g-get the b-b-boats to the people."

"They already have them."

I glance back. Some Radicals dove into the water to collect the motorboats. Frenchie rounds the cargo ship, barely avoiding a collision. We slam against the opposing waves and I'm sure we'll tip.

"Should we g-get on board?" Madame looks from the ship to me.

Frenchie rolls her eyes, but can't manage a sarcastic retort through the gash in her lip. She steers us to the walkway hanging off the side, keeping pace with the ship. It's gaining speed, coasting toward our Radicals.

I try not to imagine Solomon dead, blackened, at the wheel of the ship.

"Angelique, steady the d-dinghy."

She takes her hand away from her mouth and forces words through a grimace. "I 'ave been in ze control room of a cargo ship. I know some things. I can 'elp."

"Well, you know more than Solomon probably does." We bump against the walkway. The motorboat bobs inconsistently. One foot on, one foot off, and I'm thrust into acrobatic splits that might just tear me in half.

Commit. Commit to the steps. I push off the deflating bobbing edge of the dinghy and roll to the side, clanging against the ship's hull and holding tight to the railing.

My muscles tremble. They're hypothermic weights, ready to drag me back into the sea. I force them to climb. Halfway up, the walkway lurches. Madame is on below me. Poor Frenchie, she has the hardest job since she'll be abandoning the dinghy. But she was the only one who knew how to drive the thing.

We sneak on deck, eyes and ears open. Relying on my ears won't do any good, not with the rumble of the engine drowning out the whispers and scuffles.

Here I go, God. Please let Solomon be alive. A shudder passes through me. God allowed Jude to die—well, Jude also *let* himself die. Still, chills accompany my prayers for Solomon's safety. I can't control it. Only an hour ago I realized I loved Solomon—at least, I'm on my way to love. I want to be with him, to know him, to discover him. I want him to know me.

But we need to be alive for that.

The deck is rough, black-patterned glass beneath my feet. My knees buckle when I stand and I fall against the low railing. What's wrong with me? Oh yeah, I climbed over a thousand foot wall, almost choked to death, and then swam in the coldest water on Earth after crashing a snow bike into the sea.

That's all.

A hysterical laugh bubbles up.

"Shhh." Madame waves her hand up and down at me.

Frenchie cups her hand at us, telling us to follow. "Ze bridge eez this way." We creep past shipping containers and check around corners, forcing our fading limbs to cooperate.

At one row, a shout and clang startles me. I throw out my arms to keep Madame and Frenchie from advancing, then peek around the corner. Nothing. More pounding. The shouts are muffled. A few other voices join it.

It may be foolish, but I follow the sound. Past two stacks and then up another aisle of containers, I find my answer. People are inside, clamoring to get out. Did the Enforcers forget to release a container?

"Let us out!" a man shouts from inside.

I take a deep breath to respond, but Madame clamps a hand over my lips from behind. "Don't."

I squirm until my mouth rips free. "Let me go."

"Is someone there?" We all freeze. That was Monster Voice. "Hello?"

Enforcers are inside.

"Let's go," I murmur, and we leave them behind for now. The rubberband squishing my heart loosens. We're safe on board. We're on our way to saving everyone. *Everyone.*

"How did your Enforcer get them all in there?"

I shrug and we walk through a heavy white door with a circle window. Inside are solid grey stairs leading upward in a repetitive square shape. Frenchie clomps up them like she owns the place, not even glancing at the blue panel on the wall listing every important room from A Deck to G Deck.

The bridge is at the very top. The thick door is propped open, tight against the stairwell wall, and inside stands Solomon. His feet are planted shoulder-width apart on the green painted floor, his back to us, and he wears more guns than articles of clothing. The clothing he does wear is an Antarctica Enforcer outfit, complete with mask. Rifles hang over his shoulders and back, pistols pop out of every pocket and space in his belt. He holds a rifle in each hand, leveled at two people—a man and a blond woman—who stand, trembling, at a panel of controls.

The last thing I want to do is startle a man covered in guns, so I back up a bit and slam my footsteps. "It's me, Solomon."

He barely moves. "I know, I saw you crossing the deck."

We step in. I'm dizzy, but try to focus. The bridge is larger than it looked from the stairwell. It's a long rectangle stretching to my right, split down the middle by a board of computers and electronics—most of which are black and not working. The walls are angled glass on all sides, revealing the outside deck, shipping containers, and sea ahead.

"What can I do?" Frenchie steps forward.

"Figure out how to steer this thing."

"Wait, these two aren't steering it?" I gesture to the man and woman. We could crash into ice or land and then be trapped on Antarctica again.

Solomon shakes his head. "The captain's not on board. These two don't know much."

I stare at the blond woman. My sluggish brain urges me to remember something. What is it? "She's a navigation officer!"

The woman's eyes snap to me, her startle giving her away. "You are?" Solomon growls.

"The Lead Enforcer and Reece were talking about her." I don't really know what a navigation officer is, but it sounds like the type of title we need right now. My body trembles, outside of my control.

"Well, zat's great." Frenchie sits at a screen and fiddles with the buttons. "Make 'er 'elp."

The woman needs no urging. She plops into a seat beside Frenchie and gets to work. She and Reece *would* have made a good pair—they're both nervous wrecks when threatened.

Solomon tightens his hands on the rifles. "I was afraid this'd be a drone boat."

"What's a drone boat?" Madame asks.

"It means no one on the ship actually controls it. There's a virtual bridge somewhere in the USE that would navigate the vessel for us. *But* they chose to use an old-fashioned cargo ship for the delivery of Radicals. I'm betting the other Radicals won't be so lucky."

A strong shiver seizes me and I fall to one knee. I take a deep breath to relax and force myself back up. I'm so cold. *So* cold. Pieces of my hair clink together. Frozen. I can't feel my fingers.

"I'ma help pipll aboard." I shake my head against the slurs in my speech. "I'm gonna help p-people . . . aboard."

Madame and I head back down the stairwell. My knees buckle on the last steps and I land on all fours. Madame helps me up, but she's just as weak as I am. I can't shut down yet. Not until everyone is safe!

Some part of my brain flashes a warning sign: *Get warm! Get warm!*

But people need help. I can do this.

The ship is parallel to the shore. Four motorboats filled with Radicals zoom toward us. The people pour onto the boarding walkway, testing its strength.

Harman and McTavish are in the first boat. They hand up Dusten's body. It's wrapped in the communal blanket. Next, they pass up Cap and Kaphtor, who both hobble up the walkway. For once, Cap doesn't complain about being near an Enforcer.

Just as the four motorboats return to shore to fill up again, I see them. Enforcers. At least twenty of them—on *our* side of the Wall—all armed and running toward the shore. Toward my people.

"Look out!" I try to holler, pointing over their heads, but all that comes out is a slurred grunt. I try again. Some hear my indecipherable shout and look over their shoulders.

Then the screaming starts.

That's all the incentive the Radicals on shore need. They swarm the motorboats, piling in too many people, tipping one, filling another with water.

Several Radicals jump into the sea and paddle toward us, but we're so far from shore. I've been in that water. I know what they're feeling. Soon they'll be too stiff to paddle. Soon they'll all have hypothermia.

Soon they'll all be dead.

They can't make it. Not in this cold.

Cold.

Co . . . l . . . d.

The scene blurs and wavers like a photo underwater. I shake my head. My vision clears. What can I do? What can I *do?*

I should jump in and help them. After all, I'm already wet . . .

Yeah, that sounds good. As I lean over the ship's edge and the water swarms with desperate Radicals, the Enforcers reach the shore and open fire.

The surge of bullets causes chaos.

I scream for Solomon as the cargo ship coasts past the writhing, bloodied bodies of Radicals now drowning in the frozen ocean. The Enforcers keep firing and, at some point, the furious panic inside of me bursts out in tears.

I'm helpless. I scream and scream and scream, not having enough muscle control to jump over the railing and help. More shooting slams against my eardrums. Solomon fires from the back deck.

I'm sickened by the relief that comes when Enforcers slump to the ground.

At some point, a thin black woman tackles one of the firing Enforcers. He knocks her in the head with the rifle, then aims at her, but someone else shoots him first.

Get 'em, Solomon.

The sound of the cargo ship engines changes. It grinds and something in the movement of the ship throws off my balance. We stop, resting in the mayhem, the death, the murderers and murdered.

The formerly clear Antarctic sea is now an inverted underwater sunset, decorated with clouds of blood and limp skydivers. I drop to my knees. Who's dead? Is Mother there, floating face-down, her last breath one of salt water?

I can't focus—a debilitating brew of dropped body temperature and sorrow seeps through me. Everything happens as if I'm in a daze. I hear a splash and slide my blurry gaze back over the edge, only to see Solomon swimming toward one of the motorboats covered in dead bodies. He climbs in and steers the boat to the ship, handing up the bodies. Then he heads back to shore.

Back and forth, back and forth, he transfers the bodies. I lie on the deck. The shivering has stopped. In fact, I'm sleepy. How long has it been since I really rested?

I close my eyes, melding into the chill of the deck. It's not as cold anymore. I think I'll sleep here . . .

Two hundred seventy eight people died from bullet wounds and drowning. Two hundred seventy eight Radicals who never had Clocks. No one knew if this was their time or not.

Twelve people died from hypothermia. I guess I was almost one of them. I woke in some berth underneath the deck with a pile of blankets over me and Mother hugging my body tight. Two thoughts echoed in my head:

She's asleep.

She's alive.

I learned she was most responsible for saving several lives after we got everyone on board. That's my mother.

Now I'm in the stairwell on my way up to the bridge, wearing dry clothes that must have belonged to someone on the crew. A man walks past me with a bucket of tracking chips that he's extricated from people's bodies and is about to toss into the ocean.

It's dark outside. Night time.

How long have I been asleep? There was no darkness when we were in Antarctica. Where are we heading? Are we truly safe and on our way out?

I reach the bridge and walk in. Frenchie stands behind the control wheel, stitches lining her puffy upper lip, with at least four

Radical men—probably the closest thing we could find to sailors. All of them are stiff and focused. My plans to talk disintegrate. A radar screen claims their attention. Its arm sweeps in a circle, revealing an assortment of glowing blobs. Mist drapes upon the sea like a shroud, as though to disguise danger.

Eerie.

"There's one." A man gasps and thrusts his pointer finger onto the radar.

"I see eet." Where is the navigation officer? Why isn't *she* steering?

His eyes dart from the screen, to the sea, to Frenchie. "If we hit an ice—"

"Shh!" Frenchie tightens her knuckles against the wheel.

I don't want to be here. I liked the secure feeling I had upon waking. I leave and run into Solomon at the base of the stairs.

"I was just looking for you." He smiles.

"Well, here I am." I wrap my arms around my middle. It's strange, wearing clean, dry clothes when I haven't washed in several weeks. Is the smell of vomit still on me? And what in the world does my hair look like? At least the deathly dip in the ocean helped rid me of some filth.

"I wanted to talk to your mother and you. Can we go to your room?"

"I . . . have a room?"

He grins. "Where you're sleeping. I think you share it with a few people, but follow me." It takes us only a moment. Whoever shares our room isn't in here right now, but the other bunks are messy. Mother sits on the edge of her bunk, rubbing her cuticles with a towel. They're red from the blood of patients.

She nods to Solomon, then turns to me. "How are you?"

"As good as can be." Honestly, I haven't assessed that yet. I'm trying to seal away the scenes of dead Radicals, many of whom were from Unity Village, but no one I knew personally.

Still, they were my people.

"I thought I'd update you on our course." As Solomon sits on the messed lower bunk across from Mother, I sit beside her. "We're heading north toward Argentina. The projected Wall went back up only an hour after we shut it down, so we're stuck on this side. Looks like you'll still get to show everyone the West."

West. We're going home—to *my* home.

Good. It's time the Council realizes it will lose. My God has *always* survived.

He takes my hand. "So, Parvin, where is the best place for us to go?"

"Ivanhoe." The name pops out with firm certainty. "Mrs. Newton was preparing a safe house for Radicals—the Preacher gave it to her. She and I worked out how it will fit a few hundred people. Those who want to stay in Ivanhoe will be able to start a new life." And it would be on my way back to the Wall . . . to let Father through on New Year's Eve.

"Where exactly is that located?"

I scan the room as if I'll find an old map. "Somewhere inland. There will be a lot of traveling, but I was told there are cities on the coast. Maybe it's the West coast? I don't really know what the West looks like on a map."

"Angelique's been studying the electronic charts. Once we pass through this section of sea ice, we'll be traveling by map only so the USE can't track and destroy us."

Destroy? I didn't even think of them trying to blast us out of the water. Am I leading everyone to death? "What if we run out of fuel?"

He shakes his head. "This ship is mostly solar- and wind-powered. It uses very little fuel."

Thank you, Lord.

We sit silent then, staring at our hands or the floor. I told Solomon I loved him the last time we were together, but so much has happened since then. It's almost inconsequential now. Did I mean it when I said it? Did he?

"Am I doing the right thing?"

Neither of them says anything to my blurted question.

Their silence spurs me to defend it. "I mean, I still don't think I know God's plan or will for my life. He clearly wants me alive—He let Jude and Reid die so I'd live. So what am I supposed to be doing? Is it this . . . to help the Radicals escape from Antarctica? Or is it about the Clocks? About destroying the Wall? About Willow or Skelley Chase? Am I missing what God wants of me?" I look at Mother.

She shrugs and avoids my eyes. "You overthink this, Parvin. Just live."

It's that "just live" mindset that left me feeling empty in the first place. That can't be right. I have to have more purpose and vision, otherwise how can I *pursue* life?

"I disagree," Solomon says. "No disrespect meant, Mrs. Blackwater, but Parvin . . . you're on the right track. I don't know that it comes down to one specific act or purpose. I think it comes down to the greatest commandment."

My brain short-circuits. "Uh, love your neighbor?"

"Close." Solomon grins. "Love God with all your heart, soul, mind, and strength. I don't think He wants us to keep asking and dwelling on His specific plan or will. He wants us to dwell on and seek *Him*. Then our decisions will be made from our love for and relationship with Him. We are free to take action in *whatever* means we want as long as we seek Him and allow Him to guide us."

Mother adjusts the blanket and smooths the wrinkles on my pillow. Does this topic make her uncomfortable?

I roll Solomon's words over in my mind. "How do I get to know Him better? I've been praying . . ."

"His character is everywhere in the Bible. Even when it seems boring, keep reading it."

My pack rests by my bed. The contents are still dry. Mother must have brought it for me. My Bible is in there. "Wish we could read the verse of the week. You know, from the church gathering you took me to."

Solomon pulls a small NAB from his pocket. "Ah, but we *can.*"

He is amazing! "Where did you get that?"

He grins. "Chaos opens the doors of opportunity. The Lead Enforcer is going to find it difficult to contact his superiors . . . at least until he finds another NAB."

Mother's lips are a firm line. "You stole it?"

Solomon nods. "And we'll be able to contact Oliver." He turns it on, and reads, "*'Because the poor are plundered, because the needy groan, I will now arise,' says the Lord; 'I will place him in the safety for which he longs.'"* Psalm twelve, verse five."

We are poor. We are plundered. We are needy and groaning.

The Lord is arising. For us. Like a general for battle, and I want to fight as His soldier. "I don't remember Psalms being one of the days of the week. Which one does it stand for?"

"It's not one. Sometimes we just need a good reminder."

Giddiness rampages in my chest. We're free. God has arisen. He let me survive again. We saved lives. He hears. "The Council lost." I look up. "The people have seen that we can win—we can survive."

"Then it sounds like we're right on track." Solomon stands.

"Tally ho." I grin at my own usage of the phrase. I'm finally understanding it. And I like it.

NAB in hand, Solomon sends messages for the next hour–to his dad, to Father, to Fight and Idris . . .

"Everyone's okay," he finally says, peering down at the screen. "Your father and Tawny are safe. Dad says that Enforcers have come and gone from the orphanage, but Willow's still there."

They're okay. Everyone's okay for now. I can almost hear God's, "I told you so."

The trip away from Antarctica is the opposite of when we traveled to it. The air grows warmer and we mill around on the solar-panel deck. The little girl from Unity Village—I still don't know her name—spots dolphins one day, leaping alongside the ship.

I'd never seen a dolphin before. It's sleek, smooth, and seems blissful. I wouldn't mind being a dolphin.

Solomon, Mother, and I told Father of our escape and our current status. We left out specific details, of course, in case it was stolen or read by an enemy. I don't bother counting the days as we travel. For once, people aren't asking me questions about survival. They only ask, "When will we get there?" and I send them to Frenchie. Or "What's the West like?" and I spend an hour talking about Ivanhoe.

On a bright day, when the air is warming and I'm out on deck, the black woman who tackled an Enforcer during the battle on Antarctica approaches me. She smiles and shakes my hand. "In all the craziness, I haven't been able to officially introduce myself. I'm Gabbie Kenard, the editor-in-chief—well, the *former* editor-in-chief–of *The Daily Hemisphere.*"

My jaw drops. "You're alive? I thought the Council might have killed you!"

Her smile turns sour. "I trusted the Council my whole life, but they treated me like a . . . well, like a Radical! What about freedom of speech?" She glances around as if the Council might be listening over her shoulder. "Actually . . . I wanted to talk to you . . . about one last hurrah."

My heart stutters. "What do you mean?"

She lowers her voice and I barely catch her words. "Do they have NABs in this Ivanhoe of yours?"

I shrug. "I don't know. Mrs. Newton might." I don't tell her about the NAB Solomon and I have been sharing. Not until I understand her motives. "What do you mean by one last hurrah?"

She clasps her hands in front of her. "A video of you talking—sharing the truth about what the Council is doing to us—with emotigraphs and photos from our . . . survival. We can release it to the public. Maybe we could film you speaking about that Dusten boy. Show his overridden Clock."

Speaking. That word won't leave me alone. "I don't know. We're trying to *flee* the Council right now. Do you think it's wise to do something like that so soon?"

"Well, not *now* obviously. Not until we have a NAB. But until then, start thinking about what you want to say."

I haven't exactly said yes yet, crazy lady. I sigh. "I'll think about it."

She grins, and her teeth glow against the dark backdrop of her skin. "Great. When I was denied a Clock and stuck in a boxcar, I finally saw what *you* saw in the Clocks—control. Too much control for the Council. I want to help show the world the truth and show Skelley Chase the danger."

I step back. "Danger?"

She leans toward me. "*I* think the Council is forcing him to work for them." Her eyes reflect the same infatuation that Rat Nose, the receptionist from the county building, had whenever she talked about Skelley. "If he sees the *truth* of what they're doing, maybe he can escape, too."

Before I can tell her Skelley is a back-stabbing monster, she fluffs her poufy hair and crosses the deck toward another group.

• • •

We eat three meals a day, living mainly off *cooked* potatoes and chicken. Mother and Madame plant their flag of ownership in the kitchen or, as Frenchie corrects me, the *galley*.

The captive Enforcers and Monster-Voice remain crammed in a shipping container. That's where the peaceful feeling stops. I can't walk past them without hearing banging, moans, or pleas for freedom. I finally go to Mother about it.

"They will survive." She cuts up potatoes and carrots for a stew.

"But . . . it's not right."

She chops through a potato and the knife edge smacks against the cutting board with an echo. "It's *just*."

"Why is it just? Because *we* had to live through it and some of us died? It's inhumane. It's already been a week."

She blows a stray hair from her face and sets the knife down. An odd calm settles her shoulders, and she meets my gaze, composed and patient. "Parvin, you have a special place in your heart for the enemy."

"What?"

She lays a hand on my arm. "You befriended Skelley Chase without knowing who he was. You have feelings for Mr. Hawke. You care about Kaphtor now because he helped save us. You're worried about the Enforcers. You see? You cannot see the situation without bias."

I push her hand off my arm. "Of *course* I'm biased. I see everyone as a human. My entire purpose is bringing *shalom* back to this world—making it the way God intended it to be. Do you think He wants us to treat them like this?"

She returns to the potatoes. But, of course, I mentioned God. Even though she's given me spiritual words of wisdom and verses in the past, her faith is not like what Reid and I believe. It's a . . . nervous faith. Something about it isn't right. Why isn't it changing her? Why can't she see?

"Parvin, you have a wild faith. Someday it will settle in with your logic and you will understand."

Wild faith. I like the sound of that. "I'm going to ask Solomon."

I find him on the starboard side of the deck. He rests against the rail and stares out at the projected Wall.

We keep it on the starboard side of the ship to make sure we're heading in the correct direction . . . and to see if the Wall comes down again. As long it's in view, we're heading toward land.

"Solomon?"

He looks up, and the whisper of a frown leaves his face when he sees me. "Good twilight."

I like High-City language when Solomon uses it. "Good twilight. May I speak with you about something?" My question sounds formal, even to my ears. Is it because I'm nervous?

"Of course." He turns and rests his elbows behind him on the top rail.

I scan the solar-powered deck for anyone nearby. Everyone else seems occupied or distant. "Well, it's about the Enforcers in the boxcar."

He watches me, waiting for me to continue. Why did I expect that he'd know what was bothering me? Am I the only one bothered?

"Well, they're being treated like we were. Raw potatoes and everything. Do you think that's . . . wrong?"

"Yes."

My eyebrows spring up. "You do?"

"Don't you?"

I laugh. "Well, yeah. But no one else seems to. I think it needs to change."

He straightens. "That's where I get stuck. They are still a danger to us. Even trying to move them somewhere else could result in an attack that sends us back to Antarctica. I talked to Harman, Cap, and Kaphtor, but they'd have none of it. Kaphtor is bitter, Harman wants nothing to do with them, and Cap . . . well, you know Cap."

"So what should we do? Talk to everyone? Take a vote?"

He shakes his head. "That would be just as dangerous. The people are in a very precarious place right now. They don't know what they think about you, and they're all secretly terrified of arriving in the West. You need to be very careful in your actions for now."

"If they're watching me, shouldn't I be an example of how I want them to be? Shouldn't *I* be the one to instigate kindness to those Enforcers?"

"Not yet."

I don't like his answers—they don't fit with what I feel is right— but not wanting to argue or make a case for my feelings, I return to the galley. The smell of stew fills the small space. "Tonight, cook the potatoes for the prisoners."

Mother and Madame glance up from the stew. "Why?"

"Because it's right." I turn to leave, but stop a moment. "And *I* will deliver them. I'll get them before dinner."

I toss the potatoes, a few at a time, through the barred window of the shipping container. No one says thank you. No one says anything.

"Is anyone dead in there?" I'm met by silence and my heart thuds. What if they died already? I pound the side. "Hey, you guys okay?"

I press my ear against the cold metal. I think there's move- ment, then there's a voice.

"Shh!"

It's hushed, but it gave him away.

They're trying to play dead, maybe to manipulate me into opening the door. "It's not going to work."

Someone laughs. I think it's Monster-Voice.

I leave.

The next night, I make sure Mother cooks the potatoes again. When I deliver them, I include a few folded blankets. Even though the air is getting warmer, it's still cool at night. That was the hardest part for me in the container—trying to keep warm.

A few more nights pass, and Mother gets into the habit of cooking their food. I've shoved enough blankets through to carpet the floor and walls of the container. They never say anything, but I feel better. I always let the men deliver the water since I'd be too weak to fight off an attack.

The day comes when we reach the part in our course where we need to head away from the Wall. Frenchie and the blonde navigation officer—who was apparently recovering from a head wound during the fights on the ship—found a map of North America. It doesn't show much of the West side, and who knows how accurate it is? But the navigator wants to survive as much as we do, so she's been calculating distances and looking at charts like her life depends in it. Which it does.

I stand at the stern and watch the projected Wall disappear into the blue misty horizon. The longer I stare, the more emotion flames inside as if a bellows pumps oxygen into it.

When I held that rifle and shot up the controls to the projected Wall, I was powerful. I *freed* us. The Council's new "system" of getting rid of the Low Cities failed.

Maybe that was the whole reason we were sent to Antarctica— to start the change. In a weird way, the flying bullets and shattered screens were part of the process of bringing shalom.

I want to do it again. I want to get this Wall down for good. This freedom needs to continue . . . to be permanent. It's time for the Wall to stop being a death sentence and for the Clocks to stop determining the value of our lives.

All these things are used to separate us from humanity, rightness, and shalom. I snap an emotigraph of the projection, to remind myself of this conviction.

"An hour for your thoughts?"

I tear my gaze from the blue horizon and face Solomon. "Ooh, they're worth more than an hour."

He lifts an eyebrow. "Really? Do tell."

Should I? The passion is too strong to restrain, but something inside me doesn't want to share my churning thoughts yet. Not until they settle. Not until I *know* this can be done.

"I'll tell you soon, Solomon."

When we reach land, *then* I'll tell him that I'm going to destroy the Wall . . . both stone and projection. For good.

Destruction.

It is my calling.

I've never been so sure of anything in my life. I am the only one who can do this. God has provided me with everything—the connections, the passion, the purpose.

Mother was wrong. I'm not meant to just live. I'm meant to follow my passions, with God at the front.

I will tear down the Wall. Believers can cross over and find a place to worship God without the threat of Enforcers. Willow can come home. We will be reunited with Father and Tawny. The Council's control will be broken.

Maybe this is why I survived and Reid died. Maybe this is why Jude died giving up his Clock information, and I was left behind. Maybe this is why I've always hated the Wall . . .

Because I was meant to destroy it.

We reach the west coast of the old United States and spot our first city. Buildings crawl out of the ocean onto the shore, like decayed crabs frozen in time. Windows are broken, frames bend like soggy sponges, and most roofs are caved. The base of each building is covered in crusty white stuff that looks almost like snow, but the weather's too warm for snow.

The shore is lumpy and leads to brown hills with green shrubs. Similar-looking islands break up the ocean's smoothness. More like hill peaks than isles.

We navigate past and I scan the shore for life. How will we know when to stop? Perhaps I'll ask Frenchie what the map looks like on her screens. I enter the bridge stairwell–and that's when I hear her screaming. Not panicked screaming, but angry commands. "We can't turn eet on, ze Council will find us!"

"But we'll sink if we hit—" A man's voice, shouting.

"You fool! Get us away from ze shore." She lets loose a string of angry French.

The ship jolts and I'm thrown against the railing. I tumble down the few stairs I'd climbed. A deep metal screech rips through my senses. A death cry from the hull.

We've run into something.

A young man hurtles down the stairs as I climb back to my feet. His wide eyes tell me all I need to know.

"Are we sinking? What did we hit?"

He runs by without a word. The exit is two flights down, so close, but I feel trapped. I picture water streaming into the stairwell and carrying me away until I get tangled amid the railing and drown.

Drown.

Drown like when Jude and I rode the flood down the Dregs.

"Calm down." Pep talk over, I force myself upward toward the bridge. Frenchie directs the mayhem of frenzied sailors and flashing lights. She glances at me. "We are een trouble. Get everyone on deck."

"What will you do?"

"Steer ze ship toward shore. Eet is best to sink within swimming distance."

"Okay." I sprint back down the stairwell. Am I imagining the ship tilting, filling with water? It feels heavier beneath my feet.

I'm going crazy.

The deck is already packed with people. "Get everyone on deck!"

"We're here," Cap drawls, standing beside Kaphtor.

I glance around. "Everyone?" He shrugs. I don't know how much time we have, so I run downstairs toward the berths. "We're sinking! Everyone on deck! We're sinking! Everyone on deck!" Those word choices should do the job.

God, please don't let anyone get trapped in this ship and drown.

I go to the galley. It's empty, but for a few burlap sacks of potatoes rolling around on the ground. I scoop the loose potatoes into the sacks and tie the tops together, using my teeth and good hand. Then I sling the linked bags over my shoulder.

The ship lurches and the room tilts thirty degrees. I scream. Then I crawl, clawing my way back up the stairs and out on deck. Not an easy task with twenty pounds of potatoes and one hand.

I reach fresh air. People are jumping over board. Thankfully, the ship now sits so low in the water, they're not dying from the fall. Kaphtor struggles to climb the railing, throwing a couple of shrink-wrapped life rafts into the water. He helps Cap over the edge, and they leap after the life rafts. Kaphtor pulls the cords so they inflate.

I toss the potatoes into the water and look for Mother or Solomon. Mother's holding the rail and scanning the deck. My pack is slung over her shoulders.

"Mother!" I wave. "I'm here!" I run over as the ship tilts even more. "Where's Solomon?"

She shakes her head and I look around, using her as an anchor.

"We have to jump, Parvin."

"But where's Solomon?"

"He'll be fine. He's an Enforcer."

Then I see him, using a crowbar to break a lock on the container door holding the other Enforcers and Monster Voice. I hadn't given a second thought to our prisoners.

"Parvin, come *on.*"

I can't tear my eyes from Solomon. The shipping container has slid against the opposite railing and he's pounding at the locked door with all he has. Any moment, the other containers are going to tumble on top of him.

Crush him.

"I'm right behind you, Mother. *Go.*"

She rolls her eyes. "You are determined to test my limits." She jumps.

I release the rail and half-run, half-slide toward Solomon. The ship tilts even more and one stack of containers leans. Leans. The top one lifts onto its edge, poised over him.

"Solomon!"

His pounding breaks the lock. He throws one of the doors open, still crouching on the other one. The leaning container above his head shifts its balance.

"Look out!" I abandon caution, scramble up his container, and tackle him. We fly out, over the railing, separating mid air. The falling container clips my foot then follows us over the edge.

I land face-first in the water. It slaps me like a branch switch. I claw through the water, certain that the falling shipping container will land on top of us.

I hear the splash, feel the thrust of the wave. Another. Metal on metal. Water cuffing my ears. I thrash, holding my breath longer than lungs were meant to be held. I break the surface. Groaning machinery surrounds me.

Finally, my eyes open. The ship is fully on its side, sinking fast. I paddle backward, watching it dip below the surface, releasing its last bubbles of farewell. A hand grips mine.

Solomon. His dark blond hair is plastered to his forehead and he no longer holds the crowbar.

Then the cargo ship is gone. "Did you get them all out?"

He spits salt water from his mouth. "I think so."

The chaos is epilogued by stillness. Two thousand of us float in the water, staring at the spot where the boat sank. Then, as if by silent agreement, we swim toward the shore. No alarm, no panic, no arguing.

Those who can't swim or are still injured rest in the lifeboats while others pull them. The strong swimmers help the weak. Floating particles of ship are passed around and shared.

We are one.

Unified in survival.

It's a terrifying, yet beautiful thing. The calm comes from each other, from our unity—not from the Clocks or remembered Numbers. For once, we're *not* a population of second hands. We're just swimmers. Survivors. Radicals.

And up ahead is our new home.

• • •

It turns out we ran into an old skyscraper, only Cap called it a "seascraper" since it's underwater. During our swim to shore, Solomon points out the city beneath our feet. I tread water for some time, trying to spot details.

Tall buildings stretch up to meet our sodden boots. Coral-coated blacktop roads wind between the buildings. Crooked light posts sport dark shells and crusted sea art. I don't look for very long. Too many live things swim below us and my imagination threatens to get the best of me.

I've heard of sharks. Sting rays. Big squids that eat people. I want out of the ocean, despite the eerie beauty of a drowned city. But climbing onto shore is no easy task, as it isn't a true shore at all. It's a submerged town with no smooth beach, no clear exit point. I finally find an old road that leads out of the water.

The white crust on the shore buildings turns out to be salt. Cap touches some with his finger, licks it, then spits. A few other people do the same.

I find Mother wandering among the people with the two bags of potatoes over one shoulder and my pack over the other. She looks at me as I approach. "You couldn't find more than this?"

I hold up my one hand. "I have my limitations." I take my pack from her. It's sodden and I think achingly of when I ruined Reid's journal in the Dregs. Did I just ruin my Bible? "At least we're starting our new trek on full stomachs."

"With no blankets, water, or direction."

I almost call her a pessimist, then I catch my own thoughts in a butterfly net and scold them. This is *Mother*. What am I thinking? She's trying to prepare herself for the situation at hand. Besides, pessimism notwithstanding, she's right.

Madame and Kaphtor drag a life raft ashore. Inside sit Cap and Gabbie, who holds Dusten's wrapped body. I close my eyes and release a breath through my nose. I hadn't even thought of

Dusten. But someone did. I'm glad. The charred state of his body seems have a mummifying effect.

If possible, I want to bury him in Ivanhoe. I know it's not the East side of the Wall, but it's freedom and comfort. It's good we have him—maybe Gabbie Kenard is onto something. I can film myself talking, with Dusten's overridden Clock in the background. I want to *show* the people that his Numbers didn't determine his death.

If they believe me, more people might rebel against the new Clock-matching.

A handful of Unity people turn to me now that we're on shore. But others gather in groups as they did in Antarctica, forming their own plans. I'm about to call a meeting between the leaders of these groups—we need *some* form of unity in this wild land—when a voice hollers from above us.

"Oy, this is private property!"

Everyone hushes and scans the air. Atop the tallest building, balancing on a decayed two-by-four frame, are three men, somewhere around Father's age. The middle one has dirty dreadlocks, a sleeveless shirt, and cut-off pants. He's barefoot, with a couple fishing poles slung over his shoulder.

"Can't you read?"

Silence.

"Are you all mute or something?"

People. People live here on this . . . *private property.* I almost laugh, it's so absurd. "Of course we can read!" I shout.

"Then get off my land, you bottom-dwellers!"

Some of the people inch their way behind me, until I'm standing alone—the voice for the lost. I'm about to explain our predicament to this man, but hesitate. He's defensive. If he doesn't like people on his land, that means he's had this problem before. "How many other people live here?"

"The town's a mile that way." He gestures behind him with his fishing pole. "And I've had enough scavenging wars to last a lifetime. So get outta here and don't start no trouble."

He doesn't follow up with an "or else," probably because there are hundreds of us and only one of him, not counting his two silent buddies. But it's too soon for us to be making enemies.

Whispers drift from behind me and I catch someone saying, "There are people here. On *this* side. A whole town in the West!"

Oh, if only they knew. "We, uh . . . just swam to shore after our ship sank. Can you help us?"

Now it's their turn to be silent. The man with dreads picks at his teeth with a finger. "You say your ship sank?"

I nod.

"What type o' ship?"

"A cargo ship."

He whispers something to the guy on his left, then asks, "Where?"

I point vaguely. "It hit a skyscraper."

He cocks his head to the side, dreads swinging. "Where ya from? Are ya scavengers?"

I shake my head. "We're not scavengers and we're just passing through." Someone in the group behind me mutters at this.

"I'll help you out if you let my scubers scavenge the ship . . . and don' mention it to anyone else."

I can't promise that the people behind me will keep quiet, but if that's what it takes to keep us alive, then they can have the boat. I'm not going to ask what a scuber is. His eyes hold my gaze, earnest. He wants that ship. He wants it bad, but he's trying to hide it.

I lift my chin, throw my shoulders back, and plant my hand on my hip. "We've got some terms." I've been to Ivanhoe. I know how to play tough. "You'll give us food and shelter for at *least* two days. Then you'll provide passage to Ivanhoe or, if that's not possible, information on how to get there."

"That there's a high price." He spits off the edge of the building.

I jerk a thumb over my shoulder toward the ocean. "That there's a big boat."

He grins. "All righty. But I can transport only half of you to Ivanhoe. The rest will have to earn passage."

I turn around to see what my people think. Rufus McTavish, Solomon, and the other people in leadership positions all nod.

"Deal." We'll work out the details later.

"Boys, go get your gear." The other two men scramble down from the building and disappear. "So who are you, little one-handed seasnapper? You got a name?"

"Parvin Blackwater." My name is an unyielding banner, staking my claim as the voice of the Radicals. For the first time, while among my people, I'm their leader. They stand behind me, I stand ahead with a staff of tenacity.

"Named after the blackwater, huh? That name's fit for a sea leader. How'd you lose your hand?"

I continue his casual conversational tone, even though it takes an odd amount of willpower to mention it in front of my people. "Had a run-in with an albino clan near the Wall."

His lips quirk to one side. "Is that when you earned your title, Blackwater?"

"I was born with it." It's never seemed special to me, but maybe because this man lives by the sea it means something more to him.

He raises an eyebrow. "Well, my name's Chark."

"Chark?"

"Like the giant sea predator."

"I think 'e means *shark*," Frenchie says behind me. I wave for her to shush.

"Now get your soggy salt-hides over here and we'll get you into town." Chark walks to the edge of the building, where an old rope hangs down the corner.

He slides down it, strides to me, and gives my hand a firm, calloused shake. "Welcome to Lost Angel."

31

I could never live in Lost Angel.

For one, it smells like fish. If I had a specie for every time I gagged, I'd be able to buy Skelley Chase's head on a platter. Second, it's not very . . . warm. By nightfall, the sea air turns cold and the houses are breezy. Most residences are recycled ruins.

I'm viewed as the leader of the Radicals, so Chark insists I stay in his main home. Solomon and Mother join me. Everyone else disperses, either into the houses covering Chark's property or to stay with the other inhabitants of Lost Angel.

Monster Voice and the other Enforcers are brought to me. They're weaponless, ragged, and half-starved despite my attempts to feed them cooked potatoes.

I study them for a moment. "You're free to go."

They don't seem to like this idea, but I don't care. There are people in our group who would rather see them punished. But they've been stripped of their old lives, that's punishment enough.

I turn to Chark. "Can you make sure they get protected rest and food for two days?"

Chark nods and tells them where to go. As they turn to walk away, Monster Voice pauses beside me, his head hanging low. "Thank you."

Then they're gone.

The enormity of this salt-crusted city is barely dented by the handful of inhabitants. From what I can see, the population isn't any larger than that of Unity Village, but unlike Unity, the city ruins of Lost Angel seem to go on forever.

Houses are draped with drying fishing nets. Since it's now nighttime, people light fires on their doorsteps. Some houses we pass have flat roofs and I catch sparks flying from above. Roof bonfires. That sounds fun.

All the houses were flooded by the sea when the meteorite struck the Pacific Ocean over a hundred years ago. The earthquakes didn't help, either. Now people spend their days fishing for food and fixing up houses. Crab and lobster shells, clams, and conches are used to decorate.

Chark's house is further up on the hill, where most of the inhabitants seem to live, and it's *nice*. It stands on stilts with long draperies acting as walls between polished wood beams. The draperies are tied by thin cords to keep them from flapping. Candlelight and lanterns fill the house, mixed with some electric lights.

"All the glass was busted out of this house when it flooded." Chark leads us up some stairs to the deck overlooking the city ruins. "I found it looking pretty shabby and fixed it up a bit."

There's a pool out front with sea creatures swimming around. He points into the water. "There are a couple stingrings, sea stars, and a turgle—one of the biggest I've found."

Is he calling them by the wrong name on purpose? "Do you mean sea turtle?"

Chark looks at me with a raised eyebrow. "Haven't ever heard of a sea *turtle*. I think someone's feeding you fish eggs. I'm a sea master, I know what they're called."

He leads us into the house. Mother and I exchange a look, both biting our lips to keep back the smiles. Solomon examines the drapery. We pass through the green and blue draperies into an illuminated patio covered by a coned thatch roof.

Chairs made of conically woven basket reeds and log stools provide seating. Pillows lean against the walls and dot the ground for lounging. The windows are empty of shutters or glass, too, with transparent draperies over them. The ground is made of a giant slab of stone.

I'm used to seeing different dwellings like this, Mrs. Newton's house, Jude's apartment, Ivanhoe . . . but Mother's jaw hangs loose and she runs her hand over almost everything. I take her other hand.

"If any of your people want to stay in Lost Angel," Chark says, "they're welcome to apply for an abandoned house and work off the payment. That's how we do it here. If approved, they could refurbish it from scraps."

I plop my damp pack on the ground in one of the sleeping rooms. The floor is covered in pillows of all sizes. Mother places her belongings on the ground, too, then surveys the room as if lost. I want to tell her she'll get used to it, but she's already been used to poverty her entire life. There's nothing I can do to stifle the awakening.

I don't give Chark the chance to lead us to where Solomon will sleep. We need to address things now. Together. "When can we talk about getting to Ivanhoe?"

He looks me up and down. "Whenever you've cleaned yourself up. I'm around fish all day, and they're perfume compared to your reek."

Hey, wait just a minute. We bathed on the ship.

"Down the hall, to the left is a shower room. Water runs for a half hour. Then it needs to reboot."

Well, I won't say no to a shower. Perfect. Ten minutes each.

I go first and try to keep it down to five minutes so Mother will have extra time. I remember my first time in a shower aboard the *Ivanhoe Independent*. I couldn't get enough of it.

But Mother takes only five minutes, too. Always so efficient. Solomon, however, soaks up fifteen minutes of heat and water, making me wish I'd taken longer. Chark provides each of us with new clothing. It all smells like fish with a coating of salt on it, but it's fresher than what we were wearing.

I wear baggy pants made out of thin linen with a drawstring waist, and a white tank. Somewhere in my pile of new clothes, a bra and underwear were provided. I'm not about to ask where Chark got them.

We congregate out on the porch around a fire pit. Chark, Solomon, and I sit in the wicker cone chairs, while a tall, plump woman with long lashes and red hair that reaches her waist fries something behind a little bar section.

"You look nice," Solomon whispers to me. He wears a loose, button-up shirt and shorts.

I stretch. "I *feel* nice." Clean. Fresh. Wet and soapy. Ahh.

Mother sits on a pile of pillows on the ground, leaving the other wicker chair empty. She holds her dirty knitted shawl around her shoulders, covering the skin exposed from the tank. I don't think I've ever seen her wear anything without sleeves before.

"Kiddos are still out fishing." Chark leans back. "But they'll smell dinner from four miles away. Let's talk while the little seas-nappers are gone. Why do you want to go to Ivanhoe?"

Because it's my key to destroying the Wall. "That's not your business."

"Oh, I think it is. We've recently allied with The Preacher. He married my sister just a few months back. We're not going to send some crazies into his city."

Mother adjusts the pillow beneath her and glances up at me. I press my thumbnail into the tips of my other fingers. What does she think of how I'm handling everything?

"Look, I've met The Preacher. He gave me funds and helped a friend of mine find a home. Our intentions are for safety only, unless you want us all to join you here in Lost Angel."

He shrugs. "I don't care. There's plenty of room, but they'll have to learn to feed from the sea. There are a lot of seasnappers looking for mates and you just brought a whole pool to choose from."

His wife sets a plate of shrimp skewers on the glass table between us. She smiles at me before returning to the grill. Chark waves toward the food. "Help yourself."

I'm not about to argue. The cargo ship food reminded us what it was like to be human instead of caged animals, but escaping a sinking ship, swimming over a city to shore, and bargaining with a ruling fisherman has given me a hefty appetite.

"The Preacher built us a motor coach line to Ivanhoe as a trade for our alliance." Chark snags a skewer from the plate. "You're lucky that happened, Blackwater. The only way to Ivanhoe before that was walking."

"Nothing I haven't done before." I slide a shrimp off the skewer with my teeth and nibble the fat end. It's tougher and more rubbery than fish. But whatever seasonings Chark's wife put on them eradicates my hesitance. It's delicious.

Mother delicately removes the shell from the tail of a shrimp.

"The motor coaches can take a couple hundred people at a time."

Solomon grabs two skewers, then hands one to Mother. "When can we leave?"

"So soon?" Chark shoves four shrimp into his mouth, tails and all. I hear the crunch from my side of the table.

"I have friends waiting for me." I grip the skewer tight, thinking of Willow. Is she still safe in that orphanage? "We need to get to them as soon as possible." I've yet to approach the topic of the Wall with Chark, but he doesn't seem to care where we're from.

He leans back and tosses an emptied skewer into a lined trash basket. "I guess you could leave the day after tomorrow if you wanted. It's about a two day ride in the motorcoaches."

"We'll talk to the people."

• • •

It's not easy to find everyone. Some people meld into the fishy city-life like they were born for it. Some don't care to talk, they don't care to think of other options. All they want to do is fish, eat, and sit by the fire.

I can't blame them. Most of these Radicals lived in a Low City their entire lives. Then in the course of a month or two, they were stripped of all they knew, sent to Antarctica, and then escaped on a cargo ship to the wasteland they've feared their whole lives.

They deserve to relax. This is their shalom. This is how things should be . . . for some.

Not for me.

Rufus McTavish, Solomon, and Mother help round up all of our people. Chark allows us to meet at the shore where the cargo ship sank and Solomon uses the rope to haul me to the top of the decrepit building Chark stood on.

Not everyone is here, but the sea of faces below me waits. Watches. Gabbie stands on the edge of the crowd with a notepad and pen. She must have gotten them from her host family.

My stomach tries to leap out of my midsection. What am I going to say?

SPEAK.

"We've survived." Those two words suck the air from my lungs, leaving me a dry-lipped voiceless mime. But the people catch the weight of that statement just as much as it stuns me.

We've survived.

When my voice returns, it's as if the people are now ready to listen to me—to accept my words. We are one. We are unified.

"Chark has opened Lost Angel to us. If you wish to stay and live here, he will put you to work to earn a living space. If you wish to leave, I am traveling on the motorcoaches to Ivanhoe tomorrow. Three hundred of you can fit. The rest will have to wait until the next motorcoach trip. There's a safe house in Ivanhoe for us, started up by Mrs. Newton after she and her daughter survived passing through Opening Three. Ivanhoe is a city. You can find work and shelter there."

They listen intently. I'm the only one with knowledge about this strange land. "Anyone wanting to return to the East for loved ones should come. I will continue beyond Ivanhoe and return to the Wall for the rest of my family."

I don't share that I'm going to destroy the Wall. Even they can't handle that amount of rebellion just yet. "For those who want to stay here or in Ivanhoe, feel free to write down the names of your loved ones on the East side. I'll send the list to my father and see if he can contact them and bring them to this side."

My silent, peaceful father. Would he do that for me? For the people? Of course he would. And we have the Lead Enforcer's NAB from Antarctica.

"That's all I have for you. Any questions?"

The floodgates burst. I spend the next hour answering questions about Ivanhoe and about my plans for getting back to the Wall.

Three hundred Radicals jump at the offer to take the motorcoaches to Ivanhoe the next day. More will catch the second trip a week later. Those joining me—aside from Mother and Solomon—include Kaphtor, Cap, Frenchie, Madame, Gabbie, and Dusten's body, oddly preserved by his charred state.

Gabbie smiles as we step onto the lead motorcoach the next day. She lowers her voice as the engines start up and I barely catch her words. "Have you made up your mind yet?"

Now that I really am a leader, it's my duty to commit. Gabbie's video idea seems like the moment for which I've been prepared. I could publish my emotigraphs and show people what it's like to feel like cattle being readied for slaughter. Show them the injustice.

Show them Dusten's overridden Clock.

I pull the NAB that Solomon and I have been sharing from my bag. "I'm in."

She gasps so hard she chokes. "You have a NAB? That's perfect!"

"Let's reveal the truth behind the Council and this Clock-matching."

"Do you think Skelley Chase will listen?" Her question is breathless.

I wondered if this would come back up. At first I didn't bother to argue, since her words rose from a crush on the famous biographer, but she needs to know he's not a good guy. "No. He won't. He's part of the Council, Gabbie, and *he* helped enable the new Clock-matching."

Her face turns impassive. "Yeah, the Clock-matching. That Dusten boy died from the projected Wall and I . . . well, I guess I don't know what to believe now."

"Believe in God." I grasp the topic. "Maybe that sounds . . . too spiritual, but I mean it."

She waves a hand in front of her face. "Yeah, I know. I read your X-book. But the big man in the sky isn't how I get my assurance. To each her own, I suppose." She winks and plops into a bench seat. "Think about what you want to say to the USE. We'll start filming in Ivanhoe."

To each her own? My belief in God isn't just because He's my ticket to comfort. It's because He's . . . *God*. He created us. He's shown Himself to me. I sense His voice. Can't she see His hand in my life? Wasn't it clear enough in my biography?

Maybe I didn't make as much of a difference as I thought I did.

"Get me *off* this thing!" Cap grips the motorcoach seat in front of him so hard he could probably rip the cushion right off.

The ride isn't as smooth as the motorcoaches in Ivanhoe city. It's bumpy and loud and shaky. Even so, I would have thought Cap could handle it after being locked in a boxcar for a couple weeks.

I guess not.

Kaphtor sits beside him, rigid and immune to Cap's fear, but I notice a small grin. Next to me, Solomon laughs. His smile fills his entire face and releases a load of anxiety that usually presses down his eyebrows. We're heading back home.

Passage-paid.

I don't think I'll miss Lost Angel, but I *will* miss some of my people who are staying there. I'm glad they've found a home.

As much as I want to talk to Solomon, I refuse to yell and risk the whole motorcoach hearing. It's too loud for Gabbie and me to film anything too, not until we reach Ivanhoe, so I hunch over the NAB and send another update to Father.

Father,
   We're on our way to Ivanhoe. I've decided to destroy the Wall so that Radicals in hiding can escape to this side.

I still haven't shared this plan with Solomon . . . with anyone here. I need to soon.

The Council plans to fill-in Opening Three soon. Here is a list of people left on your side. Their family members are alive here with us. Please try to contact these people and bring them with you to the Wall on that date we talked about.
   -Parvin

I don't say the date just in case the message gets stolen by the Council. After that message is sent, I send him the list of names I received from the people. Mother sits in front of us, her head lolling back on the chair. She's asleep, even with the noise and Cap's screaming. It will be good to see her and Father reunited.

Gabbie sits behind Solomon and me. Her name fits her perfectly—she's a motor-mouth. I can't make out a word she says above the racket of the motorcoach, but that doesn't deter her. I catch words like *Daily Hemisphere*, and *boyfriend*, and *dancing*. At one point I hear Skelley's name and turn around, but by then she's on the topic of food.

My gaze blurs as I stare out the window at the passing scenery. The ground is brown and hot, seeming to radiate into my bones purely through its appearance. Most of the brush is spotty, like a giant scattered seeds over the desert floor. Instead of rolling hills, we pass small mountains of dark rock. Dried up water streaks run down the sides of the beasts, like mountain stretch marks.

Day two takes us through snowy hills and into *real* mountains. *Mountains.* The majestic beasts are built of rock crags and white-dusted forests. I've never seen mountains like this. They tower above us like sentinels. Even Solomon can't tear his eyes away.

The motorcoach track weaves back and forth, up mountain passes and down. Gabbie Kenard doesn't speak anymore. In fact, she's rather green under that chocolatey skin of hers.

The ground is covered in several inches of snow. Everything looks so clean and fresh. I want to run out and make a snow angel. I haven't been in the West in winter. What will be different? What date is it, anyway? I know it's mid-December, but no one's bothered to ask, or to care—a first, coming from a population usually run by the Clocks. Are people getting used to the idea of not counting their Numbers?

Finally . . . I see it.

Ivanhoe.

Home.

The Marble—an enormous ball of bustling city in the center of Ivanhoe—glistens under the winter sun. The snow on the ground illuminates the piecemeal anatomy of the metropolis. As we slow, the *oohs* and *aahs* of my people reach my ears. I want to throw my arms wide and yell, "Look where I'm taking you!"

Do they find it beautiful? Magnificent?

Does it look like a home for them? Safety? Freedom?

God, it's stunning. You're stunning.

Mrs. Newton and Laelynn wait for us there.

"I can't wait to see them." Solomon stares hard into the front of the motorcoach, as if his gaze will pull us into the train tunnel faster.

"Me too." On impulse, I slide my fingers into his. He looks at me and squeezes my hand tight for a breath. We don't have a label. I just want to know Solomon more—to be with him more. That's enough.

We arrive at a different section of the city than the *Ivanhoe Independent*. It takes me a few moments to get my bearings when we step outside, but my people wait patiently, albeit nervously, for me to lead them.

It's as though this newness petrifies them more than the wasteland of Antarctica did. They look lost and helpless. Mother's fingers are white around her shawl. She stares straight ahead, as if resisting the urge to look up and take it all in.

Open up. Let this world in. It's beautiful!

I take my gaze from her tight-lipped face and lead the procession up the sidewalk. Gabbie snatches the NAB from me and starts filming our walk. The air is crisp and icy, clawing through our beach clothing in seconds. Bicycles weave up and down the street, ringing bells and sounding tiny horns. The sidewalk is relatively clear for the busyness of the day.

Strands of electric lights wind up the streetlamps. The sun is setting and they flicker on with the first shadow. Red, green, fairy-white. The colors send a message of welcome, celebration, and cheer.

Garlands hang over the street, weaving back and forth in giant *V* shapes. More strands of light decorate those, as well as baubles of silver flowers and snowflakes.

"Eez eet Christmas?" A puff of fog pops from Frenchie's mouth. Her stitches are out and her scar is fading a bit.

"Let's find Mrs. Newton and ask." I hurry up the street to keep our limbs warm. It's a different type of cold than the Antarctica cold—a wetter chill. Antarctica sucked out our very breath, dried up our tongues, and left us withered and frozen. Here, the cold fills our bones with winter gel, expanding and chilling us from the inside out.

Please, God, let me find Mrs. Newton's address soon.

Solomon cranes his neck up almost the whole time we walk, taking in the multi-storied buildings and the bicycle racks. He's traveled the world, been to High Cities . . . I'm surprised at his awe, but thankful for it. I'm sharing a part of my story with him. Is he remembering the entries I wrote about Ivanhoe, when we still communicated through the NAB?

After a few blocks, I see the mansion. I'd seen it only once before, and forgot how big it was. The front is made of brick, with three stories of smooth glass windows. Decorative black shutters lay open on each side of the windows and planters under each window explode with red and white poinsettias. Greek columns wound with pine garlands support the entrance. Under a shadowed arch stand double black doors with a gold knocker.

The mansion fans out into another layer, and at least eight giant brick chimneys stretch like beacons from the roof, indicating the enormity of the interior. I stride toward the steps, trusting everyone will follow, but a hand grabs my arm.

"Parvin, stop," Mother says through tight teeth. "Are you sure you know what's in there?"

I look at the entrance and back at her wide eyes. "Mrs. Newton owns this place. She and I helped organize with the Preacher so that Radicals could live here."

Her gaze fixates on the front door. "I don't think the Newtons were *this* wealthy."

I kiss her on the cheek. "It was a gift from the Preacher. Just follow, okay?" Her nerves are so different than mine. When I first arrived in Ivanhoe, I loved the magnitude, the brain-stretching building designs, the newness. But it cripples Mother. It turns her into a follower instead of a leader.

Now, I'm the leader. Me, the girl who wasted seventeen years of her life.

I walk up the steps with that message floating in my mind, lift the gold knocker, and rap hard. Three times.

It takes a moment before the left door opens and there stands a fifteen-year-old with yellowish hair cut in a choppy style. Alive, healthy, albino—and one eye covered in a black leather patch.

Elm.

He's alive.

He appraises me with his good eye, barely taking notice of the three hundred people behind me. "Took you long enough."

"Elm!" I lurch forward to hug him, but he steps aside.

"Get in to the fires. Then we'll talk."

I walk in, and the three hundred people stream in behind me, but I stare at Elm. "You're alive. You're *alive!* Willow was right."

He frowns and his crinkled brow catches on his eye-patch. "Willow is always right."

A shout from Solomon snatches my attention. "Laelynn!"

Laelynn—a six-year-old girl in a pink dress with tight blond curls–launches into his arms with a squeal. "Solomon! Solomon! Mommy look, it's Solomon!"

And there's Mrs. Newton, her chestnut hair up in a loose knot, tucking a rag into one of her skirt pockets.

Mother gets to her first. It's odd for me to watch my two mothers, embracing. Mrs. Newton comforted me and listened to my story when I came to Ivanhoe. She allowed herself to be emotional, tender, and encouraging.

Mother, on the other hand, is like a brick wall with one tiny peephole into her emotions. She's a pillar and demands that those around her become pillars, too. But this trip has brought her out of her comfort zone—her pillarhood is shrinking.

Solomon hugs Mrs. Newton next. She whispers something in his ear and he pulls away with a nod. Then she comes to me and wraps her arms around me. I cling to the embrace.

"Welcome home," she whispers.

I almost cry. "I didn't think I'd ever be back."

She leans away. "Elm told me you survived."

"How did *he* know?"

She rests a hand on my shoulder. "First we'll get everyone settled. Then we'll talk."

I turn to the group crowded in the entry. "Everyone, this is Mrs. Newton. She and Laelynn survived the Wall and put this place together for you, for Radicals."

"It was mostly Parvin's idea." Mrs. Newton smiles at me.

I feel Mother's stare. "We'll get everyone settled and warmed up."

Here's when Mrs. Newton takes over. She leads us up a giant staircase with blue carpeting that makes it look frosted. Strings of blue and white sparkles hang from the high ceiling along the path of the staircase. I run my fingers through them and they clink together.

She assigns four people to a room. "I'm still putting bunk beds in. Someday I'll get six to a room. The Preacher added a small hotel-like building to the back of the mansion, bringing the count up to a hundred rooms. I didn't expect we'd use them all but"— she looks around as people file into their rooms—"I guess I was wrong. You're the first I've had."

"Once I returned through the Wall, they closed Opening Three. They're about to close it permanently, sending Radicals to Antarctica instead or selling them as slaves. We escaped."

"Let's go to one of the living rooms and talk." To everyone else, she says, "Laelynn and Elm will bring each of you towels from the main closet."

One of the living rooms? My house in Unity doesn't even *have* a living room. Mrs. Newton leads me, Mother, and Solomon back down the staircase, through the entry, and into an open living room with a giant fireplace against the opposite wall. Just as we sit down in a square of couches, Frenchie, Kaphtor, and Cap come in.

"May we join?" Kaphtor asks.

Solomon stands and embraces him. "Of course."

Kaphtor and Cap sit at one couch opposite me. "I think it's important that some other people hear what plans you're making," Cap says. "You're acting as a leader, but you're still a seventeen-year-old girl."

"Eighteen."

Cap rolls his eyes. "Woooow, an entire year."

Solomon stiffens. "She's gotten us all the way here. No matter her age, she's sacrificed a lot to rescue everyone."

Cap scrunches his nose and leans back against the couch with a huff.

I don't deceive myself into thinking I can lead everyone correctly or make right decisions. Still, I would hope they'd trust me by now. Gabbie comes into the room next. Once we're all sitting, we start.

It takes much less time than I expected to sum up the past couple of months for Mrs. Newton. Elm walks in halfway through and stands like a sentinel behind her, by the fire. Gabbie scribbles notes and, at one point, she holds up the NAB. I think she's filming.

"You destroyed the projected Wall?" Mrs. Newton places a hand over her heart.

"Not for long," I say. "They got it back up within an hour."

"We still caused a good amount of chaos." Gabbie swipes a finger across the NAB screen. "The projected Wall went down everywhere for a whole hour. The Council wrote it off as a maintenance glitch."

She scans the screen and her lips curve up. "Skelley Chase said in an interview with *The Daily Hemisphere* that routine maintenance is standard every twenty-five years." She shakes her head. "If only he understood what they're *really* doing."

Oh, he understands.

Now is the time to share my own agenda. They won't like it, but I don't need anyone's approval except God's. I meet Solomon's eyes. He looks at me and then frowns.

I would have liked to share this with him privately.

Oh well.

"I've been thinking about what we did to the projected Wall." I rub my hand over my stump. Just blurt it out. Just say it. "Gabbie and I are going to film a speech of me talking to the USE, using clips from our escape and survival, revealing Dusten's overridden Clock. We'll release it to the public, inviting them to cross the Wall and join us here.

"And"–I grip my left wrist so hard that my stump screams a warning–"I'm going to destroy the Wall."

Cap bursts out laughing. Gabbie films me. Mother's head snaps up to meet my gaze. Solomon looks at his hands.

"How can you possibly do that?" Cap asks once he's caught his breath.

"*Why* do you want to do zat?" Frenchie's confusion creases her brow.

I open my arms wide. "You've seen what's on this side. *People.* Lost Angel, Ivanhoe . . . there is rightness over here and the world can't be denied it. That Wall is used as a cage to keep people trapped in a life of Clocks, to keep countries apart, to keep fear instilled. The Council *knows* there's life on this side and they're going to close up Opening Three."

"I will go with Parvin." Elm's arms are crossed tight over his bare, albino chest. His chin is high. "We will find and save Willow."

I nod once. He acts much more like an adult than most of these around me. It will be good to have his navigation skills along for the journey. I don't tell him that Brickbat threatened to test her—might even be testing her now. I can only hope that Solomon's dad somehow protected her. *Don't think about it.*

"But *how?*" Cap asks again.

I pick at a salt crust on my pants. "I'm going to start with the actual stone Wall. When I lived in Ivanhoe, I worked for a man named Wilbur Sherrod. He makes certain outfits that can empower a person to a degree. I tested one called Brawn once. It makes a person strong. I could use it to break through the rock."

"With one hand?" he sneers.

I shrug. "Probably."

Mrs. Newton shakes her head. "If you destroy the Wall, people will invade this side. They might take over! The Council could ruin everything beautiful here."

"Do we have the right to deny half the world this taste of beauty in order to assure our safety?"

Mrs. Newton smooths a hand over her hair. "Parvin, I think you ought to talk to the Preacher. This isn't our call. This involves his city, his people. He might have a war on his hands if you open the Wall to the East."

The Preacher *does* claim that it's his Wall. So, if I have *his* permission, then I need nothing else. "I'll see him tomorrow." He won't have a choice.

"I think you're being impulsive." Mother whispers loud enough that I know others hear her.

"I've been dwelling on this for the past two weeks, Mother. And praying over it." I think back to the verse Solomon read me when on the cargo ship: *"Because the poor are plundered, because the needy groan, I will now arise," says the Lord; "I will place him in the safety for which he longs."*

God is arising. For us. For Radicals. We all long for safety, and He is finally placing my people into the arms of shalom. But He's sending me to reach the others of the world—those still deceived by the Clock. I need to bring Willow home, reconnect Father and Tawny with Mother, and reveal the lies the Council has fed people for a hundred years. I need to create a safe haven for believers—like Fight, Idris, and Evarado.

"I want to return to ze East and travel back to France. To my parents."

"I won't allow it." Madame stands in the doorway to the living room. How long has she been listening?

Frenchie puts her shoulders back and doesn't bother to lower her voice. "Eet is my choice. You no longer 'ave a coffee shop. I am not your worker or your *slave* anymore."

"Angelique, do you think returning to France is the best option right now?" Kaphtor speaks in a low voice, while staring at the ground.

She rests a hand on his knee. "Eet eez my 'ome."

Cap yawns. "Well, this was boring. I'm going to bed."

Kaphtor, wobbling on his own bum leg, helps Cap stand. Then they and Frenchie leave. Madame stalks after them, hands on hips.

Gabbie scribbles a few other things, then runs after them. "Wait, Angelique . . . can I interview you?"

Now it's just me, Mother, Solomon, Mrs. Newton, and Elm.

"You're going back?" Solomon still won't meet my eyes. "The Council *wants* you there. They want to control and use you."

I move over to his couch and grip his hand. "Don't you see? Their desire to use me will protect me, *and* give me access to the Council, if I need it. I have to go, Solomon. Father and Tawny are there. The Wall must come down."

He looks up and his eyes flit between the two of mine.

Please, understand.

"I'll go with you, Parvin."

I shake my head. "I don't ask that of you."

He gives a sad smile and tilts my chin up. "I don't ask your permission. You think I'll leave Willow, your family, the orphans, or my dad over there? Though blasting through the Wall wasn't exactly how I imagined saving them."

"Blasting?"

He rests both arms on the back of the couch. "You'll need explosives. That Wall is thick. No magic suit will get completely through it."

Mrs. Newton leans forward. "You *will* talk to the Preacher tomorrow, won't you?"

I nod. "First thing in the morning."

Mother sighs and pushes herself to her feet. "We should all get some rest then."

"I'll see you up in our room." I glance toward Elm, who holds my gaze with his one eye, the fire casting a red glow against his skin. "I want to talk with Elm."

They take the hint. Solomon's the last to take his gaze from mine. So much time together, and yet we're never alone. Tomorrow. Tomorrow we'll talk.

Elm doesn't sit. "Where's Willow?"

"In a government-controlled orphanage in northern New York, but the Council threatened to kill her. Solomon's dad is monitoring her." I don't try to talk in layman's terms. I won't insult his intelligence like that.

"I will go to the Wall with you, *only* to rescue her." The muscle in his temple tenses in quick succession.

"I understand. I've done my best to protect her, Elm."

He shakes his head. "She would not be on the other side if she didn't have to take you over there in the first place."

My eyes burn. "I know."

He seems bigger than I remember him—more muscular, taller. The only time I really got to know him, he carried my dying body to the Wall. He didn't do it for me, but for Willow, because she cared for me.

Their devotion to each other puts my ideas of love to shame. "Elm, how did you escape the Wall?"

"I put the skeleton as a message for Willow. The scar was on the wrong eye so she would know it wasn't me. Then, when the Wall doors opened, I slipped back out to my side before anyone could see."

Genius. "Then what?"

"I tried climbing the Wall, but men were on top. Men all in black, building electric things. I tried climbing in a different area, but the same thing. They are building something to stop people from climbing over."

That something sounds like a projected Wall. It fits with the Lead Enforcer's comment regarding projection towers.

"So I came back down and built your Radical station with the Ivanhoe supplies as we promised. It is safe for Radicals now. Then I took the train back to Ivanhoe to ask Newton-lady's help. I waited here for you."

The fire dims and I notice it's not burning real wood. The logs inside look fake—like they're painted. "How did you know I was alive?"

"I told your God I needed your help. So you were alive."

So many people prayed for my survival—Elm, Solomon, Reid–and God heard them. He granted my life. I was ready to die, but instead my survival proved a testament to God's presence. Because I'm alive, Elm sees that God hears.

That, in itself, is worth it.

• • •

It's snowing when I wake.

I share a room with Mother, Frenchie, and Madame. Madame snores loud enough to shatter the wide window in the outer wall, and Frenchie sleeps with a pillow over her head.

Mother sleeps on her back, with her hands folded over her stomach. I kiss her forehead. Even in her sleep she looks stern and concerned. Beneath her brick exterior are secrets that tear her up. I haven't forgotten that she has a secret concerning Skelley Chase. She said she couldn't bear for me to know. But . . .

I have to know before I return to the East to confront the Council.

I knock softly on Solomon's door. He shares a room with Kaphtor and Cap on our same floor. It's just the three of them in there—no one else wanted to sleep in the same room as two ex-Enforcers. I don't know what changed Cap's view of them. Maybe he likes the extra breathing room.

Solomon opens the door, dressed and ready to go. "Good sunrise. I hoped you'd let me join you."

What a pleasant surprise. We walk down the hall together, into the entry, where we put on our freshly washed coats, and then outside into the snow.

Our footsteps whisper against the early morning sidewalk, the only steps breaking the pattern of smooth white. I hope no one shovels the walk. The snow is so cleansing.

"The Preacher lives in the Marble," I say to fill the silence. "Actually, it's technically called *The Core*, but I think it looks more like a marble. I'm determined to get everyone else calling it that."

Solomon grins. Our arms brush, but our fingers don't touch. I want to hold his hand. I don't want to. I want *him* to hold *my* hand. Maybe.

It's odd being in Ivanhoe—the place where I originally told Solomon I couldn't talk to him anymore because I loved Jude. Now, Jude is dead and Solomon and I are here.

My stomach flips when I look at him, and goose bumps pop up on my arms. He makes me want to smile. I want to hug him. Do all of those things count as love? They seem too surface level. What else do I feel?

Safety. Comfort. Jude was a ticking time bomb in more ways than one. I could never tell when he was going to get angry with me or clam up. But Solomon controls his temper—except for when he left me behind to resuscitate Dusten on my own.

But he apologized for that.

There's a level of spiritual and inner strength in him. He's always pursuing rightness—shalom. That, at least, is a core passion we share. And, because it's one of God's passions, that's enough for me.

Besides, who says I need to figure out love all at once? It's not a sudden thing. It's gradual, creeping in like a secret and then whispering hints over the cycle of time until you step back and see that all the hints lead to love.

Mother once said love is a choice, not a feeling. But don't feelings come from our choices? Or maybe our choices come from feelings. I don't know.

"An hour for your thoughts?"

I hiccup and shake my head. "You go first." Maybe after he says something I'll come up with a good replacement answer.

"I was thinking that I'd love to take you out for a cup of Ivanhoe coffee before we go free the world."

"Were you really?"

His smile is crooked. "Yup. But then I realized you're probably better at haggling than I am, I have no trade tickets, and I can't imagine where I'd find a coffee shop in this place."

I giggle and link my arm through his, almost tripping over the lurch my stomach gives. "That's okay. It's the thought that counts."

As I hold his arm, he slides his right hand to rest it over mine. "I was also wondering if . . . when you told me you . . . loved me, well, if that's still applicable."

I glance up at him. Snow coats the top of his hair, some of it melting from his body heat. He doesn't look at me for a moment, but then seems to force himself to. Oh, those teal eyes.

Deep breath. "Nothing's changed . . . except maybe the level of my nervousness."

"Please tell me it's increased, because mine sure has."

My laugh is weak. "Yeah."

He releases a breath and it jumps away from us in a cloud. "Phew! Well, now that we've cleared this chilly air, let me assure you that I'm still quite firmly growing in love for you."

He loves me.

He loves me.

A man has never told me he loves me—not even Jude, though I know he felt attracted toward me. But Solomon's not afraid to say it. Still . . ."What does that mean to you, Solomon?"

"To love you?"

"Yes."

We reach the Marble, an enormous spherical building with over thirty floors, held off the ground by thousands of pillars. In the center of the Marble, starting from the bottom outside and rising to the very top, is the elevator chute. We're almost there, but I don't want to arrive without hearing his answer.

"That's a question with a long answer."

I give his arm a squeeze. "Can you try?"

He licks his chapped lips. "Loving you means that you are becoming the most important person in my life, second only to God. It means that I want to commit my affection and my time to you. I want to know everything about you and to share life with you."

He stops walking and faces me. "To love you to the max is to do what God calls me to do—to help you grow closer to Him, to endure with you, to pursue shalom with you, to hope for all things, to suffer with you." His voice is hoarse. "To . . . be an example of Christ to you."

I stare up into his face, watching his cheeks grow colored from the cold and from emotion. His hands grip me by the shoulders and he holds my gaze. *More . . . keep going.* Not because I need more information, but because my very breath is stolen by his intentionality.

He breathes out. I breathe in. Then he whispers, "Did I answer your question?"

It takes me two tries to get my voice working. "Yes."

His hand slides up to hold the side of my face, rubbing his thumb over my cheekbone and along my jaw. Nothing exists outside of this moment. The pounding of my heart is deafening.

I lean forward and press myself into a hug, tucking my face in the crook between his jaw and shoulder. His arms tighten around me and we stand there for a long moment. Then we separate and walk toward the Marble, this time with our gloved fingers entwined.

He might have kissed me if I hadn't hugged him. I don't know. But I'd be happy holding hands with him for the rest of my life. Nothing could beat the current of contentedness inside me.

We are a team. And everything seems less daunting with this teammate by my side. Because we both have the same Leader and He won't steer us wrong.

We enter the shadow beneath the Marble, heading toward the elevator chute. Solomon glances up at the cement belly of the Marble. "This is . . . amazing."

Thousands of light strings and sparkles swoop along the underside of the Marble, lighting up the early morning shadows like fireflies. Only they're stars and we're walking through a celestial wonderland.

"They sure know how to deliver Christmas here," Solomon says.

We reach the glass elevator and enter the one that takes us to the entrance floor. I don't take us to the top because neither of us knows how to tightrope walk and that's the only way to reach the other floors.

We step out and I'm assailed by memories. Falling dogwood flowers, Jude fighting in the Barter-Combat Arena, trading furs with Willow, and working through special outfits with Wilbur Sherrod.

The ground is made of packed dirt, and huts fill the entire floor—huts for food, trading, work placement, meetings with The Preacher, upcoming Arena battles, you name it. Only this time, instead of the feeling of spring, there's Christmas everywhere. The scents of pine and spices fill the air. Each booth has its own amount of decorations—flowers, baubles, paintings, music.

"Is that the combat arena you wrote about?" Solomon looks to our left, where a darkened archway provides a tunnel to the amphitheater of tightropes.

"Yes. Do you want to glance inside real quick?" We walk past the Arena sign of two stick figures standing on a long white line. When we exit the tunnel, we stand at the top of amphitheater seating. Down at the bottom is a large pit of sand, but in the air are at least a hundred different types of tightropes, slacklines, highwires, and ziplines.

"Looks like an intimidating place for a battle," he says.

"It is. I don't know how anyone keeps their balance when *walking* across a rope, let alone battling to knock someone else off."

I try not to picture Jude, unconscious on the sand.

We head to the stairs.

"The Preacher is near the top."

Solomon doesn't complain. We climb and climb and climb. Five stories. Ten stories. Twenty stories. By the time we reach the thirty-third floor, vendors have opened shop below us and Christmas music sweeps out the silence.

I take a deep breath before walking into the Preacher's round waiting room. Five people sit on the benches. I don't apologize or explain, I just walk straight past the woman who's supposed to take my visitation ticket, through the tall entrance doors, and into the Preacher's visitation room.

There are no guards present. Come to think of it, there weren't any the last time I visited, either.

The Preacher's on the opposite side of the long room, sitting cross-legged on a couch of many pillows. This time, instead of a woman massaging his head while he meets with people, there's a small crowd of people on either side of the room observing the requests and meetings.

Hurray. An audience.

A man with slanted eyes and dark hair speaks to the Preacher in a different language. Solomon and I stand in the center of the room, waiting for the other man to finish.

The Preacher sees us, but makes no acknowledgement. He looks the same—middle-aged, dark Mediterranean skin, and a triangle goatee. He wears a silk red button-up making him look vampirish.

The man holding the Preacher's attention finishes up with a bow and leaves. We step forward.

"Visiting without an appointment," the Preacher says. "Foolish or proactive?"

I offer a small bow. "You may not remember me—"

"Parvin Blackwater, handless girl, Clock-dependent citizen of the USE. Seeing as how you're *here*, you must have been wrong about your Clock."

Now's not the time to explain what happened. Last time we met, he liked getting straight to the point, so I'll do just that. "I want your permission to destroy the Wall."

The other people in the room suck in a communal gasp.

The Preacher lifts an eyebrow. "First you want materials to build a safe passage over the cliff for the Radicals, and now you want to destroy it?"

"Well, I don't want to destroy the bridge, just the Wall."

"Why?"

Solomon takes a step forward so that he's within my peripheral vision. The gesture gives me confidence. "To bring shalom."

"What makes you think God wants the Wall destroyed?"

"First, because it's causing rifts between His people. Second, because the Council is planning to close Opening Three, making it impossible for people to escape. Our side is growing perpetually dependent on Clocks, something you claim to dislike. Third, there are people there who want to study the Bible and be faithful to God, but are persecuted for not sticking to the law's chosen list of sermons. They need a place to come and worship freely. This side has freedom, and I think that ought to be shared with the entire world."

He glances at his fingers, as if inspecting a manicure. "You do, do you?"

"Yes." I'm struck with unearthly confidence. The Preacher doesn't know it yet, but he'll give me what I want. He doesn't have a choice, because God sent me on this mission.

"And how do you propose to destroy the Wall?"

The question hangs in the air, daring a satisfying answer. "Wilbur Sherrod has a suit called Brawn. If he'll let me, I will use that for physical strength."

"Ah, the Samson method."

If he means Samson from the Bible, then . . . yeah, I guess so.

"Those suits are not Wilbur's to give away. He is just the designer. *I* sell or disperse them among Ivanhoe fighters."

Details. Details. "May I use the suit? And possibly others that might help?" I can tell before I finish asking that he won't let me.

He grins, but it carries little mirth. "That's a broad request." The hush in the room conveys the tension behind this question of mine. "If you destroy the Wall, we have to be prepared for war."

He gestures to the people around me. "These are my Ivanhoe fighters. And the people in the Core. And civilians. It doesn't sound like a very nice Christmas gift for them, does it?"

I shake my head.

"Yet you still want to ask that of them?"

I look around and meet only glares, no smiles. "I don't want any of you to have to fight. But my people in the USE don't even have a *chance* to fight for their own freedom. They're already captives to the Clocks, to the Council, to the Wall. Many of them don't even know it. Would you ask *them* to stay that way so you can keep your own Eden intact?"

Their glares don't budge.

"You have spirit, Parvin. But to allow you to do this means declaring war on the USE and forfeiting my voice on the United Assembly."

"Then I'll do it without your permission."

He claps his hands, and his smile widens. The sound echoes through the chamber and a few observers startle. "There we go. *Now* you're a true Independent."

I scowl. "I . . . am?"

"You see? I help the people, I am their voice, but I am not their *king* or their *ruler.*"

That explains the lack of guards.

"I am one of them. They are still free to act on their own. We have a working system in place, and I help *guide* that. You still saw me as a ruler—as the man who needed to give his permission. If you were on the other side, would you ask the USE for permission?"

"No."

"Then why come to me?"

I shrug. "So you wouldn't stop me. And I need supplies."

"Your choice to destroy the Wall is your own personal passion. I think you'll need to find a way to pay for the suits."

My posture goes slack. "Pay? With what?"

He leans back on his kingly sofa and surveys me. The movement of his eyes brings heat to my cheeks. "How about a marriage alliance?"

I swallow the ball of dread in my throat and suddenly wish Solomon wasn't with me. "Marriage?"

"An alliance between the East and West. You and me."

No. No, no, *no!* Solomon is a statue beside me. "I'm nobody!" I squeak. "What benefits would I bring?"

"You mean quite a lot to the Council and to the people in the USE. If you *do* destroy the Wall, people will be looking to you. You have value, Parvin Blackwater. When Radicals come to Ivanhoe, you will guide them."

"Can't I do that anyway?"

"Marry me. Bring unity between both sides of the Wall. Those are my terms."

The hush in the room is so heavy that I almost drop to my knees. "I can't."

"Then you're on your own." He looks past me and shouts, "Next!"

I take two steps forward. "Wait!"

God, if You really want to use me to bring shalom by destroying the Opening . . . then I'm putting this next step into Your hands. I trust you.

"Lemuel."

The Preacher startles at my use of his real name.

I square my shoulders and lift my chin. "I challenge you to a fight in the Arena."

33

"You are a fool, Parvin Blackwater." The Preacher's voice echoes, gong-like, through the chamber.

A FOOL FOR MY SAKE.

There He is, popping into my head. The assurance is palpable. That's what I needed. "If you win, I'll marry you and do as you wish"—Solomon grips my forearm so hard, I almost lose my momentum—"but if *I* win, then you will provide the supplies I need for the Wall. Explosives, some of Wilbur's suits, and transportation to the Wall. Oh, and I don't have to marry you."

He rolls his eyes. "This is child's play."

You're the one wanting to marry a child. Ew, how old is this geezer anyway? Forty? Fifty? "How long has it been since you competed?" I goad. "I think I'd stand a good chance against you."

He sits straight and his mirth is gone. "I *designed* the Arena. I am the master tightrope walker of Ivanhoe."

"Really?" I laugh. Pouring every bit of mockery into my tone. "*Really?*"

He turns to the people, as if waiting for them to attest to his greatness. But they don't. Their heads swivel between the two of us. Solomon shifts his weight but says nothing. Does he think me a fool, too, or does he trust me? *I* don't trust me, but I trust God. And He will allow this test to unfold in a way that brings shalom.

My heart is right in this. He will honor that.

I lift my chin. "Do you accept?"

The Preacher opens his arms wide, as if inviting me into a hug. "With pleasure."

Everyone cheers. Not for me, of course . . .

But on combat day, we'll see who's cheering.

"What have you *done?*" Mother throws her damp towel on her bed.

I shouldn't have told her. I just got through a long walk of Solomon-silence. It almost killed me. No matter what I said, he gave no response. I don't know what to think.

Does he hate me?

"I've given you a chance to have faith, Mother."

"There's a difference between faith and foolishness."

"I don't expect you to understand what's going on in my heart right now, but I have to do this. This is the way to get the Wall destroyed. I'm being like . . . that one Bible guy—Gideon, I think—when he put out some sort of sheepskin for God. If I win this challenge, it's proof God's behind this pursuit."

She shakes her head. "You're not Gideon."

"Actually, I've been reading my waterlogged Bible and I'm quite a bit like Gideon." The fragile looking Bible survived our plunge at Lost Angel. Not a single word is smeared. "I'm a coward, I'm a nobody, and God's asking me to be a leader. God wants me to speak out, so I've been obedient."

Her voice rises and she paces the room. "You can't speak for God! You act as though you know everything about His will, like He's *telling* it to you. He doesn't work like that."

I step in front of her. "Mother." She looks up. "There's no system to God. He might interact with you different than He interacts with me. All I can know is how He communicates with *me*. I promise this isn't impulse."

She plops onto her bed. "So when do you *fight* this man?"

"Tomorrow morning. Will you come?"

"What choice do I have?"

"Whichever choice you want to make."

Solomon knocks on my door two hours later. "I've set up a slack-line, for you to practice."

I try to catch his eye as we walk outside, but his gaze is set forward. I don't ask where he got the slackline. It's only four feet off the snowy ground, but I can barely stand on the thing. Solomon holds my hand until I get steady.

After three hours of trying to balance, the most I get is seven steps forward before I fall off. There's no way I can pull this off six stories above the ground. I don't like practicing. It shakes my faith even more than it shakes my muscles.

"Why did you do this?" Solomon helps me off the slackline.

I look into his eyes, which seem a clearer teal when set against the winter backdrop. "Because I had to. I'm not afraid, Solomon."

He gestures to the slackline. "Even after this . . . practice? You're not afraid that he'll beat you and you'll have to *marry* him?"

I can't explain it. "No."

He turns his head away, watching bundled bicyclists make their way down the icy roads. "I am."

I place my hand on his arm. "Maybe instead of practicing on the slackline we should just . . . pray." I can't infuse him with God-confidence. That can come only from the true Source of peace.

I've never been in this position before—feeling stronger in faith than Solomon. Usually I'm turning to him for encouragement. Does that mean I've grown? Or does it mean Solomon's faltering?

He sighs, and we walk back toward the mansion. "We've done as much as we can today. You're probably right."

We enter the mansion to the aroma of meat and onions. In the kitchen, Mrs. Newton and at least ten other women—including Frenchie and Madame—stand over giant pots.

"Are you sure zis eez food?" Frenchie stirs the contents of her pot.

I glance in as we pass. Rice—that funny maggoty food I ate the last time I was in Ivanhoe. I was just as skeptical.

Mrs. Newton laughs. "Yes, Angelique."

Some other pots hold beef in a brown sauce with vegetables, thicker than stew. Beef—a rarity in the USE—is as common as chicken on this side. My people will be eating High-City food tonight.

I sneak a piece of meat out of the pot and pop it into my mouth before it burns my fingers.

"I saw that," Solomon says in an attempt to be more lighthearted. I appreciate the effort.

We retreat upstairs. When we come to my room, he leans a hand on the doorframe. "I'll be praying, Parvin."

"Me too."

And that's our good night.

It's not easy for me to talk to God. I much prefer listening, but then that's not a relationship. I lie on my bed in the empty room as everyone else eats dinner. I'll catch leftovers tomorrow—either as comfort food or a celebration meal.

Back on the cargo ship, I asked You to grow my love for You. And it's grown. Just a little, but it's grown. I want to do what pleases You, what will bring You glory, and what will bring the people shalom.

I pour out every concern and desire to Him. I share how Ivanhoe is home more than anywhere else in the world. I share how Mother's nitpicking and the slacklining opened the door for doubt. I share how I wish Solomon could have the same assurance I have.

God is a great listener.

Why can't I be like the people in the Bible—the ones who get passionate about putting God on the spot? The ones who speak a word and no rain falls for years. The ones who just *know* what God will do.

I'm so far behind.

I fall asleep praying. I wish I hadn't. It seems like an insult to God—like we were having a conversation and I got so bored I drifted off. But morning dawns cold and icy with blue skies and I'm still set.

A group is in the first living room, warming by the fire. Solomon and Mother are among them. I join them and sip a cup of Mother's coffee.

"I'm not afraid of the outcome." She and Solomon need to know this.

"We'll be there," Mother says. "You and Solomon go on ahead. Mrs. Newton will show us the way."

It takes Solomon and me five minutes to reach the Marble. There's a long line at the floor-level elevator. Call it intuition, but I know they're all here to watch me battle the Preacher.

The only thing is, they don't know it's *me*. They pay no attention to me, they just know someone—some average Joe—challenged the Preacher to a battle.

We get inside and enter a different tunnel to the Arena—the tunnel for the contestants. I can't get enough air. I'm lightheaded. We stop halfway in the tunnel and Solomon steadies me. "You okay?"

"Why am I nervous, Solomon? If I *really* trusted God, wouldn't I feel braver?"

"Your feelings are human, but your actions are what show His strength." He's back—the faithful doubtless believer I've come to know.

I still feel like a spiritual wimp. Nowhere in the Bible did I see King David feeling queasy prior to a battle, or the apostle Paul dizzy before speaking to the grouchy leaders.

We continue down the tunnel. It curves upward, a mixture of ramps and stairs, to the sixth-story platform. I'm about to continue on, but I stop at the first story. "I'm not starting at the top."

"You're allowed to do that?"

Only now am I struck with the thought. It's not mine, but it's nice to feel an urging on what to do. "In the Arena, I'm allowed to do anything except touch the ground." As the words come out of my mouth, my nerves lessen. I can do *anything*. I don't have to look professional. I've got one good hand and that's enough to hold on to a rope.

That's all I need.

He is strong in my weakness.

Solomon stays in the tunnel as I walk out to the wooden platform attached to a slackline stretching across the entire Arena. There are another few ropes below me, crisscrossing.

The seats are packed. The buzz of voices is so loud it presses against my lungs. In one wave, the noise heightens to a scream. I look up. The Preacher is on the highest platform, his arms raised as if allowing the cheers to nourish his pride. We are both barefoot, but he's in tight gymnast pants without a shirt and I'm in the clothes I got from Lost Angel.

He levels his gaze at me. I hold it. He smiles like I imagine the devil would before dragging someone to hell.

Charming.

"Begin!" he hollers.

Solomon slides to the floor in the shadowed tunnel, his head bowed. It's now or never.

Above the slackline to my right, at shoulder-height, is a tightwire. I hold it to keep my balance on the slackline. My hand grows sweaty in a matter of seconds. When I'm about ten steps out, I stop.

And wait.

My legs tremble and I try to still them before the slackline starts vibrating. The Preacher dives—head first!—off his platform, catches a tightrope, and swings himself in a new direction. Toward me.

But I'm not afraid.

The crowd turns feral from his display of prowess.

But I'm not afraid.

He lands on a slackline a few yards above my head, halfway across the Arena from where I stand.

But I'm not afraid.

He uses the slackline to launch himself into the air spread-eagle, toward me. He performs a front-flip, positioning his feet one in front of the other to land on my slackline.

That's when I let myself fall.

34

I thrust my feet to the side, throwing my body perpendicular to the slackline. It clips one of the Preacher's ankles and throws him into a downward spin. One of his arms gropes for a tightrope, but it's ripped from his hand by his momentum.

I cling to the tightwire with my sweaty right hand, swinging back and forth with only seconds before I'll fall.

Thud.

The Preacher hits the sandy ground.

I scrabble for my slackline with my feet, finally getting it clenched between two toes. It takes a tremendous amount of abdominal strength to lurch back up to a standing position and I almost fall again. Once balanced, I inch backward, toward my little platform, sliding my slick hand along the tightwire. A rope hangs from my platform down to the sand.

I wrap my right hand in the loose folds of my white tank, grab the rope, and slide down with my legs twined around it.

The Preacher lies on his side with his face in the sand. Not a soul breathes. The wild spectators gape with slacked jaws at their leader—their *hero*—on the ground. Defeated.

A sound fractures the silence.

Laughter.

The Preacher's laughter reverberates in the Arena. Long. Loud. Nonstop echoes. No one joins him. Not a single observer laughs or even smiles.

He rolls onto his back in the sand, clutching his stomach. Still laughing. Alone. He pushes himself to a sitting position and slaps his knee. I think he even snorts at some point.

He goes on like this until it grows awkward. I take a single step toward him. He laughs. Everyone else is frozen. Then he pushes himself to his feet, thumps me on the back, and strides out of the Arena.

I think that man is slightly insane.

Maybe even more than slightly.

As if realizing that they missed their opportunity for autographs, the onlookers flock after him, regaining their voices. I'm left in the center of the Arena with seven people still in the stands. Mother, Mrs. Newton, Frenchie, Madame, Cap, Kaphtor, and Gabbie.

I salute them and they start slow, tentative applause. *Thank you, God.*

Solomon slides down the same rope I did and joins me on the sand. "Look at you. So confident in faith." His smile is perfect.

Hand in hand, we walk up the stairs to our small group of supporters. Mother hugs me. "I'm proud of you."

Cap sits with his arms folded and his nose in the air. "What a weird place, this Ivanhoe."

I address Solomon. "I'm going to go talk to Wilbur Sherrod and get some suits before the Preacher changes his mind."

Mrs. Newton's a little pale. "He won't change his mind."

"I am coming wiz you to ze Wall. Don't forget." Frenchie pinches her cheeks to turn them rosy.

"Me too," Mother says.

Kaphtor looks at Frenchie out of the corner of his eye. "I'll come along."

Cap nudges him. "You want to go *back?* After all the stuff they made you do as an Enforcer? They'll carve your face up!"

Kapthor allows a half a grin. "Yes, I want to go back. Don't you, goat-man?"

I squeeze Kaphtor's shoulder as Solomon and I continue up the stairs. "Thank you."

I didn't expect anyone to come with me to the Wall. Now I have Solomon, Mother, Frenchie, Elm, and Kaphtor. They're not following out of obligation, are they? Then again, who *would*, when they know that destroying the Wall is full-on rebellion against the Council?

Wilbur Sherrod spits a spoonful of chestnut soup onto his sketch-pad when he sees me. "Ah now, look what ye did."

"Hey, Wilbur."

His russet afro is as large as ever, still receding, leaving him with a very exposed forehead. His floppy sneakers slap against the tile as he walks over to shake my hand. No hugs for us. We're not *that* friendly. Actually, a handshake is pushing it.

"The Preacher gave me permission to take some of your suits. I'll need at least six."

His already pale skin turns pasty. "S-six outfits?"

"Yes, I beat him in the Arena and that was our agreement." The Preacher better stick to it.

"Ah yes. I heard de Preacher was competin' today. *Ye* were after fightin' him? And ye won?"

"God wanted me to win, so I won."

He looks me up and down, cocking an eyebrow as he takes in my outfit. "Hold on now, I t'ought ye were dyin' or somet'in'."

I slide my hand into Solomon's. "That's a long story. For now, what outfits do you have? I'm destroying the Wall and need something that will allow me to do that."

"And me," Solomon chimes in.

"De Wall? Destroy it?" Wilbur's bug-eyed surprise transforms into thought, and he seems unfazed by my statement. All I have to do is challenge his skill or get his thoughts onto his suits and he's clay in my hands. "Well, I've de Brawn outfit which ye tested. It gives ye strengt', but ye need protection, too, from de falling rock." He reveals his crooked teeth in a smile. "I've somet'in new to show ye, Parvin."

We follow him deeper into his studio.

"Where are you from?" Solomon asks. "Your accent . . ."

"I have Irish."

We enter what Wilbur calls "De Closet," but it's more like a round warehouse of outfits displayed on mannequins. The floor and walls are black, the only illumination coming from the mannequin cases. Not creepy at all . . .

Across the room is the mannequin he made of me when I first worked for him, complete with stump and bruises.

It's to that one we walk.

"Isn't Ireland on the other side of the Wall?" Solomon's sifting through the same questions I once asked.

"It is."

"So how'd you get here?"

Wilbur stops in front of my mannequin and unlocks the glass door protecting it, with a few taps on a screen. "My mam and da crossed in Russia when I was a babe." He places a hand on the mannequin's shoulder. "Here we go. A new piece called Armor."

The form-fitted outfit has a metal sheen like medieval armor, but on top of the mannequin's head is what looks like a ski mask without eye, nose, or mouth holes.

"How does it work?" I run my fingers over it.

Wilbur lifts the sleeve hanging off the stump portion of the mannequin. "Squeeze de mannequin's shoulder."

It's soft like normal silky material and under my pressure sinks into the plush, creepily humanlike body of the mannequin. He presses a button on the inside of the sleeve and a red light blinks once on the wrist, then disappears. "Now again."

I try to squeeze the mannequin's shoulder, but the material might as well be carbon fiber. It has no give at all.

"It activates automatically at de sign of impact or danger. Ye can also turn it on manually. De suit withstands t'ree hundred t'ousand pounds per square inch."

Solomon pushes against it. "So it's virtually indestructible."

"That it is. Only problem is de timing limitations."

My hand drops from the suit. "Like the Epiphany suit." That suit stimulated extra brain cells in the user, but it worked for about five minutes before the red light blinked a recharge alert.

"Exactly. Dis suit will protect for ten minutes from de moment ye press de button. Then de red button will blink a one minute alert. I'm workin' on a longer one."

"How does it recharge?" Solomon looks like he'd eat the suit if he could. Inventions may not run in his blood, but they run in his thinking.

"Dat's de beauty of it. It recharges from de user's body energy. Takes an hour, but ye never have take it off."

It's perfect. "Okay, we'll take this one."

Wilbur's face falls. "It's my only one."

I wink at him. "Print a new one, genius. You're brilliant."

The flattery works, but not without a little complaint. "It takes me two months to print out dis one." He removes Armor from the mannequin.

"So, how about a Brawn suit? I need to tear down stones."

"Ah, now we have a problem. If ye wear de Brawn suit for destroyin', ye won' have enough time to change into de Armor suit for protection." Wilbur hands the folded Armor suit to Solomon and then leads us across the room.

Solomon fingers the material. "Can't you just layer the suits?"

Wilbur stops in his tracks, his sneakers squeaking a protest. He doesn't turn. Doesn't move. Doesn't say anything.

"Wilbur?" I take a tentative step toward him.

"I . . . I . . ." He turns on a heel and stares at Solomon. "I . . . never t'ought of tryin' layers." His eyes lose focus and his mouth moves in mutters. He taps the tips of his fingers like he's counting.

"Wilbur?"

He jerks out of his trance. "I . . . never t'ought of tryin' dat before."

"Do you think it will work?"

He nods four times before speaking. "I do. It should work best wit' de Armor." He rips Brawn off the mannequin and thrusts it at me. "Try it on."

"We don't have time for a simulation."

"No, try it here."

I hold the outfit to my chest. "Well, I'm not going to change in front of you two."

"Oh, I forgot. Give it here." Wilbur grabs both the Brawn and Armor suits from us and presses a spot on the collar. They fold into themselves, tightening, shrinking, until they're each a small square, no larger than a matchbox.

"That's new," I breathe.

"Aye. Portable an' easy fer dressin'. Look here." He holds the Brawn matchbox right up against my sternum and presses it hard. The material slithers out, growing and stretching, melding to my body over the clothing I already wear.

Then it stops and I'm completely dressed. Now *that's* what a one-handed girl needs.

I put the Armor outfit on over Brawn. It slithers out just as smoothly as the other. The ski mask is so thin I barely feel it against my skin. My vision is perfect and breathing is normal, even as the suit covers my face. It's as if I'm not wearing the mask at all.

Wilbur drags a heavy metal crate by one of its handles from one side of the room. It takes all his effort and he gets halfway to me before slumping to the ground. He wipes sweat from the bald portion of his head. "There now, pick it up."

I feel no different in the suit, but I've been through this drill. I walk to the crate, loop one gloved finger under a handle, and lift. Piece of cake. The weight is barely noticeable, like picking up a shoestring.

"Now lay down and turn on de Armor suit."

I obey. "You put the activation button on the left wrist."

"I was t'inkin' of ye." Wilbur directs Solomon to the other side of the crate. "It activates automatically, remember. De button is a last resort."

He and Solomon pick up the crate and hold it over me. Wilbur lowers his side, but Solomon doesn't budge. "This isn't going to crush her, is it?"

Wilbur straightens and scowls. "I've tested de suit over t'irty different times. I am a *master*. Now put it down before it be breakin' my back."

Meanwhile, I lie inches beneath a bone-crushing crate, waiting for the boys to stop arguing. They lower the crate, but I feel nothing. And I mean *nothing*.

"How is de breathin'?"

I take four deep breaths. "Fine."

Wilbur puffs out his chest. "De mask is like de suit—can't be crushed. Both are programmed to give ye enough room for breathin' whenever ye get buried."

"How comforting."

Solomon lifts his side. "Can we get this off her now?"

I sit up. "Oh let me. We wouldn't want anyone pulling a muscle." Wilbur hops out of the way and I flick the crate off with my thumb and forefinger. It topples end over end across the room into a glass-paneled mannequin stand. "Oops, sorry."

But Wilbur's jumping up and down like a kid on Christmas day. He turns to Solomon. "Will ye be wantin' a Brawn suit, too?"

Solomon retrieves the crate. "I'm a man, of course I want to destroy things with my bare hands."

"We'll need to blueprint ye." Meaning he'll scan and print out a perfect replica mannequin of Solomon. I hope they display his next to mine.

The blueprinting takes about a minute, then Wilbur shoos us out. "De outfit will be complete tomorrow. Sorry I have only de one Armor."

"It's okay. Thank you, Wilbur. I'll bring up the others who need to be blueprinted." I lead the way back to the Marble staircase and we head to the mansion.

When we walk into the entry, people swarm us.

"You're going to destroy the Wall?" someone says as Solomon and I push through to the staircase.

"Are you mad? You'll ruin this place!"

"You fought the king of Ivanhoe?"

"Why would you leave us?"

"That Wall's been there fifty years! It's a national monument!"

Someone spread the news, and I'm willing to bet it was Gabbie or Cap. I turn at the base of the stairs to face them. "I'm destroying it because we need to save those who have been left behind. The Council is going to close all passage soon and we still have people on the other side."

I walk upstairs to my room. Solomon follows until we're alone in the hallway. "Thanks for praying for me in the Arena."

"Welks. Looks like God gave us our answer."

I smile. "Tally ho." I don't want to leave him alone in the hallway, but I need to send Mother and Frenchie to Wilbur for blueprinting. Before I can feel too guilty, though, he continues on to his own room.

I walk into mine. Mother lies on her bunk, staring at the underside of mine. "Are you feeling okay, Mother?"

"There's lunch downstairs."

I close the door behind me. "I don't want lunch. I want to know if you're feeling okay."

She turns her face toward the wall and, for a moment, I spot a glimmer of light off her cheek. My gut squeezes. Is she . . . crying?

What do I do? The longer I stand here, the more uncertain and awkward I grow. I should do something. I should leave her alone, she clearly wants her privacy. Instead, I force my feet forward and I sit on the edge of her bed. "Mother, what's wrong?"

She squeezes her eyes tight. "I want to go with you to the Wall . . . but I can't go if you're just going to get captured and killed."

So this is about me. My head bows low. "I have to return, Mother. I need to destroy the Wall so people can be safe over here." I place my hand on her shoulder, gently like a landing butterfly. What's the real problem here? "Reid's death wasn't your fault."

She shakes her head. "Yes, it was . . . you don't know."

The fingers of dread pinch my throat closed. I pop my neck, forcing my voice to work. "What don't I know?"

She turns her face as far away from me as possible. This must have to do with her secret about Skelley. She said she couldn't tell me, but maybe now . . . "What happened between you and Skelley Chase?"

She angles her face even farther away from me.

"Mother . . . please tell me." I grow queasy. I don't want to know, but I *must* know.

Her breath comes in a shudder. "He told me to choose."

I choke. "Choose what?"

She covers her face with a trembling hand. "Choose which one of you to kill."

35

Mother chose to let Reid die.

My lungs strain against the tar in my chest. Skelley made her *pick* one of us?

"He said that, at the end of your Clock, one of you would die. I needed to choose who would die and who would survive—you or Reid. Otherwise he'd expose me for training you up as believers in Christ and he'd kill you both anyway."

I'm alive.

She picked me.

I break with her. "Why did you choose me?"

"B-Because you were finally doing something with your life." She sobs into her hand. "You d-deserved a chance. I didn't know Reid was getting married or that you would return to us craving death. I didn't know . . . I didn't know . . ."

If she'd known, would she have chosen Reid instead? "It's not your fault."

She nods her head, but doesn't speak.

"It's not. Reid said in his journal that he *knew* it was his Clock. He was ready to die. He even told Tawny before they married. She accepted it and married him anyway."

Her hand slides away from her face and she meets my eyes for a single blink.

"It's true. Ask Tawny when we get back to the other side.

Besides, only God can control the Clocks. Only He can add to or take away our Numbers. Skelley has no power."

She looks at me, the red around her eyes highlighting her silent guilt. "You should go get some lunch."

If words could punch people in the stomach, she'd be a professional boxer. I've been dismissed. My voice comes out defeated. "All right."

Gabbie and I film my speech that afternoon. We go behind the mansion, where Solomon and Kaphtor dug a grave for Dusten's body. He lies beside the hole, preserved by the odd black charring that covers his skin.

I kneel down and illuminate his Clock. The Numbers still tick down, his name is still there, and the word *overridden* glows the brightest.

Gabbie holds up the NAB. "Whenever you're ready."

I look into the small hole that's doing the filming. Solomon stands behind Gabbie—partly to monitor what she's doing with the NAB, and partly to make it easier for me to speak.

My breath fogs in front of my face and I shiver. "People of the USE, I am Parvin Blackwater and I have secrets about the Council that you need to know . . ."

I talk for a good half hour. I tell them how the Council forced the Low-City people to pay for their new Clocks and how those without money were sent to Antarctica. I tell how some of us were sold as slaves. I tell how the Council stole Jude's information and tried to use me as their voice. I reveal that they kidnapped Willow and threatened to torture her. Lastly, I tell how Dusten died. I kneel beside his body and show his Clock to them all.

"This new Clock from the Council is different. I don't know how, but Jude created new Clocks that can somehow be overridden. I don't know what the trigger is, but we're not bound to them anymore. Don't accept these Clocks from the Council. Don't let them control you."

Once I finish and Gabbie shoots me a thumbs-up, we bury Dusten . . . on the free side of the Wall.

The living room to which I retreat with my meal is filled with Unity people. Laelynn and the little girl from our boxcar sit by the fire playing a game with a ball and metal stars that they pick up between bounces. It reminds me of Willow playing with the cards she won in Ivanhoe.

I sit on a couch with a dish of beef chili and cornbread—a simple Unity Village dish, only we don't use beef. *The Daily Hemisphere* is open in my lap and the headline bores into me.

New Clock-Matching Comes to High Cities.

They're doing it already. Gabbie and I need to get our video out as soon as possible.

"What does eet mean?" Frenchie looks to me for the answer. "Dusten's Clock?"

She sits beside Kaphtor, even though he was the Enforcer who dragged her out of the coffee shop to sentence her as a Radical. For the first time, he's not wearing black. He's in jeans and a long-sleeved shirt. Normal clothing looks weird on him, especially with the tattooed backward *E* on his temple.

Kaphtor straightens his shirt and readjusts on the couch. "Did the Council make a mistake with the new Clocks or did the problem arise with Dusten's original Clock?" Everyone else in the room, even Laelynn and her friend, pause in their movements.

If only Jude were alive, he'd have the answer for us. "Jude changed something. That's all I know. We are all Radicals now and will be forever. Gabbie and I plan to release this truth to the world through a video."

"To take away everyone's confidence?" Cap asks from next to the fire.

"Their confidence is based in a lie, so . . . yes."

He folds his arms. "That's not very kind."

"Neither is leaving the world trapped in deception."

Frenchie sets her dinner plate on the coffee table in front of her. "You all s'ink ze USE is ze entire world. Do you know *anything* of uzzer countries?"

The spotlight swings from me to her.

She rolls her eyes. "To 'ave a Clock een France means you are *very* rich. Eet's not required by ze government. Eet's a luxury. My maman et papa saved up zeir whole lives and deedn't 'ave children until zey could purchase ze ovachips."

I cringe. Who would *want* those electronic gnats inside their body? That's the only plus side of these new Clocks—they can Clock you without having to put an electronic device in your body.

"Zat's 'ow I was born wis a Clock." Her accent grows stronger the more passionate she gets. "Zey wanted to send me to ze USE for a better future. I got 'ere and what did I find? Eet eez *illegal* to live without a Clock. Zat is why you have so few visitors to your country. You are *alone* in zis."

She fiddles with the hem of her sweater. "I was in ze USE only two months when my apartment burned to ze ground, destroying my Clock. I could not go 'ome. I was trapped, a Radical, until Madame found me and made me 'er servant."

Her eyes shrink to narrow slits, but Madame isn't in the room. "If Parvin eez right, zat ze new Clocks are incorrect, zen maybe ze Council will let me go 'ome. Back to France. Back to my maman et papa who 'ave not 'eard from me for two years."

She wipes her nose with the edge of her sweater. Kaphtor stares at her. "That can't be right. I visited France for three days last year to celebrate my ten-year Enforcerhood. Everyone had Clocks."

"Staged settlements," I tell him. "The USE sets them up. That's why I never traveled as a Last-Year wish. Nothing is authentic."

"How do you know?"

I lean back. "I read a lot."

He looks at Frenchie again, as if trying to figure out whom to believe.

"Kaphtor, why are you here?" I can't help but ask. Last year was his ten-year Enforcerhood celebration? How old is he? He doesn't look much older than Solomon.

Kaphtor raises his eyebrows. "There's only so much human abuse one can watch."

Cap unfolds his arms and wrinkles his nose. "Says the most heartless Enforcer of the bunch." His tone hints that he's joking. Does he realize it's not funny?

Kaphtor shrugs as if to dismiss the comment. "I was raised in a High-City Enforcer family. There's no room for emotion. When the new Enforcer regulations sent me to Unity Village, I saw life in a way the High Cities never meant us to see it. Suffering. Hard work. Hope and hopelessness. Once we started putting people in boxcars, I couldn't take it anymore. I couldn't go back to my family, so I joined my new one."

"Who . . . us?" Cap peers at him.

With what we're up against, there's no point in holding grudges or allowing hurt to stick. Kaphtor saved us. Frenchie takes his hand. "You can be intimidating, but zat eez gone now. I am your family."

Cap pushes himself off the couch and limps out of the living room. I hear him mutter something about *family*, but that's all. Kaphtor looks at me. "Hawke showed me family first." His eyes drop to the floor. "Even after I helped strip him of his Enforcerhood."

In his defeated posture I see Mother telling me she's the cause of Reid's death. I see Jude feeling responsible for the torture of his orphans. I see myself, failing over and over again to save Radicals from the Wall. "We've all done things we wish we hadn't. But Solomon forgives you. It's evident in his care for you. Let it go."

"Did I hear my name?" Solomon steps into the living room, bringing a cheer that doesn't fit the current conversation.

Kaphtor grasps the escape. "I hear you're going to the Wall dressed in a space suit."

Solomon laughs. "Tell you what, if you still think it's a space suit after I arm-wrestle you while wearing it, then you're allowed to rib me."

"I want one."

Solomon plops next to me on the couch. "Uh-uh, then I'll never win the arm-wrestle."

Kaphtor turns an intense gaze on me. "I want one."

He wants to destroy that Wall with me. Maybe to compensate for all the Radicals he sent through to their deaths. "Okay."

"I would like one, too," Frenchie says. "And get your muzzer one. She needs to destroy something."

It's dangerous but . . . they want to bring change—shalom. Can I deny them the chance? No way. "Let's go get you blueprinted."

"I'll need at least a week to print de suits for ye," Wilbur says.

After my talk with Frenchie and the others, Madame demanded a suit. Frenchie screamed at her for a good hour. Gabbie asked for a suit, too. "A good reporter is always at the scene." She didn't seem fazed by the fact that she'd possibly get in trouble with the Council or even crushed by tumbling stone. "Perhaps I'll meet Skelley Chase in person and I can tell him about the Council's deception."

I'm going to talk to her about this weird Skelley obsession before placing my trust in her too much.

The person who surprised me the most was Cap. I eyed his bum leg when he asked to join us. When asked why he wanted to come, he muttered something about getting back to his goats. Well, if that's his family . . . okay then.

So here I am, demanding more Brawn suits. Seven days. What might happen to Willow in seven days? And how many High-City people have been Clock-matched already?

The *Ivanhoe Independent* will leave the station the day after Christmas. I take the NAB into my room and send Father a long message, explaining everything that's happened since we arrived in Ivanhoe.

More and more people want to come with me to the Wall. Perhaps it will be unsafe for you to be there when we destroy it. You and Tawny could cross over a few days later.

Only an hour after I send my long message, Father replies.

Sweetheart,
   This thing is bigger than you. I've contacted as many people on the list you sent me as possible. They're rallying. They want to cross over the Wall to escape the Clock-matching. They're bringing even more people with them.
   I've shared no details, but I'm having people meet me in Nether Town tomorrow. Then I'll lead them to the Wall on New Year's Eve.

People are rallying? If so, we can't wait any longer. That video needs to be released *now*. I track down Gabbie in one of the living rooms, where she's listening to Elm and Mrs. Newton argue.

"Christmas is a barbaric holiday." Elm lifts his chin. "Cutting trees to lock in your house? You should all atone with your lives!"

"I'll get a fake tree," Mrs. Newton soothes. "Now go get Mrs. Blackwater and Madame to come help me in the kitchen."

As Elm stomps past me, I plop beside Gabbie. "Can we send our video in a private message to a single person without it being shut down or seen by the Council?"

"Of course," she bubbles.

It takes all my willpower not to roll my eyes. "So why don't we release it *that* way? I could send it to my Father and he could start showing people, sending it to those he trusts. And then it *can't* be shut down."

Her mouth breaks into a grin and she gasps. "Why didn't *I* think of that?"

Yeah, why didn't she? *She's* the professional. "We'll send it to Father as soon as possible. It will include the day and time we'll be at the Wall to destroy it. That way, people who want to cross to this side for safety can come."

"Well, let's finish up our filming then."

By Christmas day, the Radicals have found a routine in the Newton Mansion. Several have started looking for jobs or places to live. Harman plans to open a produce stand in the Marble. Some people talk about returning to the USE after we've destroyed the Wall—mostly those who have been separated from their families.

That morning, I send the video to Father with instructions on how to share it with others. Gabbie's finished it, putting my voice over the other videos she's gathered since I presented my NAB.

It's powerful.

Father: Meet us at Opening Three on New Year's Eve at noon.

That's when and where we'll destroy the Wall.

Carolers sing at the door of the mansion in celebration of Christmas, and we have a giant supper where we all eat together for the first time—or as together as we can be with three hundred people spread all over the building. Mother makes her fig-and-walnut butter to eat on holiday toast. The last time I ate this, I thought I was dying. What a mixture of memories.

I sit next to Elm as we eat. Over fifty packed bags rest against the wall near the door, ready for our departure tomorrow. Twenty of those are filled with Ivanhoe's best explosives.

Fifty people want to help me tear down the Wall. Only ten of us have Brawn suits because Wilbur couldn't create the rest before we had to leave.

"How are Ash and Black?" I ask Elm. It would be nice to go to the albino village to visit them and see if they've been reading my Bible, but we just don't have the time.

"Black is leader now." Elm stuffs a roast chicken leg in his mouth.

"What happened to Alder?" What happened to the scary bald albino who seemed to take delight in chopping off Jude's and my hands?

Elm forces a huge swallow of chicken. "Dead."

I drop my corncob onto my plate. "Dead? When? What happened?"

"On an early morning it was very windy. We went to the homage clearing and prayed to the trees. The wind blew a tree off its roots. It fell on Alder. We buried him at its stump."

"Poor Alder."

Elm shakes his head. "He was pleased with his death. We found him still breathing until sunset. Ash and Black were not happy. They said it was punishment because he prayed to trees and not to God."

A lump that has nothing to do with Christmas dinner lodges in my windpipe. Elm must notice my speechlessness, because he continues. "The reading you did when in our village changed many things. It made Ash and Black search for better balance between us and trees. They do not have atonement for their village. Your reading made me confused. I will talk to Willow about it."

"Are the other albinos in agreement with Ash and Black?"

He releases a single laugh. "Many left, starting their own village. The albinos who stay are confused like I am. But I am Black's brother. I will stay."

"We will get Willow back."

His eyes smolder. "We must. She is waiting for me."

We get the entire train to ourselves. Wind declares its presence through the cracks of the train walls, but not enough to keep us silent.

I'm in a car with Unity people. We squish into two booths across the aisle from each other. Bench seats face each other with a table in between. Mother and Frenchie sit across the table from me and Solomon. Elm, Cap, Kaphtor, Madame, and Gabbie are across the aisle in their own booth. We all wear our Brawn suits under our regular clothing, prepared for anything. I wear Armor on top of Brawn, leaving the facemask still enclosed in the small matchbox on my chest. The suit is fully charged.

Madame leans forward onto her table and gains my attention. "I understand why we're destroying the Wall, but why are you so set against the Clocks, Parvin? I *liked* knowing I had thirty-one years left."

I fiddle with the loose sleeve hanging from my left arm, draped over my missing hand. "When I convinced myself the Clock was mine and not Reid's, I wasted my time. I panicked at the end and it led to all of this—the Council having Jude's invention, Reid's death, all of us getting sent to Antarctica . . ."

It's hard admitting this is my fault, but I push on. "Then the Clock zeroed out and I was still alive. Now that the Clock is gone, I never know if today is my last day. I might die tomorrow. And that brings me to life."

Cap rolls his eyes. "What a cheering thought. I'm *so* glad they smashed mine. Now I can never be certain when I'll keel over."

I twirl my loose left sleeve around my finger, letting the smooth material calm my nerves. "The promise of uncertainty changes how I live. It urges me to live . . . *more,* as if the very seconds prior to every sunset will be my last. *That's* the way it's supposed to be."

I gain momentum as my thoughts spiral into the sky of clarity. "Life is like a game of tag, and you're it. You'll always be it, Cap. And you must chase it with all you've got. But the moment you stop chasing it, the game's over and you've lost. You'll always lose if you stop. What's the point of having life if you won't play?"

He leans back so that Madame's plump form blocks him from view, but I still hear his voice. "Thanks for the sermon."

Cap might be spouting sarcasm, but there's something in everyone else's faces—a relaxed . . . no, a tentative hope.

Gabbie, of course, is filming.

"Tomorrow was never promised to us. Never. God allowed us to put these Clocks in His place. He allowed us to turn them into idols and look what's happened! We don't *live* anymore. The government is turning us into livestock because of our Numbers. We labeled ourselves."

Solomon's hand brushes mine, pulling my fingers away from the entangled sleeve. His touch sparks the memory of the most recent verse I read: *"Where there is no guidance, a people falls."* Proverbs something. I breathe deep. I am their leader. "Now . . . God is rescuing us from our own handmade hell."

It's too easy.

That's all I can think as I lie in my sleeper bunk. It's morning, but I refuse to rise until my thoughts are settled. I'm not sure I can stomach breakfast before I rip down a thousand-foot Wall.

I have a team dressed in superman suits, we're only a few hours away from the Wall, and no one's stopped us. The last time I was in this area of the West, the Council's assassin had a needle in my neck and then took Jude's life.

What a different situation. Will this really work? Does the ease of it all mean God is blessing our choices or does it mean I'm missing something? What am I missing?

I pull out *The Daily Hemisphere* and check for any updates.

Nothing about me or destroying the Wall, but it probably wouldn't be broadcasted through the news anyway.

I find Solomon and Mother in the breakfast car. "Pancakes are my new favorite food." Solomon slides a plate along the table to me, but I push it away.

I lean forward as if sharing a secret. "I haven't heard from Father yet. He's had the video for two days. Do you think every-thing's okay?"

Mother's features solidify to stone. "He's probably being cautious."

Solomon watches me, but his gaze is glazed. I imagine the cells in his brain running around, piecing together the implications. Father could be caught. Father could be dead. The NAB could be destroyed. "Oliver is a silent man. From what I know of him, he's probably safe. Send him another message and ask, but do it with a password-type question."

I slide my fingers along my hairline. "Okay. Do you really think people will come to the Wall to run through once we've destroyed it? What if the Council discovers what we're doing and starts fighting our people?"

Mother folds up a pancake and takes a bite. "You're getting distracted."

"Shouldn't I be prepared for anything?"

Solomon scans the food car. "Maybe we should talk to the others."

I look out the window and watch the stiff, wintered terrain zip by. "Good idea."

Solomon stands. "The conductress said we're only five or six hours from the Wall. Let's get a group together to talk this over." He places a hand on my shoulder. "Eat something, then let's meet in the same car we were in yesterday."

For a strange moment, I don't want him to leave. I don't want to eat. I don't want to do anything but sit with him and enjoy a moment of us. Maybe he's feeling something, too, because he doesn't immediately walk away.

I look into his eyes and think about the man I've come to know. Calm, strong, and willing to sacrifice so much for the sake of shalom. What would I have done if this Enforcer had never come to Unity Village?

"You were amazing yesterday." His smile warms me. "Talking to everyone about the Clocks."

I bite my lip and allow a crooked smile. "Only because I have someone else leading me."

"I'm glad you do."

My nerves evaporate at the reminder of God's leadership. Just keep trusting that He will work out the details. He's pro shalom, even more than we are. "See you in a minute."

"Tally ho." He steps out of our car, crossing into the next. For a moment, I get a whiff of blueberry ink and thatch. Then a burst of lemon–

That's when the *Ivanhoe Independent* explodes.

36

Roaring. Flying. I am a rag doll on fire.

Crumpled metal swirls around me, swung by a beast of flame. I'm somewhere over it all. In the sky. But there is no orientation. No understanding until I slam into the ground and all goes black for a moment.

When I open my eyes next, it's to see the engine of the *Ivanhoe Independent* tumbling through the air above me. Its shadow washes over me.

Then I am crushed.

Black. Pressure.

But I am not dead. My Armor suit activated, sending the suit mask over my face—nothing else could have kept my frail body in once piece.

My head pulses like an overfilled balloon. The *Ivanhoe Independent* is gone. Yellow-painted shrapnel. Giant confetti scattered on the icy ground.

I push a leg against the train engine. It takes a small groan, but my knee lifts the engine off the ground, freeing me. It's like elevating a few two-by-fours.

Wilbur Sherrod and his suits saved my life.

I get my other foot on the underside of the engine, then kick. It rolls off me, balancing back on its wheels. I don't want to kick too hard in case it tumbles onto someone else I don't see.

I clamber to my feet and press the button to turn off my Armor suit so I that don't use all its juice—thank heavens for its automatic activation. Then I search.

"Solomon?" I spin on my heel. "Mother?"

The first thing I find is a limb. My eyes pass over it and I don't let them return. I won't guess from the look of a bloodied hand which of my people it belongs to.

Wails and cries surround me. Who do I go to first? A woman screams from my left. "Mother!" I run that way. It's not her. Another body runs from the other direction—one in a silver suit and rags of singed clothing hanging off his shoulders.

Solomon.

He's alive!

He meets my eyes, but we don't go to each other. We run to the mangled train pieces crushing other people. I haul one off a woman from Nether Town. Her chest is caved in and she holds my hand tight until her muscles fail and breath leaves her.

Blood. Again. Marking my passage in the West.

I close her eyes.

I find Solomon with Cap and Elm at a sleeper car. Only half the car remains, but the cushions and mattresses must have saved them. Blood cakes Elm's choppy white hair, but Cap is relatively unharmed. Six other people from our group aren't so lucky.

They're dead.

All around us, people are dead.

"We have to get what explosives are left," Solomon pants. "Then we need to get out of here. If the attack came from the Council, Enforcers might be coming any minute to finish the job."

"I have to find Mother!" Each breath that enters my lungs without the knowledge of her safety scrapes away my hope and my heart. As I search among dead bodies, confused guilt laps against my mind.

I should have known.

I should have *known* the Council wouldn't let us get to the Wall. Somehow Skelley knew we were coming. This is my fault. "Mother? Mother!" Is she flattened somewhere under a piece of train? Dying alone? Already dead?

I'm the one to find Madame and I wish I wasn't. She's lying on one of the sleeping bunks ripped from its car, sobbing into her hands. Her very bloody hands.

"Are you injured?" I sit beside her and the bunk teeters for a moment. That's when I see the metal shrapnel sticking out of her chest, like an arrow from a fallen knight.

She looks up. "I deserve it. Angelique was crushed—*crushed*—under all that . . . metal. And she . . . hates me. Now I'm dying. "

Frenchie? Dead?

"I forced her . . . to work for me. She didn't have a Clock and I knew . . . in the future . . . she'd thank me for giving her . . . a job. All . . . High-City employers had servants. It was . . . finally my chance to step up . . . in society."

Now's not the time to tell her that using people is a poor technique.

"Then my city found out Angelique didn't have a Clock. I was sent to Unity Village." She wipes her eyes with the palms of her hands and then toys with the metal stuck in her body, as if it's merely a piece of jewelry that's killing her. "Did you know that . . . I never even had my . . . own . . . Clock?" She shakes her head, her eyes turning vacant. "I got one . . . from the black market. I've been . . . a Radical . . . my whole life."

What do I say? *I'm sorry,* sounds so trite. She doesn't strike me as the type of person who'd appreciate empty words. "Madame, I—"

She gasps and clutches my shoulder. She shudders, then stills.

"Madame?"

Nothing. She's dead.

I know dead.

I don't cry and I don't know why I feel like I ought to cry over her. No one else will. I press the button on the collar of her Brawn suit. It shrinks to matchbox size and I pocket it. Then I cover her with a torn sheet.

Kaphtor stumbles around a corkscrewed railroad tie with a body in his arms. Frenchie. "What do I do?" He looks at her face. "She's breathing, but something's wrong."

She's alive! I direct him to a clear spot. "Set her on the ground." Mother would know what to do. Where is she?

Please God. Don't let her be dead.

Kaphtor lowers Frenchie to the dirt, despite the blood gushing from his calf, and grips her pale hand tight. I don't see blood on her, which concerns me. Her injury is internal.

"Parvin!" Solomon runs toward us. He arrives, breathing hard, and dumps two packs of explosives on the ground. Only now do I notice the bruise on the side of his head.

His voice is low, careful. "I found your mother."

I choke. "No."

He leads me by the hand to an enormous pile of twisted metal. "I pulled her out."

There she is, looking smaller and more fragile than ever. Most of her full brown hair is gone—singed away from her head. Her scalp is burned and blackened. Enormous blisters cover her face and skin curls back from her cheeks. She's barely recognizable.

"*No!*" I grope for her hand and hold it to my chest, ignoring the bleeding. "I can't lose her!"

Solomon kneels and puts an arm around me. "I think she's still alive, but I don't know what we can do for her."

"We will go to my village." Elm stands behind us. "Ash can heal."

411

I look around. More people stumble toward Frenchie and Kaphtor. Not many. Who else has died? "How far away is your village?"

"We will get there in evening." Elm reaches down and picks Mother up. Her head lolls back and a crack in her neck skin releases a fresh flow of blood.

"Be careful!" I remove my first layer of clothing and bandage Mother's burns as best I can. I follow Elm to the small group of survivors.

"Those with Brawn suits will carry the wounded and explosives." Kaphtor cradles Frenchie. He presses a button by the collar and her suit shrinks into a matchbox, leaving behind her underclothes. He removes his coat and drapes it over her, tossing her Brawn suit to someone else.

"There aren't enough suits." Solomon scans the row of gathered wounded. "I will go without a suit as long as I can." Leaving no room for argument, he presses the detract button at his collar and gives it to a young boy. He now wears only ragged pants held up by his belt. All the other clothing was torn or ripped off him. A gash across his chest bleeds, but it's not too deep.

He catches me watching him. "I'll be fine."

My throat closes. "But . . . Mother."

Solomon pulls me into a hug.

"Don't tell me she'll be okay unless you're *sure*," I cry into his chest.

"I'll pray." His voice breaks and his arms squeeze me.

I want him to hold me tighter. Tighter. Until I can't feel anything more. Squeeze out the emotions. "Me, too."

"Well, I won't." Cap limps into view with two people following him. They each carry packs of explosives. "This is all that's left."

"Cap!" Kaphtor stares at him. "You are unharmed?"

"I guess."

Solomon and I stare at the eight packs of explosives. Eight packs left . . . out of fifty.

"Do a quick sweep for other survivors," Solomon tells the others. "Then we go."

Only now do I notice the very edge of the Wall peeking through the tree-spotted horizon. We're so close.

Someone finds Gabbie. She's limping, and half her black hair is burned away. She drags three travel packs behind her—mine, Solomon's, and hers. Her face is stained with tear streaks. "Did you see the other dead people?"

I nod.

"There were pieces of humans *everywhere*—"

"Gabbie." Solomon's sharp tone cuts her off. "We're leaving. Are you able to walk on your own?"

She sniffs hard. "I think so. Let me just take a quick emotigraph." She rummages in her shoulder pack.

"Why would you want an emotigraph of *this* place?" Cap's glare is hotter than the flames licking at the train wreckage.

Gabbie raises an eyebrow. "I'm surprised you even know what an emotigraph *is.*"

Cap turns bright red. I gather both Solomon's and my packs, leaving Solomon's arms free to carry a wounded young girl. I hand Madame's shrunken suit to someone else. It doesn't fit the man perfectly, but the suits are made to adapt.

"Is this all of us?"

Solomon's head hangs low. "I think so."

Twelve.

Twelve of us survived . . . out of fifty. Three are badly wounded.

Those of us with suits pick up bags and supplies. I loop Solomon's pack and one explosive pack over my shoulders and my personal pack on my front. Then we begin the trudge toward the Wall, leaving a Hansel-and-Gretel blood trail to mark our passage.

Elm and I take the lead. It takes every ounce of willpower to keep my spine straight and my chin high. Meanwhile, my emotions are curled in a corner, sobbing.

Mother's scarred, peeling face replaces the scenery around me. I picture her, jostled and bumped in Elm's arms, while life seeps out of her.

She could die. Even though her Clock said twenty-one years the last time I looked at it, I no longer have faith in the Numbers.

What frightens me most, though, is the scent of lemon I caught just before the explosion. Did I imagine it? Was there something lemony in the breakfast that I didn't notice? If the scent *was* intentional, how could it reach my nose at that exact moment before the explosion? How did Skelley know we were on that train? I didn't even tell Father. Did the Preacher betray us?

I've had the NAB with me the whole time, so it couldn't have been Gabbie.

"It was Skelley Chase," I tell them. "I smelled lemon before the bomb."

Gabbie stumbles over a bramble. "He wouldn't do something like that!"

"It's the Council, Gabbie." Solomon adjusts the unconscious girl in his arms. "There's no denying that, and he's on the Council."

Gabbie looks ready to cry.

I shouldn't have brought it up. "We'll talk about it more when we get to the village." There's one thing I know, and it's all that's needed to beat my anxiety into pure dread.

The Council knows we're coming.

"I can't do this." Cap plops to the ground a few hours later.

"You're carrying only one pack." Gabbie glares at him. "*And* you still have your suit on."

"Even if some of us don't have injuries, we still have emotional shock." Solomon sidesteps Gabbie and adjusts the unconscious young girl in his arms. "That's exhausting enough."

"We're almost there." Elm doesn't slow.

The moon is fully risen and illuminates the forest. Cap crawls back to his feet and, ten minutes later, we enter an albino village that's very similar to the one I first entered so long ago.

Small stone huts with animal skin roofs and door flaps rest on either side of a small river. A stone bridge arcs from one bank to the other. Ash, Black, and five other albinos I vaguely recognize from my time in the albino village emerge from their huts at a whistle from Elm.

"Ash!" She is as stunning as I remember her—long, cream-colored hair, a soft face, and . . . pregnant again. "You're expecting?"

"Parvin!" She rushes toward me in a half-run. We embrace.

"Whoa! There are *more* of these white people?" Cap jumps away from them, but everyone else stays still.

"We have wounded." Solomon lays his burden on the mossy ground. His hair is plastered to his forehead from sweat.

"What happened?" Black's hair is still cropped short and he and Ash stand taller, every inch the village leaders.

Elm steps in, explaining at lightning speed Willow's predicament, our situation, and the train explosion. Then he carries Mother into a slightly larger hut. Ash directs the carriers of the wounded to pallets and beds. Other albinos run errands—gathering blankets or pouches of white pills.

The rest of us sink to the ground. I can't watch them work on Mother . . . I can't watch her bleed any more than I already have.

God . . . please let her survive!

• • •

A full day passes and I barely notice, I'm so busy sleeping, praying, and recuperating. What wakes me up is a NAB message from Father.

-*Enforcers are at Opening Three. What now?*

Of the fifty people who left Ivanhoe with me, only nine of us are functioning. I gather us together and share Father's message.

"So we've lost!" Cap exclaims.

Solomon shakes his head. "We can't give up yet."

Elm leans against a bare dogwood tree. "I shall still go. For Willow."

I voice the only plan B I have. "We must destroy the Wall, but we'll meet at a different place." Let the Council *think* we're coming through Opening Three.

Solomon nods. Cap fiddles with some stray pebbles in the grass. "Where should we do it then?"

"How about the portion of Wall closest to Unity Village?" Kaphtor suggests.

"Sounds good to me," Gabbie says.

And that's that. I send the update to Father.

Ash enters our huddle of people and whispers in my ear. "Come into my hut. Rest."

Is this her kind way of getting me alone to tell me that Mother's not going to make it? I gulp and follow her into a large hut surrounded by a dormant garden, my heart shriveling like a raisin. Inside are a large bed and a child-sized one. We sit on a stone bench resting against one wall.

"Is she dead?"

Ash takes my hand. "Your mother will heal, with many scars."

She will heal. A gush of air flies out of me. "Thank you."

Her soft smile graces her face and my anxiety melts. "You are strong. But she is stronger. Stubborn."

I laugh a little. "That's Mother. She won't die unless she decides it's practical."

"Elm said you will rescue Willow and many of your people."

I nod.

"Black and I have spoken. Our people wish to help. When you destroy the Wall and your people flee to this side, we will lead them to safety. To our village. Then we will send them to Ivanhoe."

"You would . . . do that? For me?"

Her hand absently rubs over her small belly, then drifts to a box on the end of the bench. Inside is the Bible I left them. "You brought us freedom, Parvin."

Tears singe my eyes and I shake my head. I viewed the albinos as my enemy most of the time. I only taught Ash and Black to read, then left my Bible with them. How could I have known God would work through those actions?

How could I not know?

"This could put you in danger." I clench my fist around my left wrist. "The Council might send Enforcers through the Wall. It means you won't be safe."

She stands. "It does not matter what it means for us. It means freedom for others."

Frenchie is the only one who heals soon enough to join us a day later. Even then, it's against my better judgment. Her blond hair is tussled, but she limps toward our small circle of people, her chin up. She wears an assortment of animal skins and wrapped cloth. Kaphtor rises from our small circle of people. "Angelique, how are you?"

"*Vivant.* Alive."

He helps her sit on the ground.

"*Deux* cracked ribs. Zey are not so bad zat I cannot walk." She winces and leans back on one hand. Kaphtor returns her Brawn suit to her. "But I must return to my parents. I may not fight much, but I must still go 'ome."

Elm, Black, and twenty other albinos—both men and women—join us, armed with pouches of stones and slings tied to their waistbands. Some carry ropes and camming devices to anchor them in Wall crevices for climbing. "We are ready to leave."

"Thank you." I hold my good hand out to shake Black's. He may have helped Alder amputate my arm, but that doesn't taint my gratitude. Is this what forgiveness feels like? The freedom of befriending a former enemy? The freedom to watch him find hope in life and change?

He nods.

I step into the hut where Mother rests and kiss the portion of her forehead that isn't burned. She's not awake, but I whisper in her ear anyway. "I'm bringing Father to you. I love you."

Ash and the other women staying behind as healers come to bid us farewell. "Will you come back to us, Parvin? To teach us more about the book? We are anxious to learn."

Learn? What do I know? I'm no teacher of the Bible. I take Ash's hand. "I want to come back. Someday." Let God use that as He will.

She nods. "I will care for your mother."

"Thank you."

I watch her awkward gait back to the healing hut and wish for a moment that we could sit and read through the Bible as we did the last time I saw them. I wish I could tell her more of my story.

But that is not for today. That might have to wait until we're all in heaven together.

I choke through a group prayer, self-conscious over my words, then we follow Black and Elm.

"Thank goodness," Cap says once we're an hour out. "I much prefer Ivanhoe to that place." How can he dislike the calm albino village or the people I came to love so dearly? Doesn't he understand what a safe haven it is?

"I rather liked it." Solomon falls back so he's walking next to me. He looks alive, ready to attack that Wall and the Council behind it.

We walk in silence for the rest of the day. I mull over our plan of attack. Everything feels jumbled and rushed.

No time to mourn.

No time to process.

We'll arrive at the Wall base the morning of New Year's Eve, as planned. Father will be there. Who else? How many others are desperate to escape the USE?

This feels so reminiscent of the first time I passed through this terrain, trying to return. The thoughts of my family kept me going. This time, it's the thoughts of destruction . . . of freedom.

Shalom.

Night falls and we make camp. Cap hunts around for fallen branches to build a fire. Bless his heart, it's the first selfless thing I've seen him do.

"No fire tonight," Solomon says. "Not with the Council possibly looking for us."

Cap throws the wood on the ground. "This is ridiculous! We won't be a match for the Wall if we're tired, cold, and hungry."

I toss a stick into the shadows. "I'm not asking anyone to come with me. The Council knows we're coming and we're probably going to die." There. I said it.

"Can't die," Cap mutters, settling against a dried tree.

"The point is, this is not a sane thing to do. This is risky, dangerous, and even if you *don't* die, you'll probably be on the Council's list for the rest of your lives. If you want to back down now, I don't blame you. You may leave."

No one talks. No one leaves.

Several of us look at Cap. When he notices us watching him, he huffs. "I'm not chickening out. My goats are over there."

We split the food we collected at the albino village. Then we try to sleep without freezing or despairing.

God, am I saying the right things? No divine insights come. I suppose that's His way of telling me to do my best. I have to trust Him in this, but not without one more plea.

Keep them safe.

We survive the night. When I wake, my head throbs. Solomon's bruise is black and ugly, spreading across his forehead. Gabbie works to fix her singed hair, but it's no use.

Elm leans against a tree, watching Cap snore. All the other albinos are awake. I meet Elm's gaze, trying to focus on his good eye. "Time to go?"

He nods once. "We will arrive tomorrow morning."

The day passes uneventfully, but our determination is palpable. Tomorrow. Tomorrow we destroy the Wall and change our world.

We rest for four hours at nightfall, and then rise under the moon to complete the rest of the trek by morning. The sun just lightens the sky to a dull blue when Cap asks, "If they knew where to blow up our train, won't they know where we're destroying the Wall?"

"Let's hope not." Solomon hoists two bags of explosives higher on his shoulder.

The words bring zero assurance.

God, we're breaking this Wall down to bring freedom—freedom to worship You, to live without the Clock idols. Help us defeat the Council!

"Everyone has their trackers out, right?" Solomon looks at all of us. Everyone nods.

The hiking time flies by. Maybe it's because I'm dreading the actual moment we start tearing the Wall down. I can't help feeling like things will go wrong.

Finally, we creep to the edge of the forest and peek through the short, sun-deprived trees. There's the base of the Wall. No Enforcers, no resistance.

Father is on the other side.

~*We're here,* I send to him.

~*Me too,* he sends back.

"How do you want to do this, Parvin?" Solomon watches me. "The sooner the better, I think."

The Council could catch on to our change of plans any moment. We need to be fast. "Can we pray first?"

He smiles. "Of course."

Cap folds his arms and turns away. Gabbie's distracted, taking a video of the Wall with the NAB, but Elm stands respectful, bowing his head with us. Solomon slips his hand into mine. The physical connection takes me another step closer to God.

Solomon's voice is low and steady. "Heavenly Father . . ."

How *do* we want to do this? We'll tear down the Wall, help the Radicals through, and then everyone will flee with the albinos. Except me. I'll cross with Elm to rescue Willow. And Cap will go rescue his goats.

". . . Amen." My eyes fly open and meet Solomon's smile. Drat, I should have been focusing!

Forgive me! Please protect us and guide me as we move forward.

Focus. Lead.

SPEAK.

We split the bags of explosives and the people into three groups. "Angelique, Elm, and Kaphtor . . . you take one group two hundred yards north of here." Why am I whispering? "Cap and Gabbie, you go two hundred yards south. Solomon, and I will take the Wall here."

I take an emotigraph of this moment. "We're going to destroy the Wall. We're going to unify this world again. We're going to reveal the lie of the new Clocks. Be strong."

Kaphtor nods and seven albinos follow him, Elm, and Frenchie out of the forest. "Be careful," Cap grunts to them. I can't help but think back to his hatred toward Kaphtor only a month ago.

Cap and Gabbie leave next with another group. She takes the NAB with her to film the event. She looks excited and determined and oblivious all in one.

We're all still in sight of each other. This way a large portion of Wall will come down all at once and we have a higher chance of succeeding.

We creep into the clearing. There's a long stretch, about a hundred yards, of deadened grass and rock rubble between the Wall and our forest. I expect Enforcers around every tree stump and bramble the closer we get to the Wall, but none appear.

I'm finally here.

SHALOM.

Everything suddenly feels right. My worry floats away like a dandelion seed. Mother is in God's protective arms. Father is on the other side of the Wall, waiting for me. Even if they die, I mustn't see it as loss. Jude once told me my problem was seeing his approaching death as loss. But really, he and Reid are both in heaven, just waiting for me. Whether I live or die from this pursuit, it will be good. Because it is for my Lord.

Here we are, God. Choose me.

I HAVE. YOU ARE MINE.

My eyes burn at the tenderness of His voice. It's a whisper inside my soul, not an audible voice in my ear. More of a sense than hearing. But it's Him. Maybe now I'll be worthy of being called a good and faithful servant.

Maybe.

"Let's break this thing down."

Solomon, Elm, and I walk to the base of the Wall in our Brawn suits. The other ten Radicals follow us, bringing the three bags of explosives.

"Be careful not to get crushed by falling pieces," I tell them. "The Brawn suits only give strength, not protection. I'll get inside the Wall once the hole is big enough, since I have the Armor suit on."

I press the button for the mask portion of the Armor suit, but before I put it on, Solomon grabs my hand and yanks me to him. "Whatever happens," he says against my ear. "I'm staying with you."

"Whatever happens," I whisper back.

He cups my cheek with his hand and I don't think I'd mind a good-bye kiss just now. But he doesn't give it, which means we have to survive for another chance.

He sprints to the Wall and slams an elbow into the stone. A giant crack splits the silence and shoots up the face of the Wall. We all stare at the crack.

The Wall has been weakened.

The giant Wall at which I could barely *look* a year ago . . . is coming down.

Surreal.

A few of us laugh—giddy, powerful.

Way to go, Solomon.

Following Solomon's example, I stride toward the Wall and use my elbow. I tap it first, still cringing against the idea of slamming it into stone. I feel nothing, so I hit harder. Harder. I smash a hole into the stone. Rock shards fly from the Wall.

Wow.

Only a few more kicks, punches, and pushes create a hole deep enough for the explosives.

This plan seems absurd.

But it's working.

"You get the honors." Solomon hands me the bag of explosives.

They're not like what I'd expect. Of course they're not, they're from Ivanhoe. Each bomb is a small, medium, or large metal spider with a giant abdomen bloated with explosives. When set into the cracks of stone, the contraption crawls deep, then detonates at the press of a button.

I send in three fat ones. They clamber into the crack we've made, burrowing deeper, searching for pathways with their clicky little feet.

Solomon has the detonator button.

We sprint back to the forest and wait for a go-ahead from the other two groups. Everyone's safe. Everyone has sent in explosive spiders. Kaphtor waves from one end, Cap waves from the other. I turn around and Solomon's arms wrap around my shoulders. Then he presses the button with the others.

The stone bursts.

The ground quakes and pieces of rock go flying. I know, instantly, that we're too close. We turn our backs on the flying wreckage and run just as pieces slam into the ground around us.

A second explosion takes place and more stone goes flying. That would be Kaphtor's group. Cap and Gabbie's explosion follows like an echo.

"We're *doing* it!" someone shouts.

Once we realize we won't be crushed by rubble, we stop. Someone laughs first and we all join in . . . to release nerves.

A gaping hole, an elephantine cave, mars the base of the Wall. Enormous cracks spread from the cave all the way up the face. The stone is still grinding its teeth, crumbling in spots.

Once it all settles, the albinos start climbing using the spring-loaded camming devices and ropes that Elm introduced me to in October. They insert a spider here and there in the wider cracks. Once they slide to the ground, Solomon detonates them again.

Each explosive earthquake weakens the Wall and strengthens my determination. We congregate around the biggest hole—the cave. The other two groups join us, looking up at the Wall.

It seems even thicker now that there's a giant bite out of this side.

We have one bag of spider explosives left. I shove at least six of the bigger ones down the front of my suit. "I'm going into the cave!"

I'm the only one with protection from falling rock. If we want to take this down, the explosives need to go deeper.

"What if it collapses on you?" Kaphtor asks.

"Then we dig her out." Solomon gives me a firm nod. A "go-ahead" nod. "That's what these Brawn suits are for."

I enter, crunching minor rubble beneath my boots. The sound of victorious destruction is muffled the moment I'm inside. It's eerie. Dark. I'm encompassed by an irrational fear of something being in here, waiting for me.

It's this feeling—this fear—that solidifies my desire to bring this beast down.

I go all the way to the back, stepping carefully so as not to twist an ankle. The ceiling dips and I scrape my head, but I don't feel it because the Armor suit responds by activating automatically. I deactivate it again, so I don't waste any of its time.

My hand and stump stretch out, into the darkness. How much farther until we're through? I press against the deep cave and feel a chasm with my right hand. I turn on my Clock so it illuminates my path.

A deep crack rests before my eyes.

That's where I direct my kick.

For a moment, nothing changes, then come groans as if the Wall is yawning, stretching, just before collapsing. The fissures above me snap open and chunks of rock break free, tumbling onto me, but not enough to keep me down.

I thrust the rock chunks behind me and squeeze into the chasm, clawing deeper, using my head, elbows, knees, feet, to break through.

I'm frightened for a second, alone in the darkness on my belly beneath the rocks.

"Parvin!" Solomon's voice rebounds into my tunnel. "Are you done?"

"Be careful!" I call back to him. "Don't get crushed!" I pull three explosives from my suit and send them into the gut of the Wall.

I crawl back out and we exit. Solomon presses the detonator and the explosion blows a chunk of Wall toward us. Everyone hangs by the forest watching, waiting for things to settle.

But it doesn't settle. The top portion of the Wall sways. House-size boulders break free, tumbling to the ground and shaking every squirrel out of its tree.

Pulsing awe yanks me to my knees. Is this how Moses felt at the parting of the Red Sea?

"We need more explosives in there!"

I force myself up and run back into the tunnel, letting my last three spiders loose.

Solomon climbs up the Wall and sends his last few from the bag into the cracks high in the Wall. Then we retreat deep into the forest. So deep that we can't even see the Wall above the trees anymore.

He presses the button and it's as if the Earth has a seizure.

The groans of the rock monster are so loud, we all scream. I hold my hand to my mouth and feel the soft material of the Armor suit. I'd completely forgotten I had the mask on.

The ground jolts and I stumble into a tree. More crashing and groans. I don't need to see it to know that a portion of the Wall just came down.

I can't help it—I run toward the Wall, entrusting my safety to the Armor suit. When I break from the trees, I skid to a halt. Broken Wall is everywhere. Giant dust clouds impede my vision, but a wind gust clears enough to reveal the top of the Wall. It's only a hundred feet high now.

The chunk we've been attacking rests like the yawn of a colossus, beckoning me into its throat for one last attack.

I brush the dust off and squint to see how the others are doing. Crumbling cracks and holes dot the face of their sections of Wall. Gabbie, in her Brawn suit, is throwing the fallen chunks out of the way, the NAB in one hand filming the whole thing. Cap works on the base of the Wall.

There's a wildness in their work—a frenzied excitement.

"Let's clear a path!" I shout.

Only those with suits can do this. Gabbie, Cap, Kaphtor, and Frenchie show up to help and the albinos work together as a team.

We make a path through the debris to the base of the Wall. Even with our suits, it takes a fair bit of time. The cave is still there, half-filled with rubble. "We can collapse the rest from the inside."

"Does anyone have any more explosives?" Solomon looks around.

"*Oui*, only two fat ones."

I hold out my hand. "I'll take them as deep as I can." Frenchie gives the detonator and spiders to me.

Solomon's jaw muscle works. "Don't . . . get buried."

I can't promise I won't.

I slip back into my crumbling tunnel. This time, it's a little harder to crawl deep. There's a lot of rubble, but I push it behind me. I crawl on my hands and knees, digging through crevices until I'm far past the halfway point.

With a lurch, I tumble out of the tiny tunnel and into a wide space. I press my wrist Clock and the Numbers illuminate a high ceiling like a cathedral inside the belly of this Wall beast. Small rocks and dust clouds shower down upon me.

It's weak. I am strong.

This could be a good place for the spiders. I wander to the other side and kick with my heel a few times until something cracks.

A stream of light startles me and I gasp. The Armor mask keeps me from choking on Wall dust.

The other side.

That's when I hear voices.

"Father!" I scream, losing my head. "Father! I'm here! We're coming through!"

The voices falter and I claw like a mad woman, making the fissure wider and wider, not caring when bits of rock bounce off my Armor suit.

I can see the other side. Light. People.

The gap widens. There's Father's face, pressed against the stone. A giant crowd is over his shoulder. "Parvin?"

"Father!" I'm elbowing my way through the rock, as if pushing through a forceful crowd. It's tight against my back and chest, pressing against me. The stone above me protests and bits shatter. Now is the time to destroy it.

"Hurry, sweetheart. I think Enforcers are coming."

I let the spiders drop from my hand and they scuttle to the other side of the cathedral. They climb into the ceiling, disappearing into a crevice. "Get out of the way!" I shout to Father. Just a few more feet and I'll be through, with him. In his arms. Smelling his soap and sawdust.

The sound of bullets interrupts my next smash of rock.

Someone screams.

"Father!"

People claw against the Wall, trying to join me in the fissure.

I pull the detonator from my suit, my elbows and arms scraping against the walls of rock surrounding me. "Get back!" I give them ten seconds. They're the longest ten seconds of my life. I want to be out of here, fighting for Father's life—for everyone's lives.

In those ten seconds, as people scramble away, I see a form silhouetted by the light—a form wearing a fedora, a bored smirk, and the promise of betrayal.

Skelley Chase.

The shooting stops and he steps up to the crack. "Hello Parvin."

So, he knows it's me under this mask. "Look at you, trapped in there. There's nowhere to go. You've lost."

He's so close. And only *I* have an Armor suit.

I press the detonator.

Nothing happens. Is it the wrong one? I press it again, harder. My palm sweats beneath the glove. I back deeper into the stone, back toward the cathedral, but he can still see me. "You can't hide, Parvin."

Who knows how many Enforcers are with him or what they're about to do to my people? All I know is my job. I stop moving, staying squeezed in the fissure. I press my hand with the detonator against one side of stone and my stump against the other.

Like Samson, I breathe in deep. "God, strengthen me this once. Break down this Wall that keeps us from shalom!"

On the last word, I push out with a mighty yell. My hand and stump press into the stone as if it's made of soft wax. Then I hear it.

The crack and crumble of destruction.

I scream once and, with a shove, it all bursts apart. Someone shouts my name before I'm buried in thousands of pounds of rock.

Then the bomb goes off.

37

Even with the Armor suit for protection, I must have blacked out.

I come to, but the deep rumbles and crashes continue. Then blackness. Silence. After a moment, all is still.

Did I do it? Did I break down the Wall? I don't know how much fell, but my heart surges with the assurance of God's faithfulness. He heard my plea. The rock is crumbled and Skelley Chase might have been buried in it.

This is the beginning of new things.

In the blackened silence I lie, oddly comfortable. I open my eyes wide to see if there is any sort of light—any opening for escape. I push against the rocks, but they don't budge. I'm too buried. As I come to this realization, a dim light illuminates my small tomb.

Then the light leaves. I squint. It returns. Flashing. It's . . . red. The wrist light from my Armor suit.

My time is up.

One minute. That's all I have before I'm crushed. I do the only logical thing a person about to die can do.

I scream for help.

"Solomon!" My voice is flat against the weight of rocks. I push again. Nothing. I'm going to die.

Like this, God? Is this how You want it?

I had only the time He wanted me to have. And if my last act on Earth is breaking the barriers between two sides of the world, then so be it.

With every red blink, my breath quickens. Is my oxygen disappearing? At least death by crushing should be fast. I hope.

I think I hear something outside. Something above—scrambling and moving rocks. A few shouts here and there. They're too far away to make any difference.

The red light has been blinking forever. I mentally calculate how many blinks have happened and how many I might have left in this minute. I push against the rocks again, releasing a gut-wrenching groan.

Blink. Blink. Blink.

If I can't budge this stone using my Brawn suit, I must be deep.

The shouting above grows louder. I think someone says the word *stop* and *over here.*

"Help!" I choke.

FEAR NOT.

For You are with me. A tear trails down my cheek, pressed into a mini-puddle by the Armor facemask preserving my cranium.

"Hurry!" That's Solomon's voice. He's trying to dig me out. It's not going to work. He has only ten second left. Maybe less.

Ten . . . I give a last push against the rocks.

. . . *Nine* . . . Poor Solomon. Today his rescue attempts will fail.

. . . *Eight* . . . Breathing is harder. Tighter. Is the suit fading?

. . . *Seven* . . . A distant, distant light allows me a glimpse of heaven.

. . . *Six* . . . My chest doesn't expand this time when I take a breath.

. . . *Five* . . . Dust falls on my mask.

. . . *Four* . . . More light. Enough to see bodies moving in a world above me.

. . . *Three* . . . The Wall will be my burial, on the line between worlds.

. . . *Two* . . . Here I come, God. I'm ready.

"Fight, Parvin! Fight for it!" Solomon's voice is desperate, pleading.

... *One* ... The red light stops blinking.

I'm out of breath. Out of protection. For Solomon's sake, I push against the stone one last time with every muscle that still obeys. Something creaks. Something gives, enough to let me take a free breath.

I can move the rock. I can move it?

I push harder. Stone grinds against stone. It grows lighter and lighter, as people above me throw them off my shoulders. I sit up as I heave and get my legs under me. A boulder adjusts and smashes my foot, but I pull it out with a hiss of pain.

Something is broken, I'm sure of it.

The rocks turn into bricks, then dirt, then feathers, and then Solomon's grabbing the boulder on my shoulders and throwing it off me. He pulls me out of the rock pit and into his arms.

Again . . . again I have lived when I shouldn't have. *Looks like You have more for me.*

Gabbie, Frenchie, Cap, Elm, and Kaphtor stop their frantic digging. All around me are shouts and victory cheers. We're in a groundcloud of Wall dust. Bodies fly past me, scrambling over the rubble to freedom. Hundreds of people. Radicals.

Albinos clamber around, shouting instruction. "Follow us! We'll take you to safety! Run to the forest!"

Bullets fly from the east side, but the hovering dust is too thick for the Enforcers to know what they're shooting at. Suddenly I'm transferred from Solomon's arms into the embrace of soap and sawdust.

Father.

I squeeze him tight, but we don't have time for a prolonged greeting. The mask from my Armor suit retracts. I look up into his whiskery face. He tugs a loose strand of my hair. "You're so brave, sweetheart."

"Where's Tawny?" I have to shout to be heard over the screams, cheers, and gunfire.

He shakes his head. "In Prime with the people of the underground church. She refused to come and won't tell me why."

"Then we'll go to her." I give a curt nod, as if affirming it to myself.

Black scrambles toward us from the enemy side, bursting through the dissipating cloud. "We must go."

I push Father toward Black and stumble from my injured foot. It's definitely broken. Solomon catches me. "Father, go with Black. I'll follow after I've rescued Willow."

We have to get out of here. Now. But I can't run. I can't move with this broken foot.

Father grabs my hand. "You're not coming?"

I shake my head. "I'll explain everything through a NAB message. Go. Black will take you to . . . Mother." I choke on her name. "She . . . she's injured."

Father pales.

A clump of Enforcers materializes through the cloud, advancing but seeming confused on what to do. Does that mean their leader, Skelley, is gone? Dead?

"Go!" I level a hard look at Black. Get my father out of here!

I can't breathe with too much release. Tawny is still in the East somewhere. For some reason, I had a feeling this would happen.

"Let's go." Solomon leads me toward the chaos.

I can't walk. I can't take a single step without crying out. I trip over a chunk of rock, going against the flow of fleeing Radicals. Solomon lifts me into his arms. Flight is of the essence right now and he has his Brawn suit on. He carries me up. Up. Up onto a piece of Wall that rises over the cloud dust.

"Where are the others?" We crouch behind a chunk of rock. I can see everything from here—people swarming into the forest, albinos knocking Enforcers down with their stones and slings, allowing the Radicals to escape. The gap in the Wall is irreparable.

We did it. They're free. The Wall is down.

"We'll find them. We're the only people going in *this* direction."

To the East, Enforcers give chase, but they are too far behind to catch my people. The Enforcers seem . . . hesitant. Afraid, even, to cross that gap in the Wall. Not the Radicals. Not the people running free.

They are fearless.

Freedom. Shalom. Here it is!

"We did it."

I gulp down a happy sob. "Yes we did."

Solomon shuffles down the rock as fast as possible until we finally land on flat ground. Then we run, well, *he* runs and I cling to his shoulders, wincing against the jostle on my smashed foot.

First my hand, now my foot. How much will be left of me at the end of all this?

From seemingly nowhere, Gabbie, Cap, Frenchie, Kaphtor, and Elm join us in flight.

Cap runs beside us. "We're heading to Unity, right?"

"Right now, we need to find a place to hide until all this settles," Solomon says. "None of you have your tracker chips in anymore, right?" An echo of *Nos* answers him. "Good."

It's the second time he's asked us this in as many days. Does he think one of us still has it in? I hate the suspicion that enters my mind but . . . Gabbie sure thinks highly of Skelley. But she's seemed more airhead-infatuated with him than secret-traitor-spy.

I glance over Solomon's shoulder toward the Wall. The dust is thinning. It looks like a giant rock-eater took a bite out of it. *By faith we can move mountains . . . and Walls.*

"What if ze Enforcers 'ave cars?" Frenchie asks. "Zey will catch us."

"They won't know where we are." Kaphtor leads us down a slope and into a copse of trees. The going is much slower, but at least we're not exposed anymore.

For the first time, I breathe free. All of us grin like fools. "Cap, are *vous* smiling?"

Cap scrunches his nose as he hobble-runs. "Of course not. My lips are just numb."

It is quite cold, but I know an excuse when I hear one. "You can be happy, you know."

"Not until I get my goats back."

An hour later, none of us are running anymore. Poor Frenchie looks about to collapse. Kaphtor has been carrying her the past half hour as Solomon carries me. My toes are numb, but my heart pumps steady warmth through my chest. It's been a whole hour and we're safe! Free!

"I need rest." Cap bends over with his hands on his knees.

"You've been a trooper with your leg." Kaphtor settles on the icy ground, cross-legged.

Cap rolls his eyes. "Says the man who was *shot* in the thigh."

"We 'ave one gun wound, one broken leg, some broken ribs, and one smashed foot." Frenchie looks around at us. "We 'ave a good range of injuries to be proud of."

Solomon lowers me to the ground, careful not to knock my foot against anything. I'm surprised it's not hurting more than it is. I try wiggling my toes, but they don't obey. Still, they don't twinge too much either. He presses the collar of his Brawn suit and it detracts into matchbox-size. Now he's dressed in normal clothes, borrowed from the albinos.

We are in a copse of wide-based trees. Gnarly rope vines hang from them, sprouting from the ground and climbing the trunks like long snakes. The ground is stiff and frozen, but there's no snow.

Solomon rolls his neck. "Those suits are great but . . . I'm glad to be out of it for now."

Everyone else removes theirs, and while I'd like just a moment of winter air on my skin, I like being in my suit. I feel so safe.

Still, I retract both Brawn and Armor and hold them in my hand. They look identical when shrunk, except for a stick-figure on the face of each square. Brawn shows a stick man with enormous muscles. Armor shows a stick man in medieval armor. Cute.

My loose and crazy hair tickles the back of my neck. Mother's not here to braid it for me. I dig a ribbon from my pack and use my teeth to get the knot out of it.

"Need help?" Solomon takes the ribbon from me and scoops my hair up before I can answer. "Want it braided?"

Frenchie snorts. "You know 'ow to braid?"

Solomon's fingers move through my hair, separating it into three thick strands. "Learned in an orphanage. Lots of little girls with no mothers." As he combs my hair away from my face with his fingers, I imagine him braiding the hair of all the little orphans . . . being the big brother.

Gabbie hasn't spoken since we left the Wall. She settles on the ground in silence, rubbing her hands together and then tucking them under her armpits.

"Gabbie?" I venture. "How are you doing?"

She shakes her head. "Do you think . . . Skelley Chase died?" A tear slips from the corner of her eye.

I imagine Skelley's bored smile just before I destroyed the Wall. After that explosion, it'd be a miracle if he weren't crushed. "I don't know."

"I hope so," Cap growls.

Gabbie throws a rock at him. "How can you say that? He's been *deceived* by the Council just like us!"

Not this again. I reach back and pinch the ribbon knot with my thumb and forefinger for Solomon to tie it off, my two matchbox suits still clenched against my palm. "I hate to be the one to break it to you, Gabbie, but he pretty much *leads* the Council."

Still, it doesn't settle well with me that I might have killed Skelley. Why not? Shouldn't I hate him?

She lets out a huff and turns her head away from us. "I don't believe you."

"Parvin's right." We all jump as Skelley Chase himself steps out from behind the trees.

A dozen Enforcers surround us with their rifles leveled.

"How did we not see this coming?" Cap slams a fist into the ground as we all freeze.

Maybe because we were too careful for this to happen. How? *How* did he find us? It had to have been Gabbie. We've been caught.

Skelley dabs a handkerchief against a bloodied spot on his head, just under the rim of his green fedora. "It's all thanks to Parvin, really."

"What?" I need to do something. Could I slip the Armor and Brawn suits back on and attack him?

Not with my hurt foot.

Skelley steps forward and extends a hand to Gabbie. She leans away from him, even though she looks flattered. She glances at us, panic on her face, then slides her fingers into his hand and allows him to pull her to her feet.

He hands her to an Enforcer, who presses the collar of her suit and catches the matchbox before it falls to the ground. How did he know to do that? The Enforcer then shackles her wrists and presses a gun against her head.

Skelley holds out a hand toward the rest of us. "Let's have your suits, too."

I have two in my hand, which hovers above my hair from holding the ribbon for Solomon. As smoothly as possible, I wedge one suit square into the folds of my thick braid, sliding strands over it, praying it's concealed.

In the time it takes me to do that, the Enforcers advance and haul each of us to our feet. I cry out as my foot gives way. The Enforcer handcuffs me and then peels my fingers out of their fisted position. "Here's one."

I can't see which suit it is, Brawn or Armor? He tosses it to Skelley. "Don't you see, Parvin? You can never run. We always know where you are."

"How?" My tracker chip is out and, to my knowledge, they never put another one in me. Then I gasp. I'm daft. "The medibot."

"You're getting brighter by the day."

It was me. This whole time *I* was the one giving away our locations. I blink rapidly. "But . . . if there's a tracker inside my medibot, why didn't you blow up the cargo ship?"

"I think this one's going to need a gag." Skelley waves toward me and an Enforcer complies. The gag pulls the corners of my lips back and my mouth fills with rough material.

Once we're all cuffed and contained by Enforcers, others search our clothing, the ground, and our packs until they have a handful of matchbook Brawn suits.

Skelley examines one and then puts it on. It melts around his body, forming to his clothing, covering him from neck to toe. "Fascinating." He gives me his bored smile. "Let's go."

We're blindfolded, dragged through the trees, then shoved into cars. All the while, I'm crying like an idiot. Though I don't *feel* sad in that way. Oddly, I feel very little worry.

You are still with us.

The drive takes a long time. I lose track of the hours. No one's in my car and I spend the drive praying for Solomon, Cap, Kaphtor, Gabbie, Frenchie, and Elm. Beseeching God to allow them to live. Begging Him to speak to their hearts and show them that He's worth this.

At some point, the Enforcer holding a gun to my head must get tired of doing it, because he slams the butt against my skull and I'm out.

"Wake up."

Something nudges my side. I blink several times until a cell comes into view. It's not like the cells in Unity Village. This one has no windows or doors. Everything is white. How did this Enforcer get in here?

My pack sits in the corner of the cell, looking flatter than normal. It's been searched and purged. The gag is gone and I now wear a white t-shirt and sweats. Who changed my clothing? I dare not ask.

"Follow me."

I look at the four solid walls. "Where?"

The Enforcer turns on his heel and walks through the white wall, as if it doesn't exist. But I know better.

It's probably like the projected Wall in Antarctica, ready to destroy me the moment I touch it. He steps back in, grabs me by the handcuffs, and pulls me toward the projection.

"Won't that . . . screen thing kill me?"

He yanks me through. I feel nothing and find myself in a long white hall with numbers spaced along the walls above screens. Are all of these prison cells? "Where are my friends?"

He says nothing. We travel down the length of the hall. The walls are peachy-white, with screen monitors and keypads every fifth step or so. We pass them all until we come to a thick door leading into a larger white room. In the center of the room is a sickly-green plastic recliner chair. I saw one when reading about dentist offices.

I have a feeling I won't be getting my teeth worked on today.

Along the wall, across from the feet of the dentist chair, are a bench and a door. A few roller tray-tables holding boxes and gadgets are pushed against the walls. The Enforcer thrusts me into the chair and tightens a strap around my legs and upper torso. Too tight. It's hard to breathe, let alone move.

He straps my arms to the armrests. There goes my chance of grabbing the suit from my braid. I hope it's Brawn. *God, please let it be Brawn.* Armor won't help me escape. I need magnified strength.

I'm too confined.

Vulnerable.

Then they come in. Skelley Chase, Elan Brickbat, President Garraty, and the two other Council members . . . all wearing *our* Brawn suits. They stand along the bench and look at me. Should I say something? Probably something witty or defiant.

"Let my people go." If I didn't have to keep a straight face to back up my demand, I'd giggle at how Moses-like that sounds.

"You have no idea what you've done." Brickbat's lips barely move as he grinds out the words.

"Oh, I think I do." A smile creeps over my face and I let it loose. "I saved hundreds of Radicals from Antarctica, turned off the projected Wall for an hour, destroyed a portion of your stone Wall, and freed people from your oppressing and *unconstitutional* control."

Brickbat slaps me.

My consciousness blinks out.

"Try not to do that with the Brawn suit on." Skelley Chase's voice.

"She deserved it." Brickbat.

I scrunch my face. The left half of it shrieks in sharp pain. Something's broken. My jaw? My cheekbone? My . . . skull? Everything is tight and swollen from his strike. I whimper.

The pain reminds me of my crushed foot. It doesn't hurt at *all*. I wiggle my toes. They almost feel normal. Way to go, medibot!

"She's awake." The woman Council member's voice is close, as if she's bending over me. "Let's get to it, then."

My eyes flutter open. I barely make out the two blurred forms of Brickbat and Skelley when one of them—Brickbat, I think— swoops toward me and grabs the front of my shirt. "How *dare* you undermine us with that video?"

He shakes me, but all it does is grind my bindings deeper against my skin. My blurry vision clears enough to see Skelley grab Brickbat's wrist. "We need her functioning. Any more bruises and the public will know she's being forced."

Brickbat releases me and I slump against the chair. He practically spits words at me. "You're a danger to society."

I strain against the bindings. *"You're* the ones destroying the Low Cities and sacrificing the poor."

Skelley releases a two-beat laugh. "We're just doing what you wanted in the first place with your biography—we're eliminating the sacrifice of Radicals."

"No, you're not!" Spit flies from my mouth. I hope it hits them in the faces. "You're *making* Radicals by requiring an impossible fee for a new Clock. Then you sell the Radicals into slavery—out of sight, out of mind, right?"

"Now she's getting it." Brickbat cracks his knuckles.

"But that won't work." I want to push Brickbat's buttons. I want to change Skelley's smirk into shock. The Council needs to know they can't control everyone. "You saw my video. Dusten Grunt's Clock was *overridden.*"

"You put a false Clock on that boy!" Brickbat bares his teeth.

"I did not! His *name* is on there for all to see!"

That does it. The vein in Brickbat's temple pulses so large that I'm sure it'll pop and he'll die from a brain hemorrhage. "Because of *you* the High-City people are hesitant to be Clock-matched. You've poured doubt into the minds of our entire country!"

"How can I do that?" I fix wide, innocent eyes on him. "I'm controllable, remember?"

Skelley leans forward. "We are going to fix what you started."

"You *can't* fix it!" I try to put oomph behind my words. "You can't always win—this is the *truth* we're talking about. The new Clock system is *broken*. You can't keep that from the people. This is one situation where you can't do anything you want, Skelley."

"Oh, I won't be the one fixing it." Skelley's bored warble shoves my heart into a black hole. "*You're* going to undo the damage you've done—in a new video to the public."

"I won't do *anything* for you." My voice is high and frantic.

Brickbat's face grows a deeper and deeper shade of red with each hissing breath. "Then your friends will die."

39

Friends. Dead.

Can I call them friends? People who joined me on a death-mission and are now imprisoned by the most dangerous power in the USE? Do they think of *me* as a friend?

Not Solomon. We're more than friends. We're . . . well, I don't know. But we're more.

But that doesn't matter if he's killed. "Please . . . don't." Futile words. Why do I even say them? Doing so reveals my weakness.

It shows them . . . they're winning.

"Here's how this is going to work"–Brickbat's wet, throaty voice makes me want to scream–"You will cooperate with us and speak to the public, undoing the fear you've sown. You will remain with us, doing what we ask of you—"

"Oh yeah?" I challenge. "And how will I explain away the broken-down Wall?"

Here, Brickbat smiles, and my breath turns icy in my throat. "We're already working on that. Don't you worry your little head."

I close my eyes and fall back against the chair.

"If you *don't* work with us"—Brickbat's breath hits me in the face—"then your friends here will die, Willow will die, and every other orphan in that orphanage will die. But no matter whether you cooperate or not, *your* Clock will be . . . *tested*."

That last word comes out of his mouth like whiplash to my

emotions. *Tortured*, is what he means. The Council Clock-matched orphans and then tortured them to see if they'd die before their Clocks.

Now it's my turn.

I take a deep shuddering breath. "Okay."

But it's not okay. How can this be okay? This time, Brickbat's going to hold a gun to my head and actually pull the trigger. This time I'll be strapped to a table as Skelley unrolls a long display of torture devices. Either that, or . . .

This time, I'll be allowing my friends to die.

But which sacrifice is asked of me? Do I sacrifice people's freedom by lying to the entire USE? Or do I sacrifice my friends? Brickbat will probably kill Solomon and the others anyway after I cooperate. I've seen it happen with Skelley. *Return or else I'll kill Reid.* Well, I returned. And Reid's dead.

No matter what I choose . . . I'll be tested. Every form of torture I've ever read about zips through my mind. I mentally tick off each one with a *Yes, I could handle that* or a *No, I couldn't handle* that. It doesn't matter. I won't have a choice and, from what I know of Brickbat's character, it will be all the tests I can't handle.

I trust in you, O Lord . . . You are my God. My times are in your hand.

Brickbat's voice drops a notch, sounding even more menacing in a gleeful sort of way. "We might just televise your testing . . . to show the people what happens to rebels."

Skelley steps forward. "You'll turn her into a martyr if you're not careful, Elan."

Brickbat rounds on him. "*You're* the one who said she was easy to control! *You're* the one who got us into this mess, publicizing her life and rebellion. And *now* the world has seen a video about all of this and that boy's Clock!"

Sorry, but I have no way to erase the minds of a hundred million people.

"The people adore her and follow her. They *want* her voice and her face. You still don't grasp her importance."

Brickbat leans close, spittle flying from his mouth and flecking Skelley's face. *"You* don't understand the leader you've made her into. *We* are the leaders. She . . . will be *constrained."*

I look to Skelley. I can't explain why my gaze is drawn to him—maybe because, in this den of lions he's the beast I'm most familiar with, the one I can read. "I want my friends free *before* you film me or do the testing. After I watch them stride away free, I'm all yours. I'll speak for you."

I almost choke on the word *speak.* God's been echoing it in my mind nearly every day, but this can't be what He meant. Every time I've spoken, it was for shalom. This . . . if I speak for the Council, then I'm lying. I'm going against shalom.

The woman Council member stares at Skelley, then moves her gaze to Brickbat. I know who the leaders of this band are. The question is, who makes the final call?

Brickbat pops a thumb knuckle. "Absolutely not. You'd only refuse to cooperate. Our terms, our way."

At least I tried. I lift my chin. "All right then."

A pause. Brickbat cracks another knuckle. "So you agree?"

"Yes."

"Let's get to it."

I take a deep breath. "May I . . . may I say good-bye first?"

Skelley looks as bored as ever, but he stares at me for a long moment. Finally, after I'm sure he'll say no, Skelley—the true leader of the band—nods. "Only to one."

One is all I need. "Solomon, please."

"What are you *doing?"* Brickbat opens his mouth, possibly for another shout, but Skelley takes him by the arm and steers him to the corner of the room. I catch a few words like *information* and *opportunity.*

I'm not dumb. They'll probably try to torture information about Solomon and his family ties from me, as well as anything I might say during this "good-bye" to him.

But I won't talk. I won't tell them a thing.

Skelley nods to the Enforcers around my chair. They unstrap me and, as I'm led from the room, Skelley says, "You have one hour."

When I enter the off-white hallway with numbers and screens all over the walls it hits me. I have to tell Solomon. I have to tell him good-bye.

Suddenly life seems too short. For a moment, I wish I were someone else.

The Enforcers halt under the number seven and tap several numbers and symbols on the keypad. They scan a portion of my arm and then thrust me through the wall.

I stumble to all fours, landing on my knees. My palm presses against the chilled cement flooring. I stay there, staring at my hand. Loose hairs fall in front of my face and the strands are trembling.

What have I done?

I can't look up. I hear Solomon move from across the room. Any second he'll ask me what's wrong. I can't tell him. I can't watch him break.

Is this what Jude felt when he told me his Clock was short? Was it this hard for him? I didn't make it easy on him. I hope Solomon makes it easy for me. Yet . . . I want to know he cares.

"Parvin?" His voice is soft, but unstable.

The knuckles on my hand have turned a splotchy mixture of red and white from pressing on the floor too long. I need to stand up. I need to face this. I need to speak—to tell Solomon what's going on, no matter how hard it is to do so.

I tear my gaze from the ground and lift up my eyes. He's crouched in front of me, rocking on the balls of his feet. The rims of his eyes are red and tears blur the perfect teal color I've come to love, but he's fighting it. His jaw muscle pulses.

Why did I look?

He shakes his head and clears his throat. "Are . . . are you okay?" Then he runs a hand down his face as if he knows it's a dumb question, but I smile. I don't know how, but I do. Sometimes the dumb questions are needed to ferry us into the sorrow.

He helps me to my feet.

He won't meet my eyes. In fact, he releases my shoulders and turns his back on me, facing the wall. "Parvin . . . what's going on?"

Just say it. Just get it out. "You're escaping." He doesn't move. *Just say it!* "Without me. I'm going to cooperate with the Council until you're free."

There. It's out.

Solomon bows his head. I might have imagined it, but his knees seemed to buckle for a moment. I should comfort him . . . but *I* want to be comforted. It's selfish, I know, but I need a dose of assurance. I need the whisper of, "It's okay," to cement in my mind that death isn't the end.

I feel so distant, like I caused a chasm to open between us. "Solomon?"

"I knew you'd do something like this," he croaks.

Is he *angry* at me? Defense boils away my despair. "What choice do I have?"

He turns and his piercing gaze hits me head-on. He's not angry. His mouth is open slightly and remnants of tears leave his lashes separated. His eyebrows crease . . . just a little—enough to reveal helplessness, resignation, and strength.

He takes my hand and pulls me forward until he can wrap his arms around me. "I'm staying with you."

I shake my head against his chest, bunching the white material on his uniform beneath my cheek. "No." *Yes!* "No. You're the only one who can rescue everyone." I reach up and pull the matchbox suit from my braid. I flip it over and see the stick figure.

Armor.

I press it into his hand.

"It's not right. Why don't we all escape together?"

"I can't. They'll always know where we are because of my medibot. You *have* to go, Solomon. Entrust me into God's hands."

His voice turns low and harsh. "I slipped a Brawn suit into your pack. Can't you . . . can't you get that and escape too?"

Oh, such desperate hope. "They searched my pack. All the Council members are wearing a suit. Besides, my pack's in my cell and . . . I don't think I'll be going back there."

I lean back and look up. We're so close. He wipes a tear off my cheek with his thumb. I didn't know I was crying. "Solomon, get everyone out of here. The Armor suit will keep you protected for a time. Then go rescue Willow and the other orphans. The Council is threatening them. After they come and get me, then you rescue everyone else. The Council will be busy with me."

I can't tell him what they'll be doing to me . . . or what I'll be doing for them.

We both slide down the wall and sit in the corner—his arm around me, my head on his shoulder. "Why, Parvin?"

That question breaks my dam of resolve. I tell him why. I tell him about the Council's threats, about the doubt sown in the High Cities, and I tell him I'm not afraid.

"Don't you see?" He needs to know my choice is worthwhile. "The Council will test me and, if Jude *did* make these Clocks inaccurate and I override my own Clock, that's proof. That's proof that they can't run the USE by everyone's Clocks."

He groans. "They'll get proof another way. At some point, someone else with an overridden Clock will step forward. Why does it have to be you?"

"Because this is the only way to get you and everyone else out safely."

"But even if they *have* proof, they won't do anything about it."

My smile is grim. "That's not our problem. Our job is to get the word out. God will spread it." This is when I see the connection.

God's asking me to speak again . . .

. . . only this time it's through my actions.

Solomon has no comeback. The air is hushed and heavy. I curl my knees to my chest and press as close to him as I can. He holds me tight and we stay that way for the rest of the hour. Sometimes his jaw moves and I catch whispered words of prayer. Sometimes a section of my hair grows wet from his tears. He touches my face softly with the tips of his fingers. I fall asleep to it, escaping one last time before I meet my end.

40

WHO ARE YOU?

I am yours.

WHO AM I?

You are my God. My times are in your hands.

TRUST ME.

I will. I love you.

I wake, bathed in confidence. When I rise, it is with the assurance that He is worth it. God is worth any form of testing the Council could put me through. The last time I thought I would die, it was to escape this world. Now, it is to cleanse this world. With my death, the Council will see the fault in the Clocks. They'll no longer have their tool of control.

With my death, I free my people.

This . . . this was my calling.

An Enforcer with freckles and buzzed dark red hair stands by the door. Is that what woke me? Solomon jolts awake. I'm already up, ready. I'm almost . . .excited.

I walk toward the door, but Solomon launches to his feet and grabs my arm. "No. Wait. I . . ." His face scrunches and he sucks in a breath through his nose. "I . . . what do I do?"

His plea is so broken. The Enforcer remains by the door, but doesn't hurry me. Compassion?

I place my hand on the side of Solomon's face. "Wait. Be

patient. We'll see each other again." Just as Jude once told me—death is not a loss, not when I'm joining my Lord.

I'll see Solomon soon.

He places his hand on top of mine and doesn't fight the tears this time. I smile. "See? You believe I'll die despite my Clock. Your sorrow shows me you know God is greater than the Clocks. And . . . you're right."

He takes my face in his hands, his fingers tangling a little in my hair. We're inches apart and I soak in a last look. He's going to ask if he can kiss me. I know it as if the message is telepathic.

But I don't make him ask.

I pull him down the last few inches and our lips touch. It's a firm and sweet kiss. My stomach flutters. Then it's over. Just the one.

"Good-bye," I whisper.

He rests his forehead against mine and closes his eyes. "Good-bye."

I turn away from him and take the three steps to the Enforcer. I guess our kiss *was* meant to be a good-bye.

Just before I pass through the electronic wall, Solomon speaks up. "*And through his faith, though he died, he still speaks.*"

I look over my shoulder.

His arms hang at his side and his shoulders droop, but he lifts his chin as if attempting to be strong. "The verse of the week—I think it's meant for you."

We don't break our connection until I walk through the screen. Then he's gone, replaced with a false wall. The Enforcer looks down at me. We don't move. I finally meet his eyes and see something.

Turmoil. Confusion.

"It's okay. I'm ready."

His Adam's apple bobs hard. He starts walking, inching us down the hall. Hesitant. "He used to be an Enforcer, didn't he?"

I smile. "I've found a lot of Enforcers are good men who pursue truth. It's been a nice surprise."

He leads me, with dragged steps, down the hall toward the room with the dentist chair.

Through his faith, though he died, he still speaks. That was the first verse of the week I ever read. It's a last gift from God to me. My message and calling will continue even if I'm gone.

I sit in the chair and close my eyes, releasing a long breath. The straps are familiar bindings now. I try not to think about how helpless I am against their choice of torture.

"Ready?"

My eyes fly open to see Skelley walk into the room. I meet his gaze. "Yes." I'm ready to die . . . for God's timing. For the perfect timing.

He fiddles with several things on a table to my right. I don't look. I don't want to know. It's just us in the room now. I should say something, but what can I say?

"I don't hate you, Skelley."

The noises from the table stop. "I don't care one way or another."

What a liar. No one wants to be hated, do they?

Skelley sets up a camera and a few screens flicker up on the wall. *Take your time, Give Solomon a nice long window for escape.*

I don't know how he'll do it, but I know he will. What can I do other than trust that God's hand is over those I love?

Skelley comes over and turns on my Clock. There they are, thirty-something years on it. They're meaningless.

"Those are good testing Numbers." Brickbat and the other Council members walk into the room, still wearing Brawn suits. Solomon couldn't fight his way through them if he wanted to.

It's good that I'm here as a distraction.

Enforcers line the walls around me. Good—the more who are here, the fewer there are to catch Solomon and the others. Has he escaped his room yet? The Armor suit should allow him to walk through that screen thing, shouldn't it?

"Ready to speak?" Skelley steps into the camera's view and stands to my right.

I glance up to see my face on a wall screen for a moment and then back at the camera lens. "What do you want me to say?"

Brickbat's eyes narrow. "You know what we want. Improvise. We'll film it until you get it right."

How long has it been? Ten minutes? Fifteen? That's not long enough for Solomon. What do I do?

TRUST ME.

My tongue is dry. I can't do this. *Oh God, I'm so scared.* "I . . . I . . . I can't do what you want."

Brickbat steps forward and grabs my shoulder. His fingernails bite into my skin, digging under my collarbone. "Do I need to get one of your friends in here with a knife to his throat to help you cooperate?"

I try not to wince. "It doesn't matter." A tear trails down my cheek. "I won't do this."

Brickbat jerks his chin at the red-headed Enforcer, the one who originally delivered me to the dentist chair. "Go get her boyfriend."

He hurries from the room. I wait with eyes squeezed tight. What seems like mere seconds later, the Enforcer runs back into the room. "Sir." He addresses Skelley and avoids my eyes. "The . . . prisoners, sir." His gaze flicks to mine and sweat lines his temple.

He doesn't get any other words out before Brickbat screams at him. "Spit it out, Enforcer!"

"They're gone, aren't they?" Skelley's almost smiling as he says it, not because he's on my side, but in a, "I'm-a-cat-and-you-just-made-this-game-of-chase-more-fun," sort of way.

My relief escapes on a sob.

Skelley turns off the camera. "Send a group of Enforcers to track them."

Brickbat clamps down on my shoulder one last time and I yelp. Then he releases me. "Let's get on with the testing. That'll make her obey."

Oh, I'm already being obedient . . . just not to Brickbat.

"I have it here." Skelley steps forward with a needle. Brickbat makes sure a different camera is on—probably some sort of documenting device.

"Any last words?" There's a sick glee in Brickbat's voice, like he's mocking me. He can't wait to see me hurt. What's in that needle?

Last words. Last words. "What are you going to do when I die?"

"You're not going to die," Brickbat sneers. "Haven't you seen your Numbers? We have so many lovely tests for you to go through, I'd hate for you to miss them."

I'm blessed really . . . to have a meaningful death. To have a death that I *know* is accomplishing something worthwhile. Maybe that's how Jude felt. "Dusten died before his Clock. You can't stop this. Jude did this on purpose. He *knew* you'd get the invention information and he made sure it was flawed."

I said the wrong thing. At the mention of Jude's name, Brickbat's head whips around to look at Skelley. "She knows something."

Skelley closes his eyes for a moment, like he's regretting my words for me.

Brickbat rounds on me and presses my strapped wrists against the cold metal chair arms. "What do you know?" Spit flies in my face.

His fury pushes my body against the seat in a recoil. "Nothing. What do you mean?"

"Jude Hawke told you something, didn't he?" I shake my head, but Brickbat looks at Skelley again. "Get me a pirate chip." Skelley sighs, walks to the table of tools, and opens a drawer beneath. "The terminating type."

"Elan—"

"Do it! Focus words: Clock, Jude, invention—"

Skelley fiddles with a small device I can't make out. "Jude Hawke didn't know anything. Why should she?"

"—Hawke, Numbers, church, might as well throw Solomon's name in there, too."

Skelley walks over. "Got it."

Brickbat grabs the chip from his hand and squints at it. "Is the termination set? That will be a perfect start for the testing."

Skelley doesn't look confident now. His eyes flit to me with a mild crease of concern. "Toxin termination."

"That'll work."

I hold gazes with him. "I'm going to die, Skelley."

He shakes his head, but I nod. It's coming any moment. I'm not scared anymore. How can I be scared of the pirate chip if Jude wasn't? Jude was brave. I will be, too.

"My Numbers are in God's hands. No one—not even *you*—knows if you'll have a tomorrow."

"Shut *up.*" Brickbat grabs my hair.

"It's my time to speak." Only not in the way they expect.

"No," Brickbat says, "it's your time to die."

"God can speak through my death."

He laughs. "Show me."

He nods to Skelley, who turns on some sort of NAB—probably the one that will drink up the secrets they're going to steal from my brain. But I don't have the answers they want—I *don't* know why the Clocks can be overridden. Solomon and I have only pieces, guesses.

Skelley clears his throat. "This chip has a condensed version of the toxin that almost killed you before. If, indeed, you are right about the Clocks being faulty, then you'll die, but it will be more like falling asleep."

One of the Enforcers in the room shifts his weight. This will be good for them to see. Witnesses are good—they spread truth and gossip. And that one red-headed Enforcer—the one who announced Solomon's escape—I think . . . I think he helped us.

Someone connects a few tubes to my arms and my vitals pop up on a screen to my left.

"You wanted to die so badly last time"—Brickbat yanks my head forward so my chin is jammed against my chest—"maybe your wish will be granted." He inserts the two needles from the chip into the back of my neck.

A white flash blinds me for a moment. Skelley stares at the NAB screen. I can barely see words streaming across it—my memories. My information. My mind.

Will I forget the information they're stealing?

"Done." Skelley looks up.

The pirate chip lets out a pop and I grow woozy. Brickbat removes the chip and my head flops back on the headrest. The room is blurry. My stomach churns, but the heavier temptation is to sleep.

Sleep.

Death.

The vitals monitor on my left releases a series of shrill beeps. Through the haze, Skelley's low voice drifts to my ears. "You know what we'll have to do if she *does* die."

"She won't die." Brickbat's voice is a distant echo.

"But if she *does* . . . that means the Clocks—"

"She won't die!"

An Enforcer's voice from my left speaks up. "Um . . . sir?"

I'm going. There's no fighting it. In fact, it's relaxing. I'm folding backward into the warmest, firmest embrace that's ever touched a soul.

I'm coming home. And, in doing so, I'm freeing my people.

I allow one final blink before succumbing to the warmth. In that blink, I see Skelley step forward—blurred by my mental fog. His voice comes from somewhere far away. *"Parvin?"*

I close my eyes—my last sight is that of a tear slipping down Skelley's cheek.

"Sir?"

"... can't be . . ."

"... flat-lining, sir . . ."

The beeps mesh together into one loud beep that doesn't stop. As a long breath whooshes out of me, a verse scrolls across my last flicker of consciousness. *And through her faith, though she died . . .*

. . . she still speaks.

DISCUSSION QUESTIONS

- Parvin believes God is calling her to something, but she can't pinpoint what it is. *How do I know if these are my ideas or His? I guess I'll have to do what I did in Ivanhoe, pursue what I believe is the best choice and commit it to God and to prayer.* Do you ever have a hard time knowing what God wants from you? How do you pursue clarity?

- When Parvin first returns to Unity Village after Reid and Jude's deaths, she feels like every problem was her fault and she can't fix anything. When is a time you felt things were out of your control? What helps you give those feelings to God?

- What if God called you to do something you were uncomfortable about? Like when he asks Parvin to speak or lead. How would you react?

- We tend to fear what people will think of us. What are some ways to try and overcome that fear?

- Which character in this story do you find yourself relating to most? In what ways?

- Cultures often have a habit of labeling people. In *A Time to Speak,* the Council decided that Radicals and the poor aren't worth keeping in the USE. In fact, they sell some of them as slaves and send the others off for hard labor. What dangers are there in labeling people? Do you ever find yourself labeling people (homeless, different ethnicities, "nerds," etc.) and treating them differently because of that label? What does the Bible say about this? (See *Deuteronomy 10:17-19, Acts 10:34-35,* and *Romans 2:11, 12:18)*

- When Parvin is traveling to Antarctica, Skelley Chase continues to offer her ways out. He tries to bribe her and a lot of his bribes sound pretty good. Have you ever been tempted by something that is very appealing and seems like it could even be the right thing to do? How did Parvin resist? How can you?

- At the end of this book, Parvin finds herself willing to sacrifice her life for what she believes is right. If you were in a similar situation, do you think you'd be afraid of dying? Why or why not?

Acknowledgements

My *thank yous* could fill a book by themselves. This journey is not one I've walked alone. I thank my Lord and Savior, Jesus Christ, for changing my life as I wrote these books, and for His ultimate sacrifice, which allows me to see and pursue shalom with the hope of eternity with Him. May He speak through me always.

Thank you to my handsome hunk of an adventuring husband (yes, I call him that daily), Daylen. Thank you for telling me you're proud of me every single day, even on those days I don't cook for you or I write into the late hours. You are my hero.

Thank you to:
Steve Laube—forever titled *Most-Awesome-Publisher*. Thank you for your leadership, your humility, and the round-the-clock work you put toward our books at Enclave.

Karen Ball—My hard-working friend, editor, and agent. You can cheer me up with a single word and remind me that God's called me to write.

Jeff Gerke—my incredible mentor and editor who tears my books into pieces in just the right ways so that when I tape them together again, they tell better stories. Also, thank you for the many *many* pep talks.

Thank you to Kirk DouPonce from DogEared Design—for letting me nit pick the already amazing covers you make for me!

Captain Aaaaargh (aka: Dad)—for doing awesome Dad-ish things (you know, like *taking me through the Panama Canal for the sake of book research*) even though I'm a grown-up married girl now. Thank you also to Pat, Simon, and Matt—for teaching me all I need to know (and more!) about cargo ships and the Canal. Mom—for being a constant an encourager. Elisabeth—for supplying me with more resources and research books than I could ever read. Binsk—you always claim you're "bad at giving feedback," yet your feedback is often the most helpful. Love you, little bro. To my Little Weed (aka: Melanie)—for being the epitome of excitement with *every. single. update. ever.*

Grandad and Judy—for your insight regarding Antarctica and your travels there. You inspire me to be an adventurer. I love you. My beta readers who caught all the typos—Brenda Wood (bestie!), Megan David, Angel Roman, Lisa Godfrees, Ashlee Willis, Josh Hardt, Emily Kopf, Jill Williamson, Karen Foster, and Binsk. (I'm *so* sorry if I'm forgetting anyone!)

Angie Brashear—the best writing buddy, critique partner, and friend an author could ask for. You're always the first to pop into my mind when I need writer chat and you constantly remind me of God's calling. You're an irreplaceable blessing to my life.

For the Readers of Nadine Brandes FB group—thank you for helping me brainstorm everything from FB parties, to back cover blurbs, to marketing ideas, to character photos. You're my crew.

Thank you to all the readers who picked up this book to continue Parvin's story. These books would get nowhere without you. I'd give all of you a hug if I could. May your faith and your relationship with God grow so deep that He speaks through your lives—and, one day, your deaths–for His glory.

ABOUT THE AUTHOR

Nadine Brandes learned to write her alphabet with a fountain pen. In Kindergarten. Cool, huh? Maybe that's what started her love for writing. She started journaling at age nine and thus began her habit of communicating via pen and paper more than spoken words. She never decided to become a writer. Her brain simply classified it as a necessity to life. Now she is a stay-at-home author, currently working on next book.

Visit her web site: www.NadineBrandes.com

Facebook - @NadineBrandesAuthor
Twitter - @NadineBrandes
Goodreads - @NadineBrandes
Instagram - @NadineBrandes

If you enjoyed the story (or even if you didn't), please consider writing a brief honest review on Amazon and/or Goodreads. Reviews are the greatest gift you can give an author, as they help get books into the hands of new readers!

THE **OUT OF TIME** SERIES

A Time to Die

A Time to Speak

A Time to Rise

Available Now!